THE GILES AMENDMENT

Cathy!

I'm trying to learn :)

All The Best,

G Henley

THE GILES AMENDMENT

❀

A Novel

Stirling Scruggs

iUniverse, Inc.
New York Bloomington

The Giles Amendment
A Novel

iUniverse books may be ordered through booksellers or by contacting:

iUniverse
1663 Liberty Drive
Bloomington, IN 47403
www.iuniverse.com
1-800-Authors (1-800-288-4677)

ISBN: 978-0-595-47091-4 (pbk)
ISBN: 978-0-595-91373-2 (ebk)
ISBN: 978-0-595-70927-4 (cloth)

iUniverse Rev Date 11/03/2008
Printed in the United States of America

Dedication

With Love for
Roy and Jason
For their courage and commitment
And
as always for Harumi

Acknowledgments

For their encouragement and help, I thank Tony Donato, Michelle Goldberg, Alex Marshall, Paul and Ann Micou, Stafford Mousky, Patti and Roy Scruggs, Jill Sheffield, and Catherine Shutters. Some read various drafts of the text and made thoughtful suggestions along the way while others read the completed manuscript and provided helpful advice. They were all wonderful. I thank Drs. Nafis Sadik and Elliot Nadelson for their medical advice and Ben Chevat and Tim Rieser for their guidance about Equal Rights Amendment (ERA) legislation and House and Senate rules. The National Organization for Women (NOW) was created to champion the ERA, and champion it they did. Much of my historical research came from the NOW Web site and its references.

I especially thank two very special people: my wife, Harumi, who formatted, corrected, advised, and helped me shepherd Giles from start to finish, and my good friend, Richard Snyder, who read and provided advice and editorial assistance after each chapter. They were wonderful.

Chapter 1

"You're killing your baby. Don't do it; please don't do it. God will punish you. It is your own flesh and blood!" The woman was holding a poster with sonogram pictures of a fetus at its monthly stages of development.

Suddenly a man screamed, "Whore, you will burn in hell! Repent, you still have time! God is love. Don't murder your baby. God is love. God will take care of your baby. That bitch with you is a killer!"

The group of protesters, about twenty or so, Shiloh guessed, was too close to them. The people's venom was worse than she had ever seen; Shiloh could see the rage burning in their eyes. Usually the group in front of the Mid-State Women's Clinic was more respectful and always peaceful, as if they were just going through the motions of protest. But this group was different, she thought. They were more agitated and frightening as they boldly closed in on the patient and her escort with their chilling taunts.

Then she saw him: Jerry Skyler, a nationally recognized leader of Operation Savior. She had seen him on TV. Operation Savior was known for its take-no-prisoners approach at antiabortion demonstrations, and Skyler was the organization's star attraction. Shiloh knew that pro-choice advocates around the country feared Skyler. He had been arrested many times for his antics. He would come into a town at the request of a local antichoice group as a hired gun to provide his unique guidance. He was a hero to the radical side of the antichoice crowd. Everywhere he went, he made news and brought attention to their cause. Skyler's MO was to use foul language and intimidation to scare already frightened women.

"This is a crusade for life, people!" Shiloh heard Skyler say in a thunderous voice. "In this struggle, you must be tough; either we stop the slaughter, or someone dies. Standing around mumbling and hanging your head is pathetic. God is with you; always remember that you are working for God."

He was effective; she had to hand him that; he certainly scared her. *Just imagine how the poor patient must feel*, she thought.

Skyler approached Shiloh and her charge. He looked like he would explode any minute. His sinister smile, bulging neck veins, and sweaty, red face were menacing.

Shiloh whispered to the patient, "Just a few more steps and we'll reach the door. Don't look at him; just focus on the door."

Skyler screamed at Shiloh, "Killer! Whore!" Then to the patient, he yelled, "Save yourself from this evil woman; don't let her force you to murder your baby. There is still time. Don't go into that killing chamber."

Before Shiloh could react, Skyler threw a coffee cup full of blood in Shiloh's face and pushed her shoulder, trying to separate her from the terrified patient. Shiloh almost lost her balance but regained it in time to guide the young woman toward the door where two clinic staffers and a security guard were waiting. They pulled her inside and closed the door as Skyler lunged at Shiloh in his attempt to stop the patient. Shiloh noticed that the police had arrived but were too far away to stop Skyler.

Suddenly, Skyler grabbed Shiloh's hair and pulled her down as he screamed something at the departing patient. He was in a rage, and saliva dripped from the corner of his mouth. The man who was with Skyler was pushing him forward. His look of cold hatred alarmed Shiloh more than even Skyler, who was threatening enough. Shiloh could tell Skyler was a well-rehearsed act. But the other guy looked truly demonic. Shiloh surmised that this guy would do anything to stop her and her patient, even kill them. She felt a sudden chill.

Shiloh pushed the thought aside as she concentrated on getting her hair from Skyler's grip; in a catlike motion, she straightened up with a looping swing and brought a tightly balled fist down on the bridge of Skyler's nose. She heard a loud crack and could almost feel the pain she had inflicted as her blow landed square on his nose. He fell to his knees, and blood gushed over his shirt. Shiloh, also covered with the blood Skyler had thrown at her, stood over her assailant.

She was torn between the urge to lash out again at Skyler and her compassionate, gentle side that told her to help him. For a moment, she just stood there like a statue. Then she knelt down beside him and gave him her handkerchief.

When the crowd saw the police, they immediately backed off—except for the man with the demonic eyes who Shiloh didn't recognize. He was about five foot nine, she guessed, slightly built, with a full head of light brown hair.

His look was determined as he addressed the police, "My name is Reverend James Robert Lawson, Jr. We were here demonstrating, trying to save a poor, wretched, young woman from killing her baby when this person," he disgustedly pointed at Shiloh, "attacked my colleague. We were exercising our constitutional rights when …"

"Whoa," said the smaller of the two patrolmen, who seemed to be in charge and whose nametag said Officer Williams. "We saw exactly what happened. Your friend is lucky he isn't hurt worse off than he is. If we had been closer, I would have used my stick on him when he grabbed this woman's hair." He was pointing down at Shiloh who stood up to meet the police officers.

Skyler stirred and finally stood, wiping blood from his chin and neck. He was still a bit shaky but compensated with a loud, blustering voice. "I am an American citizen. I am defending the life of an innocent child. This woman and the others inside are murderers."

"Can it, pal," said Williams forcefully. "You'll have your chance to talk later."

To the crowd he said, "If you will all gather over there next to the concrete planter, my partner and I will talk with you in just a moment."

He asked his partner to put Skyler and his colleague in the backseat of the patrol car.

Shiloh watched nervously as two TV crews and a print reporter were already talking to the crowd. *There goes my career,* she thought.

Williams turned to Shiloh. "Ma'am, are you okay?"

"Yes, officer, I'm fine. The blood isn't mine."

"Yes, I know. I saw him throw it. It's probably some kind of animal blood," said Williams. "Do you think you'll want to press charges, ma'am?" he added.

"I don't know," said Shiloh,

"You probably have enough to put him away for a year. You have plenty of witnesses including me and my partner."

Shiloh sighed nervously, "I suppose I should, but it takes so much time talking to lawyers, going to court, and trying to do my job. Plus it would probably mean publicity I don't need."

Williams continued, "Ma'am, I'll need a statement from you. But I really believe you should use the law to send a message to this guy. He has disrespected women and the law that he's so quick to quote when it suits him."

Shiloh nodded. "It's a difficult enough situation for women without all the interference and confusion caused by folks like him." Shiloh glanced toward the police car where Skyler and Lawson sat in handcuffs. "I know I should do it. I owe it to women and to what I believe. But I am an Episcopal priest; it could cause troubles for my pastor."

"Well, ma'am, you can't hide it, not with all these press people here."

"I suppose you're right, Officer Williams. It's just that I hate the thought of embarrassing my boss. He went out on a limb to hire me."

"Many people are like that … afraid to press charges," said Williams. "But this pest deserves a taste of his own medicine."

"Yes, I know, sir. I'll let you know tomorrow morning, is that okay?" asked Shiloh.

"Yes, ma'am. Just call me at this number." Officer Williams shook hands with Shiloh and gave her his business card.

Shiloh was unable to sleep that night. She kept tossing and turning as she replayed the day's events. She worried about her job and the grief she had brought to All Saints Pastor William Jacobson. All Saints was a relatively liberal church, and Bill Jacobson was certainly on her side. *But*, she thought, *this is Tennessee; this is the Bible belt.* All Saints was an old church. She knew that its vestry had thought long and hard about being out front by hiring the first female clergy of any denomination in the Nashville area. Bill had insisted to the vestry on breaking the gender barrier in Nashville. What would they say to her boss about his woman priest now?

When Shiloh picked *The Tennessean* up off her front step the next morning, she noticed the article about the demonstration just below the fold on the front page. There was a picture above the article of Shiloh standing over Skyler; "Local Episcopal Priestess KOs National Antiabortion Agitator," the caption read.

Anxious to find out more, she took the newspaper inside and sat down at the table to read it.

> Reverend Catherine Shiloh Giles, an Associate Pastor at All Saints Episcopal Church, broke the nose of Operation Rescue national leader Jerry Skyler yesterday afternoon in an altercation in front of the Mid-State Women's Clinic. Skyler was in town at the request of the local Operation Rescue affiliate to lead a demonstration at the clinic.
>
> The incident occurred when Giles was escorting a clinic patient, whose name has been withheld for reasons of privacy, through a crowd of demonstrators.

Nashville Police, who arrived on the scene during the melee, arrested Skyler and a companion, James Robert Lawson II, the pastor of the nearby Crown of Thorns Evangelical Church. Lawson is the leader of the local Operation Rescue group. He told *The Tennessean* that he had invited Skyler to Nashville to train the local group on demonstration techniques.

According to the arresting Officer, Clarence Williams, Rev. Giles acted in self-defense when she responded to Skyler's assault on her and the woman she was escorting. Witnesses stated that about 20 to 25 people participated in the demonstration.

Giles made news last year when she became only the second woman in Tennessee and the first in Nashville to serve as a clergyperson. The Rev. William Jacobson, Pastor of All Saints Episcopal Church, said last night that Giles has been a tireless worker and is well liked by the All Saints congregation.

A native of Tullahoma, Tennessee, Giles received her undergraduate and theological degrees from The University of the South in Sewanee, where she graduated with high honors. Giles took up her current posting at All Saints last September after serving seven years as an agricultural and medical missionary in the Philippines.

Shiloh fielded calls from reporters and friends for the rest of the day, before finally calling her second father, Barry Whitfield, in Tullahoma. Barry was consoling, which is what Shiloh needed. Shiloh was looking forward to seeing him in Tullahoma the next week when she would go there to visit her grandmother.

* * * * *

Shiloh saw the newspaper on Bill Jacobson's desk when she entered his office the next morning. Jacobson, in his midsixties, was an even six feet tall. He had been a decent athlete during his youth, but over the years, he had grown comfortably into middle age. He was a slightly plumpish man who was best known for his warm, fatherly smile and jocular personality that immediately put folks at ease. A full head of gray hair was a perfect fit for his personality and status. Bill, or Father Bill as he was known to everyone, was loved by his congregation and respected in his field, often being asked to give lectures at the seminary at Sewanee and to comment on the affairs of the day locally where he was a regular Rotary speaker and media source.

"Is it true, Champ, that you will be giving a karate demonstration Sunday night at the Young People's Service League meeting?"

Shiloh noticed that Bill had a twinkle in his eye as he motioned Shy to the coffee maker.

"Tell me what you know that I don't know. Did I hear on the radio that you were going to appear on the Larry King Show? Will that be in New York, or is he in Washington these days?"

"I'm sorry, Bill. I never dreamed that this would cause so much of a problem. I guess Skyler is a big name," Shiloh said.

"It's not Skyler; it's you. Stop and think for a moment. A woman punches out a man nearly twice her size; she is protecting women's rights, and throw into the mix that she is a priest, the first woman minister in Nashville. That is the story, my dear."

"I'm so sorry. I know that you'll have problems from the vestry. Some of them weren't too happy about me in the first place, and here I've potentially harmed the man who had enough confidence in me to give me a chance."

"Don't worry, Shy. I have confidence in myself too. I can handle the vestry. Susan kept score last night. Every time I got a call, she would ask pro or con. According to Susan the pros have it twelve to three. And, I might add, Susan was prouder of me last night than she was when I asked you to come to All Saints in the first place. Are you ready to press charges?"

Shy looked pensively at Bill. "I don't know about pressing charges. I don't want to cause you or the church any more problems."

"I think you should. Don't worry about the church. You were right—he needs to be taught a lesson. I called Judge Barker last night and asked him what he thought. He said it could be a bit of a production. On the other hand, throwing blood on someone and accosting a woman so blatantly on film could be embarrassing to the other side. By the way, was that a karate blow? Joe Bartlett says that if it was really karate they may try to say that you provoked him in some way because you knew you could hurt him—if, in fact, you were trained in martial arts."

Shiloh laughed for the first time in what seemed ages. "My father taught me a few things to do if I was attacked and couldn't get away. It was part of his talk on the birds and bees. He told me to scream, to try to make my attacker lose his balance if possible, and to aim my fist at his nose and swing as hard as I could. He said that if you hit someone in the nose, they become disoriented due to the tearing effect, the pain, and the sight of blood. Somehow, when Skyler was pulling my hair all I could think of was his nose.

"My dad also told me where to kick," she added, "but I didn't have a good shot."

Bill roared with laughter, "Just imagine the headlines, Shy: Priestess Castrates Antiwomen Fanatic. Wait till I tell Susan."

In a serious vein, she added, "Thank you, Bill. I know that it hasn't been and won't be easy for you. Whatever happens, please know that I'm committed to you and to All Saints. And yes, I'll press charges."

Reverend Jacobson nodded. "Don't worry, and good luck with Larry King. If you have any questions or thoughts that you'd like to talk through, please don't hesitate to ask."

Shiloh finished her coffee and left to get ready for her interview with Mr. King.

* * * * *

The CNN taping was to be at three o'clock that afternoon at a local station. After that, she planned to go home and figure out how to handle the next month or so. She needed to talk to the church attorney, decide how to handle future interviews, and ponder what, if anything, the events of yesterday would mean for her work and her future. She had already received several speech requests and even a job query from the local Rape Crisis Center to consider replacing its retiring executive director.

The Larry King interview went well. They discussed what happened, her past work, and women's rights. King was good at his job. He had a way of making people feel at ease while still asking probing and interesting questions. When he'd closed her interview, King had said, "Reverend Giles, I have a feeling that we will be hearing about you again someday."

* * * * *

James Robert Lawson II, the man who was arrested with Skyler at the Mid-State Women's Clinic, had become an outspoken abortion opponent in the late '70s. He'd graduated from a religious college in Virginia and had gone on to attend its seminary. He was a dedicated follower of the school's founder and president, who was a nationally known televangelist. Lawson considered the man to be his mentor, and, like his mentor, he believed that women, blacks, and Hispanics were God's chosen minorities, and he treated them that way.

He took up the reins of a small, fundamentalist church, the Crown of Thorns Evangelical Church, on the outskirts of Nashville, in the early '80s. He faithfully distributed his mentor's weekly *Fact Sheets* every Sunday. They contained national political news with instructions about what his adherents were supposed to follow or act on and various bits and pieces about the work of his graduates. They almost always included his standard message of contempt for women and minorities and absolute hate for abortion for any reason. Lawson also kept a copy of his mentor's equally caustic *Ninety-five Theses for America* pinned to his office bulletin board. The *Theses* contained ninety-five policy statements that represented his mentor's manifesto for the political, moral, and social conduct of America.

Lawson had become an active member of the Moral Majority during his college days. The zeal he felt for his cause knew no bounds. He ignored tax laws, as he not only told his congregation how they should vote, he also passed out what he called the Real Christian's Voting Slate at major political events around Nashville. He was arrested once for shouting down Al Gore when he was campaigning for the Senate and again when he disrupted the Tennessee Assembly during a debate on the funding that was required as the state's match for Federal Title X family planning funds for the poor and the young.

His church was small, and its members were as fundamentalist as they come. He preached that men should rule the family. He believed in a vengeful God and interpreted the bible as the literal word of God. "Anyone who does not follow the exact words of the Bible will burn in hell. Je-ee-zzz-zus will make it so."

He had contacted Skyler and asked him to come to Nashville. When they were arrested, he'd told the police that he was working for God and that Skyler was God's avenging angel, to which Officer Williams had said, "That's fine, as long as you and your angel friend obey Tennessee's laws."

What would a black cop know about God and abortion and putting women in their rightful place anyway? Lawson had thought. *These people stick together. That woman Giles and the cop are enemies of God.* He knew God was testing him, but he would figure out a way to exact God's vengeance against these nonbelievers.

Lawson would tell his congregation about his arrest the next Sunday and that they should follow his example and speak out against abortion, even if they had to sacrifice their freedom. He had already rehearsed what he would say. "The people who force this murder on women are vile and should be abolished from this earth. God will reward you for fighting this horrible sin. Sometimes violence like abortion requires violence. Remember Sodom and Gomorrah. Smite thy enemy. Smite sin. My arrest and Mr. Skyler's was an abomination. But we will prevail, my dear friends. We will prevail because God is on our side."

After being released from jail, Lawson had returned to his church and sat in his small office seething about the events of the day. He hated Shiloh Giles with every fiber of his being. She was the devil incarnate, a woman so vile he couldn't utter her name without the taste of bile in his mouth. The mere thought of her repulsed him. Murderers he could accept; liars, harlots, and whores he could accept; thieves, crooks, and fornicators he could accept. God was merciful and compassionate and believed in redemption. And so did he.

But Catherine Shiloh Giles was beyond redemption, beyond contempt. She did not murder in the heat of passion or to save her life. She led the unborn to the shadow of death and proclaimed their slaughter a human right. She convinced mothers to do the most unnatural act mankind has ever known—kill their offspring—then aided and comforted them as though they had done a noble deed. She was Jezebel, put on earth by Satan to do his bidding and to betray God and his children, but only worse.

James Robert Lawson II was born in Sardis, Mississippi, in 1951. His father was the pastor at the Sons of Zion Church, his mother the preacher's dutiful wife. His father, The Right Reverend James Robert Lawson, was a legendary figure, a God-fearing man known far and wide for his fire and brimstone. People came from miles around just to hear him say, "Jesus," which flowed from his mouth in three unforgettable syllables. "Jee-zzz-us," he'd intone, reveling in the collective gasp of the congregation that was so awestruck it could barely manage a weak "amen" before he unleashed another, more impressive "Jee-ee-zzzz-zus," and so it went, until the congregation was his to command.

The Right Reverend Lawson's sermons were works of art. His pulsating delivery interspersed with soft, gentle, and sometimes even tearful murmurs cast a spell over his congregation until he owned the destiny of each and every one in the congregation and their future generations yet unborn, including his own impressionable son, Jimmy Bob II.

The indoctrination of Jimmy Bob II started when he was still in his mother's womb, when his father decided to add two roman numerals to his name instead of Jr. "Jr. would pay homage to his father," he was fond of saying. "But James Robert Lawson II pays homage to his true creator, the Lord Jesus Christ—in him, by him, and for him." The Right Reverend's voice trembled when he said this and tears welled in his eyes.

When he was a child, the reverend had sat little Jimmy Bob II on his knee and talked about the wonderful works of Jesus and how God had chosen him to minister to a world full of sinners.

"I too am a sinner, my boy," his father would say, "but you are special; you have a special role to play in life. You are pure, innocent, and chosen by God."

Little Jimmy had listened to every word. At first, he was proud of the attention, but as he became older, he feared making a mistake. He read the Bible constantly and prayed for strength to do God's bidding. When he went to church with his father, he quoted scriptures to the revered reverend.

He talked about God's laws and the world of sinners and how they must be punished before they could be saved.

In school and among his friends, Jimmy Bob II concealed his divinity well. He was a small, shy, weak kid given to long bouts of depression, which in the Lawson household was defined as the reward for serving God. For Jimmy Bob II, it was a certainty that a crucifix would have been easier to bear than the II that followed his name. The burden of his father's expectations was a constant reminder of his weakness. He constantly tried to live up to his father's expectations and was haunted by his ineptitude. On the one hand, he tried to be strong in front of his father, but among the rest of his family and with schoolmates, he was shy and introspective.

As Jimmy Bob grew, he seemed to get smaller, shyer, and weaker. But his threshold for sin got bigger and bolder and stronger, especially when it concerned girls—soft, pretty, feminine girls who loved to flash a coquettish smile his way just to see him squirm in a self-righteous superiority he could neither suppress nor control. The prettier the girl, the more come-hither the smile, the softer the curves of her body, the greater the sin he committed alone in his room at night. For other boys his age, it was a necessary and pleasurable release of tension, a small respite from their raging hormones; for Jimmy Bob II, it was eternal damnation and the beginning of a long night of self-degradation. He considered his feelings of lust as God's test and God's punishment for his lack of discipline and self-control. *If I can't control this, how can I ever carry God's word to the world and smite the sinners as Jesus smote the moneychangers in the temple?* he had often asked himself.

All this flooded into his head as he sat on the edge of his bed the night of his arrest at the Mid-State Women's Clinic cursing that harlot Shiloh Giles. Why did she have to be so pretty? Shiloh had dark, shiny hair that was slightly wavy and cut shoulder length. Her radiant blue eyes were wide and alluring, and her face was creamy and smooth like porcelain. She had a slight overbite, which added to her appeal. She was slender. Her breasts were proud and proportionate to her body, and her hips were athletic yet perfectly rounded.

How could any creature put on this earth be so soft, so desirable, and yet so deadly? Was she sent by God to test his worthiness? Or was she a tool of Satan sent to test his faithfulness to God? Either way, he knew he was in for another night of self-doubt and self-abuse. He was faithful to God, to be sure, but he was as yet unworthy. He would win this trial by fire, but it would take time. Purifying the soul required true sacrifice and pain.

"Shiloh Giles, I hate you!" he yelled at the top of his voice as he began what would become his almost nightly ritual of exorcising her, or some other harlot, from his thoughts as he dropped off to sleep. When he awoke and during the day, he fretted about his weakness and his lack of accomplishments. How would he ever prove to God that he was a worthy servant? What must he do?

* * * * *

Meanwhile in New York, Seth Richards had read a short blurb in the morning's *New York Times* about the confrontation in Nashville and the tough woman priest. He had smiled as he'd thought to himself, *Good for you, Reverend Giles.* He had imagined a tall, tough woman not unlike his third-grade teacher who had taken him by his ear to the principal's office when he'd glued the hair of the girl who sat in front of him to the back of her desk.

Seth Richards was a mid-level external relations specialist, editor, and fundraiser at the United Nations Population Fund, UNFPA, when Shiloh made news with her altercation at the Mid-State Women's Clinic.

Seth had generally planned, when he thought about his future, that he would like to be a college professor or to even join the Foreign Service. But as he'd scrambled for jobs during school, he'd found himself drawn to writing and editing. While working on his PhD, he'd had more time to work and had been able to pick up a few good editing jobs at UNFPA. The more he'd done for them, the more they'd wanted. Before long, he was not just editing but also writing policy papers and speeches. Soon it became more than just another way to pay his bills. The population field intrigued him. He was especially drawn to women's rights and health.

When he was in Vietnam, he remembered seeing women in the villages. They were all bone thin and seemed to be working constantly. And he remembered an Air Force pal who'd married a young Vietnamese woman who had died during childbirth because there was not a hospital nearby that could provide the cesarean section she needed.

When he finally agreed to UNFPA's offer of a permanent job, he was asked to go to the field several times and help UNFPA's far-flung field representatives write assistance programs. During some of those trips, he visited villages and learned firsthand about the need for family planning, safe deliveries, and adequate hospital care. He also began to understand the burden that women bore because of their lack of status, which so often relegated them to forced marriage, sex against their will, and inadequate schooling. The more he learned, the more he understood UNFPA's mission. Soon he became committed to its cause and decided that this was honorable work and a profession that he could be proud of, even though it came with the dreaded tag of bureaucrat.

Seth was well liked and respected by his colleagues and friends in Trenton. He was an easygoing guy who masked his sharp intellect with quiet humility. But in time, people who knew him well learned that he was bright, a quick study, and a natural leader. He moved quickly up the bureaucratic ladder and made many friends around the world. He wasn't particularly ambitious; he just wanted to do something that he felt good about. And without the pressure or responsibility of a family, he could "hang loose," as he told himself. Seth believed in fate. But he would think sometimes when he was lonely, *It sure as hell takes its sweet time finding me.*

That evening as he sat in his one bedroom apartment on Manhattan's East Side channel surfing the news programs while he waited for the West Coast Yankee game to come on, he stumbled across the Larry King show and saw Shiloh Giles, the minister from Tennessee whom he had read about that morning. He watched her and thought how beautiful, how poised, how articulate she was. *She's not big and scary at all,* he thought. The wonderful creature on his TV screen mesmerized Seth. She had a combination of spunk and grace that he found quite appealing.

In time, though, Shiloh Giles, the reverend from Tennessee, became a hazy memory. Seth was a good man and dedicated to his work and the mission of his organization. It was, some would say, his life. Surely it gave his life meaning. Seth was comfortable in his skin.

But something was missing in Seth's life: a person to share his life with and to come home to and spend weekends with exploring the city's many parks and museums or driving through the countryside and going for hikes and bike rides. He even thought about starting a family. But like many singles in New York who worked hard, it was difficult to do much on the weekends but rest up for the workweek ahead. He marveled at how his married friends were always on the go enjoying full weekends and attending their children's events. He smiled when he heard them say, "You singles have it made."

Ah, but they have short memories, he mused.

Chapter 2

It had been three days since the "event." Shiloh was kept busy with interviews, queries about jobs, requests for speeches, and questions from friends, family, and church members about how she was coping.

When she actually had a minute to catch her breath, she found herself thinking about what had brought her to this place in life. After seminary, Shiloh had taken a job in the Philippines. Her post was located in Northern Luzon with a multidenominational program, which included United Methodist, Presbyterian, American Baptist, and Episcopalian representatives.

The missionaries had each trained for three months before coming to the Philippines. They'd served for seven years on a rotational basis with folks coming in and out of the program every year or two. Their training was in language and agriculture with a focus on rice. They'd also received extensive training on the culture and folkways of the Philippines in general and Northern Luzon in particular. They continued language lessons among themselves, and one of the missionaries, Sally, gave workshops every month to the group and served as their resident aggie expert.

There were twelve of them. Brian and Sally McCurley were the old timers with almost six years under their belts. Patrick and his wife, Julie, and their two kids had been in the Philippines for five years and Shiloh for three. The other seven were more recent arrivals. They worked in different villages but lived together in the same mission house. The mission house was located in the small town of Burgos. The missionaries were each assigned to cover different villages within the Burgos area. Sometimes they helped each other with seminars, bulk purchases for their co-ops, and joint thresher-machine rentals after harvesting and drying had been completed.

Shiloh's initial assignment had been to help organize local farmers in the barrio of San Rafael into co-ops, or as they were called there, farmers' clubs. The clubs pooled their resources in order to buy the new "miracle" rice seeds that were being produced as part of the so-called Green Revolution. Norman Bourlag had worked for years at the University of the Philippines's International Rice Research Institute (IRRI) to develop and test new varieties of rice seeds that were fast growing and disease resistant, produced larger yields, and were shorter than native rice so that they would not "lodge," or blow over, during frequent typhoons. The results were incredible. Yields doubled and, in some cases, even tripled if the farmers could afford enough fertilizer, and the length of the growing cycle allowed for two crops per year instead of one.

The farmers harvested by hand and dried their crops on palm mats that they placed on the roadways or the concrete slabs at the local markets. They tested the dryness of their seeds the way it had always been done, by biting the seeds. That method seemed to work as well now as it had for past generations and was always within a few percentage points of the instrument that the missionaries used.

Very few people owned land, and if they did, they owned only a hectare or maybe a portion of a hectare. Most of the farmers sharecropped on a sixty-to-forty basis from owners who lived in the towns. Sixty percent of the harvest went to the tenant, who was responsible for seeds, fertilizer, harvesting, and thrashing. In bad times when there were severe typhoons, locusts, disease or pest problems, the tenants borrowed from the owner, which perpetuated their sorry plight. The miracle seeds were making a difference, but land reform and a fairer system of land use were needed before they would be able to prosper much beyond the subsistence level.

The people in all the villages where the missionaries worked liked the missionaries and appreciated their work, but they would complain about the taste of the miracle rice, although they loved the output and their greatly increased income. And as new varieties were invented, the taste improved. The folks in San Rafael soon grew to adore the perky lady who was helping them. She and her missionary colleagues mastered the local language, Ilocano, ate their food, and were always cheerful and helpful. Shiloh wasn't afraid to roll up her pant legs and get behind a water buffalo and plow or harrow rice paddies. But she drew the line at sitting around with the men in the evenings and drinking their dreadful gin and coconut wine. Instead, when the workday was over, she would often have coffee or tea with the women and talk about their lives and families.

She heard stories about sickly children and women dying from various problems during birthing or shortly afterward. And she knew that many of the children were malnourished. In fact, she could not remember ever seeing even one overweight person in San Rafael. The children were often sick, and very few adults lived long lives. The people were always clean, they were happy and kind, but they were dirt poor. Some families, in which the men were ill, unable to work, or lazy, were very poor and had to depend on odd jobs and charity to get by.

The women almost always wanted to talk about America. Shiloh was always embarrassed when the women told her that they wished that they were rich and beautiful like her. As for being rich, she was embarrassed. She knew that her salary, although barely above the U.S. poverty standard, was many times more than any of them earned as a family. That was true even for the few who ran small businesses selling soap, oil, and other daily needs in their little sari-sari stores, or even for the fortunate few that owned the jeepneys that provided most of the local transportation. Shiloh had her own jeep, which only added to her image of wealth. None of the farmers she worked with even dreamed of owning a private vehicle. That was simply out of the question. Most had only ridden in jeepneys or buses. Very few had ever been in a car or private vehicle of any kind.

The village women would often tease Shiloh, telling her that she looked like a movie star. Shiloh would always blush and deny their claims. But she understood that to these poor village women, she must seem to have everything, and in their eyes that meant that she was beautiful.

Shiloh was always clean and fresh, but she didn't wear makeup or dwell on her looks. When she thought about such things, it was usually when she looked at her calloused hands and broken nails and tried to imagine what her grandmother and college friends would say about letting herself go.

She loved talking with the women and often felt sadness that she couldn't do more to help them. She was keenly aware that she would leave someday and return to America where air conditioning was standard, where food was varied and plentiful, and where electricity and transportation were not luxuries. A few families in San Rafael owned small generators and a refrigerator, but the majority used kerosene lamps and, if they could afford it, bought blocks of ice to preserve their food and cool their drinks.

One evening after work, before she left to go back to the mission house, she was having tea with a few of the ladies when one of them, Letty, blurted out, "Shy, tell us about having babies—I mean, about how not to have babies. Our husbands always want to *have contact*," her friends giggled, "and we always have babies. I have heard that women in America can decide when to have babies, that they can do something to stop babies from coming until they are ready for them and still have contact anytime. Is that true?"

Shiloh took a moment to collect her thoughts. She had been there for almost three years of her seven-year assignment and had never discussed sex or having babies with the women. The women were timid, and she was focused on her farming work. Food was basic for survival, and some of these folks lived barely above the survival level.

Shiloh began slowly. "Well, preventing babies is called birth control; one method is little pills that women take every day. Another is something that a woman uses inside her body each time she has contact with her husband. It is called a diaphragm. There is something else that stays inside permanently, but I don't know the name of that method. And there are rubbers, or condoms, that men use. Using these things is called family planning. They allow you to plan when to have babies."

They all started to talk at once, but Letty prevailed, "Shy, where can I get this birth control? I want family planning."

"Me too," said the others in unison.

"You get most of them from a doctor," said Shiloh.

"We can't afford doctors. No wonder rich people have only a few children," said another woman, whose name was Loling.

"Let me check on it," said Shiloh.

Thus Shiloh's new career in family planning began.

Shiloh talked to her colleagues that night at supper in the mission house. She asked Patrick James, the in-charge person of their mission, if she could try to help the women in San Rafael obtain family planning.

"Only," said Pat, "if you don't limit yourself to San Rafael."

The others nodded their assent. Brian McCurley spoke up. "Shy, I hear stories all the time about problems with pregnancy. The men I work with are constantly worried when their wives are pregnant. And their children always seem to be sick from one thing or another."

"Yes, that's my experience too," agreed Sally, Brian's wife. Brian was a United Methodist Minister. Sally was a legitimate agricultural expert, having graduated from Moo U, as Brian called Michigan State, with a degree in horticulture.

As a first step in her quest to help the women with family planning, Shiloh asked around and found a doctor in a town about forty kilometers away who was trained in obstetrics and gynecology. Doctora Luisa Encarnacion readily agreed to see Shiloh's "patients."

Shiloh then went to Manila and was able to get pills, IUDs, and rubber gloves through the U.S. foreign aid program. She was eventually able to talk the UN office into a grant for family planning and maternal health, which included training midwives for deliveries and prenatal and postnatal services and, of course, family planning.

In the early days, she focused on San Rafael and the barrios where her missionary partners were working. But by the time she completed her assignment, the program had extended throughout the province with U.S. Peace Corps, Japanese, and UN volunteers helping out.

Local Catholic priests even got into the act by discreetly organizing seminars for Shiloh and her colleagues in the barrios under their care. They too had seen the needless suffering caused by malnutrition, poor maternal care, too many pregnancies, and pregnancies spaced too closely together.

About three weeks after that fateful discussion with her friends over tea, Shiloh was ready to begin her first family planning seminar. She was freshly schooled in the methods of contraception and had charts and brochures provided by a Boston-based private group by the name of Pathfinder. In their eagerness, Letty and her friends arrived at the big event early, which is not a Filipino trait. They settled in to wait for others and for Shiloh's presentation.

Mercedes Paat, the principal of the grade school, had offered a classroom for the evening session, and the town crier had gone throughout the barrio the night before to announce the "miss-i-nary sim-er-nar on baa'bee planning." Shiloh was more nervous than she had been in the fifth grade when she had to deliver Patrick Henry's famous 1775 House of Burgesses speech before the entire student body. Learning agriculture was one thing; talking about sex was quite another, Shiloh thought. *And me a virgin. Give me family planning or give me unwanted pregnancy and possibly death*, she mused as she stood there watching the women enter the classroom.

She smiled at the thought of her Grandma Alice and her brother Sam and the ribbing they would give her if they could see her now, standing here thousands of miles away talking about birth control. They'd laughed at her as a farmer. She remembered Sam asking her if she knew the difference between corn plants and tomato plants. *And now*, she thought, *I am a sex education teacher. What next*, she wondered, *auto mechanics, fish farming?*

The crowd was standing room only. Several women were even standing outside the waist-high windows leaning in, while many men stood under the mango trees that adorned the front of the schoolyard smoking and talking quietly among themselves.

Shiloh glanced at Letty, who was sitting ramrod straight on the front row with her eyes glued on her friend. Their eyes met for an instant, and the flicker of a nervous smile crossed Letty's face. Shiloh knew that Letty had talked to almost all of the women in the barrio about her American friend. "She will help all of us have healthier children," Letty had told them. "She will help us be stronger, and she will give us confidence to be with our husbands at night."

Shiloh couldn't let them down. But what she had to say was so elementary, so basic. Surely they knew about reproduction. Surely they knew about sexuality and their periods and ovulation. Suddenly she felt foolish. *Who do I think I am anyway, some great savior from America?*

But she brushed away her fears and stepped up on the small platform. "My friends, I am here tonight to talk about something very personal." Shiloh could feel the perspiration trickling down her back and sides. The room was like an oven in the sweltering Philippine evening, which, combined with the body heat of the audience, added even more humidity. She plowed on.

"Sex is intimate. It is one of the most intimate actions in our lives. Sex brings pleasure, it expresses love, and it often produces children. Sex is the way we reproduce; it is the way we continue the human race. Many of you have asked me to talk tonight about how you can have sex and meet your obligations as a wife and still prevent babies that you are not ready to have. I know that when I marry," there was a chuckle from the crowd, "when I marry, I want children when my husband and I are ready. I want them when my husband and I can take care of them properly, when we know that we can afford the medical care they will need, and when we know that we can provide adequately for their schooling. It is a big decision, perhaps the biggest one any of us will ever make.

"Being a parent is a full-time job. Children depend on their parents for everything. Unlike a dog or a cat and other animals that wean their young to become self-sufficient after a few months, our children stay with us until adulthood. Yes, pregnancy is a big decision. Until recently, most of us depended on luck or on what we might know about women's menstrual cycles and when a woman can become pregnant and when she cannot. But now there are ways you can be intimate with your husbands, have contact, and at the same time be almost certain of avoiding pregnancy. That's what we are here to discuss tonight."

Shiloh was beginning to hit her stride. She could tell that her audience was listening carefully to every word. "I know that you are interested because of the stories Letty and the others have told me about your hardships." Letty beamed at the recognition. "I can also tell that you are interested because so many of you are here. I can even see many men outside under the mango trees." Shiloh gave a quick wave to the men, whom she could see through the open windows. Half of them turned away in embarrassment while the other half giggled. A few waved back.

She pointed to a large chart of the female reproductive system that was taped behind her on the blackboard. She explained the menstrual cycle including its purpose, ovulation, and pregnancy. She then began to discuss different methods of birth control and how they were used and how they worked. When she got to the last method, the condom, she held up a large chart of the male reproductive system. The penis was erect. Every face in the room turned red, and the room erupted in nervous laughter. The men seemed to move further back into the shadows of the trees. Many of the women turned to watch the men's reaction as a new wave of laughter filled the room.

Shiloh passed around the different contraceptives for the women to see. She asked Letty to take a set out to the men. Finally, after answering countless questions, she made an announcement, "Doctora Luisa Encarnacion, who has a clinic in Cauayan, has agreed to see as many of you as we can get to Cauayan next Wednesday. I have asked Romy and Cirilo to have their jeepneys here at the school at seven o'clock Wednesday morning to take anyone who wants to go. The U.S. government has provided the contraceptives, and my mission group is paying for the doctora's services. You will have to pay for your own jeepney ride."

The room filled with applause as almost everyone came to the front to thank Shiloh for her presentation and her help. Even a few men came in to thank her.

The first trip to Cauayan was a circus. Over eighty women showed up at the school by 6:30. Unfortunately, the jeepneys could only seat fourteen each, and Shiloh's jeep could squeeze in just four more. That left over half without a ride. In time, all that wanted to go, about 70 percent of the reproductive-aged women in San Rafael, were able to go and see the doctora. The UN eventually bought a jeep for Doctora Encarnacion so she could visit the barrios where someone would turn their house into a clinic for the day. By the time Shiloh had completed her seven-year commitment, the infant and maternal morbidity and mortality rates had begun to go down. The birth rates were down, and school attendance had begun to rise. The mission added maternal and child health and family planning to its mandate.

When Shiloh left, a special banquet was held in her honor, hosted by the governor at the provincial capitol. Letty and her friends also arranged a big bash for Shiloh in San Rafael. When Shiloh finally left, she did so with a heavy heart. She was returning to the land of plenty and leaving her poor friends behind. She felt guilty, but she wanted to see what else was out there for a woman priest to do. She was young and had the world at her feet. She wrote to her grandmother and brother that she had a long time yet to decide what she wanted to finally do when she grew up. It was her way of telling them that she may someday return to missionary work.

The opportunity to go to All Saints in her home state was perfect. She liked and respected Reverend Jacobson. She had attended a few lectures that he had given at Sewanee when she was in seminary and had talked with him a few times. He was a thoughtful clergyman who balanced his ministerial role of teaching the articles of faith with his pastoral role of counseling troubled members of his flock. He was down to earth and yet somehow came across as a man of consequence. He was someone Shiloh considered a model of the kind of priest she hoped to be someday.

Apparently, he remembered her too. When her name went out to churches as her term was ending in the Philippines, Jacobson immediately contacted her with the offer of an assistant's position at All Saints.

Someone nudged Shiloh out of her thoughts. It was time to do another interview

* * * * *

When Shiloh finally got home, she poured a glass of wine and sat down to take stock of the last twenty-four hours. A ringing phone soon broke her reverie. "Shiloh Giles," she answered.

"This is Walter Cronkite."

"Sam, you devil. I was going to call you as soon as I got a breather."

"Yeah, right. I'm only a minor lawyer in the big city of Trenton. Why should you bother with a little fish like me?"

"It's nice to hear a friendly voice."

"How bad is it?"

"It's so bad that I was sitting here in the dark just thinking about what to do."

"Believe it or not, sis, I didn't know a thing; none of us did. Father Gunn called me to find out what was going on and how you were. That's how I found out. So, Shy, what are you going to do?"

"I don't know. Father Jacobson told me that I can stay here forever. I've learned a lot from him, and I believe that he likes my work. He and his wife, Susan, treat me like their daughter. But the phone won't stop ringing: interviews, speaking requests, even a job offer. I can't believe this has caused such a firestorm. Quite frankly, I don't know what to think. But I'm going to Tullahoma next week to see Grandma and Uncle Barry for a few days."

"What about me?" said Sam in a phony wounded voice.

Shy laughed, "Poor baby, I was going to call you as soon as I turned on the lights."

"Whew," Sam sighed, "you have a full plate. I'll bet the Philippines look good about now."

Shy laughed, "Yeah, plowing behind a water buffalo certainly doesn't get press attention."

"Catherine Shiloh Giles, I think you are enjoying this."

"What is this, confession time? I didn't know you had been ordained."

"Seriously, Shy. Is everything okay? Our old friend Father Gunn has an opening now. I know that it's yours if you want it. He can provide a safe harbor away from the storm."

"If I were to leave, it would look I was pushed by this incident. I guess that's why I need to take a few days in Tullahoma. I need to think things through. May I call you for your wise counsel after I return, Mr. Counselor?"

"Of course, Shy. Better still, come for a visit."

Shiloh laughed, "Thanks, Sammy. I love you. It's nice to hear your voice."

"You too, Shiloh."

* * * * *

After her conversation with her brother, Shiloh got out some cheese and crackers to go with her wine and continued to sit in the dark. She thought about how unexpectedly her life was turning out. When she had arrived in Nashville, she had been full of energy and ready to settle down in her role as assistant parish priest. It would be a new challenge. She knew it would be an entirely new life and experience. She had especially been anxious to see how life for women had changed or at least what had happened in that regard in the seven years she had been in the Philippines.

She had known from growing up in Tullahoma and in her studies during high school and college that women were unequal in her country and that women were often discriminated against and mistreated. But she had not been prepared for the hardships women faced in the developing world.

Women's social status in most developing countries was far behind their sisters in the developed world in education, in health, and in economic opportunities. Options had been severely limited for many who were raised in crushing poverty. And in numerous countries, women were maligned by harsh, male-dominated cultural standards; few choices were available about when and who to marry or even about whether or when to have children.

Shiloh remembered talking about these subjects with her grandmother and how much change had occurred in her lifetime in America. *How long,* she wondered, *would it take for change to happen in the developing world?*

It had been especially good to take a posting in Nashville because it put her close to her Grandma Alice, who was getting up in years and had become frail. Shiloh smiled as she thought of her.

Alice was the most important person in Shiloh's life. During the bad times, when her mom was in trouble and during her parents' divorce, Shiloh had always depended on her grandmother. Grandma Alice had actually been her surrogate mother. She'd given her youngest granddaughter the unlimited and unconditional love she missed at home. Now it was time for Shiloh to be there for her grandma.

As she sipped her wine, her thoughts turned to her childhood and the year everything changed. Shy was seven years old when her brother Sam, who was only sixteen, and their mother left Tullahoma. Shiloh had been left alone to cope with a new family.

*****

"Grandma, are you going to die too?"

Alice's sister, Bertha, had just died, leaving Alice as the only surviving member of her immediate family.

"Of course I'm going to die, Shy; we all die someday," replied Alice.

"But when are you going to die, Grandma? I remember when Pappy died. I was five years old then. I'm seven now. How old will I be when you die, Grandma?"

"None of us know when we will die, sweetie. Your Grandfather Pappy died unexpectedly. He died in his sleep from a heart attack. Aunt Bertha had been ill for a long time. We knew she was going to die soon, but only God knows exactly when she would die or when any of us will die."

"Grandma, have you ever met God?"

Alice exhaled a sigh. "Shy, I've never really met God, but I believe that I've felt his presence and his love. Why don't we have a glass of iced tea, sweetie. This heat is unbearable."

It was July in Tullahoma; the porch where they sat was shaded, but it was still hot. The day was still and steamy as the dew burned off of the grass, the kind of day that was normal for mornings in Tullahoma in midsummer.

Shiloh watched a mocking bird drink at the birdbath while Alice was inside pouring iced tea. When she returned, they both took a long swig of tea.

Shiloh broke the silence. "Why do you call me Shy, Grandma?"

"It is short for Shiloh and easier to say," Alice explained. "Your father is named Charles Clayton Giles. Chase is short for Charles, and we all call him Chase. Now how about lunch?"

*****

Shiloh sat at home, remembering the many hours she had spent on Grandma Alice's porch. She was taking some time off next week to spend a few days with Grandma Alice. She would also pay a visit to Uncle Barry, her father's law partner and her godfather. Barry Whitfield was Chase's best friend. They had sports and law in common, they had both fought in the war, they attended the same church, and they each had children about the same age. Since her father died, Barry was the closest thing to a father she had had.

She remembered those early years when she had had both her parents. During those years, Shiloh and Sam would go grocery shopping with their mom. Sam would push the cart, and Shiloh would help her mother decide what to buy. It was fun. She loved her mom and remembered her kindness and the warmth of her love. But her mom, Ruth, was an alcoholic. Her affliction eventually destroyed the Giles family.

Shiloh's family was happy during the nondrinking times. But there was always tension at home when Ruth drank. Ruth was very pretty and almost always attracted men. When they went shopping, men would frequently say things to their mom that would make Sam angry. More than once, he warned men to stay away from his mother. "Don't talk to my mother," he would say as he tried to sound gruff.

Shiloh knew that she had missed the problems of the early days when Sammy had been younger. He hadn't said much, but she was smart enough to figure out that he had been hiding his pain and acting upbeat for her benefit. Even when he was ebullient, she could see the pain in his eyes. Sam had protected his little sister. She loved him so much.

"Why are Mom and Dad getting a divorce, Sam? Grandma Alice said that they've been married twenty-one years."

"I don't know," Sam had answered. "But there isn't anything we can do about it."

"But I heard you tell them not to get a divorce."

"I know I did. But they didn't listen. I guess they don't love each other anymore."

Chase had taken an apartment close to his office while the divorce business got settled. Shiloh and Sam lived with Ruth. Sam had protected his mother from Chase and had insisted that he and Shy stay with her during the divorce proceeding. Sam was blind when it came to his mother. He would blame his father who, after years of trying to hold his family together, had started drinking too. Shiloh could remember times when her mom and dad would yell at each other and Sam would intercede, sometimes standing between them before there was violence.

The summer of the divorce she stayed with Grandma Alice every day. She would play with neighborhood friends and spend hours "helping" her grandmother with baking, cooking, and doing other household chores. Sam stayed busy playing baseball, carrying papers, being an acolyte, and taking care of their household. Ruth worked downtown at a candy store. Sometimes she came home and cooked; other times Sam cooked. On the nights Sam cooked, Ruth would not arrive until late. She was almost always drunk, and sometimes she could barely walk.

In July, she hit a fire hydrant in her car on the way home one night. The police chief, one of Chase's high school buddies, had called Chase. Chase had brought Ruth home. They were yelling when they came into the house. Chase had said, "You goddamned slut, who did you screw this time?"

Ruth turned and tried to slap Chase, who slugged her in the eye. Sam lunged over his mother's sprawled body and hit his father in the chest with the full force of his fist. Chase staggered backward. It was obvious that he too had been drinking.

Sam grabbed a poker from the fireplace and ordered his father out of the house. Chase glared at Sam.

Shiloh jumped in. "No, Daddy. Don't!"

Sam stood his ground; Shy could see him shaking. Sam had tears in his eyes. "Get out, Dad, now."

Chase looked at Shy and said, "I'm sorry, Shiloh. I'm leaving now."

Shy ran to her dad and hugged him. "Thank you, Daddy."

Chase left, and Sam told Shy to take care of their mom. He made coffee and called Father Gunn.

Father Gunn arrived about thirty minutes later with Jenny Miller, an AA member who knew the Gileses' situation. They all had coffee. Ruth held her cup in shaky hands. Jenny called and made arrangements with the Oakwood Sanitarium. She took Ruth there the next morning.

Shy had felt so proud of Sam. When Father Gunn had asked Sam if he could take care of Shy by himself, he had answered, "Yes, sir."

For the next two weeks, Sam and Shiloh stayed alone. They ate with Grandma Alice a few times and once with the Gunn's. Barry came by one evening and brought hamburgers and ice cream. Shiloh remembered him telling Sam that their father felt badly. He told him that he should consider taking Shiloh and moving in with their dad, but Sam refused. "We can't leave our mom, Barry. Someone needs to be with her."

But Ruth had continued to get drunk after she returned from the sanitarium. Sometimes her mom came home, and sometimes she didn't. Shiloh would go to the bus stop and wait for her. Ruth was no longer allowed to drive. It was a sad time. *Poor Sam*, Shiloh thought all these years later. He was so young to be worrying about things like that. Tears welled up in her eyes as she thought about the childhood Sam had missed.

When Shiloh and Sam awoke Christmas Day, Ruth was gone. She left a note that said Sam and Shiloh should go live with their father. Sam was devastated. He had no idea where his mother had gone. Reluctantly, he'd called his grandmother. He took Shiloh to her grandmother's house, and then he went to stay with a friend. The next day, Grandma Alice told Sam that Shiloh had gone home with her father.

A few days later, Sam's uncle, George, Ruth's brother, had come and taken Sam to Alabama to stay with his family. Uncle George worked at a factory in Chattanooga, and his wife, Betsy, worked off and on at a local grocery store. Uncle George and Aunt Betsy were nice people and treated Sam like a member of their family. They had five children; the eldest was ten years old. It was a big and happy family. Sam started school there after the holidays. He stayed until June.

One day in March, Uncle George met him at the school bus stop in his car. "Come with me, son," said Uncle George. "We have to go down to Calhoun Georgia to get your mother."

On the way to Calhoun, Uncle George told Sammy that Ruth was in jail. "They called me today at work, son, and said that she had been beaten and was hurt, badly hurt. There was no place for her to stay except in the jail infirmary under police custody. The person or persons that beat her left her in a motel. She had apparently been there for four or five days and is just now able to travel. I called Doctor Blankenship, and he said that he would make arrangements for her at the hospital in Fort Payne for when we get back."

Ruth had stayed in the hospital for four days. She had also had an illegal abortion in Georgia that had not gone very well, which had added to her pain. But by the time she got out, she seemed much better and was in good sprits.

But all of a sudden, Ruth disappeared again. Sam wrote to Shiloh and told her, "This morning, I went out to milk ole Gertrude, and Mom was with me and helped me feed and water the chickens. When I came home from school, she was gone. Aunt Betsy said that a man came for her. She had told Aunt Betsy to tell me good-bye. And that was it."

By the time the school year ended, Sam had turned seventeen and decided to join the military. He had called Shiloh to tell her.

"Take me with you. Dad's new wife, Margaret, hates me."

"No, you can't come; I don't have any money," he'd told Shiloh.

"Joining the army is best for me, Shy. You should stay with Dad. He'll take care of you," Sam had said, "and Grandma Alice is a short walk away. I'll always write"

Sam wrote to Shiloh and Grandma Alice when he got to boot camp. He told them where he was and that he would be fine. "I'll get my high school diploma here with something they call a GED test, so I'll be able to go to college later."

It was 1970, and Sammy was seventeen years old. He would soon go to Vietnam, and Shiloh would not see her big brother for almost ten years.

As Shiloh remembered all of this, she reflected on how life must have been for her mother and her affliction. Sam had not told Shiloh the details about how their mom had come to Alabama when Sam was living there with his aunt and uncle until he came for Shiloh's graduation from high school.

Shiloh felt pain and sorrow whenever she had seen similar situations in the Philippines and even during her short time at All Saints, which reminded her of her mother. Alcoholism was a terrible affliction, especially for the families and it was almost always difficult for women because they were so often abused. Abuse and violence were frequently present regardless of whether the woman was an alcoholic herself or was a family member of an alcoholic.

She took in a deep breath and said a prayer for her mother.

Chapter 3

It was a clear, bright day when Shiloh left her house at 6:00 a.m. for the three-block walk to All Saints. This was the first Sunday she would see church members since she had become a local celebrity. *I wonder what folks will say*, she thought as she made her way. She was assigned to officiate the early service this week and to read the lesson and assist with communion at the eleven o'clock service.

Her head was clear and her walk determined as she headed down Willow Lane. Early May was a wonderful time of year in Nashville. It was not yet oppressively hot. And Mother Nature had painted everything in bright colors. The azaleas were still gloriously hanging on, the dogwoods were in bloom, more white than pink as usual, and even a few early roses were beginning to bloom. She saw magnolias just getting started, and there were tulips and perennials leafing out in every garden.

An evening shower had washed away the dust, making the world around her sparkle. Birds were everywhere, singing and flitting around; it was like being inside her own private aviary. Robins were flitting around on lawns looking for early morning worms, blue jays were squawking, and wrens and sparrows were filling the air with their sweet songs; she could even hear doves cooing. And, as usual, mocking birds were dive-bombing to protect their nests from naughty blue jays, cats, dogs, and unsuspecting priests.

She felt a new confidence about who she was. Was it a kind of inner pride, she wondered. She had done something, quite accidentally for sure, but nevertheless, she had done it, and she was pleased. It was difficult for her to fathom, though, that this one act of courage could have had this much of an influence on her life. She was someone with values and principles, someone, she thought, who had stood her ground and had spoken out. But others would have done the same thing. She was just at the proverbial right place at the right time. For what, though? Was there a hidden reason or a grand plan? Had she changed somehow? No, she was still Catherine Shiloh Giles from little Tullahoma, Tennessee. She hadn't changed, she wasn't different, but now people knew her better than they had before. She was happy about that in a way she didn't quite understand.

Yes, she decided, she was proud of herself. But that was not necessarily good. *Calm down, Shiloh. Don't get heady. Maybe it's self-confidence that I'm experiencing*, she thought, *but I've never lacked self-confidence*. With this situation, she had publicly acted out and increased her status. She had gone from being an assistant parish priest to being an assistant parish priest whose opinion would be sought. She had become an expert on women's rights and a somebody overnight. She was still answering calls for interviews.

But I'm still Shiloh, she told herself. She felt radiant and happy, a bit bewildered perhaps, but ready for whatever might come. *Another beautiful day*, she thought, *and a new me*. She smiled to herself.

She thought about her work with young people as she walked, this was another part of her work at the parish that she loved. It awakened in her a passion for counseling. Teenagers were the most difficult to fathom. Most were trying to cope with the changes that occur during the process of maturing, especially the effect of hormones and the pressures to succeed and be liked, while at the same time struggling with their place in the family and in society as they knew it at their age. Some were worried about problems at home, some about how they were seen by their peers and adults, and still others about their schoolwork and religion. One thing was certain; Reverend Giles was popular. Her schedule was always full of youngsters who wanted to talk. At twenty-nine, she she was close enough to their age for them to identify with, and yet old enough and important enough to take seriously.

The most difficult problems were the ones that involved the family. Divorce was common. Youngsters frequently thought that it was somehow their fault. It rarely was, but it was hard to be convincing when the real reasons were not always known to anyone but the parents themselves. The saddest problems involved drugs and alcohol. Parents with these problems seemed to always make a hash of their lives and in the process, the lives of everyone around them.

Even though Shiloh had her own personal experiences to fall back on, it mattered little. In most cases, all she could do was to be a friend and try to help the kids stay focused on their responsibilities as students and members of their family. She counseled them to prepare for their own life ahead and try to be as understanding as possible with their parents. Her strategy was to encourage them to work on the things they could do something about so they would not dwell so much on the things they could do little to change. She realized that was what Father Gunn had tried to do with her and Sam. It had worked with Shiloh, but Sam had been so protective of his mother that he had been unable to cope rationally.

When it was the child that had the drug or alcohol problem, it seemed easier to handle or at least to find solutions. In these cases, she worked closely with parents, who often instigated the contact in the first place.

The most frustrating problem she confronted was with young women who came to her perplexed about their gender.

"Why are we considered less fit than guys for serious careers and colleges?"

"Why are we always considered first for our appearance rather than our personality or academic achievements?"

"Why aren't we given the same opportunities as men when we are just as qualified?"

One young woman came to Shiloh, complaining that she had been turned down for a senior internship at a local manufacturer. When the young woman interviewed with the personnel director, he had told her that their internships were serious, that they were intended for serious students and potential engineers.

"You are a pretty young woman," he had said, "you'll go to college and probably marry before you graduate. You wouldn't want to take the place of a serious young man, now would you?"

Shiloh asked her, "Beth, what do you want to do about it?"

"There's nothing I can do. I spoke to my father, and he told me the same thing, go to college, and learn what you can and see what happens. You may get a marriage proposal."

"And?" said Shiloh.

"And I don't like that. I want to be an engineer. I've dreamed about being an engineer since I was a little girl. I love math and science and want to try."

"What does your mother say?" queried Shiloh.

"She's proud of my grades and accomplishments. My science projects have been in the top three in my class since ninth grade. I won twice. But Mom also tells me to listen to my father. She also told me to go on to college and study hard and that maybe my dad will see that and be more encouraging."

"That's a good start. I had a similar situation with my counselor in high school, but my father was very supportive. I just ignored my counselor and went my own way. But that's not always so easy. Maybe your mother's idea is the best road to follow for now. Go to college and do your best and maybe your dad will be more understanding."

"I guess I don't have much choice."

"Oh, but you do."

"You're right. I shouldn't worry so much about being slighted and just go to college and do my best."

"Good," said Shiloh, "and maybe someday we can get the ERA passed and adopted, and then, in time, it will get easier to change minds."

The Equal Rights Amendment had never been adopted, and the situation for women in America, while much better in the twentieth century than ever before, was still far short of real equality. Shiloh wanted to do something, but how?

For now she counseled and encouraged girls. She wanted to find a way to do more, but nothing came to mind. She remembered the time she'd challenged her status at church. She giggled now thinking about her tenacity at such a tender age.

* * * * *

"Grandma, I want to be an acolyte like Sammy. But he told me that he's never seen a girl acolyte before. He said that he'd ask Father Gunn if it would be okay though. He's a nice brother."

"Yes, dear, Sammy is indeed a good brother. But he's right; there aren't any little-girl acolytes."

"That's not fair," said Shiloh. "Why shouldn't I be an acolyte? Why should acolytes be just for boys? I know Father Gunn will listen to Sammy. It shouldn't just be boys, Grandma; that isn't fair. Boys aren't any better than girls. I'll do a good job. I know I can do it, Grandma."

"You're right, Shy. Girls can do it just as well as boys. And your Grandma Alice will be proud to see her little Shy up in front during church."

Sammy had indeed talked to Father Gunn, who had reluctantly agreed to try his sister as a junior acolyte. Sam had told Shiloh about his conversation and asked her to be sure and thank Father Gunn for allowing her to be an acolyte.

"This may open up the flood gates, Sam," Father Gunn had said. "Once other girls see Shy up there in front of the church, they'll all want to do it too."

"But you'll be making a lot of little girls happy, Father," Sam had said. "I'll help train them."

* * * * *

Before she knew it, she was in the vestry getting ready. She went to the sanctuary to make sure that everything was set out in its proper place: the flowers and candles on the altar, the communion implements on the credence table, the gospel marked at the appropriate places for the reading and the service. It was all ready; the altar guild was perfect. She thought they were like silent angels preparing God's house for his worshippers.

The morning communion was for the folks who preferred a short, quiet service; a few families would come to the early service on their way to parks, lakes, and other family outings. Some folks would be heading to work or were on the way home, and there were always a few golfers with early tee times or folks who were going fishing and wanted to be on the water when the fish woke up. She liked the early service. It was peaceful. You could hear the birds singing and occasional traffic sounds, although it was light at this time of day. Later services were always crowded. The rustle of the congregation, the whispers, and the starched clothing made a sound that you only heard in church.

At the later services, folks frequently wanted to talk after the service, ask questions or make appointments. But there was precious little time to do any of that because of the large numbers. Conversely, at the early service there was plenty of time to chat when she greeted people at the door and to minister to those with problems or requests. She liked the special intimacy that was so evident at these quiet morning worship services.

During the service, she focused on the solemn aspects of the Eucharist. She had forgotten for a moment about the excitement of the week, but when the congregation, a bit larger than usual for this hour, reached the door after the service to shake hands, she was besieged with compliments about her adventure at the clinic.

"I saw you on TV, Reverend Giles."

"You were great on *Larry King*, Shiloh."

"Wow, I couldn't believe that someone I knew was on national TV."

And on and on.

Shiloh's slight fears of rebuke were obviously misplaced. No one mentioned the actual situation or the reason for the hoopla; they focused instead on Shiloh and her performance on TV or seeing her name in *The Tennessean*.

She thought to herself, *so this is what it's like to be "public."* Folks want to know you, to see how you act and what you look like up close. Imagine what it would be like to be a politician or an actor, she mused.

The eleven o'clock service was more of the same. Even the few vestry members, who Bill had told her were grumpy, were all smiles. Some folks asked her to pose with them for pictures. One woman said that she wanted to send a picture to her son who was away at school. She noticed Bill looking at her once with a smile on his face. She couldn't tell if he was proud of her, amused, or both. She was looking forward to a late supper that evening with Bill and Susan after the youth meeting. Shiloh would leave for Tullahoma the next morning for a few days off.

When she arrived at the Jacobson's for dinner, Susan met her at the door and gave her a big hug. "Let me look at you," said Susan. "Let me see this karate priestess up close."

Bill joined them at the door. "I suppose you could use a stiff drink, Shy, after the week you've had?" asked Bill.

"A nice glass of cold, white wine would be wonderful," answered Shiloh.

"Me too," said Susan as she headed for the kitchen to check on dinner.

"I noticed that you had a lot of admirers at church this morning. I was thinking of taking up a special collection next week so we could hire a PR person to handle your appearances," laughed Bill.

Shiloh suppressed a giggle. "Perhaps we could hire one of those Madison Avenue firms, and while you're at it, could you get me an agent too?"

"Good idea," Bill said, stroking his chin. "Maybe we can ask that Skyler fella to pay another visit to the clinic to make it more interesting. I read that he was shocked that you were a priest. I believe he was quoted as saying that he couldn't imagine what kind of church you were from."

"The church," said Shiloh, holding her nose high in the air, "that has produced more presidents than any other denomination in the United States."

"Indeed it has, my dear. Indeed it has."

They clicked their glasses and moved to the parlor where Susan met them with a tray of hors d'oeuvres.

"So what has happened on the interview front?" Bill asked.

"Well," said Shiloh, "things have calmed down a bit. Skyler's lawyer, after learning that I was pressing charges, said that they would pursue a civil case against me."

"What civil case?" queried Bill.

"He's claiming that I incited the crowd and forced the issue and that I tried to usurp his constitutional rights," replied Shiloh.

"Oh bull; surely he can't get anywhere with that baloney?" exhorted Bill.

"No, of course not. Tony Hill told me that his lawyer was just bluffing to try to get me to drop the charges. Tony said that he and Judge Bartlett had spoken and that y'all had talked, as you told me earlier."

"Yes, that's true," replied Bill. "The judge thinks it's a can't-miss for you."

"Tony also said that you and he were for making a stand too."

"We are indeed, dear. We'll run interference internally if any is needed, which I doubt. Didn't some people offer you help?" Bill continued.

"Yes, the ACLU and Planned Parenthood. But Tony said that wasn't necessary; unless it gets serious, his retainer from the church will handle it without any additional charges. I'd be reluctant about taking time from my job if that is required. But Tony said that if that were to happen, I could back out later."

Bill frowned. "Don't worry about the church, Shy. We'll be fine. I'm delighted that you're going after that bully—again," he exclaimed, laughing at his own joke.

"Here, Shy," offered Susan, "try this cheese spread. It has chives and green olives. I love it."

After a wonderful supper of pot roast and apple pie à la mode and conversation about church and gossip about several of its members, they moved to the parlor for coffee.

"Would either of you ladies like to join me for a brandy?" asked Bill.

They both said yes.

He poured the drinks, and they all took a sip.

Bill spoke first. "What makes America different is that we're a nation of laws where church and state are separated. Jefferson said in a letter to the Delaware Baptist Association in 1802 that, and I quote. 'The legislature should make no laws respecting an establishment of religion, or prohibiting the free exercise thereof, thus building a wall of separation between church and state.' Thus, the principle of separation has been upheld by our courts and legislature since that time.

"Your incident at the clinic is a perfect example of the influence of fundamentalism where American citizens are banding together under a religious banner to usurp the legal rights of their fellow citizens. Maybe incidents like this will sober our fellow citizens and remind them from whence we came.

"When our church and several other mainline Protestants submitted amicus curiae briefs in the abortion case in 1973, we made it clear that we did not necessarily support abortion but that we believed all citizens must make their own decisions based on their own beliefs and articles of faith."

He held out his hand for emphasis. "That's what the separation of church and state means. These fundamentalists, like Lawson and those TV preachers that push a strict and literal interpretation of the Bible, are ruining our country. They're so intrusive and dogmatic. If they were really in charge, there's no telling what might happen. They'd be just as bad as those folks who run Iran and Saudi Arabia. What they really want is a theocracy."

Bill leaned forward in his chair. "We have a lot at stake. If these people gain any more political power, I shudder to think what may happen. I could go on, but I thought I might take a good long swig of this brandy and let you two have the floor while I drink. It's just that your incident at the clinic and being together away from church is a good opportunity to get that off my chest." Bill rested his case.

They all sat in silence for a few moments.

Finally Shy spoke. "I agree. Americans are struggling for answers to questions of faith. We lost in Vietnam, drugs are everywhere, unmarried teenage girls are getting pregnant, President Nixon was forced to leave office in disgrace because of Watergate, and all of this on the heels of our proudest moment as a nation when we saved the world from fascism in World War II. After doing so well, everything seemed to go off the tracks, and no one had any answers to fix things.

"All of a sudden, life seems more difficult. People can't cope with the uncertainty and confusion. We want easy answers, and there are none. This has opened the door for nondenominational evangelical churches, which have sprouted like mushrooms after a spring rain."

Bill nodded. "They have simple answers to complex questions. They aren't bad people, but they are promoting a political ideology that condones intolerance and rigidity and a doctrine that interprets the Bible to suit their black and white philosophy. Rather than promoting faith and goodness, religion is becoming an instrument of governance with its own social agenda and foreign policy."

Shiloh tilted her head to the side, deep in thought. "Our government was founded on the principles that all of its citizens are free to worship God or not and in the way they choose, that all people are equal, and that we all have the right to life, liberty, and the pursuit of happiness. We may speak out on issues we believe are wrong or immoral such as war, segregation, abortion, or the low status of women, but we leave the actual policies up to our government. We teach that the way to correct problems is by solving them, not by wishing them away through a rigid doctrine."

Bill took another swig of his brandy. "You're right. Our laws and policies are designed for the betterment of all people, not just a few or a certain group. We may abhor abortion, but we don't usurp a woman's right to abortion, instead we promote birth control and responsible behavior. We realize that our way of government allows our religion to exist. We do not have a state religion. That's one of the reasons our country is so great."

Shiloh smiled. "Quite frankly, this week has left me a bit frustrated. It's made me want to do more to fight the Skylers of the world. But I'm worried about being seen as grandstanding, as using my position as a priest and pushing too hard with what I think is right. Is that too much caution, or is it true?"

Bill remarked, with a warm smile, "You were simply being conscientious. I wish I were in your shoes. I respect you a great deal for fighting back."

"I agree," said Susan. "Someone has to draw the line somewhere. Why not you? Why not now?

Shiloh reflected on Susan's strong words. She appreciated how passionate both Susan and Bill were about women's rights. Bill had been adamant about having Shiloh join All Saints when she had been not only the first woman clergy of any denomination in Nashville but also the second woman ordained in her faith in Tennessee.

Susan told Shiloh how impressed her husband had been when he'd first met her at Sewanee years ago. "He admired your intellect and, since then, has admired your mission work," she said. "And now that you're here, we've both found that you're even better than we thought possible."

Shiloh felt herself blush as Susan continued. "I must say, my dear"—Susan looked directly at Shiloh—"that your mere presence here has lightened the hearts of many women in this church. Not only are you a woman, you're good at what you do. Bill frequently talks about your intelligence. I know that it isn't your job to go out and preach from a soap box, but you may want to consider writing an op-ed for the *New York Times*. Who knows, they just might print it. An op-ed in the *Times* or the *Washington Post* could be duplicated and used by activists far and wide and encourage others to stand up for our nation's founding principles. It would allow you to say your piece without feeling that you are detracting from your work. What do y'all think?"

Shiloh was too embarrassed to speak. Bill's and Susan's praise caused Shiloh's natural modesty to surface.

Bill picked up where Susan left off. "I think Susan's right. An op-ed would be just the ticket. You'd still be available for comment except that then you would have a well-circulated piece that would state exactly where you stand and would serve to encourage others."

Shiloh nodded. "I can try to do that if both of you will proofread and advise me. Maybe then the calls will slow down, and I can earn my pay."

"Now," asked Susan, "why didn't I know more about how you felt about the politics of the right, Bill, in fact, how our church feels about these social issues? I knew about the court briefs and that many mainline Protestants were involved then, but there's little talk in the literature these days about the hard issues like abortion, women, race, and such."

Shiloh spoke up. "We as a church seem to be more focused on keeping our members and our missions intact. We stick to the safer issues, if I may say so."

"You may," said Bill with a grimace, "and of course you're right. Our church and many others have been losing members over the past several years. There are two schools of thought, actually three, for why we've been losing members. The first is that we're politically on the wrong side of social issues. Actually, we're where the majority is, although the majority is shrinking. We believe in the separation of church and state. We believe in limits and morality, for sure, but we also believe in tolerance and compassion—and I'll say it again, the separation of church and state."

Bill paused. "The so-called fundamentalists are making social issues, especially abortion, and homosexuality, lighting-rod issues to recruit supplicants. They use buzzwords for race and welfare, linking them to taxes, morality, and our American way of life. They reach out better than we do. They have television stations and radio shows that preach constantly about what's wrong with our country. They don't deal with cause, just problems and fear. Fear drives people more than just about any other emotion.

"This leads me to my theory, the third reason: mainline Protestants don't offer easy answers. It's like you mentioned before, Shy. It isn't that the other side isn't smart. Many are, but they view the world differently; they don't want to see gray; they want to see things in black and white, wrong or right. Oh sure, they get abortions, and they take advantage of state largesse, but they don't advertise the former and don't admit the latter."

Shiloh nodded. "It's much easier to be against something than to try to figure out how to make things better, to make corrections, or, for God's sake, to help someone.

Bill scratched his head. "I think that it may have started when we lost in Vietnam and forced a sitting president to resign, as you mentioned. Those were difficult, confusing days. I may be oversimplifying, but that's my fifteen-cent answer. The two-dollar answer would require a Margaret Meade dissertation. The bottom line is that our country is becoming divided, and where we'll end up is anybody's guess. We're not the America that I believe our founding fathers imagined. We've had detours here and there for sure. But generally we've marched forward. I just pray that reason will eventually prevail and keep our great nation moving forward."

The discussion went on into the night until suddenly Shiloh gasped. "I'm so sorry; it's past midnight. I've kept y'all up."

Susan frowned. "You're sorry? We are, my dear; we've kept you here late, and you're driving home tomorrow morning."

"Don't be foolish," implored Bill. "All we're guilty of is enjoying each other's company and solving the world's problems."

"Bill, all I know for sure is that I want to stay right where I am for as long as you'll have me."

"The feeling is mutual," said Susan, beating Bill to the punch.

Bill nodded with a smile. Susan and Bill insisted on walking Shiloh home. It was a beautiful, warm spring night, and they all needed the fresh air. Susan and Bill hugged Shiloh at her steps and wished her a good week.

Chapter 4

Shiloh left for her hour-and-fifteen-minute drive to Tullahoma at 8:30 the next morning. She had planned to leave earlier but had slept in after the long day at church and the late supper with the Jacobsons. She was anxious to see her Grandma Alice. As she was driving, she thought about Alice and about her childhood.

Shiloh knew that her father had tried for years to make his first family work, but in the end, he had succumbed and joined Ruth in her drinking. Instead of staying with Ruth and working on AA together, which Ruth would struggle with for months at a time and one time for over a year, he became moribund and depressed. His spirits ebbed as Ruth's problems grew worse.

Chase never seemed to try that hard to make his second marriage with Margaret work. He appeared to Shiloh, in retrospect, to have only gone through the motions. He had been crazy about Ruth. Yes, Shiloh thought, she was his dream and his albatross. Shiloh believed that her father's early death resulted from an accumulation of his drinking and his depression. In the end, he had been a respected and successful senior partner at the law firm, but his ambition for politics had been dashed on the rocks of an intense relationship that he could not control or escape.

Margaret was nothing like Ruth. She was pretty and came from a prominent family, but her ambitions were all about status and her place in the local social pecking order. She was, thought Shiloh sadly, a southern belle, who had little concern for anything other than her children and making sure that they were firmly ensconced in the appropriate social circle.

Margaret hadn't been unkind to Shiloh, more like disinterested. Shiloh and the Giles family didn't fit the social mold. They liked sports, loved politics, and cared about what was going on in the world.

Shiloh had felt alone. She had lost her brother and mother all at once. She'd loved her mother, and she loved and depended on her brother. Suddenly both were gone and she was thrust into a home that was foreign to her. At first, she felt like she was in a battle: Shiloh the loner against the three "others."

She developed a chip on her shoulder and stayed to herself. And Margaret didn't make much effort to mother Shiloh. Rather, she focused on her children and let Shiloh fend for herself.

The relationship was something like a marriage of convenience. Each went through the motions. After the first several months, when Shiloh had been recalcitrant, she settled down and went her own way. She had Grandma Alice, her father, and church. School also became important to Shiloh as well. Over the years, Shiloh and Margaret had coexisted.

Years later, Chase and Margaret divorced.

One day it had all come to a head. Shy remembered Chase coming home and arguing with Margaret about why her son had not done the yard work Chase had instructed him to do. Margaret had informed Chase that that her son was too old for that now—that it wouldn't look right for her son to be out in the sun working like a common yardman. That was followed by another blowup when Margaret had sent what Chase thought was far too much money to her daughter when she went away to college, so she could buy new clothes that would assure her entry into the sorority she wanted to join.

"But she had several suitcases full of expensive new clothes when she left for college," Chase had complained to Margaret.

To which Margaret had replied, "No, Chase, you don't understand. They just weren't right for that sorority. You will never understand class."

The next day, Chase took his clothes, his briefcase, and his papers and left Margaret. He sent signed divorce papers to her, giving her all they had. He essentially started over. He was alone and lived a secluded life, slipping further into his own gloomy world.

Shiloh had been twelve at the time. The marriage had lasted five years. Shiloh had gone to live with her grandmother, where she remained until she went away to college.

Before the divorce, Chase had told his children to give back to society, that they were lucky to be born well. He'd believed in service and helping the community. He said that hard work was a virtue for which one should be proud. She had enjoyed the rare moments with her dad when they would discuss life and values. But after the divorce, she couldn't talk to her dad.

When they were together, it was superficial; he didn't really know how to talk to Shiloh. Grandma Alice and Sam were her only confidants.

For the first few years after Sam left home, he and Shiloh wrote to each other almost every week. That gradually became fortnightly, until e-mail came along when their exchanges became at least weekly again. They'd remained very close over the years, and they both appreciated that they had gone through an intense experience together. Neither one of them forgot that, nor how much they meant to each other. He was always her loving big brother, then and now.

Something he had written to her a few weeks before he shipped out to Vietnam had stuck with her the rest of her life. She kept that letter tucked neatly inside her Episcopal Book of Common Prayer where it still resided today.

> April 26, 1971
> Dear Shy,
>
> Thank you for your recent letter. I'm sorry that I can't be there to be an acolyte with you or to join you on Sunday afternoons for Grandma's great pecan pie. I miss you and Grandma every day and wish I could see you and see how much you have grown. Grandma writes to me often and keeps me updated about all of your shenanigans that you don't tell me about in your letters. She says that you have been growing tall and that you will be a beautiful woman. She also hints that you are not doing as well as you could in school, and you just told me in your last letter, once again, that you are miserable living with Margaret and her children.
>
> Shy, I went through some of that too. I felt like the world was against me and that life wasn't fair. I spent too much time hating Dad and even, at times, Mom and what she had done to all of us. But I had you and Grandma Alice and Father Gunn. You do too. I know it has been easier for me because I could escape. But you not only should do well, you must. I know you can do it, and you know you can do it. Don't ever let anyone rebuke you because of your position in society or because you are a woman. You are as good as anyone and can go wherever your talent and dreams take you.
>
> I discovered something about myself recently, Shy. I went to Mexico with some of my pals to drink and to be with girls. The bars there don't care about age, and all of

us thought manhood meant booze and women. I got very drunk and didn't remember what happened the next day when I woke up with a terrible hangover. I rode back to Fort Hood in the backseat of a friend's car. By the time I arrived I was a different person.

I thought about Mom and what it would be like if I became that way. I felt sorry for myself and thought if I let it, booze could take me too. Well, when we got back to the Fort, I went to the chapel and sat alone on the back pew for hours. That Sunday night changed me. I thought about the past, about you, Grandma, Father Gunn, the people who really cared for me, even Dad. I thought about all that I had learned in church and the pride I felt for Dad and his accomplishments, for you as the first girl acolyte, and for Mom and her kindness as our mother. I cried, Shy. I suppose it was because I felt bad about what should have been for both of us and for our family. After a long while, I sat there in the dark and gritted my teeth and said quietly to God, "I will do better with my life. I can and I will do better. Please forgive me for being weak."

I know this sounds like a bunch of mush, but it is true. I became a new person right then and there. I realized what my values really are and that it is okay to dream because dreams can come true if you try. Oh, I still go out with my buddies and have fun, but I never get drunk or mistreat anyone. And I am always respectful of women, like Dad taught me to be. I even go to the library where I read history and study, can you believe it, math and English.

We can determine who we are and who we are going to be. We can do whatever we want.

Everyone who succeeds in life must work hard. It takes time. Let us both work hard and prove that we are just as good as anyone else. Let us prove that we can succeed. We love each other, Shy. We have Grandma and Father Gunn. And you have Dad. Maybe someday I will too. We can do it if we just work hard. Don't worry about what others say. Prove to yourself that you are better than all of them.

I love you, little sister. No matter what, that will never change.

Sammy

He had been seventeen when he'd written it, and she had been eight.

Her Grandma Alice was the most important person in Shiloh's life but her brother was her special friend.

Sam had been wounded in Vietnam and sent to Germany for treatment and therapy. But he did not include that in his letters until he was discharged from the hospital. Sam told Shiloh that he had become friends with a guy from New Jersey: Mario Donato. They enrolled in college together, finished in three years, and started law school.

As for Shiloh, she moped around when Sam first left home, but once she received his letter, she decided that she was going to study hard and follow Sam's advice. She still had the church, and Father Gunn was always there to help her over rough spots.

After a few years, her stepmother more or less left Shiloh alone. Shiloh knew her reasons. To her father, she could do no wrong, and what did Margaret care if Shiloh wasn't interested in the country club and planning her debut at the club's annual debutante's ball? She had her own two children to worry about.

Shiloh became a star student, joined the debate team, and participated in sports, an activity Margaret thought was undignified for young women of a certain class. Her lack of support only made Shiloh try harder. Shiloh often told Sam she couldn't wait to go to college, and he would always advise her to work hard and plan for college but enjoy high school first. And she smiled as she thought now, *I did, big brother, I did.*

The first time Shiloh saw her brother again was at her high school graduation. Sam had gotten married after college. He had never come back to Tullahoma, but nothing would keep him away from his little sister's high school graduation. He and his wife stayed with Grandma Alice. Sam had told Shiloh about his reunion with their grandmother.

Grandma Alice had been standing at the door when they arrived. Sam had brushed away his tears and said with a smile, "It is so good to see you, Grandma, so, so good. I've missed you so very much. This is my wife, Barbara."

They had hugged.

"Sam, you are a lucky man."

"She's the lucky one, Grandma."

"Pshaw, you haven't changed a bit. Young lady, you have my condolences."

And so it started. It was a wonderful homecoming for Sam and his wife.

An hour later, Shiloh came in from school, and as soon as she saw Sam, she squealed and ran to his arms. She cried for joy. She remembered looking at Sam's crooked smile and his brown eyes thinking that he hadn't changed at all. And she'd remembered welcoming Barbara to the Giles clan.

"It is nice to meet you, Shy. I've heard so much about you," said Barbara. "Your brother's been talking about his little sister all the way down here. Somehow, though, I was expecting a little girl. I think Sam still remembers you as a child, not a beautiful young woman."

They had a wonderful evening together. Father Gunn and his family came over and filled Sam in on the goings on at the church. "We have a waiting list for acolytes now, Sam. Almost half of the current group is girls. Your sister started a trend."

They talked long into the night. After the Gunn family went home, Shiloh and Sam went out to the porch and talked for another several hours.

Shiloh smiled as she remembered what had happened the next morning while she and Barbara had been out shopping. Grandma Alice had found Sam alone the next morning on the porch with a glass of her iced tea.

"And a good morning to you, my sweet grandson," Alice had greeted Sam. "Did you and Shy ever go to bed last night?"

"Yes, but not too long ago, I'm afraid."

As the conversation had progressed, his grandmother had demanded that Sam go see his father. After a few minutes of trying to talk his way out of it, he had agreed. Chase was expecting him, and they stayed together the rest of the day.

When Sam returned that evening, he told Shiloh about what had happened and how good he felt. Shiloh had been so happy that Sam and their father had reunited after so many years. But he also told Shiloh that he was worried. "He looked bad. He's drinking too much."

She and Grandma Alice had also been worried about Chase's health.

The next day, they all had attended Shiloh's graduation. It was hot and clear on that memorable late spring day, just what you would expect for that time of year in Tullahoma. Shiloh looked cool and radiant in spite of the heat. Her valedictorian speech was about women's equality.

After Shiloh's speech, back at Grandma Alice's house, Chase and Sam had congratulated her, but Grandma was confused. "Shiloh," she had said afterward, "why all the business about women? I suppose you are all for abortion being legal, aren't you?"

"Yes. Why not? You've known women who have had abortions haven't you?"

"Yes, but I just wish it wasn't you, dear."

Shiloh had touched her grandmother's arm. "Don't worry, Grandma, I won't go overboard. It's not my time yet. But I care about women's rights, racial injustice, and other issues too. I'm proud that Tennessee approved the

Equal Rights Amendment. It's just too bad that the right-wing people have succeeded in stopping ratification in other states. It's still a few states short of adoption."

"Chase," Alice broke in with a proud smile, "what are we going to do with this hellion you have raised?"

"I agree with her, Mom," answered Chase. "Women should be equal to men in every respect." Chase made a joke of clearing his throat. "But it is you who has influenced this young lady. Where else did she learn to become such a tiger? I remember a lady, sitting right here in this parlor, who said that if she could get her hands on that minister on TV who said that all women should stay home and take care of their families and mind their husbands, she would punch him in the nose."

"Yes, and I still would," replied a feisty Alice. "If women didn't do all the work, how would men survive? And to think, that preacher was caught in a motel room with an underage girl. What a piece of work."

They all laughed.

"Shiloh," Grandma Alice began in a sober tone, "nothing is more important for women than the ERA. It would solve many problems. When it is your time," she said, as she smiled at her granddaughter, "you should show these men a thing or two about the ERA."

Sam had told Shiloh that night about her mom's abortion. He told her about getting their mom out of jail in Calhoun when he had been living with their Uncle George and his family and the kindly doctor in Fort Payne who treated her for her beating and the infection caused by her illegal abortion.

Chase had known too. Uncle George had told Sam that Chase had paid the hospital bill. Shiloh and her brother agreed that the Supreme Court decision legalizing abortion had saved many women's lives.

Shiloh had never seen her mother again. Sam had lost touch with Ruth after he had joined the military and finally tracked her down several years later through a missing persons firm. They reported that she had died in San Marcos, Texas, in 1986.

Chase had visited Sam and Barbara a few months later and had taken them to New York City for the weekend. Sam had been a struggling law student then. Chase and Sam had worked hard at building bridges and making up for lost time. They called and wrote to each other weekly, but time was running out.

The next year in March, Shiloh called Sam from college. She was crying, "I have bad news, Sam. Dad died this morning. He had a stroke."

It had hit both of them like a ton of bricks. Shy knew that it was especially sad for Sam since he and his dad had just reconciled after all those years.

Chase's was the biggest funeral anyone in Tullahoma could remember. The newspaper ran stories about Chase's high school and college sports feats and his military record. There were stories about his law firm and cases he had won. The paper was full of Charles Clayton Giles and his family. He had died at the age of fifty-eight, leaving behind his mother, an eighteen-year-old daughter, and a twenty-seven-year-old son.

A few days later, Barry Whitfield, Chase's best friend and "uncle" to his children, read the will. "Your dad left all of his money in trust to me to pay primarily for the needs of your Grandma Alice. As you know, he turned over almost everything to Margaret when they divorced, but he has accumulated a bit more since then. He left forty thousand dollars in trust to me for Alice and another account to pay tuition for all of Shiloh's educational expenses and the remainder of Sam's law school expenses as well as ten thousand dollars to Sam to help him get a leg up when he starts his own practice with his friend, Mario—unless you change your mind and come here to practice law, Sam; you and Mario would be welcome here anytime. Your dad had planned to give the cash to you for your graduation."

Shiloh and her brother were grateful that Grandma Alice was provided for. That was their biggest worry. Shiloh remembered her brother thinking of his little sister first. Sam had said, "Thank you, Uncle Barry. But, please, split my money with Shy so she can have a leg up too."

"I can't," replied Barry. "Your dad was firm. I am sure there will be a bit left over for when Shiloh graduates."

As time passed, Barry occasionally wrote notes to Sam and included a hundred-dollar bill. Barry and Shiloh became much closer. She considered the Whitfields her family, and she knew they felt that way about her and Sam too.

Barry had already declared for the state Senate when Chase died. Chase had been handling his campaign. Barry had no opposition in the democratic primary, and his opponent, who had held the seat for donkey's years, was just going through the motions.

Barry ran and won easily. Shy had come home on the weekends to help. Sam couldn't come until the final weekend due to the demands of law school, but he came and stayed until the results were in on Tuesday night and then rushed back to school.

* * * * *

After a reflective drive from Nashville, Shiloh was on Grandma Alice's porch by 10:30. Grandma Alice was waiting with iced tea. The day was cool and overcast with a threat of rain. But the flowers were gorgeous. Pink Roses of Sharon covered the front and left side of the porch, leaving a beautiful entryway that over the years had formed into a lovely spring and summer archway of pink and green. It was also a haven for bumblebees that Shiloh remembered chasing with a water pistol when she was a little girl. On the right side, there was a fragrant sweet shrub and a flower box full of red petunias. Beyond the porch stood a birdbath surrounded by marigolds, ornamental shrubs, two majestic oaks, and a privy hedge that bordered a large front lawn.

It was almost summer, at least it would seem that way later in the day when the weather changed and the heat returned. After living on a relatively cool mountaintop in Sewanee, Tullahoma, seemed more like the Philippines than the Tennessee she had grown to love and idealize in Sewanee. But Tullahoma was home. Unlike the Philippines, Grandma had air conditioning and electricity and never ran out of iced tea or pecan pie.

"How is my little girl?" a smiling Grandma Alice asked her granddaughter.

"Fine, your little girl is fine."

They both laughed and embraced.

"Why don't you drop your bag inside, and we can sit here on the porch for a spell before you go to meet Barry for lunch."

Shiloh did so and rejoined her grandma.

"You look great, Grandma, just like a million dollars," exuded Shiloh.

"Ah, pshaw, you sound just like Barry. I know I look like an old, rusty penny. You're the one who looks great.

"By the way, young lady, is it your time?"

"What do you mean?"

"You told me after your splendid graduation speech that it wasn't your time. Remember that?"

"Yes, I remember. Why do you ask?"

"Because all I see in the newspapers and on TV are stories about a woman priest who bops men in the nose."

"Oh, that," said Shiloh through her laughter.

"Yes, dear, that. Did you think I wouldn't see it?"

"No, I'm sorry. I just didn't want to worry you."

"Good for you," replied Alice, brushing off Shiloh's apology. "Good for you."

They chatted until it was time to for Shiloh to meet Barry.

When she called Barry to say that she was coming down and before she could ask to see him, Barry had told her to please save Tuesday afternoon for him. They had met for coffee a couple of times in Nashville, but home ground was somehow different. She was curious about why he wanted to see her. She hoped that it wasn't something bad about Grandma Alice.

They met at Barry's office and just as the weather folks predicted, it had become still and sultry. Barry offered Shiloh a seat after their initial greeting hug, her how are you and Trudy, his have you heard from Sam and how is your grandmother, and the rest of the requisite small talk.

"Shiloh, today we are going to talk about you," started Barry.

Shiloh's face flushed. She felt like she was in the principal's office.

Barry saw her reaction and started again. "I'm sorry if I startled you, dear. I guess I sounded a bit overbearing, didn't I?"

"A bit like my elementary school principal when I was horsing around and broke the flower vase in Mrs. Gandy's room," replied a smiling Shiloh.

"Well, I guess I feel like your father in some respects. I really have no right to say such a thing except that I couldn't love you any more if you were my own flesh and blood."

Shiloh grabbed Barry's hand. "Oh, Barry, Sam and I both think of you as our second dad. You've been so wonderful to us. We love you and Trudy dearly. You were there for us during the difficult days, when Mom and Dad were having troubles." Shiloh breathed deeply. "And you may have been my father-in-law, if … if," Shiloh's eyes filled with tears. She paused to regain her composure.

"I know what you were going to say. Barry confided in me the day he left." Barry looked away. He wiped tears from the corners of his eyes.

Shiloh remembered that day like it was yesterday. The younger Barry had returned to college; it was the last time either of them had seen him alive.

"Barry told me everything, Shiloh, about the intimacy of your relationship, his love for you, and his plans to somehow make it work out. He said that he couldn't imagine finding a better woman to share his life with. He said that he wanted to propose to you when he graduated. I tried to say something about his age and especially yours, but I couldn't disagree with his choice, then or now."

Shiloh looked down and held up her hand for Barry to stop. He came over, knelt down in front of Shiloh, and took her hands in his. He offered a box of tissues. After a long moment, Barry suddenly sprang to his feet and started to pace around the room. "Damn, and I want to run for governor. How can I do anything right if I can't even talk to one of the people I most love in the world and not make a hash of it?"

Shiloh laughed through her tears. "I needed to hear that. I've needed to let it out for a long time. Maybe we both have." She got up and hugged him. Shiloh knew that both of them needed to move on, each with their own thoughts and their own pain. "Your son was wonderful. Not a day goes by that I don't think of him. He was kind, considerate, and almost as handsome as his father."

"I think of him too," said Barry. He held Shiloh a moment before continuing. "How about we go to Frank's Place and get a burger and a beer or two?" Barry suggested. "We can finish our conversation there."

Frank's Place had become a habit with Chase, Barry, and their gang years ago and included their families, who carried on the tradition.

"Great idea," said Shiloh. "Or three."

They headed for Frank's, two blocks from Barry's office. Friends and neighbors greeted them as they walked down the street. One of Barry's partners stopped them and shook hands with Shiloh and then brushed her cheek with a light kiss and a slight southern bow.

"Barry," he said, "I see you brought your bodyguard down from Nashville. Congratulations, Shy. You have done a great service for this country by poking that turkey in the nose. I read up on him after your recent run-in. His exploits around the country are creepy. He's a nasty bully. He especially likes to bully women. What a jerk."

Shiloh spoke up. "It's good to see you, Alan. How are Marcy and the kids?"

"It's a struggle to make enough money with two in college and one getting ready. Marcy and I plan to go on bread and water when Brad goes away."

"I'll bet," said Shiloh with raised eyebrows. "From what I can tell, you guys mint money at that poor old firm of yours."

"We make some, but Barry spends it all in Nashville on taxes," Alan said with a wink. "Y'all have a good lunch. And, Shy, don't be a stranger. We were all worried to death about you when you were over in the Philippines with all those snakes and diseases, but we were sure proud of you—still are. Don't forget where you're from now, you hear?" Alan waved and headed back to the office.

"It is a standing joke in the firm," laughed Barry, "that I make more money for the firm when I am in Nashville than I do here but that I tax them to death and take it all away. Those jokers say that my status brings in more clients than I ever did with my lawyering."

Shiloh nodded. "I wish Dad were here to see how well you have done. Did I hear you say governor in there? That's twice I've heard that since I got here."

"Oh," said Barry.

"Yes," said Shiloh, "Grandma says you should be governor too."

They arrived at Frank's and were seated in an alcove in the back where they could have some privacy. "Speaking of governor," said Barry in a conspiratorial whisper, "if I can get Alice, I can get anyone. She is a wonderful woman."

"The feeling, Mr. Governor, is mutual. And thank you for all you've done for her all these years while Sam and I were AWOL."

"Enough of that," said Barry. "She's my family too—and I might add, quite a teacher and counselor. She has more horse sense than anyone I know."

They ordered burgers and beer. "So did it feel good to bop that no-good on the snooze, Shy? Tell me the truth."

"Oh, of course it did. For an instant, it felt wonderful. But just as quickly, I felt awful."

"Just as I figured; you're a humble priest with the heart of a lion."

Shy laughed. "I guess that you would have liked it more than I did. To me, he is a pathetic bully, to borrow one of Alan's descriptions."

"He has a real thing about women," said Barry. "He's a poster boy for what it would be like in this country if zealots of his ilk ever gained power. They'd become our moral police."

They sat in silence for a moment and contemplated Barry's words. The food arrived.

"You first," said Barry.

Shy smiled. "Okay, counselor. I really don't have much to say." Shiloh paused. "Actually, that's not quite true. I guess what I need is some fatherly advice. I became a priest for a simple reason. I care about helping people, and that seemed the good way to me. Father Gunn and the church were godsends in my life, and I wanted to return the favor. I loved the Philippines and the close association with the people I worked with there."

"But?" inquired Barry.

"But I was ready to leave. I wanted to see how I liked working in a church in everyday America."

"In comfortable, middle-class America?" asked Barry.

"Yes, maybe. I had worked with the poor and the illiterate; how would I be able to cope with people who had an education equal to mine, who were, in some cases, the powerful, the elite, and even the notables?"

"And?" Barry asked.

"And I need another beer," said Shiloh.

The second round arrived immediately. Shiloh looked surprised.

Barry smiled. "I signaled Mabel a few minutes ago. Continue."

"Well," Shiloh continued, "this last week kindled, or, to be honest, rekindled, a desire in me to be more visible; no that's not it … to have a bigger say in the affairs of my community and my country. I have received queries from several nonprofit advocacy and public policy groups to be a spokesperson for women's rights and even a few offers to consider jobs.

"I'm already on the board of the local Planned Parenthood and have been asked in the last few days to be on the boards of the local Rape Crisis Center and the YWCA. I know that this is what is called one's fifteen minutes of fame. And I know that it's because I'm a woman priest and because I bonked Skyler. I don't mean to sound like my ego is running my mind, but I do want to at least think about what it might mean to do something someday that may somehow influence policy and justice and have a positive impact on society. Actually, I don't really know what I'm talking about for sure. I like my job now. Maybe this is just a fantasy hangover."

"So," Barry intoned with a smile, "you want to discuss careers and the future—how you can be comfortable, have your privacy, and yet make a difference in the lives of your fellow citizens, in a way, how can Shiloh have her cake and eat it too. Is that about right, Reverend Giles?"

Shiloh smiled. "Does that sound immature? Am I just caught up in my own glory and self importance?"

Barry's demeanor softened. "I wasn't being sharp or condescending. I was just reminiscing a bit. Your dad was my best friend. He went all out to get me recruited to the firm. He used several of his chips with the senior partners to get me on board. The firm had just hired him two years before. Tullahoma isn't exactly the legal capitol of the world. They could afford another young lawyer, but they certainly didn't need one.

"Sure, I had some notoriety from football and the war, but I was another green law grad. I was scared as hell to let my best friend down or to let down the firm. I felt like I had been thrown into the deep end of the pool. But here I am.

"In short, I know somewhat how you feel. And now you have, in a different way, been given a platform like I had all those years ago. Your Philippine experience has given you an understanding of the world that I will never have. You are at All Saints, when all of a sudden people not only wanted to listen to you, they felt like they needed to. So your dilemma is that you like being there, but you aren't quite sure what to do next. Do you have the confidence it takes to actually take on more responsibility, and if so what? Something like that anyway. Do you agree?"

Shiloh furrowed her brow. "Yes, that about nails it. I'm a bit frightened to think about my future. At All Saints, I'm fairly confident that I can handle my job, but moving in another direction is a bit unnerving."

Barry signaled Mabel.

"Coffee this time for me, Barry."

"Me too," said the future governor. "Mabel knows."

Shy cleared her throat to speak.

Barry signaled with a raised hand and a boyish smile. "I'm not finished yet, dear."

Shiloh chuckled. They clicked coffee cups, and Barry continued. "It may interest you to know that I wanted to see you to discuss the same subject we are in fact discussing. My thoughts are fairly well formed, so I'll just speak freely."

Shiloh nodded.

"For what it's worth, my view is that you should stay where you are for now. The experience will be good for you, and it'll enhance your mystique. But you do need to keep yourself out front."

Shy looked at Barry quizzically.

Barry continued, "I spoke to a PR guy I know in Nashville a few days ago about you. He has helped me on my campaigns and is on the secret team that is plotting my run for governor."

"Secret?" said Shy.

"Well, we don't have a store front office yet. I haven't declared and won't until next year. That is, if I decide to. But no more interruptions about me. This is your career we are discussing, at least until we switch to mine." Barry couldn't help but chuckle at his own excitement.

Shiloh's eyes met his knowingly.

"My PR friend, Charlie Bates, says that you are now and can continue to be, a hot commodity. In political speak, that means, for future political office."

Shiloh's pulse jumped a few beats.

"Charlie suggests that you do an op-ed in *The Tennessean* and agree to an occasional speaking engagement, if any come your way."

Shy nodded, to signify that they had.

"You should bide your time. I know for sure that Bill Rogers plans to resign the House. So his seat will be open in just about three years. The next election will be his last. He's getting up in years. And he wants to enjoy his grandkids and kick back, catch a few crappies, and sit on his porch enjoying some of Tennessee's finest corn squeez'ins. My dear, that seat would be perfect for you. He is your representative, so you wouldn't have to move a muscle to run."

Shiloh was flushed with excitement. She took a deep breath. "Gosh, Barry. I don't know. Did you just think of that?"

"No, my dear, I must confess that I had those thoughts long before you came back from the Philippines. You are bright, Shy, the valedictorian of your class. And you're attractive, but that doesn't begin to describe you. You have guts—not because you whumped Skyler, although the public liked that."

Barry paused before continuing. "Your childhood was not easy, Shy. You saw way too much of your mother's business and the difficulties between her and your father. That would be rough at any age, but especially for someone so young. And anyone who could live in the Margaret Giles household and thrive as you have has to have some kind of incredible intestinal fortitude. Plus you spent seven years in the Philippines, which was certainly not an easy thing to do. And finally, my dear, you are damned articulate. You reason well, and you express yourself like a seasoned pro. My dear, you're made for politics. From a national political platform, you could make a real difference."

Shy started to speak, but Barry held up his hand to silence her.

"Just think about it and bide your time for now. We have plenty of time to talk later. If you agree, I think that we can make it happen. But for now, try to keep some of the visibility you have. Rest assured, this conversation about you is far from over, my dear."

Shiloh smiled. "I'm glad you're considering running for governor. It would be great for our state and the country. I know the kind of man you are. And I want to help. But before we get into that, and, at the risk of sounding self-absorbed, I want to finish the conversation you've begun."

"Shy," intoned Barry, "the reality is that you are a treasure. You have God-given talents and, in my view, a political philosophy that is right for this moment in our history, probably for any moment in history. The reality is that you need to sit on it. You need to think about the issues of the day, to study beyond the headlines and to bide your time."

Shiloh frowned. "But it seems so planned. It feels, I don't know, kind of wrong to be talking this way."

"Shiloh, Shiloh," said Barry with a smile on his face and a trace of exasperation, "Did you live your life up until now without planning? It isn't wrong to plan. Sure, your current flash of celebrity wasn't planned, but everyone plans, dear, especially for politics. Most people who decide to run, even John Glenn who the whole world knew, planned. He didn't just walk into the election board and say, 'I'm John Glenn, and I want to be a senator.'

"I know it's new to you. But I saw your reactions earlier, and I know in my heart you have thought about it. You admitted as much earlier. Well, I have too," he paused, "for a long time. I'm in the state Senate, and maybe I'll be in the Governor's Mansion someday, because your dad and I planned, first for him and then for me."

Shiloh paused for a moment. "I understand. And now, since I know when Bill Rogers will leave, I have time to think and decide and yes, to plan. And if I decide yes, I have time to work on whatever that means too."

"Exactly," smiled Barry, and he reached over the table and squeezed Shiloh's hand. "Exactly, my dear."

"And now, Mr. Governor," Shiloh smiled and took her queue.

Barry told Shy about his plans, asked her to join his secret committee, and told her to learn about the workings of the Tennessee state government. He went into some detail about how he intended to run his campaign. He would let the speculation mount and the rumors swirl until just after New Years, and then he would announce. By then, his campaign would be designed, set, and ready.

"Amazing," said Shiloh when Barry finished.

After another cup of coffee they parted. It was a little past four o'clock. They would meet in a few hours at Grandma Alice's for supper.

Chapter 5

Shiloh left Tullahoma Wednesday morning after breakfast and a dreaded extra cup of Grandma Alice's strong chicory coffee. She almost never braved a second cup, but this trip was special. She knew that her grandmother appreciated the visit and their last conversation on the porch before departing. It was part of the ritual her of childhood. Grandma Alice was always there; she was never without a word of encouragement. Shiloh brushed back a tear when she saw Grandma Alice waving good-bye as she pulled out of the driveway. She knew that Grandma Alice wouldn't be there forever, no matter how much they both willed it.

As Shiloh began her drive, she thought about Grandma Alice and her best friend, Hattie. Alice had been Shiloh's de facto mother for most of her life, and Shiloh felt a special affection for the woman who helped her grandmother take care of her big house. Hattie had always been a part of Shiloh's life, from her earliest memories. She too was like a grandmother to her. Both women were as soft and gentle as they were strong and determined.

Shiloh guessed that Hattie must be at least seventy-five. Hattie had helped Grandma Alice for as long as anyone could remember. Theirs was an odd relationship. Hattie was a slight built, black woman, with a small, wrinkled face; gray hair pulled back in a fierce bun; and a ready smile that never seemed to change. She had always been Aunt Hattie to Shy. She was a sweet lady who was kind and considerate. She would never join them at the dinner table, though. Even last night, Hattie had eaten in the breakfast room. Chase, Sam, and Shiloh had all tried to change this anomaly. But Alice had told them it would make Hattie uncomfortable. And when each in their turn had discussed it with Hattie over the years, she had always flat out refused. Yet she frequently joined them in the parlor after supper.

Alice knew all of Hattie's children and grandchildren. She never missed sending them cards for their birthdays, and until this day, she always enclosed a five-dollar bill. The two attended weddings and funerals of each other's families. Hattie would come over and visit Alice almost daily and have tea or even some of Alice's coffee. They were best friends, and yet they were creatures of the Old South and would never change. Shiloh felt sad about that. These two women had been best friends for many years. And yet they were separated by a culture and a tradition that would only die when they did.

Shiloh remembered Hattie babysitting her and telling her stories about her grandfather Albert and father Chase. One day, when Shiloh was playing with friends and Alice was at the grocery store, Shiloh had fallen and cut her head. She was bleeding profusely. Hattie had fixed a compress with a wet towel and rushed Shiloh to the emergency room. A nurse had delayed treatment while she asked Hattie several questions. Hattie had become quite angry and balled up her little fists and demanded immediate service for "her child." A doctor who was a friend of the Giles family happened to be nearby and responded. After tending to Shiloh, he called Chase to tell him that Shiloh was okay.

Chase went to the hospital to retrieve Hattie and Shiloh. When he spoke to the doctor, he told Chase about Hattie's determination. From then on, the Giles family referred to Hattie as "Champ." Shiloh smiled at the memory, which Grandma Alice had told for what must have been the hundredth time last night.

Shiloh had been close to Hattie growing up and sometimes confided in her about her problems. During high school, she even discussed discrimination with Hattie and how Hattie had coped with racism.

Shiloh loved and respected Hattie and was happy that her grandmother had such a wonderful friend. But she could never get Hattie to discuss her own personal feelings and why she would not eat with the family when she knew that she was welcome. That discussion made Hattie uncomfortable; she wouldn't discuss that subject, and that was that. Shiloh didn't suppose that even now she would ever get a straight answer on that question from either woman.

* * * * *

Shiloh arrived in Nashville fresh, excited, and eager to get back to ministering. Before going home, she stopped at the church to check in with Bill. He was officiating at a funeral and the other assistant was making hospital rounds. Feeling guilty, she changed into the appropriate attire and hurried to the sacristy to wait for the right moment to appear. As the service ended, she offered her condolences to the family and friends of the deceased. Her eyes met Father Jacobson's. He nodded a welcome and whispered that he would call her after the graveside service. She went home to unpack.

When she arrived, she found several phone messages and letters from former classmates and church members. She returned the calls and enjoyed reading the letters.

Over the next few days, Shiloh stayed busy with her church work. The All Saints congregation numbered well over a thousand. That was a big flock to attend to, even for three priests. She also wrote her op-ed for *The Tennessean*. Father Jacobson looked it over and didn't change a word. She followed Barry and Charlie Bates's recommendation, although she had not yet met Bates.

"Focus on home for now," Barry had said. "Charlie Bates will make sure that your op-ed gets around to all the right folks such as the party faithful, national women's advocacy groups, religious circles, and the like. Don't reach too far yet; that'll come soon enough."

Shiloh welcomed their advice, even though she felt a bit uneasy about writing an op-ed. On the one hand, she felt like she owed it to her church and the community to explain her actions. On the other hand, since her talks with Father Jacobson and Barry and the unknown Charlie, she thought that an op-ed might be too contrived; she was calling more attention to herself. *Of course I am*, she thought. She was taking the advice of three mentors, one who wanted his church to speak out on an important issue. The other two held similar views, but their reasoning was more complex. They were thinking about Shiloh's future as a politician.

Shiloh's op-ed was accepted and ran the Friday after she returned from Tullahoma.

THE NASHVILLE TENNESSEAN
By Catherine Shiloh Giles

Two weeks ago Tuesday, I was involved in an event at the Mid-State Women's Clinic that was covered widely by local and national media. I was assisting the clinic as a volunteer escort for women who had an abortion appointment.

Why did they need escorts? Because a group known as Operation Savior (OS) was picketing in front of the clinic in order to try to convince these women, on their way from the clinic parking lot to its front door, not to have an abortion.

The usual tactic of OS is to stand across the street from the clinic and hold signs and speak in a respectful voice about preserving life in an effort to change the women's mind about getting an abortion. Sometimes, they also softly sing religious songs.

The OS group is active around the country. Until last Tuesday, the group here in Nashville has always stayed across the street from the clinic, but recently, they've begun to take pictures of the women who come to the Mid-State Clinic and to raise their voices in an effort to discourage these women. That is why the director of the Mid-State Clinic asked for volunteer escorts to assist patients when they walked from their cars to the clinic doors.

The escorts are not there to convince the patients who arrive for their appointment to have an abortion. No, the patients make the final decision once they are inside the clinic, where their medical history is taken and where they receive counseling and a medical examination and, finally, sign or do not sign their medical consent form. The escorts are there simply to help the patient navigate the 100 feet or so from her car to the clinic door. In short, they are there to ensure that the patients are not intimidated to the point where their right to an abortion is usurped by harassment or threat.

Until last Tuesday, OS demonstrators in Nashville had never crossed the street or assaulted any of the patients. But on the day in question, they did both. A national leader of OS, Jerry Skyler, was asked by the local group to visit Nashville. He has visited many other clinic sites around the country "training" OS devotees on harassment techniques like those mentioned above.

Since the *Roe v. Wade* U.S. Supreme Court decision that legalized abortion in 1973, women in this country have had the constitutional right to abortion. This right is the right of all American women. It has been held by our courts that citizens may try to dissuade women from seeking an abortion under the free speech clause of the First Amendment of the U.S. Constitution, but at a distance. The rights granted dissenters in the court ruling did not include intimidating, frightening, or harassing the women with tactics such as taking pictures and using threatening language, and they certainly did not include physical assault.

Mr. Skyler, the man who caused the incident at the clinic verbally assaulted the woman I was escorting that day and tried to prevent her physically from entering the doors of the clinic. During his terrifying and uncivilized rampage, he threw what turned out to be chicken blood on my face and chest, he spit on me, and he physically assaulted me when I tried to protect the patient.

I regret to say that I struck back at Mr. Skyler when he tried to grab the woman I was escorting and pulled my hair and pushed me to the ground. My response was reflexive. I was trying to protect the patient and myself from harm.

I regret striking Mr. Skyler. I apologized to him then, and I apologize to you now. That is not the way to solve a problem. It is not an appropriate example to set for our children, especially for a member of the clergy. We have laws and courts that decide these issues.

But I must say that, if I were faced with a similar situation, my response would probably be the same because I was acting in self-defense. On the day in question, a raging man almost twice my size attacked the woman I was escorting and me. He was attempting to force his views on a person whose decision about whether to have an abortion is hers and hers alone to make. That was wrong, and soon Mr. Skyler will answer for his lawlessness in court.

I was not acting on behalf of my church. I volunteered as a clinic escort in my own capacity as a private citizen. That is my right as an American citizen and as an Episcopalian.

In the Episcopal Church, we study the Old and New Testaments of the Bible. And throughout the calendar year, we worship God through the examination and celebration of the life and teachings of Jesus, from his birth to his crucifixion, death, and resurrection. We believe that the individual search for meaning is best served in a community of loving support and intellectual challenge.

We do not force beliefs on our members. We believe that their decisions are theirs to make within the structure of their faith. You will find members of our church who have different views on the abortion issue. We believe that individual members have the right, in a pluralistic society, to make their own decision. We support the founding principles of this country, including the separation of church and state.

That is not to say that my church promotes, in any way subscribes to, or condones abortion. What that means is that we (the church) have no right to make that decision for someone, nor does any other faith in a free society. I know of not one individual in my church who believes that abortion is good. We believe that our society should do everything in its power to prevent the need for abortion.

Issues like sex education, abortion, and women's rights are best settled through thoughtful discussion and the decisions of our courts and legislatures. That is the way a civilized society operates. No one has the right as a citizen to determine what is appropriate for another citizen. To speak out is fine; that is a cherished value. To act out against a fellow citizen is wrong. Mr. Skyler was wrong to do so, and so was I. We must all learn from such experiences and treat each other with respect.

In response to Shiloh's op-ed, there were several letters to the editor the next week; some were sympathetic, but most were outspoken on one side of the issue or the other, including a letter from Reverend Lawson, who had been arrested with Skyler. He wrote that the ends—stopping abortion—justified the means, which in this case meant trying to stop women from committing murder.

Shiloh received several supportive notes and letters from members of the congregation, and in the weeks following, she heard from women and organizations around the country.

Father Jacobson told Shiloh he was proud of her and how she had responded. The vestry never mentioned Shiloh's incident formally, although many of them spoke to Jacobson privately. They were pleased with how the Giles affair had been handled, especially the op-ed that most agreed cast a favorable light on their church. A few were unhappy with the limelight, but in time it dimmed, along with the immediacy of Shiloh's celebrity status.

Shiloh had made it into scores of Rolodexes around the country. For the moment, her national fame was restricted to the memory of a brave woman minister who lived somewhere in the south. But the first step had been taken. As Barry had predicted, the plan had worked. Shiloh took a few speaking engagements but mainly concentrated on her work and Barry's "secret" committee.

Barry's full committee met once a month to touch bases. The twenty-person executive committee met or held a telephone conference call weekly. The executive committee included Charlie Bates, the PR guy; a few party regulars who had worked on many other campaigns, a pollster/strategy expert, Brenda Jones who worked with Bates; and folks who had the connections needed for fundraising and finding support around the state, especially for the primary.

If Barry won the nomination, the party would focus all of its attention on him, but until then, the party faithful would choose sides based on reputation, issues, geography, and their view of who had the best chance to beat the republicans. In early polling, Barry scored well against potential democratic primary rivals. His likely primary opponents would be the mayor of Memphis, George Blaylock, and the state attorney general, Jim Clancy. There were a few others who might consider running, but Blaylock and Clancy were the serious contenders.

The Republican candidate would likely be Congressman Robert Keller from Knoxville. Barry was slightly ahead of Keller in head-to-head polling. Keller was well-known in his district, but Barry was better known statewide from his years in the Tennessee Senate, especially as chair of the finance committee.

Shiloh was assigned to the health and social services and the PR subcommittees. She also sat in on the finance committee at Barry's request, to broaden her education in this essential area. She was expected to contribute significantly to the health and social services committee, both because of her experience in the ministry and her work in the Philippines.

Each committee prepared briefing books on their subject areas, which included important current issues; Barry's record, if he had one; available polling data; the positions of potential Republican and Democratic rivals; and a chairman's section, which included what the subcommittee thought were the most important talking points for the candidate to consider. The chair would make subcommittee assignments and conduct conference calls. It was a whole new world for Shiloh. She particularly enjoyed the PR subcommittee, headed by Charlie Bates.

Charlie Bates and Brenda Jones made a good team. Charlie, in his mid-forties, was a veteran of Democratic politics in Nashville and was usually the first person a potential candidate would call for advice about costs, organization, and, of course, Charlie's availability. He had known Barry since Barry had first come to Nashville. In his view, Barry was a perfect candidate. He was thoughtful and considerate of the people around him, he had solid Democratic positions, and he came across as strong, as well as concerned. He gave the appearance of someone who could be trusted. He was sincere about doing a good job, and it showed. He listened to his advisers. Charlie often complained about how he hated to work with candidates who thought they knew it all. Polling, message development, strategy, and PR were critical to the success of any campaign. Charlie explained that the candidate and his or her issues needed to be packaged in a pleasing way to get the candidate's messages out to the voters in a manner that was easily articulated and understood.

After their first subcommittee meeting, Charlie asked Shiloh to have coffee. As they walked across the street from the capitol, Charlie asked Shiloh, "So, what do you think of behind the scenes politics?"

Shiloh laughed. "It was interesting, educational, and a bit overwhelming." She gathered her thoughts and continued, "I never dreamed it was so complicated. I guess if I had thought about it more seriously, I would have guessed at least some of what is needed to run a viable political campaign. I was naïve. And to think that Barry thinks that I can do this—run for office I mean."

Charlie smiled. "It's not as hard as it looks if you have volunteers and enough money. The formula is really pretty simple."

"Right," said Shiloh. "That's easy for a pro like you to say."

They both laughed as they walked into the Hyatt Coffee Shop.

They ordered coffee, and Charlie continued, "Believe it or not, the hard part is the candidate. After fifteen years in this business, I am very selective about the candidates I agree to help. With Barry, it was easy. I actually asked him a few years ago to let me help him if he ever decided to take a shot at running the state. I like Barry. He has integrity, he's smart and respected, and he has views that I support.

After refills Shiloh spoke. "I can see why you'd like Barry, but how did you get into this unusual line of work in the first place?"

Charlie shot back, "What drove you to become a clergywoman?"

"Touché," replied Shiloh with a smile. She liked Charlie.

"Actually, I started out as a journalist. After college, I got a job at a small paper in Bristol. About eighteen months later, I moved to the evening paper in Chattanooga, but I hated their editorial policy. After three years, I left. (It took me awhile to get the guts to leave.) Anyway, I finally did and went to work for peanuts on Jake Walker's failed campaign for the Senate. That did it. I was hooked.

"I started my own company with one employee—me. I started off slowly, very slowly. I almost depleted my meager savings before I had a payday. In the early days, I worked with large firms on ad campaigns and consulted for companies about their image or products. I still do some of that, and now I even help an occasional nonprofit group on the cheap, if I have time and can afford to do it. But the truth is, I live for politics. It's in my blood. Now there are twelve of us who work for Bates and Associates. Brenda Jones is my business partner. You can't do this work without good polling. We merged about five years ago." Charlie paused. "Now you, Reverend Giles."

"I knew that was coming." Shiloh smiled. "It's really quite simple. I wanted to save the world from politicians and guys who help politicians bamboozle the poor electorate."

"Come on, the truth."

"Okay, the truth. The church was important to me growing up. I was an altar girl."

Charlie interrupted, "You mean acolyte, or were you raised Catholic?"

"Sorry, Episcopalians have to explain what an acolyte is so often that I just refer to acolytes as altar boys to non-Episcopalians."

Charlie studied her quizzically. "Shy, I see you every week at All Saints. I sit near the back and sneak out during the recessional."

"Touché again. How could I have missed you so many times?" replied a slightly embarrassed Shiloh.

"Not to worry, Shy. I leave very early in the recessional and don't really care to stand in line after church. Now, please continue."

"Okay, Charlie. But I am really sorry I missed you." Shiloh was perplexed but smiling broadly. "Anyway, I was an acolyte and was close friends with the rector and his family. I went to Sewanee for undergraduate studies, and the more I was exposed to the church there, the more I became convinced that working as a priest was what I wanted to do. I stayed for seminary and only had to move a few blocks from my undergrad dorm. After seminary, I spent seven years as an agricultural and health missionary in the Philippines and have been here at All Saints for a little less than a year."

"And that nose-crushing, overhand smash that you used to whip up on that bully you kayoed a few weeks ago—where did you learn that?" asked Charlie.

Shiloh was into her story now. "That came from my home-taught sex education class. When my dad had that talk with me that all parents dread, he talked very little about the birds and bees and mostly about self-defense."

"I can see why—if you will forgive my brashness—" said Charlie, "you are quite a stunner."

Shy blushed slightly. "That isn't much of a compliment coming from a PR guy who works in politics."

Charlie smiled ruefully. Before parting, they set up a meeting for the next week.

* * * * *

The following day, Shiloh heard from Wendell Rawlins, chairman of the health and social services committee, who gave her an assignment to write a think piece about women's special health needs including birth control and abortion and a few talking points for their pro-choice candidate. "It would be good, Reverend Giles, if you could send me something before our next meeting in two weeks."

"Doctor Rawlins, please call me Shy or Shiloh."

"I would be delighted, Shy. Please call me Wen." He chuckled. "That's W-e-n, Shy, not w-i-n-d as in long-windedness, which I am accused of by my wife and children."

They were both laughing as they rang off. Shy didn't know how old Wendell Rawlins was, but she remembered him as the state commissioner of health from her elementary school days. It was nice, she thought, for him to work so hard on such an effort. She knew that he was retired. She had been impressed by what he had to say at the committee meeting. He was a dedicated health professional who knew his business.

Over the next two weeks, Shiloh kept up her busy schedule. When the health committee met, Shiloh discussed her assignment on women's health at the request of Dr. Rawlins, who seemed very pleased with both the paper and her presentation.

After the meeting, Charlie and Shiloh went to supper together. It was a small, quiet Italian place. They just made their eight o'clock reservation and were seated in an alcove booth at the rear of the restaurant.

After consulting with Shiloh, Charlie ordered a bottle of Chianti and toasted a successful meeting. It was approaching July, and the weather was hot and humid. It hadn't rained lately, and the dust was thick with humidity, which made the wine taste especially good. This was the fourth time that they had been together alone over the past few weeks, but it was the first time that they had eaten together and drank alcohol.

Shiloh was beginning to feel affection for Charlie that she thought might go beyond friendship. *It's about time something stirred me other than work, family, and politics*, she thought. She was looking forward to spending more time together like this.

They talked about the campaign and the earlier meeting. Charlie raked his hand through his hair. "I'm pleased with the progress so far. This campaign seems quite advanced for being this far out from the election. Only reelections are this advanced at this stage. Our candidate is doing quite well, and we can be proud of our work as a committee. Each of the chairs obviously knows their business."

"Did you like the reports today?" asked Shiloh, looking for the compliment she thought was due.

"Yes, they were all pretty good," said Charlie. "Your report was excellent. The research was superb and gives us a lot of meat to work with in preparing the eventual briefing kit for Barry. The talking points were fine too."

"Fine," Shiloh tried to hide her disappointment.

"Oh, I'm sorry. They're very good. That was a poor choice of words. I was talking like I was at the office."

"You're making it worse," she said with a phony smile.

"Yes, I suppose I am. Your work was excellent. I couldn't expect more. Besides, if it were perfect, I wouldn't have a job."

He was trying hard, thought Shiloh.

"Let me explain what we'll do now, but first let me rephrase what I said about your talking points. The talking points, plus your report, provide, as far as I can tell, all we need to move forward into the strategy and message stages. We'll plug all of your information into a formula, which asks some basic questions that we will use to craft appropriate messages for various audiences.

"First, we look at various audience demographics such as age, income, race, religion, and region. The messages we craft will include different amounts of specificity, depending on polling data and candidate preferences. But it will all be developed from your material. The statements will be basically the same with nuances. For example, suppose that you were trying to provide information to young people and the altar guild and, say, the vestry or a journalist about one of the teachings of Jesus or about sexuality or, for that matter, even a recipe for chocolate cake. You would use words that met the audience's level of education, experience, and perhaps gender. It would also be crafted to address what we know through polling, experience, and observation. You basically say the same thing to every group but with words and examples that they understand."

He took a sip of his wine and continued, "The main criteria for good messages are to be honest, to know your facts, and to stick to the message once you have decided on it. Don't wander around with your words like you just thought of something. That'll get you in trouble. The hardest job we have is to convince candidates to stay on message and to be a messenger and teacher rather than a lecturer. We also train them on how to work with the media and on how to debate their rivals. But the main thing is the message. Always stick to your message. Don't ever freelance with a question; if you don't know, don't guess.

"It is always better," Charlie said with a professorial air, "to say you will find out the answer or investigate then to make a mistake by giving the wrong answer off the cuff."

Shiloh respected his opinions and knew that she would learn much from Charlie Bates.

"Next, you look at what allies you have, who you may be able to quote or bring along to help. Finally, you test all of this with the various demographic groups to see if you're right. Then you discuss what you've put together with the committee members. Depending on their comments, the messages are tweaked one final time.

"Am I boring you, Shy?"

"Of course not," said Shiloh, and she meant it, but she was happy to see that the food arrived.

After a few bites to quell her initial fear of starvation, she spoke. "I apologize. When I was doing the research and writing the paper, with a lot of help from a friend at Planned Parenthood, I thought, just how difficult could this be anyway? All Barry needs to do is read this, and he's set. Boy, was I wrong."

Shiloh continued to work on her arugula salad and strip steak.

Charlie smiled. "And I didn't even mention printed materials, posters, radio and TV commercials, and the biggest task of all, candidate preparation. It all has to include candidate positions and words that he's comfortable using."

Charlie poured more wine for Shiloh and refilled his own glass, as an Andrea Bocelli CD played love songs in the background.

Shiloh liked this restaurant. It was cozy and relaxed and one didn't feel rushed. Its décor featured muted earthy colors with pictures of Italian villages surrounded by tall mountains, vineyards, and deep blue lakes. Perhaps it was Tuscany, she mused. She was in great spirits.

They changed the subject to college life. Charlie was an alumnus of UT Knoxville, an avid Volunteer football fan, and a man who loved the mountains of east Tennessee.

It was 11:00 by the time they had finished coffee and an outrageous double chocolate dessert that featured warm chocolate cake filled with hot fudge.

On the drive home, Shiloh replayed the evening. She concluded that the evening had gone well and was fun. She liked Charlie's company. She liked Charlie. He was a southern gentleman, she thought. He'd kissed her on her right cheek, as was the custom in the south as a greeting, when they'd said good-bye before. Maybe tonight would be different.

"Charlie," Shiloh asked as they arrived, "why don't you come in for a night cap? I have some liquors here that you may be able to help me identify."

Charlie agreed. "Sure, I'd like that."

She walked in and went straight to the kitchen. "I keep my liquor in the kitchen cabinet," she said as she opened the cabinet door.

"Good Lord," said Charlie. "That is one hell of an assortment you have there."

"Father Jacobson prepared me for this, just before last Christmas. He said, as you can see, several parishioners give the rector and the assistants bottles for Christmas."

"Really," said Charlie. "I always give cash in a special envelope that we receive from the vestry in early December. I understand that half goes to the rector and a quarter each to the two assistants."

"Yes, that's true," said Shiloh. "The liquor's extra. Some folks just want to give us something personal I guess. Bill has enough to start a liquor store in his home."

"I guess that's why we're called Whiskeypalians," laughed Charlie.

Shiloh nodded. "What would you like?"

"Let's see, how about that one there—Remy Martin?" suggested Charlie.

"And what would I like?" inquired Shiloh in a rather breathy voice.

"Grand Mariner; I think you'll like it. It tastes like oranges."

Shiloh looked up at Charlie. He had to lean over her to reach the bottles on the second shelf over the counter. Shiloh didn't move. Charlie got the bottles. Shiloh moved very close to Charlie and leaned into him as he tried to open the first bottle. She looked up and noticed that Charlie had tears in his eyes. "Charlie what is it?"

"Oh my God, I thought you knew. I thought everyone knew. I'm gay."

* * * * *

The next day was hot and sultry and compounded by a light drizzle. In a word, it was dreary. The drizzle wasn't cooling; it was just wet and inconvenient. It matched how Shiloh felt. What a fool she had been. She had an ironic smile as she focused on her thoughts: wet and inconvenient.

She and Charlie had stood in the kitchen holding each other. Charlie had cried from frustration and Shiloh from embarrassment and thwarted desire. They sat and talked on the coach in Shiloh's living room until after 2:00 a.m.

His sexual preference was generally known but never really discussed. He was not presently seeing anyone and had not for a few years. He had told Shiloh the night before, "It isn't easy to be gay in the south. I had a partner, but after three years, he decided to take a job on the West Coast. We're still in touch, but he just couldn't take being so secretive all the time."

"Have you ever thought about joining him?" Shiloh had asked.

"Oh sure, but my family is here. My mother isn't well, and I enjoy my work and being my own boss. It would be hard to start over," explained Charlie. "My Tom just couldn't handle a secret life. He wanted to be public, but people are not very tolerant about gays around here, at least visible gays."

"That's terrible," she'd responded, telling him about a friend of hers in college who had come out to her parents only to have them disown her. "I just can't understand how parents could turn their backs on their own children. But I understand that that is a fairly common reaction."

Shy had opened up about her sex life too, or lack thereof. "I have spent so much time fending off men in my life that I couldn't recognize the difference between a gentleman and a man who was sexually disinterested. I guess my inexperience is showing through. Actually, I'm a virgin," she'd confided. "I surprised myself at how forward I was a while ago."

"Wow," is all Charlie had said at first. Then he'd added with a smile, "I didn't know that there was such a thing as a thirty-something virgin."

"Twenty-nine, Charlie," said Shiloh trying to look stern through her big smile. "If you are ever crazy enough to try to estimate a woman's age again, for goodness sakes err on the low side. That may save your life."

"I must admit, I wished at that moment that I wasn't gay or that you were a guy. I really like you," said Charlie as he took a sip of his brandy. "It must be quite difficult being who you are, an attractive woman who happens to be a member of the clergy."

Shiloh waved him off. "There you go again with the PR jargon Charlie. But I appreciate the complement. Actually I am happy enough, but ..." Shiloh's voice trailed off as she struggled with emotions she rarely experienced.

Charlie sighed as he gazed at Shiloh. "Companionship is important. I've tried to get used to being alone, but it hurts sometimes, especially when I want to relax and celebrate. These days, that usually means a couple of cold beers at a sports bar, alone, watching whatever is in season on one of their TV sets. And I visit my mom at least once a month."

"Me too," said Shiloh. "Not the beer and the sports bar, but maybe a glass of wine and some quiet time reading. I usually drive down to Tullahoma every other Monday to have lunch with my grandmother. Do you ever go out to see Tom?"

"I went twice, but he's in a serious relationship now. We stay in touch, but just as friends."

When they'd parted, Charlie had bussed Shiloh's cheek and hugged her tightly. He'd whispered, "Shiloh Giles, you are a good person. I hope that someday you do indeed decide to run for Congress. Our country needs more people like you."

* * * * *

Shiloh was busy, which helped her get over her embarrassment. She was working hard at church and loved it. She was also learning about the world of politics and how to run a campaign.

Shiloh appreciated Barry's desire to serve and admired his integrity; he was a great role model for her. Being around Barry made her think about her own future candidacy. She knew that there were tradeoffs; she knew she'd lose things like privacy and the more comfortable life as a parish priest. But she was also excited by the possibility of being in Congress and serving on a bigger stage.

Shiloh had never entertained a thought about church politics. She had no desire to be a bishop. National politics was different. She liked the idea. She tried to convince herself that it wasn't her ego driving her, even though deep down it felt good to imagine herself as a congresswoman.

She and Barry spoke by phone weekly and occasionally she went by his office for coffee. Once in the fall when Trudy was in the capitol for the weekend, Shiloh invited Barry and Trudy to dinner at her home on Sunday night with the Jacobsons.

Barry and Bill had met briefly when Barry had attended All Saints a few times when he was in the capitol for the weekend but had never held a real conversation. Shiloh had introduced Barry to Bill after a service on one of those occasions. They had not met each other's wives, but Shiloh knew that Trudy and Susan would hit it off.

It was mid-November. The remaining leaves were brown; it was the time of year when every gust of wind would bring more to the ground, signaling the arrival of another season. It was a bright, sunny day.

After the last service that morning, Shiloh rushed home to prepare for her first attempt at formal entertaining. She was having roast chicken with stuffing. She had watched Grandma Alice and Hattie cook roast chicken all of her life. How difficult could it be anyway? She had looked up a terrific cornbread stuffing recipe and was all set for a splendid evening. After tonight, she would be known as the world's greatest cook and hostess, she mused.

At 2:30, she put the chicken in the oven to cook. She prepared the fixings for her hors d'oeuvres and set up her bar and dinner table. She thought she was ready. She went off to church for the evening service and the Young People's Service League.

She was back by 7:30 after leaving the youngsters earlier than usual. Her guests were arriving at 8:00. She put the finishing touches on the hors d'oeuvres, put ice in the ice bucket, and the doorbell rang. It was the Jacobsons, and the Whitfields were pulling up at the curb.

They greeted each other on the front stoop, moved into the small parlor, and took their seats. The men started talking about the Vandy-UT game, while the women complimented each other on their outfits and Shiloh on her house. Shiloh took drink orders. After bringing the drinks, she joined the conversation for a few minutes before excusing herself to check on her meal.

Ten minutes later, Susan and Trudy came in.

Susan spoke first; she was stiffing a giggle, "That is either a nice, large quail or a very anemic chicken."

They all laughed at Susan's quick wit and Shiloh's predicament.

"Don't worry, dear, we can find something here to fix those two little boys in the parlor. They'll never know the difference," said Trudy as she dabbed at her tears.

"There isn't much here," said Shiloh. Instead, Shiloh called and made reservations at the nice Italian restaurant where she and Charlie had eaten their first meal together.

"What do you normally eat, dear?" asked Trudy.

"Mostly I eat salads, an occasional hamburger. I cook bacon and eggs every now and then, but as you can see, I don't cook anything complicated."

"How long did you cook that poor bird anyway?" asked Susan with a smile.

"I put it in at 2:30. How long should I have cooked it?"

"About a fourth of the time it cooked or a little less," advised Trudy. "You stuff it, add seasoning a little water, set the timer on the oven, and go about your business."

"What timer?" asked Shiloh, which produced another round of laugher.

"Let's freshen up the boys' drinks and tell them that we are going out to eat. Stove malfunction we can call it," said Trudy.

They drove to the restaurant and ordered their meals. The conversation consisted of small talk until the meal arrived. Then Bill turned toward Barry. "So how is your campaign going?"

"Pretty well, I think," said Barry, "but you never know. And just like sports, you can't let up until the final buzzer. There's no such thing in a campaign as over-preparation,"

"I can tell you," offered Shiloh, "I've learned a lot. The process is incredible. So many issues, so much research, so much for the candidate to learn and be ready to discuss."

Barry nodded. "Shiloh's right. The candidate must be ready for anything. People look into whatever interests them, or they get a feeling about a person based entirely on how they speak, their sincerity, their posture—even their shoes if they get close enough. Almost anything can trigger momentum in either direction. Of course, the press is critical in this process. They are always looking for a tic here or a slip up there. If that happens, you go into crisis mode trying to explain what you really meant. It's an exhausting process."

Trudy wiped her mouth with her napkin. "Barry seems to have his nose in briefing books of one kind or another constantly. Or else he's asking me how this or that phrase sounds. I suppose I'm learning too."

"Just imagine running for president," said Bill. "I didn't vote for Nixon, but I felt sorry for him being judged on his five o'clock shadow. Or in the last election with Mondale and Reagan when Reagan parroted the Wendy's commercial, 'Where's the beef?' That cooked Mondale."

"When will you officially declare, Barry?" Susan asked.

"Right after the bowl games in early January," said Barry. "That's usually a dead time media wise, unless we declare war or something."

"It really is a game of chance, isn't it?" asked Susan.

"I'm afraid so," said Barry. "Being prepared is essential, but even then it's a turkey shoot. Look at all the times that shoo-ins have lost. And there isn't much you can do until it happens. At least if I lose, I can later claim that I helped start a great career for the first woman to be elected to Congress from Tennessee's Fifth District, right Shy?"

Shiloh reddened as all eyes turned to Shiloh.

"What do you think, Bill?" Barry asked quickly to save Shiloh the embarrassment.

"Well, I hadn't really thought about that, but as I do, I must admit that you may have something there."

Shiloh had regained her composure, but she was stymied about what to say. Finally she blurted, "Barry has big plans for me."

"And?" asked Susan.

"And I must admit that I'm intrigued. I've thought about it quite a lot since Barry first mentioned the possibility."

Warming to the subject, Bill followed. "Catherine Shiloh Giles—now that is a political name if I ever heard one. I think Shy would be a terrific representative for the Fifth District." He turned to Shiloh. "You're bright, you're capable, you speak well; yes, I think you would be terrific."

They discussed politics awhile longer, and then Trudy changed the subject. "Shy, this restaurant was a great choice; the food is delicious and you don't have to worry about dishes."

"Yes," smiled Shiloh, "but I still have to bury that poor quail."

The women laughed as Trudy explained what had really happened to the "stove."

Bill chuckled. "I remember those days. We had some humdingers when we first married. That tiny stove we had in our apartment in seminary didn't help much either."

Trudy told everyone about Barry's first backyard barbeque adventure. "He almost blew up the neighborhood."

"Why is it that women are always the cooks?" asked Shiloh. "When I marry, I want a man who will do the cooking."

"Speaking of men," asked Barry, "any prospects?"

Ever the quick mind, Shiloh asked, "Did Vandy finally beat Tennessee?"

They all laughed and stood up from an enjoyable evening.

Over the months and years to come, the Whitfields and Jacobsons would become close friends.

Chapter 6

December was a busy month for Shiloh. She visited Grandma Alice every Monday now. Alice's health had begun to fail around Thanksgiving. She had become more forgetful, not knowing sometimes whether it was day or night; she slept longer and her heartbeat was irregular. Her doctor had told Shiloh that her grandmother was wearing down. Shiloh decided to visit every week.

Shiloh was busy with Christmas preparations at the church, including the pageant with the young people, and she was attending weekly meetings of three of the campaign subcommittees. She came home every night exhausted. She enjoyed her work and helping with the campaign, which was fun and educational, but Grandma Alice was constantly in her thoughts.

She called Hattie every day now; she could sense that Hattie was tiring under the pressure of taking care of her failing friend. Shiloh was ill at ease when she thought about Grandma Alice. She felt like she should be there with her, and yet she knew that being there full time was impractical and also that neither Grandma Alice nor Hattie would stand for that. They would both insist that she had her own life to live, although each looked forward to her Monday visits. When Shiloh arrived on Mondays, Hattie would take a short break and tend to her own affairs. As usual, Alice was always eager to see her.

The full committee met on December 20 to plan Barry's announcement, now scheduled to take place the second Monday in January. All the subcommittees had completed their assignments. They were all excited with the growing confidence that their guy could win. Barry thanked his team and told them that he would do his best not to let them down.

"I'll work hard to win and work hard as your governor when I do win," Barry told his team. "I've asked Bill Sawyer to be the campaign manager. Charlie and Brenda will handle press, outreach, campaign materials, and damage control, and I hope all of you will be able to find some time to help out in other capacities. Now," Barry smiled, "I invite all of you to join me next door for a little toast."

They all followed Barry to the next room, where food and drinks were waiting. Trudy was there with Bill and Susan and a few other close friends.

Once everyone had time to get drinks and raid one of the food tables, Wendell Rawlins clicked his glass with a spoon. "Friends and colleagues, we are on our way to electing a great governor." There was warm applause. "I've known Bill since he came here to serve many years ago. I was younger then, about legal retirement age I would guess." Everyone laughed. "I've served under several governors, and I've watched many elected officials come and go during my years here on the Hill. And I've never met anyone who works harder, who has sounder positions, who is better prepared, or who is more honest than Barry Whitfield." The applause was loud and sustained.

"Now," continued Wendell, "a toast to all of you who have worked so hard these last several months to bring us to this place and for the work you will do during the campaign." More applause filled the room. "And of course, a toast to our candidate, Barry Whitfield, the man who will lead us to victory, the next governor of the great and wonderful state of Tennessee."

The room erupted again. There was long, sustained applause as Barry shook hands again with Wen.

Shy finally worked her way up to Barry and Susan. She hugged them both.

"Well, Shy, what do you think of all of this?" asked Barry.

"I'm excited," Shy answered.

"Me too," Barry replied. "Now the hard part begins."

"Yes, but you'll be ready," Shiloh answered confidently.

"Just imagine losing," said Barry. "There will probably be ten or twelve folks in the two parties who will announce. One or two will do nothing more than that, and a few will drop out early. Except for one of us, the rest will all be disappointed."

"Don't be so depressing, dear," whispered Trudy.

"It's true," said Barry. "Governing is a great responsibility, but not letting down the folks who helped you is very important too. You have to stay focused on your briefs and daily changes in the political climate. And you must maintain a high level of energy in a race like this or in any race for that matter."

Barry shook hands with one of his guests and continued. "But big ones like this require more help, more money, and carry more expectations."

"Is that a word to the wise?" asked Shiloh.

"Yes, I suppose it is. I feel stronger than ever about your run for the House and your abilities. I hear great reports about your work and your ability to articulate your ideas. And I've known for years about your character and sincerity. You are, in a word, a natural. The other side of the coin, however, is the people who work hard on your behalf. You should always thank them and not forget that there will be other elections. You'll always need help. If you win, they win; if you lose, they lose. It's a big responsibility."

Shy went home that night thinking about what Barry had said and about the possibility of a campaign of her own. But those thoughts quickly turned to Grandma Alice, the All Saints Christmas pageant, and the Christmas shopping she had not yet started. She even had a fleeting thought about her nonexistent love life and wondered if she would ever fall in love.

Shiloh finished Christmas week exhausted. She assisted Bill with the Christmas Eve midnight service and handled the service at 7:30 on Christmas morning. Then she assisted with the Christmas day service at 11:00, which was usually fairly sparse after a long midnight service. She made hospital calls that afternoon and left for Tullahoma at around 5:00, arriving at Grandma Alice's by 6:30 to a group of hungry family members who had waited on supper for her. Sam and his family had come down from Trenton, and of course Hattie was there.

When Shiloh arrived, she asked Sam how Grandma Alice was doing.

"Okay, I guess. She seemed very tired last night and came out late this morning."

Hattie had nodded. "She's not an early bird like she used to be," she said with a sigh. "She sleeps late in the mornings and takes long naps in the afternoon."

Grandma Alice didn't get up from her favorite winged back when Shiloh arrived, but her smile was radiant, and she made Shy stand in front of her so she could look her over. "Such an angel," said Alice.

"Are you talking to me?" asked Sam.

"Pshaw, I said angel, not devil."

They all laughed. She was as spunky as ever. They ate supper in the parlor holding the plates in their laps, something that Alice would never have allowed under normal circumstances. She didn't move from her chair. Hattie covered her shoulders with a shawl and sat next to her in one of the straight-backed dining room chairs. Shiloh and Barbara cleared the dishes while Sam stayed with the children in the living room. When the dishes were done, they all gathered around Grandma Alice to open presents.

They opened them one at a time going around in a circle, which was their custom. Grandma Alice demanded to see every present. She patted Chase on the head when he showed his great-grandmother the chess set that Hattie had given him. She laughed as Jill examined the multicolored T-shirt from Chase. "Will you wear that shirt in public, dear?" smiled Grandma Alice.

They laughed as Jill thanked her little brother for the "neat" shirt. Grandma asked them to sing Christmas carols. She listened and smiled.

It was Hattie who noticed that Alice had left them. She gently used her fingers to close her friend's eyelids. Shiloh noticed what Hattie was doing and burst into tears. Sam knelt at his Grandma Alice's side and put his big hands over her small frail hands. Hattie was quietly sobbing. Barbara put her arms around her children's shoulders and told them that their great-grandmother had passed away.

The funeral was well attended, even though Alice hadn't been to church in over seven years. One day she had just decided not to go anymore. It had been too much of a strain for her, and she didn't like to cause a scene when she needed help to get up and down the church steps. Father Gunn and later his successor, Father Stevens, gave her communion at her home every two weeks, just like they would for someone in a hospital or a nursing home. Only the older folks at St. Luke's remembered Alice. But many others came out of respect for the family. Father Gunn drove down from Kentucky and co-officiated at the funeral with Father Stevens. Barry read the Twenty-third Psalm, Alice's favorite.

At the graveside, Chase and Jill stood between their mom and dad. Shiloh stood on the other side of Sam. They held hands and silently said their last good-bye to their grandmother. She had outlived all of her children and helped raise two of her grandchildren.

* * * * *

Shiloh was still in a fog of grief when she went back to Tullahoma for Barry's announcement for governor. Barry had asked Sam to come down from New Jersey, which he readily agreed to do. Shiloh and Sam arrived the day before and stayed at the old homestead. They went through Alice's things and bundled her clothes to give to the Salvation Army. They took a few mementos for themselves: pictures, Alice's ring for Shiloh, a few special dishes that held little value but many memories. Each took an iced tea glass, and Sam took the old footstool that his grandfather Pappy had made. It was a sad day for them both. They were now the last of the Giles family.

* * * * *

Barry had asked Shiloh and Sam to stand with Trudy, Susan and his brother, Hal, during his announcement for governor. "You're my family," he explained, a sentiment that his best friend's children shared.

But it was a bittersweet day for both of them. They were happy for Barry but still sad about the passing of their grandmother. Shy thought about what might have been: the early death of their father and the tragedy of their mother's illness and her death. Life had been good and bad for her family, she thought. *I must remember the good and learn from the bad.*

The day was cold with intermittent sprinkles of bitter cold rain. *It'll probably freeze by nightfall, making driving treacherous,* thought Shiloh. By the time Barry introduced his family, and began his speech, a light snow had begun to fall. As the snow began to fall harder, about five minutes into Barry's speech, he stopped talking and looked out at his audience.

He began again. "My dear friends and neighbors," he said with a smile, "You know me, and the state will know me better soon enough. I am running for governor; I hope you will all support me. I pledge to do my best to make our great state even greater. Now let's get into the courthouse and out of this weather. I believe we have some coffee and hot chocolate in there to warm us up. I want you all thawed out so you can vote for me in the primary and, hopefully, next November."

There was hearty applause and several "Barry for governor" shouts from the crowd.

The courthouse foyer filled with well-wishers as volunteers passed around coffee, hot chocolate, and cookies. Charlie whispered in Shiloh's ear, "That was a nice touch out there. The print reporters will use the release and speech, and the radio and TV folks have enough for a few good sound bites. They were cold too. He had a good round."

Shiloh smiled. "The ever instructive Charlie," she said. "You're good at this. I agree. Barry did a great job out there."

That snapped her dark mood. She mingled with the crowd and became her old self again.

After the reception, Shiloh and Sam went to Barry's office to await his arrival. Several interviews later, he joined then.

"Great show, Mr. Governor," said Sam.

"Yeah, what a ham," said Shiloh as coffee arrived.

Barry smiled and put his arms around both of them. "Of course you'll both join Trudy and me tonight for supper. I'm afraid that there will be a houseful—Charlie and his team, Bill Sawyer, the crowd from the firm, maybe even a few reporters, so don't tell any family secrets. And before you say no, I insist."

They both laughed and nodded. "Okay, now Alice's will. She had very little money left in the trust, a little north of two thousand dollars the last time I checked. She left that to Hattie. The house and contents go to the two of you jointly."

"Barry," Sam cleared his voice. "Shiloh and I are certain that you've paid much more for us and Grandma than we'll ever know. We figured it out. Dad couldn't have had all that you claimed he did when he died. We want to thank you. The money you gave me helped Mario and me start our firm, and we are sure that you personally supplemented Shy's tuition."

"Now …" Barry held up his hand, "even if that were true, you are my family, and what I do with and for my family is my business and Trudy's. I don't ever want to have this conversation again."

"Yes, sir," said Sam.

"Thank you, sir," Shiloh spoke softly. "We love you and Trudy. You're both saints."

"Enough," said Barry. He was smiling and had tears in his eyes. "Enough. Now, what do you want me to do with the lovely old barn of yours?"

Sam and Shiloh looked at each other. Shiloh spoke, "Give it to Hattie. We talked it over last night. We want Hattie to have it. She can live there, or she can sell it. She was Grandma's best friend, and she's like a second grandmother to both of us."

"Are you sure?" asked Barry. "That's a fine ole piece of property; the house could use a little paint here and there. But it was a beauty in its day and could be again."

"No," said Sam. "We want Hattie to have it. We'll both be fine."

"I can see that you're determined. I'll ask one of the youngsters here at the firm to draw up the papers. Why don't we drive over to Hattie's place now and tell her?"

And they did.

She protested to no avail. She finally gave up, and through her tears, she kissed and hugged each of them. It was a happy occasion. She talked about the old times when "Miss Alice" and she were younger and when Shiloh and Sam were children. They left Hattie's around six o'clock, insisting that she join them for supper. They were full of coffee and ready to brave the accumulating snow.

The next morning, Shiloh and Sam sat in the breakfast room of the home they had given to Hattie and drank some of Grandma Alice's strong chicory coffee for old time's sake. Sam spoke quietly, "It's just you and me now, sis. We can never forget that."

"I know, Sammy; and I could never forget our little Giles family. But you also have Barbara and your children. Maybe someday I'll have a family too."

They hugged each other and left—Sam headed for Trenton and Shiloh to Nashville.

* * * * *

Barry's primary campaign went well. He won 54 percent of the vote, a landslide. The party circled its wagons around Barry.

November was no different from the primary. Barry ran another solid campaign and won over his republican rival with 58 percent of the vote.

"Another great victory," Shiloh enthused when she saw Barry on election night.

"Thanks for all your help, Shy. I'm happy and anxious to get started on my new job."

As they parted that evening, Barry whispered to Shiloh. "You next, my dear."

* * * * *

"Preparation sure paid off," exclaimed Shiloh over dinner with Charlie.

"I know, and Bill Rodgers announced yesterday that this would be his last term."

"I saw that," said Shiloh.

"And?" inquired Charlie with a smile.

"And I'm not sure," said Shiloh. "I don't need to decide right away."

"While you're thinking, take these things with you and tell me if you like the colors." He handed Shiloh a large thirty-by-twenty-four-inch envelope. She looked inside and found a large red, white, and blue poster: GILES FOR CONGRESS, dedication service integrity.

"Dig deeper," said Charlie.

There was a button: Shine with SHILOH.

"You devil," Shiloh said with a wide smile. She tried to look harsh but failed in a peel of laugher. "You rascal," was all she could manage. She stood and gave him a big hug.

* * * * *

A few days after Barry's inauguration, Shiloh went to see Father Jacobson in his office. "Nice coffee; is it a new brand?" Shiloh inquired.

"If you think I don't know why you are here, with an appointment nonetheless, you are crazy, young woman," said Bill with a knowing smile.

"Of course you have my blessing to run for Congress. Barry and I have talked about it several times. We both hoped that you would decide to run."

"Yes. I think I'd like to run, but I wanted to talk to you before I decide for sure. I have a whole list of things to discuss. I have responsibilities here. I like what I do."

Bill interrupted her gently. "What you need to know, Shy, is that I'll support your decision to run for Congress. Yes, we have some details about All Saints to discuss, but I encourage you. I know you and I know your integrity, I know your positions. I think you would make a great representative. Washington is a much larger platform than you have here. You can do a lot of good there. You can help a much larger flock than you can here."

"I really do want to do it, Bill. I guess I just have the jitters. Once I jump, that's it," responded a thoughtful Shiloh. "Maybe I'm just living up to my name: Shy."

Bill reached over and patted her hand. "Remember you have your boss's blessing and the support of the governor. Plus, my dear, I've heard many people mention you and politics in the same breath. Even some of the old toads on the vestry agree that you would be great in Congress."

Shiloh was shocked. All she could manage to say was a weak, "Really?"

"Really. People are waiting for you to announce. The rumors have been around since your altercation at the Mid-State Clinic, and folks have been discussing you seriously for the last few months. You handled your notoriety well. And when you decided to prosecute and won, especially when Skyler was given thirty days in jail, that sealed your fate. You handled the hearing firmly and with grace.

Shiloh knew Father Jacobson was referring particularly to the Lawson incident near the end of the hearing. The guy had jumped up and yelled at her when she was on the witness stand, and she had kept her cool. When he had barged through the gates and approached the witness stand, she'd been proud that she hadn't even flinched.

"This Lawson fellow is out of control," Father Jacobson added. "His ten days for contempt served him right. Yes, my dear, you will find a receptive audience."

"I-'m floored," Shiloh smiled nervously. "Losing your privacy. People talking about you." Shiloh took a deep breath. "I guess this is it, huh?"

Bill smiled warmly, "You'll get used to it. I know it may be hard to believe, especially for someone as humble as you, but you have talent, and people believe in you. You're smart, and you've learned many things in your short life that will be useful in your new calling. You're an example for women, and they'll support you. I'm proud that I know you, Shy."

Shy stood and hugged Bill. "I've learned so much from you. It is I who am honored. Thank you so much for your support."

Bill gently walked Shy back to her chair and then seated himself next to her. He wanted to talk politics.

"Now, Barry," Bill continued, "thinks that you may be unopposed in the primary if you get out front early. His endorsement will carry a lot of weight. The general election will be different, though, Barry told me. The other party may decide to fight hard for an open seat. It's difficult to tell now, but they've never been overly strong in the Fifth District except in statewide races. We all loved Howard Baker in the statewide races, Democrats and Republicans alike. Al Gore and Bill Rogers are both pro-choice and always won handily in this district, but they didn't go around punching out people who disagreed with them," Bill said with a smile. "So you may receive special attention from the fundamentalists. When Lawson got out of jail, he announced that you were an enemy of all decent people and that your so-called church was a den of iniquity. I expect that you may well hear from him and his kind during the campaign. But a well-managed campaign and plenty of stamina will handle them. So it is my guess and Barry's advice that, if you're going to do it, you need to get started." Bill leaned back in his chair, clearly feeling proud of his insight into the world of politics.

"I voted for Baker myself," replied Shiloh. "I know I shouldn't admit that too often. But he is a good man."

"Me too," replied Bill. "He was a great senator for his state and for the country. You'll be good too, Shiloh. You have talent, you have integrity, and you are attractive. But it isn't just you folks are thinking about. It's politics too—our community and country. They want good government, and many people think you can carry on the tradition of good leadership in this district. Politics are the lifeblood of a country like ours: democracy, the rule of law, justice, tolerance. That isn't a bad calling, is it? You can even call it your duty to serve."

Shiloh sat up in her chair. "Yes, I've thought about those values and my role in promoting them as a member of Congress. It's just that the being out front and in the limelight is neither in my nature nor does my ego demand it. On the other hand, I have pictured myself fighting for what I believe in on the floor of Congress. So I guess that my ego isn't on life support yet"

"Good," said Bill laughing. "Then get going, lady."

"It's all just happening so fast," said Shiloh.

* * * * *

For the next several months, she busied herself at church and met several times with Charlie to plan her campaign. The biggest job was setting up a committee. Barry had offered to assist with that task. He knew that his influence would help, especially with someone who was running for the first time.

Shiloh set up a committee in June under the tutelage of Barry and Charlie. She didn't need to start as early as Barry had, but, as Barry and Charlie had advised, she would declare earlier than usual in an attempt to scare away primary rivals. She was timid at first, but she soon warmed to her work. She used money from her own savings and two thousand dollars contributed by Sam and Mario to get started. She offered to pay Charlie a down payment for his services, since she had not started fundraising yet, but Charlie refused.

"Remember, this is a labor of love for me. Don't worry; I'll spend plenty of your money later."

Her committee was similar to Barry's but smaller. She and Charlie used most of Barry's briefing books since her positions were essentially the same, and they added foreign affairs, defense, intelligence, and national health and education to the list.

Charlie and Brenda and their team would have to change Barry's messages to better match their new client and work on new ones for the new areas, but a congressional district was much easier to contest than the entire state.

Her initial campaign expense was for refreshments at her first campaign committee meeting, which she held in her small, two-bedroom home.

Barry teased her, "Whatever you do, don't cook."

Shiloh recruited a few of her Sewanee professors and a member from her church who was retired from the defense department for her committee. A professor from Vanderbilt also joined. The first thing she learned from one of the attorneys on her committee was that she couldn't use her house again for the meetings.

"It belongs to a religious institution," the woman had advised her. "I know you pay a modest rent, but this is a gray area that you are best to avoid."

Charlie called the first meeting to order and introduced the governor. Barry stepped to the front of the room. "My friends, everyone here knows Shiloh Giles, one of the assistant pastors at All Saints Episcopal Church. You know her from working with me or from personal contact with her. If there is anyone here who does not know Shy, you may remember her as the lady who punched out the big bully at the Mid-State Women's Clinic a while back."

Everyone laughed on cue.

"What I can tell you," Barry continued, "is that I have known Shiloh all of her life. She is smart, articulate, and tough. I believe she would make a superb representative and will endorse her when she announces. Yes, Shiloh is like a daughter to me, but I am not here because of that. I'm here because she will be good for the Democratic Party, good for the district, the state, and our nation. To put it simply, Shiloh Giles is a winner."

There was warm applause as Shiloh took the floor in her cramped parlor. Barry found a place on the carpet and sat down.

"Thank you, Mr. Governor," said Shiloh. Looking at her audience she continued, "I'm overwhelmed that ya'll are here. I'm overwhelmed that I'm here."

Her audience chuckled.

"To run for Congress is a great responsibility; to tell you that I'm running and to know that y'all are here because of that is both humbling and exciting. I have three messages for tonight. First, I thank you from the bottom of my heart for agreeing to help me and for being here with me on this fine evening—even if the governor cajoled most of you." More chuckles filled the room. "You're here, I hope, because you want good representation in Washington from the Fifth District of Tennessee and think that I may be able to provide that. I know what it means to give your time in a campaign like this—hard work and many hours. I thank you again, my dear friends.

"Second, I pledge tonight to do everything I can humanly do to win this election and, if I do, to work hard every day I'm in Washington for the people of this wonderful district."

Shiloh paused for a moment before continuing. "My third message is to tell y'all a little about myself, who I am." Shiloh continued with a brief biography. She mentioned her family, her education, her time in the Philippines, and finally, she talked about her time in Nashville.

She ended with a statement about issues. "Many issues concern me. I want better education for our children, especially minorities and the poor. I want to work to improve race relations. I believe in a strong national defense to be used only in the gravest of circumstances. I pledge to be responsive to my constituents if I'm elected. Government can be daunting, and most folks are intimidated. I want to serve the individual constituents.

"Finally, I know why I'm here before you tonight. I'm here because I stood up to a bully. I stood up to a man who was attempting to force his will on a woman. That's wrong, and I'll work every day to change that. Women's rights are essential if we are ever to become a real democracy. The ERA for women has not been ratified by the required thirty-eight states to become a part of the U.S. Constitution. That is something I hope to someday help to change. With that, dear friends, I thank you again for being here. I'm humbled by your presence and eager to get started. Thank you."

* * * * *

Shiloh had declared at the Davidson County Courthouse the Monday after Thanksgiving. Mondays weren't the best news days, but it was easier for Barry, and Charlie had assured her that word would get out. Sam was by her side. Barry introduced and endorsed Shiloh, and Charlie did his usual with the press.

Word had indeed gotten out. It was the buzz at church that Sunday. Charlie had faxed the press release to the same list he had used nationally to send out Shiloh's op-ed, plus he included a few political action committees that were interested in women candidates.

Shiloh was overwhelmed with well-wishers everywhere she went. The national press occupied much of her time the next week. Their rolodexes did indeed have her name, plus they had the press release Charlie'd sent reminding them who she was. Charlie was delighted. He made sure that the district press learned about the national attention Shiloh attracted.

The money poured in. The first check came from Barry, and many more followed from members of All Saints, Barry's law partners, and, in time, after filing in many questionnaires, from political action committees. The first PAC check came from Emily's list.

Their strategy worked. On March 31, the final date to file, Shiloh learned she was unopposed in the democratic primary.

* * * * *

The first death threat came in April. "Those who kill babies will die by the hand of God's avenging angel," was the message of the cold voice on her phone.

The police came, but there was nothing they could do. The phone company said that the call had been placed on a pay phone. Several more calls came, until Shiloh asked for an unlisted number. She was shocked that she had encountered such venom. *From whom?* she wondered. Someone like Lawson she suspected, but she was nonplussed. She refused to take such cowardly calls seriously.

Then in May, someone threw red paint across the front of her house and left a sign staked in her yard: "Death to Baby Killers." Whoever it was did the same thing at All Saints. There was a picture and story in *The Tennessean* the next day.

Taking no chances, Charlie hired a twenty-four-hour security service to protect Shiloh's home and a plainclothes guard to stay with her throughout the day. Charlie also asked Gwynne Wyler, the finance chair, to send out another fundraising letter. Security wasn't cheap. Several committee members called their friends to help with funds. The National Party also sent a nice contribution, and the fundraising letter was a great success.

But the death threats continued. They were coming in the mail now, and Shiloh's church was receiving phone calls.

"Why," Shiloh asked Charlie, "why is abortion such a consuming issue? It's settled law. It's only one of many important issues."

"I know it seems that way," said Charlie. "It isn't that big of an issue here—yet. It's important only to a tiny percentage, but they're vocal. It's beginning to become important nationally to the Republicans, not because rank-and-file members care so much about abortion. In fact, the rank and file generally support a women's right to choose. But this small group of fundamentalists is becoming more powerful within their party. They are led by the so-called televangelists, who own radio and TV stations and use them to rally their flocks.

"Their power was first felt in 1980 when six Democratic senators lost by very slim margins, which most pundits attributed to letters from national televangelists to churches in those states where the senators lived. These letters were read to many congregations the Sunday before Election Day. They're reaching more and more people with each election. Even though their numbers are still small, relative to the entire population, they have become a major force in some parts of the country. Just imagine being able to virtually guarantee 2 or 3 percent of the vote in a tight election."

"Will it hurt me?" asked Shiloh.

"I don't think so. Abortion barely registers in Brenda's polls. The anti-groups here are not yet so savvy politically. They're like that group that pickets the clinics and yells, and in some cases, becomes violent. That has been counterproductive so far. But they are learning. I expect the more vitriolic types to fade in favor of folks who will utilize more sophisticated tactics. Then we'll have problems. But here the radicals are still holding sway. And as I said, their numbers are still small." Charlie took a deep breath.

"Shy," Charlie finally said, as he looked at his friend over his coffee cup, "I suspect that you'll always have to deal with the abortion issue. It'll always be part of what defines you. People are getting to know the real you, but the incident that gave you the spotlight will always be with you. And your victory in court further angered your opposition. Not only did you get positive publicity for punching Skyler in the nose, he had to pay a fine and sit in the Davidson County jail for thirty days. Heck, that weasel Lawson even got a few days. You won on every count, and when it received national attention, that set them back. They're not going to let this go."

"So be it," said the perplexed candidate. "I won't change my mind about abortion. I just don't understand how people can be so focused on one issue. There's so much more to worry about. Why do we have to continue this endless debate? Don't people remember the violent deaths of women that occurred when it was illegal? Abortion should not be an issue. Instead, it should be a clarion call for contraceptive research and access to birth control and sex education—and for women's rights."

"Too bad the other people don't share your logic. They're against abortion, and many of them are also against the remedy to reduce it," exclaimed Charlie. "They're interested in what they think is right for everyone. Their religion demands that."

Shiloh sighed. "But they must use family planning."

"Many do," agreed Charlie, "but their right to privacy protects them from you knowing that. Ironic, isn't it?"

"Ironic indeed," Shiloh said. Then she leaned forward. "What if it were their teenage daughter or their forty-something mother who might die from another child or a poor welfare mother who already had one child she was raising alone but has enrolled in a college or trade school and is trying to break the welfare cycle and make a life for herself and her child? Like the woman I escorted that day with Skyler." Shiloh was agitated.

"Life's unfair," said Charlie, "We both know that."

"Yes, I know," said Shiloh. "Unfair for the world's women too. We're a lousy example of human rights for the rest of the world, aren't we?"

"Yes, we are," agreed Charlie. "The debate will go on, often at the expense of other important issues that get pushed to the side."

* * * * *

The Republican primary was nasty. There were four candidates. Shiloh's early announcement seemed to have scared off as many potential Republicans as it had Democrats. She received good press and was good on the campaign trail. Everyone wanted to hear and see the attractive lady priest.

The four Republican candidates slugged it out for a month or so, and then the two serious candidates dropped out. All four were behind undecided in the Republican polls, and Shiloh was running well ahead of each one of them in head-to-head polling. The two who dropped out could read the tealeaves; plus they were more than a little embarrassed by the tactics of one of their opponents.

That left two Republicans in the primary. Marcus Jennings, an older gentleman with a modest law practice, was a perennial candidate. Some quipped that he had run in every primary since the founding of the republic.

The Tennessean referred to Jennings as the Harold Stassen of the Fifth District. He always attracted a few votes with his diatribe against taxes, but he was a nonfactor.

When Shiloh had announced, Lawson had decided that the only way to stop her was to run himself. He'd no doubt told his small congregation that the race would pit good against evil. He'd written to Shiloh saying the same thing.

Perhaps, Shiloh thought, *he thinks he can scare me into backing out.* She was curious about what made this madman tick. It certainly wasn't his strategic prowess, she mused to herself.

His single-issue attacks against Shiloh did not resonate among registered voters. Nevertheless, he was ahead of Mr. Jennings, his only remaining opponent. His supporters got out what vote there was and, unbelievably to his party members and to the local press, Lawson won the Republican primary. It was the smallest percentage Republican primary turnout in history, which hurt Republican candidates running for other local offices. Many who did vote did not mark their ballot for a congressional candidate.

After the primary, the campaign turned from bad to worse. There were ugly demonstrations almost everywhere Shiloh spoke. It was usually the same people who demonstrated against Shiloh yelling the same reactionary jargon—"Baby killer," "Satan," even "Whore"—and holding the same nasty signs—"Down with the Devil Woman," "Join God," "Oppose Giles," or "God's Party Says No to Giles."

She was disappointed that the election had become such a farce. What's happening to our country and our state? thought Shiloh.

Although it was obvious she would win, she didn't want to go to Congress like that. But she kept slogging along, giving speeches throughout the district and patiently answering questions. As a priest with experience in the Philippines and in Nashville, she understood families' daily problems and concerns about money, health care, and education. Shiloh had a good grasp of global issues. She had lived abroad and traveled to several countries. She could talk about the rest of the world in a knowledgeable way, but what seemed to impress people most about Shiloh, according to what Charlie told her, was her warmth and sincerity. "On all counts," Charlie told Shiloh, "you are a splendid candidate."

* * * * *

One week before Election Day, there was congressional debate at Tennessee State University. It was a feature of each congressional election as far back as anyone could remember. It was televised locally, and many people tuned in just to watch the fireworks. Shiloh was relatively well-known in the district, and now folks wanted to see this lady priest who was mentioned so often on television and in the press. Others wanted to watch the crackpot running against her to see if he would rant and rave as he had done so often during the campaign. Shiloh had a feeling they would not be disappointed.

The moderator was the leading news anchor at the TV station on which the debate was telecast. There was also a panel of three local journalists who would ask the candidates questions. The two candidates stood at individual lecterns twenty feet apart on the stage facing out toward the audience. The moderator and the three panelists shared a table facing the candidates. They were fifteen feet away from the candidates.

The moderator began, "Tonight, ladies and gentlemen, we have the one and only televised debate for the candidates representing the two major political parties in the November election for the office of Representative to the United States Congress for the Fifth Congressional District of Tennessee."

Shiloh was wearing a dark blue suit with a light blue, high collar, cotton blouse. She was calm and appeared ready. Lawson was wearing a light gray suit with a white shirt and a green tie. He also stood calmly behind his lectern. Shiloh was amazed. Was this really Lawson looking so serene standing there as her debate opponent? Shiloh had only seen him as an agitated demonstrator and courtroom wild man. *Maybe we'll really debate the issues,* she thought.

"Reverend Lawson, Reverend Giles," said the moderator, "the rules for tonight's one-hour debate are as follows. Each of you will have two minutes for an opening statement, which will be followed by questions from the panelists. Each of them will ask you questions on a rotating basis. You will have two minutes to answer. The other candidate will have one minute for rebuttal, and then we'll go to the next question. There will be no commercial breaks. The debate will fill the entire hour. I'll tell you when you've used up your time. Each candidate will have two minutes at the end to sum up. By way of a coin toss, Reverend Lawson will start with his opening statement."

Shiloh watched as Lawson reached into the space for papers under the surface of his lectern and pulled out a manila envelope. From it, he took out a Bible and placed it on the lectern. Then he pulled out a white, blood-smeared butcher's apron and put it on. Slowly he stepped to the side of the lectern where he could be seen by the audience and cameras. "I stand here before you tonight," he thundered, "as the only person who can stop this abortionist, this evil woman, from going to the United States Congress and representing the decent people of the Fifth District of Tennessee. You've seen her in the newspapers. She's pretty, and she's smart, ladies and gentlemen. She has fooled many people. She claims to be a minister, but what kind of church would allow a Jezebel like her to attend to the needs of its flock?"

Shiloh looked on with mixed emotions; she was horrified that the election had become such a circus and frustrated that any chance of addressing a large TV audience with a legitimate discussion of other issues would be lost.

He held up the Bible. "Not a church that believes in our Lord and Savior, Jesus Christ. This woman is a killer." Lawson paused and his voice became even louder. "Look at the blood on my apron; that's what you'll see every day in the abortiontoriums of this country. That is what you'll see right here in Nashville. This is the blood of innocent children. This is the blood of Jesus. This woman must not win. She and those like her will be judged by our savior and condemned to burn in hell for eternity. She is an evil woman!" he screamed and paused before going on. "She must not go to Washington. She must be stopped. You must stop her."

He faced Shiloh and pointed his bible at her. "This woman should be ..."

"Mr. Lawson," said the moderator in a loud voice, "your time ..."

She was drowned out by Lawson as he picked up a newspaper clipping and yelled, "This woman has said that abortion represents a social failure to provide family planning, appropriate education, and ..."

"Mr. Dawson, please give ..."

Lawson continued at the top of his voice, throwing down the clipping and grabbing the Bible. "She is the social failure. She is the Antichrist. We must stop her!" he screamed

The moderator tried to break in when, suddenly, a section of the audience, about fifty people, began to chant, "Lawson, Lawson, Lawson!"

A policeman rushed down the steps of the auditorium to try to quell Lawson's followers.

"Death to the abortionist!" shouted Lawson's followers, ignoring the pleas of the police officer.

Another police officer rushed onto the stage and stood next to Shiloh, where she was joined by her plainclothes security officer. Lawson's followers would not stop chanting. They had taken over the event.

Several minutes ticked by before more police arrived. Finally, the police began to wade into Lawson's supporters and ask them to leave or face arrest. They slowly headed for the aisles.

The moderator stood and faced the audience. "Ladies and gentlemen, I'm sorry to announce that this debate is over. This exercise in democracy has unfortunately been ruined by a group of people who refuse to abide by the First Amendment."

Already thirty-five minutes had elapsed. Lawson glared at Shiloh and walked off the stage to join his followers.

Shiloh could feel her heart racing. *What have I gotten myself into?* she thought. *Is this going to be my life now, always abortion, the Antichrist, no issues to discuss? Is this really the way I'll be defined?*

The panelists and moderator joined Shiloh to make sure she was protected. The police finally escorted Lawson and the rest of his group out of the auditorium to a chorus of boos from the audience. Soon after, the rest of the audience slowly filed out into the warm, fall evening.

Shiloh relaxed a few minutes with the journalists in a room behind the stage. They talked about the surreal turn of events. Charlie had given Shiloh a signal not to talk. She joined in their banter but did not say anything quotable. She did not answer any questions, because there were none—not even for reaction. The reporters were talking like any other spectators would at such a bazaar incident; theirs resembled the talk one hears after a sporting event when viewers recall special moments or their reactions.

Finally one reporter did ask a question, "So, Reverend Giles. How do you like political debates?"

They all laughed and suddenly became focused on their jobs.

Shiloh decided to ignore Charlie's advice. "It was frightening," she said in an even voice. "Not Lawson. I wasn't in fear of him or his supporters. I was frightened about what this means for our democracy, to our way of life. Debating issues and honest discourse between political opponents is a sacred tradition in America. Hate politics and religion mixed with politics like it was tonight is dangerous. I hope this serves as a lesson to us all about what it means to be an American. And," Shiloh finished with a warm smile, "thank y'all for coming to my aid."

They wrote furiously and another asked, "Reverend Giles ..."

Charlie broke in before the reporter could finish, "Come on, it's been a long night, at least an exciting one. Why don't you let me take the candidate home so she can write in her journal about her first TV debate?"

They laughed. They all they needed to file their stories. Shiloh thanked the journalists, her student hosts, and the policewoman who had run up on stage to protect her. Shiloh, Charlie, and Shiloh's security man were driven to Shiloh's home in a Nashville police cruiser.

Barry came straight to Shiloh's house from the airport after returning from an event in Memphis. His driver had filled him in after watching the debate on TV at the airport VIP lounge while awaiting the governor's arrival. Bill and Trudy had come directly from the debate. Bill had keys to Shiloh's house, and the three of them had gone inside to await Shiloh's return. Two Nashville police cars arrived and waited outside along with a few reporters and several of Shiloh's neighbors. By the time Shiloh and Charlie arrived, there were three Nashville police cars parked at the curb, along with the state patrol car that Barry had requested. It was quite a welcoming committee for a candidate for Congress.

Charlie tried to handle the press while Shiloh thanked her neighbors for their concern.

When Shiloh finally entered, Barry was in the kitchen filling glasses with ice. "I don't know about you, but I need a drink," Barry deadpanned.

Shiloh rushed into the kitchen and hugged Barry tightly. "It's really good to see you."

Shiloh got out some chips and peanuts and poured soft drinks for her security man and the patrolmen.

She talked to the others while they waited for Charlie to finish with the press. When he came in, he headed straight for the kitchen to fix a drink. He barely acknowledged Shiloh's guests. When he joined them, he looked flush with excitement. He shook hands with the two men and sat down with a sigh. "Nice debate huh?"

"What now?" asked Bill.

They all looked at Charlie.

He smiled, "Well, my friends, I believe it's safe to say that Shiloh will win. She handled herself well tonight. She has proven on the stump that she knows the issues and that she can deal with controversy, to say the least. But I'm beginning to worry about these anti people. If they ever get organized, they will be a real problem for us and for the country. The abortion issue just won't go away. I'm afraid that it will be a mainstay in American politics for a long time. I hope I'm wrong, but judging from this Lawson character, they're determined. Maybe I dismissed them too quickly before. Time will tell."

They talked for a while and finally left Shiloh in the capable hands of her security man. On this night, Shiloh was comforted by his presence. And on this night, he had plenty of company. One of the Nashville police cars remained along with a state highway patrol car.

Chapter 7

Several supporters called Shiloh the day after the debate to encourage her. She even received a call from the vice president. She admired him and hoped that he would run for president someday. He was dynamic, smart, and a down-to-earth man. She was impressed with his views on defense and the environment. He had represented the Fifth District in the House before Bill Rogers. Rogers had come to the House late in life, after serving twenty-six years in the House of the General Assembly of Tennessee. Rogers also called the next morning along with countless other friends and supporters.

The election was anticlimactic after the excitement of the debate. Shiloh kept her security detail until a week after the election. Election Day, with the exception of a few Lawson followers spread out among a handful of polling places, was peaceful. Even the demonstrators, it seemed, were only going through the motions. The result was a foregone conclusion; Catherine Shiloh Giles became a freshman member of the Congress of the United States. After the dust settled and she had time to thank her supporters and the members of her election committee, she took some time off. She visited Hattie and made the rounds in Tullahoma. Barry's partners had been especially generous with campaign contributions. She knew that her dad would have been proud.

She made a down payment on a two-bedroom condo in Nashville and arranged to have her things moved from the house on Willow Lane. The vestry gave Shiloh a generous Christmas check and a letter of appreciation that was circulated to all All Saints members. Bill and Susan had been wonderful. She stayed with them for a few nights during the packing and moving process.

In mid-December she went to Washington for a briefing session with the other freshmen. She learned about her office budget, staffing, the rules of the

House, franking, and all the other things that come with being a member of Congress. The Speaker met with each new member privately, and he and the minority leader cohosted a reception for the new members at the Capitol rotunda. Her party would be in the minority when Congress convened in January. This would be the first time in eons that the House would be controlled by the Republicans.

The president dropped by the reception and welcomed the new "class" to Washington and posed with each individually for pictures. Shiloh was overwhelmed every time she thought about where she was and what she was doing here. The only thing that seemed to calm her was that every other new member was just as excited and confused as she was.

The bureaucracy was similar to college, and getting the committees you preferred was like trying to get into the right classes during your freshmen year. She would return in January to set up her office, hire her staffers, get sworn in, and go to work. In the meantime, she had to find a place to stay in Washington and organize her district office.

* * * * *

Shiloh had spent Thanksgiving with the Whitfields and Christmas with Sam and Barbara in Trenton. Before returning to her new job, she took a long walk with Sam. She was still uncertain about this turn is her life.

"Thanks for inviting me, Sam. It's so nice to see you and your family and to get away from what my life has become. I have so many doubts. Did I run too soon? Do I really want to do this? What was I thinking? I never in my life thought much about politics until Barry mentioned it to me. Did I do the right thing? Can I really do this job?" she asked Sam.

Sam grabbed her shoulder. "Hold on, little sister. I know you've just gone through a couple of bad months; no privacy, threats, in the public eye constantly, being careful of what you say. It's been a pressure cooker for you, but I don't for a minute think that you went into this without careful thought. Of course Barry and Bill nudged you. And they probably even got a little rush of their own from your victory, but they would never have encouraged you if they didn't think that you were the right person for the job. You're feeling the downside now. It's too late to doubt your ability or to think about that comfortable, private life you had at the church. Remember what you hoped to accomplish."

"Maybe," said Shy. "It's just a lot to swallow. My whole life is different now."

Sam frowned. "Shy, tell me why you ran."

"Oh come on," said Shy, "don't play the psychologist."

"Just say it," argued Sam. "Why did you run?"

"Okay, fine. Because I wanted to help us have better health and education, because we can do more for our senior citizens. I'm for a cleaner environment and a sound energy policy. I ran because I want to speak out for women's rights and because I believe in a strong military and a strong economy. I believe in a prudent foreign policy that will protect our citizens and lead the world based on the principles of our constitution and respect for human rights. And I believe in international development that will help uplift the lives of the poor and bring peace and justice around the world. And, finally, I ran because I believe that I have the ability to promote the issues I care about and that are right for our country. How's that for a stump speech?"

"Great," replied Sam. "Do you believe what you just said?"

"Yes, and it helped to say it. Maybe you should be a psychologist after all." Shy smiled at her brother.

They embraced.

Sam whispered in Shy's ear. "I love you, Shy. Our little family is small, but we are strong. I am always here."

"I know."

* * * * *

When Shiloh returned to Nashville, she met with Bill Rogers to discuss local staffing. The Nashville district office was set. Most of the staff had been there for at least one term, knew the issues, and were good on constituent services. Whatever Shy did as a member of Congress, her constituency came first. She wanted to be responsive to anyone who contacted her, whether it was to discuss a policy issue or to seek help on a personal issue such as social security or veteran's affairs.

Wayne Long was the Nashville chief of staff. He had been with Rogers in the Tennessee House and had moved with him when Rogers was elected to Washington. He was happy to stay on with Shiloh. Wayne was in his late forties and took his job seriously. Wayne and Shy hit it off immediately. *So far, so good,* thought Shiloh.

Shiloh went to Washington after New Years to look for housing. She was lucky to find a two-bedroom townhouse about six blocks from the Hill. A senator who was retiring had previously rented it. It wasn't cheap, but it was manageable. She was set.

By luck of the draw, she got an office on the backside of the cannon building on the second floor. A few of the freshmen ended up with basement offices. She soon realized that seniority was king. Longevity and chairing a committee or being the ranking minority member of a committee or subcommittee had its perks: corner offices and more staff and, of course, more status.

Senior committee staff had more clout than freshmen members and sometimes even better offices. Shiloh and her freshmen colleagues soon learned that they were small fish in a large pond. Being in the minority didn't help either, especially with this Speaker, who wanted the Democrats to pay for their years of lording it over the Republicans. Shiloh got appropriations, which she had asked for, and veteran affairs and science, which she had not.

Staffing was a problem. Rogers's Washington chief of staff had taken a committee staff position as soon as Rogers announced that he was going to retire. And most of the other staff had either left Washington or found staff jobs with other members. The only two who had stayed were a secretary and a legislative aid. The secretary, Carol Smith, was an old-timer. Shiloh and Carol became fast friends. Carol understood how the bureaucracy worked, knew how to get things done, and, it seemed, was known and admired by everyone in the House.

The legislative aide, only twenty-four years old, had been there for just a year. She planned to work for another year and a half until her husband graduated from law school and then go back home to Pennsylvania.

Shiloh called Barry and asked for suggestions. Barry told her that his former Senate chief of staff had moved to Washington with her husband when he had landed a good job at the Justice Department. "Her name is Sarah Bartlett. She was a lobbyist here on the Hill before I hired her. She's very good. She's smart, has good interpersonal skills, and is a terrific negotiator. She's also a good supervisor. You'll like her," Barry had told Shiloh. "She's loyal and isn't afraid to work. I believe Sarah is in her third year of law school at Georgetown. She may be interested. Several senior staffers in Washington are lawyers." Barry sent Sarah's contact information to Shiloh.

Shiloh called Sarah Bartlett, who agreed to meet her to discuss the job. When Sarah came for her appointment, she congratulated Shiloh on her victory. "My husband, Abe, and I were rooting for you. It's nice to meet you in person, Congresswoman Giles."

Shy was taken by Sarah's looks. Her short hair and flawless ebony complexion highlighted her high cheekbones. At five foot seven, she was a few inches taller than Shiloh. She had an attractive physique that suggested regular time in a gym or perhaps jogging on the mall.

"Please call me, Shy. Everyone does. I feel much more comfortable that way," Shiloh smiled.

Sarah nodded. "Yes, ma'am."

They both laughed.

"So," said Shiloh, "tell me about Sarah Bartlett."

"Well," Sarah started, "I was born and raised in Chattanooga. My parents are schoolteachers; they will both retire in a few years. I went to Vanderbilt on a scholarship where I met Abe. He is from Knoxville. His mother is a nurse and raised six children by herself. His mother is one of the strongest women I have ever known. She retired a few years ago. She is Abe's hero. My mom and dad are special too. They've had to deal with discrimination all their lives, and yet they do not allow that to affect the way they teach. They care deeply about racism and politics, and they always preach perseverance, love, and forgiveness to their students.

"When I was at Vandy, I volunteered for NOW. After I graduated, I worked for them as a public affairs officer, primarily liaising with the legislature about women's issues. After a year, I joined Governor Whitfield's Senate staff and helped put Abe through law school. We were as poor as church mice during those years. My salary was very small at NOW and not much better as a Senate staffer. We could probably have qualified for food stamps. I didn't earn a decent salary until I became Barry's chief of staff.

"When Abe graduated, he caught on with the attorney general's office in Nashville, and after six years there, he landed a job with the justice department. I graduate this summer from law school."

"Barry recommends you highly and says that he hated to lose you," said Shiloh. "Are you at all interested in joining the rat race here?"

"Of course," replied Sarah. "It's in my blood. I just have a semester to go in law school, and if need be, I can spread that out over a year by opting for night school. What do I need to do to apply?"

Shiloh spoke. "Carol, the secretary, says that you need to fill out an employment form and that I have to talk to the employment folks. Once that is done, they hire you."

"You mean that you're offering me the job, just like that?" exclaimed Sarah.

"Yes, I guess I am," answered Shiloh. "I need someone, Barry sings your praises, and quite frankly, I like you. As for affirmative action, I don't plan to interview anyone else. As Carol says, they make the laws here, but they don't necessarily follow them. Besides, from what I hear, good staff members, especially chiefs, are hard to come by. So when someone comes in, they grab them and don't let them escape." Shiloh smiled.

But then she became serious. "Sarah, I hope you'll take the job. It doesn't pay as much as you could make by practicing law, but it isn't bad. It's more than I made as a priest, and I'm sure it's better than the salaries for staff on the Hill in Nashville. We'll get to know each other soon enough. My only rule is that I want to do as good a job as I can for my district and for the country. And I would expect that to be your goal as well."

"I'd love to work with you. You don't look like a priest, but I hope you act like one." Sarah said.

Shiloh smiled at her chief of staff, and they shook hands, Shiloh turned Sarah over to Carol to fill in the appropriate forms. *Wow,* she thought, *I have a chief.* If everything else is this easy, I could get to like this place.

* * * * *

Shiloh performed well in Congress. She was in her third term and approaching the tender age of thirty-seven. She was close to many of her colleagues and enjoyed working on good legislation. She always looked forward to the to and fro of debate. When it came, she loved the sweet taste of victory, but she was not a rabid ideologue and soon learned that getting something done required compromise. Even if the bill wasn't perfect, it was usually better than existing legislation. She respected the institution of Congress and its responsibility for upholding the democratic principles of the republic, especially the separation of power.

Shiloh was not known in Congress as an abortion radical. For sure, she was pro-choice. And many people knew some of her history on abortion, but as a member she was respected as a thoughtful legislator and colleague, even among those with whom she disagreed. She was firm and would speak out and vote against bad legislation. But she still remained friendly with her colleagues with whom she disagreed.

She worked on several education and health bills. She was a strong supporter of the military and worked hard on environmental, trade, and foreign aid issues. From her spot on the Subcommittee on Foreign Operations of the Appropriations Committee, she fought hard for women's health programs and policy initiatives in the foreign aid bill each year. And she always spoke out forcefully on women's rights. In fact, all of her colleagues knew that if they ever crossed swords with Shiloh on women's issues, including health and abortion, vitriol wouldn't cut it. Shiloh knew those issues well and would have her opponents roped and hog-tied before they got out of the gate if they tried to wing it. She wasn't vicious or reckless, just thorough, convincing, and determined.

* * * * *

Shiloh was midway through her third term. Her life was good, and she was having fun. In her last election she had remained unopposed; according to Charlie, this had much to do with her having utterly crushed Lawson in her initial election. Because of her trips to the district every other weekend, she was able to see the Whitfields and the Jacobsons frequently and would always stop by to visit Hattie when she went to Tullahoma. On rare occasions, she would see young friends from All Saints, and she always made a point of seeing Charlie at least once a month.

Being in Washington put her quite close to Sam in New Jersey. They both took advantage of that. She visited Sam and his family frequently, and they would occasionally visit Shiloh in Washington and see a new exhibit at one of the museums or take in a play or sporting event in Washington or Baltimore. But her love life remained virtually nonexistent. She was beginning to believe that she would never find a life partner. Men seemed afraid of her.

Shiloh had been angling almost since she had arrived in Congress to get appointed to become a U.S. public delegate to the UN. Every year, the White House appointed five people to attend the UN as U.S. public delegates during the fall session of the General Assembly. It would usually be three private citizens and two members of Congress, one from each party. They rotated between the House and the Senate every year. One year, two senators would be selected and the next year, two House members. They could go whenever their schedule allowed during the General Assembly session, which ran from about September 1 to December 15.

This was Shiloh's year. The minority leader had selected Shiloh to be the Democratic representative from the House. She attended her first UN meeting to listen in on plans for the five-year follow-up and review of the 1994 Cairo Population Conference.

Shiloh was sitting in Conference Room Three in the basement of the UN Building listening to a debate about whether the United Nations Development Program's (UNDP) work plan should include poverty eradication as its major focus for the next several years. UNICEF was about children; the Food and Agriculture Organization (FAO) was about food; WHO worked on health issues; the World Bank was mainly about economic development; the United Nations Population Fund (UNFPA) was about population, which primarily focused on women's reproductive health.

The latter is why Shiloh was there today. She wanted to hear the discussion about UNFPA's proposed plans for 1999 to examine the lessons learned, the successes, and the failures in implementing the global program of action that had been adopted in 1994.

But UNDP's poverty proposal was taking a lot of time. As the largest UN development organization and the one with the most far reaching agenda, UNDP was generally the coordinator of UN meetings in the field that tried to ensure collaboration within the UN family. By focusing on poverty, the ultimate goal of all development, UNDP would orchestrate the efforts of all the UN organizations through advocacy, coordination of programs, and government negotiations. It sounded like a reasonable proposition to Shiloh.

However, it seemed to Shiloh that each of the UN's 191 countries had something to say about various aspects of the organization's proposal. Donor countries felt generally one way, while most developing countries felt another way. No one knew quite what France wanted. They were ignoring the umbrella under which the European Union usually spoke. France had spent all its speaking time complaining about the quality of the French documents that UNDP had prepared for this segment of the committee meeting. So far, the country's representatives had not mentioned what it was that they found objectionable or agreeable about UNDP's plan. The French delegate kept on talking; it seemed he had not given any thought to reading his prepared statement. *I guess,* thought Shiloh, *this is what they mean by the French being French.*

All UN development organizations covered almost every aspect of social and economic development. Thus, working together, they addressed the major issues related to poverty. The donor countries thought that UNDP should coordinate so that the issue of poverty, which they believed was the predicate of all development, would receive more focused attention. On the other hand, the developing countries did not want any more cooks stirring the already complicated development pot in their countries. The General Assembly's Second Committee, the committee charged with "programme matters," had begun this discussion at three o'clock the proceeding afternoon, and it looked to Shiloh that they might go on with this one agenda item for the remainder of the current fall session of the General Assembly, which had another three months to run.

"It's like watching paint dry," Shiloh sighed in frustration in the general direction of the person who was sitting to her left.

"You got that right," replied her neighbor.

She examined her interlocutor with an exasperated smile and a nod. He was a handsome guy. He looked to be close to six feet tall and built strongly with broad shoulders—*like a rock,* she thought, remembering a TV commercial for trucks. His hair was a thinning mixture of black and gray. He had a ready smile that highlighted his blue-gray eyes. His ruddy complexion betrayed hours in the sun; probably a tennis player or jogger, Shiloh surmised. *He looks kind yet rugged and self-assured,* she thought, *natural and genuine.* She hadn't noticed him before; she'd only had a faint notion that someone was sitting next to her. She did now. Something stirred inside her.

"Hi, my name's Seth Richards. I see from your ID card that you're a delegate. Why aren't you sitting with your delegation instead of back here in the peanut gallery?"

"Don't accuse me of being a part of this. My name is Shiloh Giles. I'm, thankfully, only an observer."

"And an American one from somewhere below the Mason-Dixon line I would guess," replied Seth.

"Yep, Tennessee. I'm attached to the U.S. Mission. So what's with the blue ID? Do you work here?" inquired Shiloh.

"I'm with UNFPA, the UN Population Fund. I'm waiting on the next agenda item. That may not be until tomorrow the way they're going on about the UNDP program."

Shiloh's first impression of Seth was good. He was pleasant and seemed to have a warm personality. Best of all he, had a sense of humor. She had heard so much about the slow pace of the UN that she somehow expected all the organization's employees to be bleary-eyed bureaucrats.

"That's why I'm here too," replied Shiloh. "I'd like to learn more about UNFPA and this particular agenda item. Do you have a few minutes to escape all the fun here and get some coffee?"

"You read my mind. We can probably drink a few pots of coffee before they get around to UNFPA. How about the Delegates Lounge instead of the proletariat Vienna Café?" offered Seth as he stood. "It's quieter there."

Shiloh removed her earphone and grabbed her purse. "Lead the way, maestro. I've never had the pleasure of visiting either place, but I can handle bourgeois."

Seth stood in line to get two cappuccinos while Shiloh found a table on the lower level under the huge tapestry depicting the Great Wall of China; she guessed that it was about thirty feet long and twenty feet wide. It had been given to the UN in 1971 by the Chinese government, and Shiloh reckoned that it had not been cleaned since the day it was hung. Even so, it was a spectacular piece of art. The Delegates Lounge was almost as quiet as a library. Its forty-foot windows commanded an expansive view of the beautiful UN Gardens, the East River, and in the distance, the massive Queens Borough Bridge, which at night was a stunning sight when bright lights silhouetted its superstructure.

Seth arrived with the cappuccinos and said, "So, Shiloh, how long have you been here?"

"Shy, please, that's what everyone calls me. I arrived two days ago to observe some of the fall session. What about you, how do you stay awake in these boring meetings when they don't involve you?"

"Don't be so tough." said Seth. "The UN is stodgy and cumbersome for sure, but it succeeds in establishing international goals and standards; it does good work in the development field; it helps the world's nations to talk rather than fight; it fields peacekeeping missions; it responds to emergencies;

and all of that for about three or four days worth of the funds that are spent yearly for military armaments. As for its efficiency and effectiveness, well, that depends on its members. It has not had time yet to recover from the vestiges of the cold war, which have dominated all global affairs since the end of World War II."

Shy smiled. "I didn't mean to ruffle your feathers. I adore the UN and all that it stands for. But I don't think I have the stamina to sit through endless boring meetings."

"Yes," replied Seth, "it's burdensome sometimes—especially when you know that some delegates are only posturing. But the world of pinstripes actually facilitates progress, and as I said, it often keeps folks from fighting it out on a battlefield. But it can be mind numbing."

"So, what do you do for UNFPA?"

Seth shrugged. "Oh, I keep track of the UN and its goings on; I work with UNFPA's Executive Board and do some advocacy and fundraising, both of which are aimed more often than not at Congress. Unfortunately, UNFPA is known in Washington for what it doesn't do, assist coercion in China, rather than what it does, which is save women's lives. There are some grandstanding members of Congress who make points with fundamentalists misrepresenting UNFPA—not to mention some of our presidents. But that's another conversation."

"So, you must come in contact with our government quite a bit," Shiloh remarked.

"Yes, I do, and it's easier now with Democrats in charge of the executive branch. Actually, I was at the meeting you were attending to see what would happen to our report on our plans for next year's review of the work in our field since Global Cairo Population Conference; 1999 will be the fifth anniversary."

Shiloh was smiling. "Me too. But before we discuss that, tell me some more about our lame Congress."

Seth smacked his forehead with his hand. "Oh, I forgot that you're attached to the U.S. Mission. I hope I didn't offend you."

"No, not at all," said Shy. "I fully agree with you. I was just curious about your take on Congress and the UNFPA issue."

"That's easy. Congress has been relatively good except for a few notable exceptions. They are, as you say, the lame ones. But in spite of the few crazies, Congress always appropriates funds for UNFPA. Still, until this president, who agreed to refunding, the two previous presidents used a law passed in 1985 to refuse funding to UNFPA because of our work in China. No other country has ever done that. A few members of Congress say that UNFPA is involved in coercion and forced abortion in China. It isn't, of course, but the truth doesn't seem to matter. It is easy not to fund UN organizations since they have no real constituency here in this country, at least not a vocal constituency. And with the Republicans in power, we are fodder for their fundamentalist pals.

"We don't support abortion anywhere, although I suppose that we would provide technical support to countries to make abortion safe if they asked, but it seems most countries want to keep us away from even more controversy. UNFPA rigidly upholds human rights. What those few in Congress say about UNFPA is just not true. If we were involved in coercion and forced abortion, don't you think that the Brits, the Germans, the French, and the Nordics, among others, would deny funding like the U.S.? What the U.S. does is slanderous and causes great harm because we don't get the funding to save women's lives with reproductive health services and to prevent AIDS. Former presidents have canceled us out of the appropriations bill each year, which curries favor with their rightwing base." Seth stopped for a moment. "Sorry, Shy, I can get heated about this stuff."

Shiloh smiled and urged him to go on.

"Just imagine," Seth continued in spite of his apology, "if I attacked you publicly on the Internet about some fictitious crime that I claimed you had committed. You would want to shoot me, but first you would have to tell your employer, your family, and your friends that it wasn't true. Would they believe you? Some may suspect you or at least become concerned about your integrity. So you fight back. But in time, people begin to believe that where there's smoke, there's fire. That's how it is for UNFPA and the people who oppose us. It is pure ideology, and we lose. More importantly, women lose."

Shiloh could tell that Seth was very passionate about his work, and his contempt for Congress was justified. She felt the same way about the UNFPA issue, which she had tried unsuccessfully to change. She felt badly for deceiving him. She looked Seth straight in the eyes and said, "I'm so sorry, Seth. I wasn't completely honest with you when I asked you about Congress. That's where I work. And I agree with everything you've said. I just wanted to hear the unvarnished version, which I certainly have. It makes me want to work that much harder to help."

"What do you do? Are you a staffer?" asked Seth.

"Well, no," Shiloh squirmed. "I'm a member. I represent Tennessee's Fifth District—the vice president's old seat once removed."

"Oh!" Seth paused and squirmed in his chair. "You said the magic words: work harder. I'd be happy to help you with that. But that was a nasty trick you played on me." Seth smiled as he said this. "So," he paused, "to make amends, I'd like to invite you to dinner tonight so you can apologize, especially since

I know that members of Congress would never go to dinner with a mere voter."

"I'd love to go to dinner."

"But," said Seth.

"No buts; what time?" said Shiloh.

"Er, ah great. Where are you staying? I can pick you up at 6:30 or so."

"The Hyatt at Grand Central, and 6:30 is fine."

Shiloh tried to hide her excitement. She liked this guy. He was honest and believed in his mission. "Do you think that the UNDP decision will be taken today? I really want to listen to the UNFPA debate, but I have some calls to make and a welcoming lunch with the ambassador," inquired Shiloh.

"Probably not. But you never really know. I'll assign someone for this afternoon's session, and they'll call me and I'll call you if the UNFPA item comes up. If not, I'll come by for you at 6:30."

"Great," said Shiloh.

They shook hands and went their separate ways. Shiloh went to the U.S. Mission, and Seth back to his office in the *Daily News* building two blocks away, which many New Yorkers call the Superman building since it had been the model for the *Daily Planet*.

Seth called Shiloh's room from the lobby of the Hyatt at 6:30 sharp. When Shiloh appeared, she could tell by the look on Seth's face that he was stunned. Earlier that day, Shiloh had worn a blue pants suit and gray blouse. Now she was wearing a beautiful cream and beige silk dress that highlighted her perfect figure. It had a short V-neck and flared slightly at her waist. Her thick hair was pulled up, which accentuated her beautiful neck. Seth sucked air through his teeth as he quickly recovered with a crooked boyish smile and stammered, "Good evening, Congresswoman."

"And good evening to you, Mr. Richards," replied Shiloh.

There was a pregnant pause before Seth said, "You, uh, you look terrific. Your dress is beautiful."

"Thank you; you look nice yourself."

"I'm still wearing my uniform from this morning, but it's my best suit so I guess I would have picked it out if I had time to go home to dress for dinner." Seth replied with his ever-present smile.

On their way to the restaurant, Seth told Shiloh that the UNDP debate had finished about an hour before and that the UNFPA item would begin at 10:00 a.m. the next morning.

Shiloh was a bit nervous. She was attracted to Seth. It was the first time she had felt anything like this since that night with Charlie several years ago. Was it her heart fluttering or an alarm bell? *I guess I'll find out soon,* she thought.

They arrived at the restaurant after a twenty-minute cab ride. Seth had chosen Erminia, a cozy Italian restaurant on East Eighty-third Street just off Second Avenue. Seth told Shiloh he had discovered it years ago when friends had taken him there for some long forgotten occasion. He remembered that the food was great, but mostly he remembered the atmosphere and the superb, nonintrusive waiters. He told her he had been lucky that their always-full reservation list had a cancellation.

They were seated, and the waiter asked if they wanted drinks.

Seth looked at Shiloh. "What would you like?" he inquired.

"Wine would be nice," smiled Shiloh.

"Red or white?"

"You decide; either is fine with me."

"I thought that all priests were wine experts," Seth quipped.

Shiloh smiled. "How did you know I was a priest?"

"I Googled you when I returned to the office."

The waiter was staring at them. Seth looked up at the waiter. "We'll let you decide, maybe a nice red that a UN bureaucrat can afford."

"Yes, sir," he replied, "I have a nice California pinot noir. Is that okay?"

Seth and Shiloh nodded in unison.

"I also found out that you were a missionary and an accomplished boxer. I was intimidated enough that you were a member of Congress who I insulted, and then I discovered all these other things about you that make me even more nervous."

Shiloh spoke quietly, "So, shall I hear your confession or tell you about my prowess in the ring?"

"Certainly not the former," laughed Seth, "but I would love to hear about your work as a missionary."

They each ordered the house salad and the pasta special. The pasta tonight was penne with mushrooms and shallots in a creamy white wine sauce. After the pinot noir, they switched to a smooth French chardonnay to wash down their meal. They finished with coffee and split a scrumptious piece of New York cheesecake.

They talked about their childhood and families, work, colleges, and even reproductive health and UNFPA. Almost three hours later, after several cups of coffee, they reluctantly decided to give up their table. Neither wanted the night to end.

When they went outside, Seth suggested a stroll down Second Avenue to walk off their meal. Shiloh readily agreed.

"Are you married, Seth? Do you have children?" Shiloh asked nonchalantly.

"I was married once when I was very young, for less than a year. She was my high school sweetheart. I enlisted in the air force and eventually went off to Nam. She sent me a Dear John letter a few months after I arrived. She had found someone else, apparently before I even shipped out. We didn't have any children. After that, I became a serious student. I dated and even had a few steadies, but nothing ever seemed to work out. So here I am, fifty-two years old and single."

"Me too," offered Shiloh. "I was in love once, but he was killed in a car accident. I was quite young too. After that, I finished high school and went off to college and later to seminary. I dated a few times, but I guess my profession and maybe my personality kept men away—at least men who I might have liked."

It was a warm, calm fall evening. As usual, the streets were full of folks hurrying about. New York City seemed to always be awake and exciting to tourists and visitors. They strolled in silence, neither knowing quite where to go with this conversation.

Finally Seth said, "It must be difficult to be in your profession, even as attractive as you are, and not intimidate potential suitors. I know that when I looked you up on the Internet, I was, if not intimidated, certainly awed. It leads to all kinds of questions. I immediately thought of my parish priest."

"Are you Catholic?" Shy said as she chuckled at his comment.

"Yes, I am," he replied. "Maybe it's the term priest," said Seth. "To me that means robes, celibacy, confession, and such—maybe even a beard." He snickered. "That image is not the sort of person I conjure up in my imagination when I think about companionship."

They walked on in silence. Shiloh had enjoyed their wonderful evening together. They seemed to click intellectually and philosophically, she thought. But what was it that she was feeling deep inside that she couldn't quite identify. Was it passion? Was she intrigued? They kept walking. Shiloh was trying to think of something compelling to say. Was she excited? Whatever it was she was unnerved by this strange new feeling.

Finally Seth asked, "Shall we get a taxi? We're approaching Sixtieth Street."

"Really, already? Sure," said Shiloh.

They rode in silence to Shiloh's hotel. When they arrived, Seth walked her to the lobby.

As they walked, he said, "Thanks for joining me, Shy. You're a special person, and I hope it wouldn't be presumptuous if I asked you out again sometime."

Shiloh responded immediately. "How about tomorrow night, unless you already have plans? And this time, my treat."

Seth turned to face her. "It would be wonderful to have a repeat performance tomorrow night. I'm not busy at all. I was just going to sit around and read some executive board documents and drink warm milk." Seth stammered with a giggle. "And even if I were busy, I would cancel."

"Terrific," said Shy with her own giggle. "Same time okay?"

"Yes, but I'll see you tomorrow at the UN too, won't I?"

"Yes, of course," she replied.

Seth bussed her cheek and watched her walk to the elevators.

* * * * *

When Shiloh went to bed, she lay there thinking about Seth. She had been in love once in her life, but so far it had never come again. When Barry Jr. had returned home from college after his freshman year for summer vacation, one of his first stops had been to meet Shiloh at Grandma Alice's. He and Shiloh had been friends all their lives. But their relationship was like that of a brother and sister. They had spoken on the phone that morning and set a time. But Barry Jr. soon discovered that his "sister" had blossomed while he was away at school.

Shiloh and Alice had been sitting on the porch when Barry'd arrived. He was a handsome young man. He was six feet tall. He had light brown hair and a quick smile. His build was strong and wiry from his years of running track and cross-country. Barry Jr. was a good student and a good person.

He was speechless for a moment before uttering, "Er, ah, hi, Shy. Gosh, you've changed."

They had played together often when they were younger. She remembered the time it had snowed and school had closed. It had been the largest snow anyone could remember: eight inches. Schools were closed for a week. The town only owned one snowplow, and other neighboring towns were in the same pickle. The kids had flocked to Wheeler's Hill with sleds, plastic laundry containers, even an old car hood to slide down the hill.

Shiloh had been eleven then, and Barry was fourteen. She and Barry and a few other kids went over to the ridge on the north end of town to sled. She was on the front of Barry's sled when they went whizzing through the trees. All of a sudden, a tree jumped out in front of them. They scored a direct hit. Shy had a big goose egg on her forehead, and Barry had bled all over his coat and all over Shiloh from a smashed nose.

Margaret, predictably, had been angry. "There you are," she had said, "the perfect picture of a tomboy."

Shiloh smiled now thinking about hitting the tree.

Shy and Barry had been inseparable that special summer after Barry's freshman year. They'd gone hiking and swimming during the days and must have seen all the movies that played in Tullahoma and all the surrounding towns at night. Shiloh could tell that Barry liked her in a different way, and she was sure that she felt that way about him. She was falling in love.

Barry tried almost every night the last week of summer to make love to Shiloh, but she always stopped him. Barry was always a gentleman. He was kind and considerate. For her part, Shiloh was sure she had found the man she would marry. She knew that they would make a great family together. Shiloh decided that, on his last night before he went back to college, she would let Barry Jr. take her virginity. She had always wanted to wait until she was married, or at least until she was engaged, before she had sex. She'd never really thought much about love and marriage or much else in this sphere, until Barry had come along that summer. On her few dates, she'd never even come close to having sex. She had only been kissed a few times and never petted. She did not believe in having sex without a commitment. When she thought about such things, she imagined that love would find her in due course.

On their last night, she and Barry had gone to CJ's Drive-In for burgers. They'd sat and talked for hours about their future, college, their friends, and even church. Church was always in Shiloh's thoughts. Father Gunn was her friend and counselor, and she loved the church. It held a special place in her heart. She was still an acolyte, and she served at the Wednesday and Sunday early services.

Later that evening they drove to their favorite parking place. It overlooked a beautiful valley in the daytime. At night, only a few farm lights shone way off in the distance. Barry put his arm around Shiloh and kissed her full lips passionately. She felt his tongue meet hers as she willingly joined in his embrace. He fumbled with the buttons on her blouse.

Quickly he moved to her left side away from the steering wheel on the bench seat of his dad's Oldsmobile. When he moved, she quickly unhooked her bra. Shiloh could see Barry's surprise. He kissed her breasts; she could feel his hardness against her thigh. He felt under her dress and touched her gently and kissed her ears and neck.

"Shy," he said through gulps for air as he panted in his frenzy. "Shy, I love you so much; please, let me make love to you."

"I love you too, Barry. I love you too."

It felt to Shy like he was caressing her everywhere all at once, and it all felt good. He lifted her dress and gently pushed her legs apart and manipulated himself into a position where he could penetrate her.

Shy began to sob quietly as tears rolled down her cheeks. Barry's erection turned to jelly. "Why are you crying? I thought it was okay."

"It is Barry; you can do it," she said through her tears. "I want to make you happy."

After a long moment, Barry said, "I can't. It torments me to think that I may be hurting you"

"I'm so sorry, Barry. I love you so much."

"I love you too, Shy, more than I can properly express. But I can't do this until it is, well, more proper. We're both young. Our first time should be perfect. Our life together shouldn't begin like this. I need to finish college first. And you need to finish high school."

They got dressed and held each other. When they finally drove home, they vowed to marry someday. They professed their love to each other again the next morning when Barry stopped by to say good-bye.

Shy would never see her first true love again. They'd written for a few months. Then Barry had been killed in a tragic car wreck.

Shiloh was still a virgin.

Barry Jr. had made Shiloh feel something that she had never felt before. The thought of really being in love had never seriously crossed her mind until that summer with Barry Jr. Thinking about it now, she didn't think it was puppy love. Being in love had been wonderful. She realized that she must have thirsted for affection and companionship that wasn't available anywhere else in her life. Being with Barry would have meant a new family eventually, a new chapter. It had been a wonderful feeling, but as soon as it was there, it was gone. She had wondered if she would ever feel that way again. Maybe now, with Seth.

Two years after her summer with Barry Jr., Shiloh was at Sewanee. Barry was still haunting her thoughts. She had worked hard in high school. She was focused on building a strong academic record and on giving herself a solid foundation for college and an eventual career. She was interested in the opposite sex but only in a casual way. She was focused on her future, college, her grandmother and father, and the church, which continued to be an important aspect of her life.

She clung to the memory of Barry, perhaps to fulfill her private needs and perhaps to focus on her academic goals. She knew that Barry was gone, but she wanted to cling to his memory for now.

During her sophomore year at Sewanee, she was at a party one Friday night. As was her custom, she left before it got too wild. When she was leaving, a guy Shiloh had danced with, who was well on the way to being drunk, grabbed her arm. "Where to, baby?" he said. "I thought we had something going there."

"It was nice dancing with you," replied Shiloh, "but I need to go home now."

The guy leered at her. "I've seen you around before. You are a classic. You're the kind of woman that likes to rub up against a guy and then walk away. Goddamned bitch."

"Good night," said Shiloh. She left, feeling very unsettled.

She went back to her dorm room, went to the bathroom and changed her pad, brushed her teeth, washed her face, and went straight to bed. She looked forward to sleeping late tomorrow. It had been a long week of study, and the cross-country meet yesterday had been tough with her period. She needed to rest so she would be ready to work in the library on her research paper the next afternoon.

She had just fallen asleep when the covers were pulled from her bed. Before she could respond, the now totally drunk guy from the party was on top of her. He was naked from the waist down. He pulled up her nightgown and pulled at her panties. She hit him in the face, but he was big and powerful. She yelled, "Get off of me, or I'll scream."

He paused and looked into her eyes and said, "You do, and I'll hit you so hard you'll never scream again, bitch." He held one of her arms and ripped off her panties and tried to force his penis into her bloody vagina. She slapped him, and he hit her back with an open hand. "If you do that again, I'll kill you." His voice was cold and threatening. She could feel his anger and hate. It felt like he wanted to hurt her.

She gave up her struggle, closed her eyes, and prayed that it would quickly end. He shoved hard and pushed through her hymen. Soon it was over. He cleaned himself on her nightgown, pulled on his pants, and left.

Shiloh, shaken and bleeding, staggered over to the bathroom. The place where he had slapped her was red, but it didn't look like it would bruise. She hand washed her sheets and cleaned the mattress where she had bled. She turned over her mattress, put on clean sheets, took a shower, and finally tumbled into bed. She lay in bed crying most of the night, unable to sleep.

Shiloh had called Father Gunn the Saturday morning after she had been raped, and he had driven over with Barry Sr. that afternoon to spend time with Shiloh. Barry was angry and offered to represent Shiloh in a civil case if she decided to press charges as well as to work with the local prosecutor.

"But it would be difficult," he counseled, "because you did not go to the police immediately, and a medical exam was not conducted. And you destroyed any other evidence that might have existed when you washed your sheets."

Barry's fatherly instincts were in overdrive. Father Gunn had been calmer and discussed the impact of a trial and the mark it would leave on Shiloh in a society that somehow blamed women, especially pretty women, for rape. The issue had been left undecided as to whether or not to press charges. In the end, both men said that she should go to the dean on Monday and that they would support whatever she decided to do. They both called her for the next few days. And they both saw her whenever she came home for the weekend. She didn't tell Grandma Alice. She had thought a lot about her mom during those days and wished that she had been there to talk to now. She somehow knew that her mother would have nurtured her.

On Monday, she went to the dean's office and filed a complaint. She didn't know her rapist's name. She had not seen him on campus before this year, so she suspected that he was a freshman. She looked at the freshmen pictures and found him.

The dean looked at his picture and then said, "Thank you, Miss Giles. I'll take it from here."

Two days later, the dean called Shy to her office. Two other coeds were there. The dean started, "Ladies, you are here because each of you has complained about being molested by Wayne Franks. If you wish, you may press charges with the police. I should tell you, though, that these kinds of issues are difficult for women to prove, and it will be embarrassing. On the other hand, Franks has been expelled and left campus yesterday. He is from out of state and has gone home."

The four women talked for a long time. Franks had groped the other two women and one had a witness, but Shiloh was the only one who he had managed to rape. They all decided not to press charges and to move on with their lives.

As she lay in her hotel room, she wished that she had pressed charges, if for no other reason than to protect other women. She wondered now how many women Wayne Franks had hurt in his lifetime. Suddenly she thought about Lawson. There had been something sadistic about the rapist that reminded her of Lawson. Lawson seemed literally to hate women or at least to hold them in contempt. The look in his eyes at the debate reminded her of her rapist. At least she had pressed charges against Skyler.

Shiloh had never had sex with a man since that night years ago when she was raped. She wasn't opposed to sex now, and she had certainly dated; she just had never found a man that she actually wanted to have sex with. She eventually wanted to marry, and she didn't think she would be necessarily opposed to an affair at this stage of her life with the right man, but somehow she suspected that her vibes and her profession seemed to scare men away. She was, she thought now with a hint of remorse, a walking no-sex advertisement.

Damn, she thought with a rueful smile. *Maybe it will be different with Seth. Maybe he will like me. Maybe, maybe, maybe,* she thought, as she drifted off to sleep.

* * * * *

The UNFPA item was approved at 5:00 p.m., and after good-byes to delegates, Seth made his way back to his office where he waited impatiently for the clock to move to the time when he would walk over to Shy's hotel. Shiloh had left the UN at 4:00 to go over to the U.S. Mission and catch up on her e-mail.

When Seth arrived, she was waiting in the lobby. They walked to the restaurant. Seth had made reservations at the Algonquin on Forty-fourth Street between Fifth and Sixth Avenues.

When they had been seated and ordered drinks, Seth asked, "So, what did you think of today's meeting?"

"I must admit," Shiloh smiled, "it was interesting. Not only did I learn something about how the UN works, I was impressed by the knowledge and commitment of the delegations. And, of course, you did a great job on the podium."

"That's what I was fishing for—a compliment from a person who is a pro at debating global issues," Seth said through his laughter.

"No, I'm serious. It was eye-opening for me. I really learned a lot."

They spent another two and a half hours talking and enjoying the food. Seth was feeling jittery. He wanted to somehow find the courage to take their relationship a step further. He was only inhibited by his fear of failure. *Damn*, he thought, *a congresswoman and a priest.*

They leisurely began their eight-block walk back to Shiloh's hotel at Grand Central. The closer they got, the more agitated Seth became. His feelings were all over the place: hesitation and desire, bashfulness and affection, worry about ruining their relationship and excitement.

As they were walking along Forty-fourth approaching Vanderbilt, Seth finally reached out for Shiloh's hand. They stopped. Seth faced Shiloh, put his arms around her waist, and gently pulled her into his embrace. He kissed her rather quickly, and she responded. They kissed again—this time deeply and passionately. Seth didn't want to move. He didn't want this moment to end. They kissed again. Then, reluctantly, they walked the rest of the way to the Grand Hyatt.

When they arrived, Seth walked in with Shiloh. As they were riding the escalator up to the lobby, he spoke. "I'd walk you to your room if I was a

Southern gentleman, and I'd like to anyway to show you that we Jersey boys have manners too."

How corny was that? he thought. He felt clumsy and awkward. As they walked toward the elevators, Seth could feel the tension. Was she angry? Had he pushed too hard?

"That would be nice. I think I like New Jersey manners," Shiloh said.

Seth was conscious of his breathing. It seemed like they reached her door before they got off the elevator. *Now what,* wondered Seth?

Shiloh fumbled in her purse and found her card key. She turned to face Seth and before either could utter a word, Seth put his hands on Shiloh's shoulders and pulled her willingly into his embrace. Their kiss was electric. When they finally came up for air, Shiloh turned and opened the door. They entered and embraced again. Shiloh pulled away slightly and breathily said, "Don't turn on the lights."

They continued to kiss and began to undress. Seth was eager and frightened. No thoughts came to him, only intense desire. They fell onto the bed. The air was thick and sweet with their caresses, and Seth felt the joy and excitement of their passion.

Minutes later he broke the silence. "I ... I ... oh, Shy, you are so wonderful."

They talked in whispers and made love again before they finally fell asleep in each other's arms.

Hours later, Seth finally got up and fumbled around for the light switch. It was 6:15 a.m. He made coffee in the little coffee pot in the room and ordered breakfast. He left at 7:30 and rushed home to shower and dress for work. He felt happier than he'd felt in years—maybe ever. He got to the office by 9:30, gave a few instructions to his secretary, and rushed off to a meeting at the UN.

He and Shiloh had agreed to meet at the UN again, even though the rest of the agenda did not concern either of them.

* * * * *

When Seth arrived, Shiloh was already there and had saved him a seat. They sat and talked in a whisper. Finally, they returned to the delegates lounge for a three-hour coffee break. They were goofing off and loved it; nothing seemed to matter to them but being together. Shiloh felt light and free, but she was curious to know more about this new man in her life.

Shiloh grilled Seth about his work. "How do you design programs? How do you determine which countries get how much money? What contraceptives are used? Do you train doctors and midwives?"

She was full of questions, as was Seth, asking about the working of Congress.

They spent every minute they could together during the next few weeks until Shiloh had to return to Washington.

* * * * *

Before Seth, Shiloh had normally gone back to her district every other weekend. She continued that practice, alternating now with New York where she would visit Seth, instead of staying in Washington or visiting Sam and his family in New Jersey. Seth also visited Shiloh in Washington.

On one such occasion, they had gone out to a play at the National Theater and stopped at a local pub for a drink afterward. While they sat at a dimly lit table, Seth looked at Shiloh and said, "My dear Congresswoman, I can't believe my last few months with you. You've taken over my thought process. Every time I think about my work or read the paper about some global crisis or even look at the movie listings, I think of you. If that isn't love, I don't know what is. I love you, not just a little, my darling. I love you like I never knew was possible."

Seth paused for a moment.

Shiloh held up her hand and looked straight into Seth's eyes. "I feel the same way. At first, I thought this may be an affair or that you may not be serious. My inexperience led me to believe that it was too good to be true."

"It's true for me," interrupted Seth.

Shiloh reached across the small table to hold Seth's hands in hers. "I know that now. I think I knew it before, but I was afraid to say so. Anyway, darling," she leaned over and kissed him, "anyway, it is wonderful, and I love you too, Seth. I love you too."

Shiloh was finally and unmistakably in love. She had lost her virginity at the tender age of thirty-seven. The rape was against her will; that didn't count. Seth had been astounded when she'd told him that he was the first person to make love to her.

"I believe you," he had said. "But you're so beautiful. You must have had many offers, if not demands. Why now? Why me?"

* * * * *

As she sat in her DC office, Shiloh remembered his corny statement that night that they professed their love for each other: "I love a priest, and she loves me back. Wow, look at me." She chuckled to herself as she remembered that night.

She thought about Barry Jr. Her feelings for Seth felt the same to her. *Oh sure*, she thought, *I am different now; times are different; but basically it's the same feeling. I'm in love; I feel the same passion, the same trust and the same commitment.*

When Shiloh and Seth were together, they spent most of their time joking, laughing, and discussing the affairs of the UN, the world, and their beloved country.

When they were in bed one night, Shiloh remarked, "Now what? We have a relationship made for a TV drama—you in New York, me in DC and Tennessee. My, do we ever have a complicated situation. It's a study in modern male and female dynamics. I love it."

Seth's lips had turned up at the corners. "Me too, sweetheart, me too."

But they never seemed to get any further in conversations about the future.

Chapter 8

Sarah had proved to be all that Shiloh had hoped for and more. She was a perfect supervisor for Shiloh's team of staffers. She explained Shiloh's thinking on every issue thoroughly to the staff. At the same time, she encouraged enough face time with Shiloh to go over their research, what they were hearing from other staffers about their bosses, and even gossip about the other side. She was open and yet protective of her boss.

In time, they'd become real friends. Shiloh got to know Sarah's husband, Abe, and envied Sarah her happiness in her marriage. She had mentioned her loneliness on occasion to Sarah, who had offered once to set up a date for Shiloh, but Shiloh had demurred. "I want to find whoever it is or will be myself."

She had invited Sarah and Abe to supper to meet Sam and Barbara and their kids and had often joined Sarah and Abe for movies, plays, and museum visits.

After one of her weekends to New York, Shiloh finally told Sarah about Seth. She had kept it to herself for several weeks, but she felt sure enough now to spill the beans. They sat in the office late into the night while Shiloh jabbered like a teenager about being in love.

"He's so wonderful, Sarah. He's sweet and gentle and outgoing. He even pretended to be intimidated by my position as a member of Congress and as a priest. I think he just went along for the ride to see what I was like. But I sensed right away that he liked me and I liked him almost immediately. We laugh a lot and seem to agree about all things political," Shy effused. "He's coming here the weekend after next so you can meet him then. Can you and Abe come over for dinner?"

"Of course, we'd be delighted. I can't wait to meet your man." Sarah was smiling at her boss. "I feel very happy for you. But what's next?"

"We see each other as often as possible, and I suppose we'll see what happens."

"So," queried Sarah not hiding her smile, "what do you want to happen?"

"Well, I want to be with him as much as I can."

"And?"

"And see what happens. Yes, I'm thinking about marriage. Yes, I know that I'm inexperienced and that he's the first person I've cared about since high school and that I'm worried about being an old maid. But in my mind, he seems like he could be Mr. Right."

It was late, and Sarah rubbed her eyes. "I'm sorry. I didn't mean to sound like your mother. I'm very happy for you. I'm just concerned about how fast your courtship has developed. So tell me more."

"Well, Seth is from New Jersey. His father did something in insurance, and his mother was a schoolteacher. Seth is the baby of the family. He's ten years younger than his brother and eight years younger than his sister. He married his high school sweetheart and went off to war. His wife divorced him while he was gone. He was married for less than a year, but that was thirty years ago. Since then, he has just dated but never married again. He seems like the confirmed bachelor type. Anyway, he came back from Vietnam in one piece and earned his PhD in political science. He ended up at UNFPA. He's very smart and speaks several languages. He likes his job and is committed to women's health and the UN. I think you'll like him."

"And?"

"And, yes, I enjoyed *that* part of it a lot. It's so wonderful, and he's so tender." Shiloh's face flushed as she smiled at her friend.

* * * * *

When Seth visited Washington, Sarah told Shiloh she could immediately see the attraction Shiloh had tried to explain. Seth had a great sense of humor, and he was great with her kids. He was knowledgeable about Congress, and he was committed to women's health. He understood the big picture globally.

"Yes," Sarah told Shiloh after Seth returned to New York, "your beau looks like a keeper. Hang on to him, girl."

* * * * *

During Christmas week, Shiloh and Seth met each other's families. They had a great couple of days that included dinner at Sam and Barbara's. They flew to Nashville on the twenty-ninth and checked in with Wayne Long. They stayed at Shiloh's condo, attended All Saints, had dinner with the Jacobsons, and went to Tullahoma for New Year's.

They stayed with Barry and Trudy. As they were finishing New Year's Day dinner, before settling down for the bowl games, Seth cleared his voice and said in a nervous but serious voice. "Barry, Trudy, Hattie, I'm delighted to be here with Shy. She has told me so much about all of you. She looks at you as her parents and grandmother, and while this may seem rather formal—chalk that up to my Irish/German Catholic upbringing—I, well, I'm madly in love with Shy, so I'm asking her and all of you for her hand in marriage as soon as possible."

Shiloh just sat there, flush faced and smiling as she looked at Seth. She was speechless.

They had not ever specifically talked about marriage although she had thought about it constantly. She had sensed that their relationship was "the one," but she had been afraid to rush things for fear of making a mistake or of scaring Seth away. But now she knew Seth was ready; they weren't teenagers after all.

Barry cleared his throat and said, "Thank you, Seth, for your gallant proposal. Shiloh, do you love this mackerel-eating Yankee?"

Shiloh was nervous. "Yes, Barry I do." She looked at Seth and said, "I do love you, darling, so very much."

Barry walked over to his bar and came back with five liqueur glasses and a bottle of Jameson's single malt. He mumbled, "This is much better than brandy." Then he added, "What do you think, Hattie, Trudy, shall we let this carpetbagger take away the blossom of Tullahoma?"

Trudy gushed, "Yes, of course, you crazy redneck, absolutely."

Barry looked at Hattie, "Well?"

Hattie was crying. "I'm so happy for you, Shy. I only wish Miss Alice could have met your future husband." Then she turned to Seth. "Seth, you can have her; just make sure you keep her in shoes and watch out for that right overhead punch of hers."

They clicked glasses, and Barry commanded, "Down the hatch."

Seth shook hands with Barry and hugged Trudy and Hattie.

Shiloh hugged them all and wrapped her arms around Seth. "That was very nice, darling." She felt unbelievably happy.

Seth looked at Barry and demanded another shot. "Wow, this is great. I've heard so much about you all, y'all that is; I've been practicing my rebel talk." And then to Shiloh he teased, "Even for a rebel lass, you have a great family. I haven't seen a shotgun, and the governor hasn't said a word about the great southeastern conference or about lousy Yankees or the weakness of the Big Ten. So I guess he is a southern gentleman."

With that, they clinked glasses again and cleared the dishes from the table. Barry put his arm around Seth's shoulder and led him into the den, saying, "Now about those Yankees …"

As they left the next day for the airport, Barry whispered to Shiloh, "I like your fella, Shy. I think your wait was worth it."

Shiloh couldn't have agreed more. They hugged again.

* * * * *

Shiloh and Seth were married during the Memorial Day recess at St. Luke's church in Tullahoma. Father Gunn and Father Jacobson officiated together. They invited family and a few friends, including Shy's office staff from Nashville and Carol and Sarah from Washington. Seth's brother, Alex, was best man, Sarah was the maid of honor, and Sam's daughter, Jill, was the flower girl. Sam and Chase were ushers, and Barry gave Shiloh away.

The reception was held at Hattie's home, the old Giles homestead. When Hattie had offered on New Year's Day, Shiloh had jumped at the invitation, but she'd insisted that everything would be catered. Including all of Hattie's children and grandchildren, there were about eighty guests.

Shiloh and Seth honeymooned for two days in Nashville at Shiloh's condo and then went back to their respective jobs. They planned a two-week trip to Banff during the August recess.

In the meantime, they continued to commute from Washington to New York and to Nashville. They talked every day by phone, sometimes two or three times a day. Shiloh didn't like this arrangement, but it would have to do for the immediate future. She was in love and happy. In fact, the only cross words ever spoken between them were directed at late planes and bad weather. Shiloh continued to love her job, but she began to think about how nice it would be to have a baby. It was late for her, but not yet too late.

Neither had made a formal announcement about their marriage; Seth had told the personnel folks at UNFPA that he had recently been married, and Shiloh had done the same in Washington. Sarah and a few congresswomen had held a surprise reception for some of Shiloh's colleagues and her staff, and a few of Seth's buddies at work had taken him out to dinner one night to celebrate.

Several months later they attended a reception for UNFPA's executive board. They went through the receiving line, and the executive director said, "Hello, Shy. Is Seth trying to talk you into U.S. funding?"

Seth looked surprised. "I didn't know you two knew each other."

"Yes, we do," said Shy. "I forgot to tell you; we met a few weeks ago in Washington."

"Well," Seth said smiling, "I'll bet I know one thing that my boss doesn't know, but she'll have to finish the line here before I tell her."

Half an hour later, the executive director cornered Seth and Shiloh. "I just have to know. Are you talking about your marriage, Seth, or is it something else?"

Seth was shocked, "How did you know?"

"Because I'm your boss, and it's my job to know. Congratulations! I wish you the very best. Let me know when you're ready to leave, Shy. I have plans."

Shiloh smiled at the look on Seth's face. He looked really puzzled. He had no idea what his boss and Shiloh has conspired in Washington.

When the reception ended, they went together to the executive director's apartment for another reception to celebrate the marriage of Seth Richards and Shiloh Giles. Most of UNFPA's staff was there, along with a few local members of Congress, Seth's brother and sister, and Sam and Barbara. The executive director, on behalf of Seth's friends at UNFPA, gave Seth and Shiloh round-trip tickets to Hawaii.

Seth took the tickets and looked at his many friends. "Thank you all; this is a great surprise. Shy and I will always cherish the memory of your kindness. You are all wonderful."

For once he was at a loss for words. Shiloh stood with Seth and felt proud of her husband. It was obvious that he was loved and respected by his colleagues.

* * * * *

It had been eight years since Shiloh had come to Washington. The Republican Party was much stronger now and held the Congress. And they did not want to concede anything, especially in the district of the former presidential candidate of the other party. They had money, they were well organized, and they were hungry.

Shiloh had heard rumors that one senator had said, "We don't want to just hold power, we want to hunt down the Democrats and destroy them. We want to make a fundamental change in the policies of this country, and that starts with getting rid of as many weak-kneed Democrats as we can. America is the strongest nation in the world, and it's time we act like it."

Shiloh could sense an ill wind blowing in Washington. The civility that had marked her first several years had given was to intense partisanship. She still liked her job and hoped that the rabid partisanship that she was living through would end with this presidential election.

The upcoming election was the first time since Shiloh's initial election that the Republicans ran a candidate against her. Shiloh was now running in the newly redrawn Fifth District. The Republican candidate's name was Jake Sheraton. He was a physician, a deacon in his church, a Rotarian, and antichoice, although not outspokenly so. Shiloh had met Dr. Sheraton several times at various events around Nashville. They had served together on a committee that had been set up by the governor in 1997 to recommend legislation to increase employment opportunities for Tennesseans. The economy had grown significantly in Tennessee and around the country during the 1990s, but it didn't seem to be reaching the underclass, who had to depend on minimum-wage jobs and even welfare to get by.

Governor Whitfield had hoped that by appointing a committee with broad experiences he could begin to find answers. The welfare rolls had dropped slightly, and crime statistics had improved. But the underclass was desperate, and the minimum wage was so low that most people who worked and had families still needed food stamps to make ends meet. Health care costs were exploding, and a growing number of Americans, especially children, were without health insurance. It was a problem that many governors across the country were trying to address.

The committee had worked for over a year and gave the governor a report that contained several significant recommendations. They had suggested programs to keep kids in school, to strengthen technical schools, and to make sure that all children received routine medical exams in schools. They suggested the creation of job programs through the parks and public works department, similar to programs that had been initiated during the depression to ease unemployment. The main emphasis though was on health, education, and training. One proposal was to provide better sex education, not only to prevent pregnancy, but also to prevent AIDS and other sexually transmitted diseases. The teen pregnancy rate, in spite of state and federal programs, was still quite high. AIDS was relatively low but could become a big problem unless the public and public health officials were vigilant.

Shiloh and Jake had gotten along well and even had coffee together after a few of the meetings to discuss their work. They generally agreed on all the issues the committee discussed, with the exception of sex education. Dr. Sheraton was not overbearing on the subject; he just did not believe in abortion and sincerely thought that sex education may have the opposite effect than the one intended. They'd discussed this issue one day over coffee.

* * * * *

Shiloh had been emphatic. "Jake, I agree with you for the most part about everything the committee has recommended. I just wish you were willing to go forward with sex education. Your minority report may give folks a reason to object and cause all that we have accomplished to be questioned because of this one issue."

Jake replied courteously and in a calm voice. "I know that you dislike reliance on abortion and want to see it become rare. I admire that about you. But where I differ is how to make it that way. I just can't believe that teaching children about birth control and how to prevent pregnancy would do anything but make those who are not sexually active want to try it because it would be safe for them to do so. Don't you understand that, Shy?"

"Yes, Jake, I do understand what you're saying, but experience is different. Study after study shows that sex education delays sexual activity and dramatically lowers the incidence of abortion and sexually transmitted diseases. Among industrial countries, the United States has the highest rate of teen pregnancy and abortion by a wide margin. The reason that we do is because we are the only industrial country that does not have good sex education in all of our schools. A few kids may experiment because of sex education, but for the vast majority, it promotes abstinence and responsible behavior. They delay sexual activity, and they do not get pregnant."

"But don't you think," Jake inquired, "that if there was no sex education and if abortion was illegal except for authentic medical reasons, that teenage sex would be dramatically reduced?"

"I know you know better than that. Don't you remember what our maternal mortality ratios were like before abortion was legal? Special wards in our hospitals were set aside just to treat the effects of illegal and self-induced abortion."

"Yes, I remember those days, but that was before. Now we have stronger religious influences in this country, and we can start those abstinence programs that are being used in Texas. Can't we just try that?"

"I have no problem with abstinence," Shiloh said with sincerity. "I believe all sex education should start with the premise that abstinence is best, but I do not believe that we can rely on abstinence alone. I respect your views. But I can't agree that this is the way to move forward. I guess that we'll just have to agree to disagree."

"Yes, I suppose so. I suppose so."

* * * * *

Now, over four years later, Dr. Jake Sheraton was challenging Shiloh Catherine Giles for her seat in Congress. He had called Shiloh when he'd accepted his party's request to run. He wanted to assure her that it was not personal, that his decision to run was philosophical.

"Yes," he had told her, "I am a Republican, and I believe in smaller government and many of the other things that separate Democrats from Republicans. But first and foremost," Dr. Sheraton had added, "I want to end abortion in this country, and I plan to make that case at every opportunity."

"I understand, Jake," Shiloh told him. "I guess we'll let the voters of the Fifth District decide."

"No ill will," Jake had said before ringing off.

"None whatsoever. This is a democracy, and we both respect that," replied Shiloh. "It's too bad that some other races aren't as collegial as ours will be. I'll not wish you good luck, though," laughed Shiloh, "just good health."

"And to you too," her rival replied.

* * * * *

Lawson had dogged Shiloh many times when she spoke in the Nashville area since that evening in 1994 when he had caused such a ruckus at Tennessee State University during their debate. His message was always the same: abortion, abortion, and abortion. He seemed to get more vitriolic as time went by, and every time there was an election, even though Shiloh was unopposed, she would receive hate mail, which she was relatively sure he had inspired. As the head of the Nashville branch of Operation Savior, he was frequently seen at the Mid-State Women's Clinic, where his antics were nothing short of outrageous.

In spite of Skyler's time in jail and his own, Lawson seemed to get more agitated as time passed. He had learned Skyler's tactics well and had pushed OS past the limit of the law. He filmed patients, screamed at them, and often came within a few inches of touching them. The clinic had taken to picking up some of their patients who were worried about being seen and dropping them off at the clinic's front door. They covered their heads when they got out of the car at the curb and were quickly escorted into the clinic.

Lawson had filmed one young patient and traced her license plate; he'd sent her a picture of herself and threatened to send it to her family, but he never did. He must have consulted a lawyer, who would have told him that he could go to jail if he did that.

When he learned that Dr. Sheraton was running against Shiloh, Lawson had gone to see him to offer his services. Sheraton had declined. But James Robert, Jimmy Bob to his friends, planned to "help" anyway.

Lawson printed a brochure that was titled: SHILOH GILES vs. MORALITY. It accused her of living in sin before her marriage to Seth. It said that her future husband had spent the night with her many times in Washington before they were married. It also said that she had a homosexual partnership with her chief of staff and had even had an affair with her homosexual campaign manager, Charlie Bates. She will try to pass a sex education bill that encourages same-sex experimentation to determine your sexual preferences. She plans to legalize and encourage same-sex marriage.

It replayed her Mid-State Women's Clinic episode and her support for unrestricted abortion. Finally, it accused Shiloh of being an enemy of the American family and parental responsibility.

* * * * *

Since 2000, the tactics of the majority in the House and its leadership had increasingly frustrated Shiloh. They had become quite vicious under their new highly partisan leadership. She was appalled by the growing lack of civility of the majority party. They refused to debate their proposed tax cuts for the wealthy and ignored her party's minimum-wage bill. Most of all, she was enraged at the way the new administration with its mean spirited majority in the House played on people's fears. They did whatever they pleased with foreign policy. The run-up to the Iraq War was all about patriotism and had very little to do with diplomacy. The idea of war with Iraq made no sense to Shiloh, especially when the country had not yet finished the job in Afghanistan. She couldn't believe that she longed for the days of the former Republican leadership team in the House and their Program for America. At least her party had held the White House then.

Once when she had spoken on the House floor for increased Title X funding for domestic family planning, the majority leader had walked by when she was about to speak and said, "Don't waste your breath, sister, ain't no way."

That was totally unacceptable language on the floor of Congress—even in jest. Decorum was essential. Even if your speech would have no impact, it was your right to speak. It was your right and duty to speak. This was still a democracy. She had thought about commenting on his manhood but instead had spoke well beyond the allowed time in spite of the chairperson's request that she end her statement.

On another occasion, she was speaking against the abstinence-only sex education bill and for a program that also taught about reproduction, contraceptives, and the prevention of sexually transmitted diseases. She had quoted an abstinence education study from Lubbock, Texas, where the president had introduced abstinence sex education as governor of Texas. He had used funds from a 1996 congressional appropriation, which was being renewed on this day. The study showed that the program was not having the intended effect.

When she finished, the majority leader quipped to a colleague, "That little cutie-pie needs to be out somewhere being un-abstained instead of here wasting our time." Unfortunately, his mic was open.

Shiloh glared at the majority leader.

He smiled and said, "Sorry 'bout that."

No one smiled. Even for the haughty among them, that was too much.

Yes, thought Shiloh, *times have changed*.

But the pendulum would swing. These zealots would overreach, and the voters would eventually throw them out. She was at a loss for why the country had gone so far right. The people seemed to be marching in lockstep with the fundamentalists. She was even more appalled by the United State's loss of reputation overseas. She couldn't imagine what the other party would do next.

* * * * *

The early part of her campaign was uneventful. Charlie told Shiloh that she should make it without breaking a sweat. The voters loved her. Sheraton, while respected, was not well-known. And besides, Shiloh was genuinely perceived as representing her district well. *The Tennessean* had written several favorable articles about her work, and the fact that she had run unopposed in the past proved the point.

Then the majority leader came to town. When he spoke, he talked about many issues: taxes, terrorism, welfare, and the no-child-left-behind centerpiece of the president's educational program. Then he turned to the issue of abortion: "My friends, abortion is wrong. We all know that it is wrong. You can do something about it by electing Jake Sheraton to Congress. He fully supports the Republican platform. America is not a place for abortion. With more people like Jake Sheraton in Congress, we can do something to stop the abortion plague in this country. His opponent is a leader in Congress on the abortion issue. She thinks it's fine for our youngsters to have abortions, even without their parent's knowledge. She even opposes abstinence education. She is not a moral person."

He went on to admonish the citizens of Nashville for sending such a degenerate to Washington. And he said, "The time to change that is now. This will be a new country, a country of God, a country of morality, and a country that follows the lead of men like Jake Sheraton. We don't want a country that reveres same-sex marriage like your congresswoman. It is time for her to go and for Jake Sheraton to represent this district."

The majority leader held up Lawson's brochure and continued speaking. "You should get one of these when you leave. There are some folks outside with them. It will tell you something that you may find very interesting about the character of you current congresswomen, the one that you will replace on Election Day. I stand before you in all humility, my friends. The Republican Party is returning morality to American life and to America's policies. Help us by electing Dr. Jake Sheraton to represent you in Congress. Remember, this is one nation under God. We must keep it that way."

The press scrambled to get the brochure. When they discovered that it was the one Lawson had been passing out, they were disappointed, but they had a job to do. The story aired that same night on the local news.

* * * * *

Shiloh felt sick about the speaker's comments because she knew Jake Sheraton had run a clean campaign. In fact, Sheraton had called to talk to Shiloh but had reached Brenda Jones in Charlie Bates's office. Charlie was with Shiloh. Brenda called Charlie and told him what happened. Charlie motioned from the back of the hotel ballroom where the Belle Meade Rotary Club was meeting and signaled for Shiloh to speed it up.

Charlie filled Shiloh in about the majority leader.

"Don't worry, Charlie, people will see through that kind of garbage. He's forever a nasty pit bull. We will survive."

Shiloh was talking as she and Charlie drove to Charlie's office. Suddenly Charlie's phone rang. It was Jake Sheraton. Charlie handed the phone to Shiloh.

"Hi, Shiloh, it's Jake. I guess you've heard about the majority leader's speech. I had no idea that he would say something like that or that he would advertise that dreadful brochure of Lawson's. He was outside the hotel when we went in and gave a copy to the majority leader. What a mess. I'm so sorry."

"Yes, it's a mess. I know that you would never sanction such a thing, Jake. What do you plan to tell the press?"

"That you're an honorable and moral person," Jake exclaimed. "And that the brochure is not from my campaign and that I disavow it."

"Thanks. I really appreciate your position. I plan to say that I'll not discuss such scurrilous attacks. How in the world does one deal that kind of filth anyway?

"Anything goes these days, Jake." Shiloh continued. "Lawson is a dreadful human being. He seems to hate me. Ever since he ran against me in '94, he has tried to sabotage my every move. I just hope his latest attempt won't put you at odds with the majority leader."

"Don't worry about that. I got into this, and I'll see it through, but not at the expense of my values," replied a contrite Jake.

"Thanks again, Jake. I'll see you tomorrow night at Tennessee State. Good health to both of us, friend."

"Yes, and to you too, Shy."

Shiloh handed Charlie his phone.

"Well," said Charlie, "so much for a clean campaign. At least Sheraton is a decent man. It could be a lot worse."

"You don't think this will be a big problem, do you, Charlie?"

"No. But it won't be pleasant."

"I'm sorry, Charlie. Attacking me is one thing, but attacking you and your sexuality is awful."

"Not to worry, I'll be fine."

But Shiloh could tell by the tautness of his mouth that he was nervous.

He dropped Shiloh off at her condo. She was due to speak at a Democratic fundraising dinner at the Opryland Hotel at seven o'clock.

Shiloh changed and got ready for the dinner. She thought about the events of the day and her life. Most of all she worried about Charlie. How could a so-called man of God smear good people like he did with that brochure and those stupid posters?

What makes his hate so intense? she wondered. It upset her that anyone could see her as an enemy. *What would Jesus think?* she mused. She was right in her positions; she knew she was right. They were moral. She was confident in her faith, but how could others be so hateful? She read the same Bible they did.

"Oh well," she said aloud. "Press on, press on. Can't stop now, girl." She chuckled to herself as the doorbell rang.

"Charlie," she greeted, "6:15 sharp. I'm ready."

In the car, Shiloh asked, "Did you call your mom?"

Charlie nodded. His mouth was set in a rigid line. "Yes, she had seen the coverage and was fine. She knows about me, of course. I just didn't want her to worry about my safety. As it turns out, she was more worried about you than me."

"She's so sweet. You're a lucky man. I called Seth. He's coming down tomorrow and will stay through the debate. He was really angry—not so much at Lawson but at the majority leader. He thinks he, in his words, is exhibit A of the reasons why this country is in such a mess."

"I can't disagree with that," agreed Charlie. "Get ready, we're almost there. Remember what we agreed."

"Okay, boss," said the candidate with a smile.

When they pulled up to the curb, they saw four TV cameras, about twenty reporters, and Lawson, who was leading a group holding several signs. Shiloh took a minute to read them: "Abortion Is Murder," "Shiloh Lesbian Giles," "Homosexuality is a SIN," "Support the Family," "Giles out of Congress," "Wipeout Homosexuality," "Abortion and Giles."

"Here we go," said Charlie.

Shiloh opened the door and stepped out.

"Congresswoman, Congresswomen, who …

"Why …"

"Do you …"

Charlie held up his right hand, "Hold on, friends, one at a time. Emma?"

"Congresswomen Giles, what is your comment about the majority leader's speech today?"

Everyone was silent, even Lawson's group.

Shiloh looked serious as she spoke, "First, I am saddened that this country, this state, and this city has to witness such a raw display of gutter politics. Second, I am angry that someone who holds an honored position in the Congress of the United States of America would discredit his office and the great institution of the House of Representatives that we are both privileged to serve. Third, I will continue discussing the important issues of the day. And fourth, my opponent is an honorable man. You can count on both of us to finish this campaign with personal dignity and respect for each other and the electorate. We have many important issues to discuss in this campaign, and I will not again waste your time or mine discussing the majority leader's remarks, nor the scurrilous brochure that Mr. Lawson has been distributing. Thank you."

For a moment, the silence continued as the print reporters scribbled and the others stared. Shiloh glanced at Charlie. He was trying hard to suppress a smile. When she saw that, she knew she must have nailed it perfectly.

The silence was broken as Lawson screamed, "Bitch, queer! We will stop you this time!"

Then his group began chanting, "Down with Giles! Down with Giles …"

Charlie grabbed Shiloh's elbow and steered her up the stairs. The press followed them. The police, there in force, kept the demonstrators at bay.

Inside, Shiloh was greeted by a standing ovation. Barry and Trudy had just arrived from Tullahoma, and the Jacobsons were there. Both couples greeted Shiloh with hugs and kisses. Shiloh relaxed, and the evening was a great success.

Shiloh and Charlie had drinks at the Jacobsons' home, where the Whitfields were spending the night. At the house, as they stood around pouring drinks, Charlie turned to the Whitfields. "I didn't expect to see y'all here tonight."

"What do you mean, Charlie?" Barry said with a hurt voice. "Do you think I'm too old to drive or that we stopped living when my second term ended?"

"No," laughed Charlie, "I just thought that an old guy like you would be at home watching reruns of *The Honeymooners.*"

The governor smiled. "What do you think, Charlie?" inquired Barry. "Will this brochure mess blow over?"

"Yes, but Lawson won't. He'll be a pain for as long as Shy is in Congress. What an awful man."

"He scares me, Charlie. That man is evil," Barry said.

Shiloh and the Jacobsons remained silent until Trudy changed the subject. They sat around for hours and discussed politics and old times. The overall theme was sadness at the turn of events since 9/11, war with Iraq, secrecy, and the country's steady move to the right.

* * * * *

Seth arrived the next day to spend the weekend working on the campaign.

They sat at the table having a late lunch when Seth turned to Shiloh and smiled. "I can't believe how polished you are as a campaigner, darling. Folks from Jersey could never match that southern charm of yours. Is it in your genes, or did you learn it?"

"Don't give me that, Mr. Richards. You know plenty about charm. You played me like a fiddle when we met, still do. You're just trying to charm me into buying supper tonight. Aren't you?" Shiloh gave him the cute little-girl pout. They had been married for over two years now and Shiloh still felt like a teenager when they were together.

"When do we need to leave for the debate?" Seth asked, changing the subject.

"Charlie's coming by at 4:30 for a drink, and we'll leave around 5:15."

Seth frowned. "How's Charlie doing after the flap about the brochure?"

"He's fine; in fact, he seems tougher now than ever before. Plus he's happy. His former partner is coming to visit after the election. He's tiring of the West Coast and has broken up with his partner there. Charlie still misses him and hopes they can reconnect."

"Good for him," said Seth. "Charlie is one hell of a political operator and a good man."

Shiloh nodded, "Yes, but don't call him an operator when he's here. He has thin skin about the morals of politics. He prides himself for always playing it right. He doesn't believe in dirty tactics."

Shiloh walked over to her husband and put her arms around his waist. "I don't mean to be rude, but we'd better get ready, Seth."

"Okay, sweetie. Shall we get reacquainted first?" he said with a sly smile.

"Why do you think I said let's get ready now, dear?" Shy asked innocently.

After the couple finished getting reacquainted, Seth went to the living room to read Shiloh's debate notes.

The chimes rang, and Seth answered the door. "Charlie, welcome. It's good to see you. I was just telling Shy a while ago how much I admire your work."

Charlie took a bow. "Thanks for the compliment. With Shy it's a piece of cake. She's on my top-two list of great candidates, and she's better looking and sweeter than the other one."

Shiloh walked through the door. "You don't have to butter me up, Charlie. I'm bringing your wine. And here's your beer, Seth."

"What about you, darling?"

"Not before the debate. I don't want to do anything that might slow me down. Plus I'm driving."

Charlie frowned. "I want Seth to drive. Is that okay, Seth? I hate to do this to you."

Seth shrugged. "Sure, I know you want to brief the candidate."

"I do," replied Charlie. "I understand from a media source that Lawson is coming tonight and bringing a crowd."

"Oh boy," sighed Shiloh.

Seth crossed his arms and his brow furrowed. "Good, I haven't gotten to meet him when I've been here before. I'd like to take this man's measure."

Shiloh patted his arm. "Just be sure that you take his measure at a distance, sweetheart. It won't do for you to get agitated. That would play right into his hands."

"Of course, dear," said Seth with mock humility.

The setup was the same as when Shiloh had tried to debate Lawson eight years ago. The trio entered through the back and missed Lawson and his gang, who were out front passing out brochures and holding their signs. They were allowed to enter, but only without their signs.

Both candidates knew their material and did well, but it was obvious from the applause that the crowd was with Shiloh, especially when Lawson's group clapped so loud and long for Sheraton and on a few occasions booed Shiloh. The crowd sensed what was happening, and they cheered even louder for Shiloh. Shiloh suspected that Jake was not at all happy with the support he was getting from the Lawson gang.

The candidates and their teams, including Charlie and Seth, had coffee with their student hosts, the media panel, and other journalists after the debate. Shiloh enjoyed meeting the students who had worked so hard to put the debate together.

She and Jake congratulated each other.

Jake sighed, "I'm glad that the brochure incident died quickly. I got a nasty message from one of the majority leader's staffers for not continuing the attack."

"Thanks again, Jake," replied Shiloh. "You're a man of integrity, and I do respect your position on the issues where we differ. Whatever happens next Tuesday, I hope we stay in touch."

"You're very kind. I'm expecting that you'll win. That's what my pollster says anyway."

"Don't be discouraged if I do win. Two years go by quickly."

"I guess we'll see. Shy, I respect you too and wish you well either way."

They smiled and shook hands, a photo op which an enterprising photojournalist snapped. The photo appeared the next day on the front page of *The Tennessean* over the article about the debate.

When they finally left, Seth, Charlie, and Shiloh went out the rear entrance with a few journalists and students. Lawson was waiting. His gang was there too with their ever-present signs. As soon as they saw Shiloh, they held up their signs and crowded in close.

Lawson spoke in a loud voice, "Here she is, my friends—the homo abortion queen. This is the evil woman who the idiots in this district want to send back to Washington—again."

He was coming closer.

Shiloh gripped Seth's hand tightly. She could feel Seth tense up as Lawson approached. She whispered, "Be calm, sweetheart."

Seth was silent.

Shiloh's buoyant mood from the debate quickly turned to anxiety. She did not like the look in Lawson's eyes or the restlessness of his companions. She could sense Seth's anger building. *I must defuse this quickly*, she thought.

Lawson came within a few feet of Shiloh. Shiloh was expressionless as she looked Lawson straight in the eyes. His gang moved in behind him.

Lawson said, "I can't stand the sight of you, Giles. You're a disgrace. You kill babies like it's nothing. You're a pervert. You're what is wrong with our country. You're the Antichrist. You make me sick. We'll get you, one way or another, pretty Miss Shiloh."

The three journalists who'd left with Shiloh were scribbling Lawson's words. The situation was tense. Shiloh could feel her heart beat faster. She could smell Lawson's breath when he spoke. But she kept her eyes locked on his.

One of the people behind Lawson said, "Your days are numbered, Giles; one day you'll be alone when we find you."

Seth shifted his weight.

Shiloh spoke quietly and evenly, "Why don't you all just let us be? We're leaving. We should all just go home. I appreciate your position, Mr. Lawson, but this isn't the place for a discussion."

Suddenly Lawson spit in Shiloh's face.

Shiloh felt a tremor of rage course through Seth as he nudged Shiloh behind him.

That's when Lawson made a careless mistake. "I'm not through talking to you, Giles," he said, and as he spoke, he put his hand on Shiloh to block her way.

Seth sprang so quickly that Lawson never knew what hit him. Seth's punch crushed Lawson's jaw. Lawson dropped like a brick. Blood gushed from his mouth. Before anyone could react, Seth said, "You'd better help your friend before he drowns in his own blood. If any of you so much as look at the congresswoman, you'll be joining your pal there."

Charlie moved quickly between Seth and the crowd, and Shiloh knelt to help Lawson. Two of his followers moved him to a better position. Lawson began to come around just as three policemen came crashing through the door followed by the student who'd gone to fetch them.

By the time the police had completed their interviews and Seth was finished at the hospital, it was past midnight. He had broken two of the knuckles on his right hand. Seth apologized to Shiloh at the hospital at least a dozen times, and he even apologized to Charlie.

Charlie had told him not to worry. "This episode will probably get more ink than the debate. Politically, my guess is that it will help. You were just acting like any husband would act."

Shiloh, while understanding, was less forgiving. "You don't have to keep apologizing. It's okay. I know that you acted on instinct, and I appreciate it. It's just that I abhor violence, especially when it could easily have been avoided. But I love you just as much now as before, and I know that you love me. Let's just let it go."

"Oh, sweetheart, I'm so sorry, you're absolutely right," stammered Seth. "It was mostly instinct. But I even scared myself. I wanted to hurt that

SOB. I couldn't stand the way he approached you, spit on you, and was so threatening in front of his group of followers. I guess I wanted to draw a line for them. But I'm really sincerely sorry, Shy."

On TV news the next morning, they learned that it had been a good debate, and the analysts who commented afterward gave both candidates good marks, while conceding that Sheraton would be lucky to get 40 percent of the vote.

Charlie was right. The story about the confrontation was given equal importance to the debate, and as Charlie had predicted, the Lawson episode played well for Shiloh. The paper was full of letters over the next few days, praising Seth and pledging to vote for Shiloh.

Shiloh won 67 percent of the votes.

Chapter 9

Shiloh's Nashville office was quick to respond to constituent queries and requests. Shiloh genuinely liked meeting individual constituents on her twice-monthly visits to the district, and she held town hall meetings every few months to discuss the issues that were being debated in Washington and to explain her votes. After she trounced Jake Sheraton, *The Tennessean* opined that Congresswoman Giles couldn't be beat. Why, they asked, would anyone want another horse when they already owned a thoroughbred?

Shiloh had often been mentioned and had even been approached privately by party leaders to run for the Senate, but she was happy being in the House. The House, Shiloh thought, while quite partisan under its current leaders, seemed to her to be more amenable to independent member action than the more stogy Senate with its arcane rules and procedures. She felt freer to explore and to take bold initiatives as she planned to do now

On a rainy Sunday afternoon, she had told Seth about her idea to introduce the ERA. They were sitting in his apartment in New York. They had slept late that morning and enjoyed a lazy brunch at Chiam. They returned home to spend a lazy afternoon reading the *New York Times*.

Shiloh had been thinking for several months about something she wanted to do and decided that now was a good time to tell Seth about her idea and to get his always-valuable feedback.

She had known about the Equal Rights Amendment for Women, almost since before she could remember. It had become a national issue when she was in elementary school. When she was in junior high and high school it had been stuck in the ratification process, falling short of the number of states needed for adoption as a constitutional amendment. Her civics teacher had discussed it extensively in her class, and Shiloh had led the debate team that argued for adoption. She was proud that Tennessee had adopted the amendment but wasn't sure that it would again today.

She remembered talking to Grandma Alice about the ERA and being surprised that she was so committed to it. Alice had reiterated to her the stories of the hard life that women like her mother and Shiloh's great-grandmother, Tennessee Carolina, had led and how unfair it was that women had to wait so long to vote. Grandma Alice had even spoken out in her church about a woman's right to vote in the teen years of the twentieth century, when it was a hot issue.

Shiloh had seen gender discrimination all her life and was surprised and angered that the ERA had essentially been placed so far out of sight on the back burner since the 1970s that it was all the way off the stove today. Things weren't right for women in America for sure, but in most developing countries it wasn't even discussed. Her days in the Philippines opened her eyes to what Grandma Alice had told her about Tennessee Carolina's life and even Alice's young life. America had improved but not nearly enough. And what kind of example did America set for the rest of the world?

It had gnawed on Shiloh for years, and now here she was in Congress, she thought, the very place where action could be taken for the ERA's adoption.

"Darling," she said, as she brought coffee into the living room, "may I tear you away from the sports page long enough to tell you about my special dream?"

"Sure, sweetheart, I'm all ears. But I thought I was your special dream."

"No, you are my extra special dream come true."

"I see," replied Seth. "What did you want to do now, enroll me in cooking school?"

"No," said Shiloh smiling, "if anyone needs cooking school it's me. Actually, I want your take on a bill I'd like to introduce."

"Uh-oh. I'd better put on another pot of coffee; this sounds serious."

And so Shiloh told Seth about the history of the ERA and her desire to reintroduce the bill on the floor of Congress. "It can't be introduced as a normal bill, Seth. That has been tried repeatedly. It will take a lot of hard work and support, but I believe there may be a way to put women's rights back on the national agenda. It has been rattling around my head since my Grandmother Alice mentioned it the day I graduated from high school. She commented on my speech about women's rights that she wished that I wouldn't speak out so much on these sorts of issues. I told her not to worry, that I wouldn't go overboard because it wasn't my time yet. Then she mentioned the ERA. She said something about how, when it was my time, I should work on the ERA and show men a thing or two or some such. Well, now it's my time."

Then she explained to Seth what she thought it would take to do it.

Seth sat in shock as he listened to his wife. "I had no idea that the ERA had such a checkered history. It's unbelievable that something so just and so right wasn't adopted, at least along with the Fourteenth and Fifteenth amendments. How can that be?"

After a moment of thought, Seth added. "It would be good for women, good for the country, and good for the world. It will take a lot of work and many allies, but we can do it. When do we start?"

Shiloh smiled at Seth. "We?"

"Yes, we. I've devoted a large chunk of my life to women's health and equality. So I do mean *we*. I've reached the minimum UN age for retirement. I can move to Washington and work on this with you 100 percent of the time. You'll need more help of course, but at least I'm cheap. All you have to do is keep loving me."

"Oh, that would be wonderful, darling. We can finally be together full time. I should have thought of this before."

Shiloh smiled now as she looked at her husband and remembered their conversation that dreary Sunday afternoon that had started their journey toward the Equal Rights Amendment.

* * * * *

Shiloh and Seth were sitting in her office waiting for her appointment with the party's leader in the House to discuss her ERA idea. Seth had joined her in Washington and would wait for her in her office when she was called to go and see her leader. He had already put in his retirement papers and would leave at the end of the year. He had come down early this weekend and was just as excited as Shiloh about the ERA. If the leader said no to their proposal, Seth would find something else to do, but he'd look here in Washington. They had both grown tired of their two-city marriage.

Shiloh shifted in her chair. "So much has brought me to this meeting today. Several years ago Bill Jacobson told me he was worried about the growing power of the fundamentalists. What Bill feared has come true. Their brand of black-and-white religious demoguery, combined with their now open politicking, is a direct contradiction to the separation of church and state, tax-exempt laws that religious organizations are supposed to honor, and the American founding principles of tolerance and religious freedom."

Seth nodded. "And I expect that they'll put you on their political hit list if you're allowed to go forward with the ERA."

Shiloh shrugged. "I'm ready, even eager for the fight. Someone needs to take them on. The well-known president of Lawson's alma mater," continued Shiloh, "founded a new coalition after the recent election to champion moral issues."

"Yes, I read that," lamented Seth. "He said the coalition was designed to take as much ground as they can while they have friends in high places. Their religious views, combined with the neocon vision of an Imperial America, scare me, Shy. How could the world's human rights champion become a country that tortures war prisoners and ignores human rights out of convenience? To promote what? Global dominance? We've got to reverse this arrogant disregard for American principles and multilateralism before it's too late."

"Exactly," Shiloh said forcefully. "Will America lead a multilateral world that values justice, health, education, fair trade, environmental protection, and human rights? Or will we ignore the commonality of nations and the other 96 percent of humankind when it suits us? I have a platform that should allow me to address these issues, but the new Speaker and majority leader use their power like dictators. What was a collegial institution has become an authoritarian aristocracy; 9/11 became an excuse to pursue the neocon agenda."

Shiloh sighed in frustration. "At a time when America should have been gathering together allies in a war against terrorism, we have a president who says, 'you are either with us or against us.'"

Seth leaned forward. "I know. Remember what the French president said on 9/11? 'The French are entirely with the American people,' and *Le Monde*'s headline on September 12 was 'We are all Americans today.' We both believed that the world would unite to fight an American-led war on terrorism."

Seth went on, "The French support symbolically guaranteed that all countries would rally to this critical international cause that America would lead. But later, as the U.S. began to push for war against Iraq, ignoring the 'multilateral' resolution of the Security Council, France and many other nations asked legitimate questions about how best to prosecute the war on terrorism. For this attempted negotiation, the leader of the free world sharply criticized one of America's most important allies."

Shiloh closed her eyes. "He rebuked the very nation that helped secure America's independence. And the country that gave America the Statue of Liberty as an indication of its respect for America's democracy and its position in the world as, indeed, the land of liberty."

Shiloh lamented, "'You are with us or against us' was more than rhetoric. This administration allows no compromise or even serious discussion. It bullies, internationally and domestically, anyone who questions its policies, including me. If anyone questions the administration's thinking, he or she is branded as unpatriotic. Never has America launched an unprovoked war against another country."

Shiloh's was getting angry, and Seth reached over and held her hand.

"I can't understand it," Shiloh continued. "there was no violation of the Monroe Doctrine, no attack on American soil by another country, no ally to whom America was bound that needed help—nothing but flimsy intelligence and the grand design of a handful of neocon intellectuals. They were willing to sacrifice American blood, even though most of them had never been in harm's way themselves, to advance American political and economic interests."

Seth nodded. "Their ideology alone was their justification for sacrificing American lives and principles. America's stature as the leader of a multilateral world has been altered. It was a philosophical coup to shift American policy away from our historical principles and a foreign policy framework that was tried and tested. It's like we've learned nothing from the great world wars and European history."

Shiloh felt exactly the same way. "Yes, darling, and even more so domestically. The rich become richer while the poor struggle just to make ends meet. Where will this arrogance take this great nation that has stood for so long as a shining light of justice, tolerance, and liberty? Are we destined to become another lost empire choked on its own excesses? Science, technology, and even diplomacy are taking a back seat to the avarice of the powerful. And the thing that infuriates me the most is that religion is often used as justification."

Shiloh believed that America's greatest strength was in its diversity and its freedom, its love of the underdog, and its can-do spirit. These things seemed to have been cast aside by a new neocon/fundamentalist class that was just as frightening to Shiloh as fascism, fundamentalist Muslims, or any others in history who used ideology to maintain power. They were following a blueprint for global religious and military dominance.

Shiloh sighed. "Every day we in the opposition are speaking out, but it's almost impossible for us to win even small battles. This is a democracy, but it seems to have become a democracy in the hands of one group that isn't about to compromise. Maybe, darling, maybe we can strike back."

Seth smiled. "We will strike back. Your plan will expose a glaring inadequacy in American law and principles. You have the potential to galvanize the American people and embolden our youngsters to once again pursue equality and justice."

To Shiloh, the ultimate sin of humankind and more recently, of the United States, was the degradation of women and backsliding on the grand, noble, and moral goal of gender equality. God put us here, she believed, with the capacity to solve our own problems. The great religions of the world and their founders respected women and did not in any way promote inequality among women and men. But over time, men in power had corrupted and skewed these beliefs.

"Did Jesus," Shiloh mused, "preach that women should be unequal to men, that blacks should be inferior to whites, or that poverty should be a punishment for being born into circumstances beyond one's control and into a system that did not provide adequate tools for escape? Did Jesus say that the rich and powerful would inherit the earth? Is this philosophy of theirs," Shiloh said, only half-jokingly, "a precursor of intelligent design?"

Seth chuckled. "I know. Recent elections, Shy, especially presidential elections focused so much on social issues, like abortion and gay rights, that they virtually ignored education, tax policy, and the environment. Clever advertising and dishonest PR steered people away from issues that could legitimately be addressed, issues where common ground could be found for at least some improvement. Instead, we've focused on issues that cause divisive, visceral reactions. People have become so focused on these things that they can't see the elephant in their living room."

Shiloh could tell that Seth was wound up as he continued his tirade. "Abortion is legal. That's a fact. But it could be dramatically reduced with better sex education and universal access to birth control. But the people against abortion—who, ironically, can chose not have an abortion while having the guarantee of privacy to have one—have also worked against the known methods of making abortion rare."

"You nailed it," agreed his wife. "The American people are against gay marriage but support civil unions. That seems a fair compromise for this moment in history. But it isn't likely to happen with this government. As it stands now, gay partners are often denied the right to visit their partners in a hospital or utilizing joint health insurance. Is that tolerance and freedom? America executes more people than all but five countries in the world, and DNA evidence has shown that some who were scheduled for execution were not guilty. Why isn't anyone addressing these issues?"

Shiloh had come to Washington because she had spunk and wasn't afraid to stand up to a bully. In her years in Congress, she had fought for women's health and rights; education; environmental protection; international development; open trade policies, if fair salaries and health benefits were included; and a strong national defense. She had aggressively supported the war in Afghanistan and thought that America had used too few troops and withdrawn far too many of those they did use for Iraq. We blew it in Tora Bora, she thought, and then moved on to Iraq. Instead of stopping terrorists, we went chasing after weapons of mass destruction that did not exist and may have succeeded in establishing a recruiting theater for even more terrorists.

She had reluctantly supported the war in Iraq because she had been led to believe that U.S. intelligence had shown that Saddam was a clear and present danger to American national security and that Saddam was connected to Osama Bin Laden and the 9/11 attacks. When she'd learned the truth, she'd spoken out against the war before it was popular to do so. For that, she'd been ridiculed for being unpatriotic.

So many things were wrong, she thought. Shiloh spoke again. "Did you know that, on the day before the report by the special prosecutor against President Clinton about his sexual dalliance, over fifty U.S. newspapers wrote editorials saying that the president should resign for his lies? This president has led America into a war killing thousands of Iraqis and American soldiers. To do so, he used faulty and perhaps even falsified information. And he changed American foreign policy principles when he launched America's first preemptive war. Is the media frightened of this government? There has not been a peep from the major media about impeachment or even investigations—not about the war and very little about torture. How can that be?"

Seth nodded. "The PR machine that the majority party guru operates is the best ever. Clever communications have replaced honesty and fair debate. In the past, the press has always helped to protect us, but apparently they are worried that they will lose too. All they do now is bring on the talking heads and see who is the loudest."

And now, after thinking through all of this, Shiloh was set to embark on what her leader could very likely call an exercise in futility. But she would try to convince her anyway. Deep inside of her, she knew that this was her moment, the reason she was where she was. Of all the problems that bothered the congresswoman from Tennessee, the one that bothered her most was gender apartheid. Women's equality would have a dramatic impact on poverty and development and even on peace and security. The notion of women's equality would attract derisive chortles from many of her colleagues in the other party, she supposed, and contempt and immediate opposition from the neocon/fundamentalist coalition, especially the fundamentalists. They would oppose her suggestion energetically with their trademark PR overkill. She hoped this time their unreasonableness would finally illustrate to America's vast middle majority that the other policies and demagoguery of this group were also suspect.

Shiloh wanted to reintroduce the Equal Rights Amendment. It had been introduced many times since the first attempt in 1923 and as recently as last February, early in this session of Congress.

"Carolyn Maloney and Jim Leach," said Shiloh, "introduced the ERA in the House in tandem with Ted Kennedy's move in the Senate. Their resolution went to the Subcommittee on the Constitution, where we all knew it would fail, as it had so many times before, but they tried anyway, with the hope that they could light a fire under their colleagues and the electorate.

"But indeed, it failed again. Neither the media, nor, it seemed, anyone else, much cared about this social issue. That has always been the problem with women's rights. No one seemed to care. And what bothers me most is that young women today, especially the ones who are from well-off families, don't understand that it is an issue. They go to good schools, get good jobs, and know nothing about their less fortunate sisters in this country and the often terrible conditions women in much of the rest of the world face."

Just then the phone rang. It was the leader's office. Shiloh squeezed Seth's hand. "Wish me luck," she said over her shoulder as she hurried over to the Capitol.

"Break a leg, sweetheart," he called after her.

* * * * *

After a few minutes of small talk, Shiloh began. "Madame Leader, I have an idea. I've thought about it for quite some time now and want to get your blessings to move forward—or not."

Shiloh imagined that the leader heard such requests all the time. Now that she was actually meeting her, she almost had second thoughts, but she plowed ahead. "I'd like to introduce, or that is, to reintroduce, the Equal Rights Amendment. But I don't want to introduce it like it has been reintroduced before, as a resolution where it would go to committee as we have in every new session of Congress since 1982. I know that would be a nonstarter."

She smiled at her leader weakly. "No, ma'am, I want to introduce it on the floor and attach it to another bill of some kind as an amendment. My reasons are twofold: the first is a matter of justice. As we both know, women in this country are not equal. There are still many continuing areas of conflict such as equal pay and enforcement of laws that demand equality but must always be proved in court.

"The passing of the ERA would also be a godsend in developing countries in such areas as health, education, and economic development. If we do it with a splash here, it will encourage other countries to follow suit. I believe that the amendment would shine a light here into a dark corner that would help condemn the everyday violations of women's human rights in all countries. And what is better for them is also better for us. There would be more local employment, less undocumented migration, less unrest and worry about breeding terrorists, and more trade and prosperity. We both know the benefits could go far." Shiloh paused to see if her Leader had any questions.

She nodded for Shiloh to continue.

"There's another reason too. Women's equality is a fundamental human right. If we line up advocates, we may be able to move this issue while at the same time causing a good case of heartburn for our friends across the aisle and their supporters. Their own record on women's issues is atrocious. How would they answer this? More fundamentalist dogma I'm sure, more divisiveness too. But maybe we could fuel a fire this time.

"I have a plan to recruit strong allies. Perhaps we could even energize a new generation of young people who have never even heard of the ERA. From the little poll data I've seen, it looks like the amendment could resonate if people had enough information."

Shiloh saw her leader smiling. She couldn't tell if her smile was that of a seasoned member humoring a less experienced colleague or if it was a smile of acknowledgement and support.

Shiloh plowed on. "Both parties used to have the ERA in their platforms. But when Reagan came along in 1980, the Republicans dropped it to appease the fledgling right wing of their party. Our party still has it in our platform, and in every new session of Congress we are still trying to move it forward. But rather than trying to resuscitate the original, which is three states short of ratification, I would reintroduce it as a new constitutional amendment so that all the states and both parties are forced to deal with this issue again.

"I know that abortion and other issues will be raised," Shiloh continued, "but in states that have enacted their own ERA, the courts have ruled both ways on abortion restrictions. I would not envision introducing it with any special caveats. It will be about women's equal rights, pure and simple. It'll take a massive effort, but that's what I propose."

For the next ten minutes, Shiloh explained her plan to her leader. "What I need, Madame Leader, is your permission to go forward. I expect that it'll take the better part of two years to get ready."

The minority leader was still smiling when she spoke. "Shiloh, I like the idea. You should try it out. It would be nice to find something besides war to ignite this country, and this issue is way past due. The ERA is more distant today than at almost any time since its inception. It's been over a hundred years since this battle was first joined, over a hundred and fifty years if you include the struggle for suffrage. I hope you can get the money you need to pull this off. I may be able to help some if you get enough traction to get started. But otherwise, this will have to be your baby until you get further down the road. If you make progress, then we can bring together some of our colleagues and secure their support. Let's move on it, Shiloh. Keep me in the loop, and let me know when I can help."

Shiloh was overjoyed. "Thank you so much, ma'am. I'll do my best."

Shiloh felt a warm glow wash over her. She hugged her leader, wished her an early Christmas greeting, and rushed back to her office. It would take a lot of work: research, fundraising, organizing, meetings, and a solid PR plan. She knew that it would take commitments from folks she did not yet know to convince her other colleagues. Both Shiloh and the allies she hoped to find would need to prepare carefully to capture the hearts and minds of the American people. It couldn't be just a ploy. It would need to be a formidable effort to challenge their arrogant opponents and goad them into action and, perhaps, into mistakes.

She wanted to win. She wanted desperately to win. She realized ultimate victory would probably take time and another election or two. But if the ERA could become an issue of significance in the press and around the country, it would expose just how reactionary America had become and perhaps hasten the day when the electorate would come to their senses.

Shiloh was ecstatic when she returned to her office. She rushed in and hugged Seth. "We did it, darling! She says to go for it.

"Now what?" she said with a big smile.

"Now we do it."

"I'm so happy!" replied a giddy Shiloh. "You're so wonderful, dear. Now your work begins."

Seth wrapped his arms around Shiloh. "Yes, but it will be a labor of love."

* * * * *

Shortly after the New Year, Seth began working on a meeting with foundation representatives to seek funding for Shiloh's plan. He contacted foundation friends from Washington, California, Illinois, and New York and set up a meeting for early February. He had rented modest office space in downtown Washington DC, and he began to collect the names of the chairs of women's studies departments in colleges throughout the country, the next group on their list. Once that was done, he would prepare an outline for what they needed in the way of background information for the campaign.

The biggest task would be to set up the national support network, which was the linchpin of Shiloh's plan. Seth had started the legal process to set up a tax-exempt public affairs organization. It would, under his leadership, prepare advocacy materials, organize meetings with allies, and serve as a command center for the new ERA effort. They called the new NGO ERA Today.

They had to be careful not to have it in anyway identified as a lobbying organization. Then it would be required to pay taxes, which in turn would mean that tax-exempt foundations could not support them. Thus, ERA Today would concentrate on the nuts and bolts of organization and building public support, while Shiloh would worry about "lobbying" her colleagues. It was hairsplitting, but the kind of hairsplitting that was necessary if they were to succeed. They had to be totally legit to withstand the attacks they were sure would come if they began to make progress.

Seth found surprising enthusiasm among the foundations. All the foundations he invited to the first meeting had a history of supporting activities that promoted women's rights in the United States and in developing countries around the world. They didn't need to be sold on the why, just the how.

Shiloh's record was well-known and admired. A few of the foundation representatives even offered to find corporate support from business groups that also supported similar work internationally. Over the past several years, business groups and individual companies used an increasing amount of their philanthropic funds for supporting women's health and education in developing countries. Their reasoning was that if more women were educated and healthy, economies would grow, trade would increase, and everyone would prosper.

As Willie Brandt had said in 1980 when he led the Brandt Commission on Development, "If countries are trading and depending on each other for prosperity, they will be less likely to find a reason to go to war."

Many business leaders who had interests in developing countries and joint ventures were often repulsed by the socioeconomic conditions that they found. Of course, their shareholders wanted profits, but a growing number were beginning to feel the heat generated by media reports of unfair third world labor practices. The foundations agreed at their first meeting to go together on an initial five-million-dollar grant. They would meet again in the fall to evaluate how their money had been invested and how ERA Today was progressing. They appointed one member of their group to represent them on the planning committee that Seth was organizing.

Shiloh and Seth were thrilled, but both knew that with these generous grants, their time was now committed for the foreseeable future. That meant no vacations and not too many long weekends until they either won or lost the first round of votes in the House and the Senate. And then of course, if they somehow won the two-thirds vote needed in the House and Senate, it would be on to the states where three-fourths were needed to ratify a constitutional amendment.

Seth set about hiring a finance person, two writers, and a secretary. He made it clear that, although they had prepared job descriptions, they would all be expected to do anything and everything to make this effort succeed. He was careful to not only hire people with skills but also people who would work hard because they believed in the cause.

For their first assignment, Seth had his team start the process of reviewing and writing a history of the ERA, which ERA Today would produce as a brochure. They started with the first attempt that was written by Alice Paul in 1921, which was introduced in the House by Representative Anthony, Susan B. Anthony's nephew, and Senator Curtis in the Senate in 1923. It failed, only three short years after women had won the right to vote with the passage of the Nineteenth Amendment. This process repeated itself during every Congress for the next forty-nine years. It came close in the Senate in 1946 and was passed by the Senate in 1950, but with a rider that nullified the desired outcome.

The Senate had relied instead, without saying so of course, on the 1868 Fourteenth Amendment, which had in its second paragraph—the paragraph that determined the number of U.S. Representatives each state would have in Congress—the term "male citizens." This, in effect, excluded women from the landmark "equal protection clause" of the amendment. That was the first time that such a denial of women's rights was enshrined in the Constitution. The second time came two years later in the Fifteenth Amendment, which was passed in 1870, and gave "all men" the right to vote. It would take another fifty years before the Nineteenth Amendment gave the same right to women. The 1950 Senate vote acceded to the pressure to vote for an ERA while at the same time assuring that it would fail.

It was not until the National Organization for Women (NOW) was founded in 1967 that the ERA began to get wings. NOW worked tirelessly around the country educating women and in Washington enlightening Congress. In 1970, NOW disrupted the U.S. Senate Subcommittee on Constitutional Amendments, demanding that the ERA be debated by the entire Congress and not continue to be locked up in committee as had been the case for most of the past forty plus years. The U.S. House of Representatives finally passed the ERA Amendment in 1971 by a vote of 354 to 24, and in 1972, the amendment passed in the Senate by a vote of 84 to 8, but the Senate set a time limit of seven years for its ratification by the states.

Seth found the history of women's rights to be both fascinating and disgusting. He read that Abigail Adams asked her husband to include in the Constitution he was helping to write the phrase, "to put it out of power the vicious and lawless use of women with cruelty and indignity with impunity," as was allowed in English law. She also said, "In the new code, remember the ladies, and do not put such unlimited power into the hands of their husbands."

Adams wrote later, "We [men] know better than to repeal our masculine systems." Adams's assessment of masculine power was proved true in a 1977 rape study that found that, "All unequal power relationships must, in the end, rely on the threat or reality of violence to protect themselves."

Seth was confounded by what he read—especially the comment of Twiss Butler and Paula McKenzie in a NOW article discussing twenty-first century efforts to pass the ERA on the case that, "In a very real sense, then, the Equal Rights Amendment will rectify a profound constitutional imbalance that may promote violence against women."

It's hard to believe that this prejudice is so secure in the thinking of a nation that prides itself on its values of equality and justice, thought Seth as he worked away with his colleagues on the brochure.

He relayed his thoughts to Shiloh, who said, "I've always admired the brilliance and tenacity of our founding fathers. Too bad they didn't include a few founding mothers for the other half of their new country, whom they conveniently left out. But I guess they didn't do so well on slavery either, did they?"

* * * * *

Shiloh, on the other hand, was busy planning her first "disciples meeting," as she called the people she and Seth had set out to convince to join their effort. The couple was sitting at home having supper and discussing their work ahead. Seth laughed at her term, but cautioned her to not use such a word publicly.

"In these times of spin and feminist bigotry, we can't give someone a chance to say that we're creating a religion or tampering with theirs. Just imagine the headline: 'Congresswoman Priest Works to Destroy the Family by Founding an Antimale Religion.' That is how one of those rightwing fish wrappers would characterize what you're trying to do if you used a word like disciples, even jokingly."

Shiloh smiled, "Surely you jest." She paused. "No, on second thought, I guess you don't." She agreed to never use the word disciples. "We've got to win. We must begin to change this culture of fundamentalist babble."

"We really must," replied her husband. "Our side is hunkered down most of the time. We're letting it happen. You really need to get those mainline protestant sisters and brothers of yours on board. They need to take back tolerance, free speech, and decency."

"That won't be easy," exclaimed Shiloh. "We've all lived in our bunkers so long that we are in survival mode, just hoping that this cycle will eventually reverse itself. We're letting the neocons and fundamentalists run our government with their bigoted morals, while we behave like lemmings."

"Well," replied Seth, "this lemming needs to get some sleep. It's almost midnight, and I have to be at the office to rally my charges at 6:00 a.m. before I fly out to Bloomington, Illinois, to meet with the chair of the Women's Studies Department at Illinois State University. I'm hoping she will be our first college ally. She runs one of the top programs in the country and is a star in the field. We need her."

They were both exhausted.

Seth hugged Shiloh. "Sweetheart, we need to figure out a way to pace ourselves, or we'll burn out before we get started."

Shiloh looked him in the eyes. "No, we won't. We will never burn out. We have right on our side."

All he could think to say in response was, "Yes, ma'am."

They walked hand in hand to their bedroom. Tomorrow would be the first day of marketing their game plan to what they hoped would be eager conscripts.

* * * * *

The Ecumenical Women 2000 is an offshoot of the World Council of Churches. It was created in 1988 to advance the UN Decade for Women. The group represents multiple protestant denominations and ecumenical groups around the world who share a commitment to human rights, especially women's rights. Each one of the staffers in the group's small Washington office was a friend of Shiloh's. When she was first elected to Congress, the organization welcomed her in Washington. They still dropped by Shiloh's office to discuss women's issues with her. Ecumenical Women 2000's primary work focused on the UN and international bodies such as the Commission on the Status of Women and the Convention on the Elimination of All Forms of Discrimination against Women (CEDAW).

The United States had not ratified the CEDAW treaty since it was signed in 1979 and in that regard had joined such other states as Sudan, Somalia, Afghanistan, Qatar, and Iran. The United States would not mandate maternity leave as the treaty required or accept the comparable worth of women in the workplace, even though it had laws calling for equal pay for equal work. Thus, women might still be denied jobs that they were deemed "unworthy" of taking, even if they have the appropriate credentials.

To say that Ecumenical Women 2000 and Shiloh were on the same page would be an understatement. They were sisters cut from the same cloth, the cloth of human rights and equality. Shiloh could not understand how the United States, which, until the Iraq war, had been seen as the world's foremost human rights champion, had not signed the CEDAW. Nor could she understand why her country had not added the ERA to its constitution. Women's rights were contained in numerous UN pronouncements and documents, and several countries, including most industrial countries and U.S. allies, had their own versions of the Equal Rights Amendment. How could the United States preach women's rights and not pass its own ERA?

When Shiloh met with the Ecumenical Women 2000 leaders and explained her plan, she received their full support and a pledge from their members to support her efforts in their states and countries. They would be especially useful allies when she and Seth began the UN part of their plan. They offered to set up a meeting with the National Council of Women's Organizations and NOW, the two foremost champions of the ERA cause, to bring them on board.

There were some among the feminist movement who wanted to specifically include reproductive and homosexual rights into a new version of the ERA, but Shiloh thought that such a strategy was doomed. *If not the current ERA,* she thought, *how in the world could an expanded version hope to pass?* That would not pass any more than the National Right to Life Committee's language would. Even though the nation's largest prolife organization opposed the ERA, it did have language prepared that would forbid women's rights to abortion or abortion funding, just in case the amendment ever got legs again. The group had used this language successfully in states that were still trying to ratify the 1972 ERA.

These issues, Shiloh concluded, would have to be fought out state-by-state and case-by-case. Perhaps after the ERA was passed and ratified, another amendment could be offered, but first things first. Expanding the amendment was just not a pragmatic strategy. She realized the arguments against her position, that some states had their own equal rights amendments and still restricted abortion. But she viewed her strategy as the only viable way to go at this moment in time, especially since the New Mexico Supreme Court had ruled on the pro-choice side of the issue. First the ERA, then more could be considered later. Shiloh believed that the abuses women suffered every day in the workplace and from violence needed to be addressed first. The equality issue needed to be back on the national agenda before the nuances could be addressed.

Shiloh had joined many of her fellow members who'd passed a House resolution to call for Senate ratification of CEDAW on March 10, 1999, but sadly, to no avail. The Senate Foreign Relations Committee had voted to send the treaty out to the full Senate shortly before the Democrats lost the Senate to the Republicans in 2002. After that, the resolution was never brought to the floor; and Shiloh figured that, since it required a two-thirds vote, it would never be allowed by the fundamentalists anyway.

The battle was still being fought for the ERA. But its proponents were losing. The Senate-sponsored, seven-year congressional limit for ratification had been extended for three more years in 1978, which the Supreme Court upheld when it overruled a lower court that had earlier held that the congressional vote for a three-year extension had been unconstitutional. However, that extension was long past. As of today, the ERA remained three states short of ratification since its passage in both houses of Congress in 1972. And it had been reintroduced in Congress every session since 1982, the end of the congressional ratification period, and each time it had been locked up in committee.

Congressman Robert Andrews introduced his own resolution as a companion to the Maloney-Leach ERA resolution in 2003 at the beginning of the 108th Congress. The Andrews legislation was designed to nullify the ten-year window for state ratification that had been set by Congress when it extended by three years the original seven years allowed for ratification back when the ERA was passed originally in 1972. Most pro-ERA observers were worried about putting the question regarding the Congress applied ten-year ratification period for state ratification into the hands of the current conservative Supreme Court. Even though the constitution gives no set time for state ratification of constitutional amendments proposed by Congress, this court may have the votes to decide in favor of the original ten-year, congressional-imposed ratification time limit. This was another reason why Shiloh thought it best to start over by passing the original ERA again and then letting the states either ratify anew or pass legislation where it accepted previous ratification.

She had explained to Seth, "Starting over will also give us a chance to restate the issue of women's equality to new generations without worrying about the ten-year rule for state ratification, which would take away meaningful debate on the real issue."

"As usual, Shy, you're right. The hard way is the only way," Seth agreed.

Shiloh thought her way would be difficult, but it had a chance, especially if all of their preliminary work paid off with their prospective allies. She was delighted with the results of her meeting with Ecumenical 2000 and was anxious to learn of Seth's fate in Illinois.

* * * * *

Seth was impressed with Sally Cohen, the chair of the Women's Studies Department at ISU. She was articulate and obviously a doer. She had many plaques in her office attesting to her work in the area of women's rights.

"Dr. Cohen, it is a pleasure to meet you. Thank you for agreeing to see me."

"Sally please, Mr. Richards," answered Seth's interlocutor. "I'm enthralled by what you discussed in your letter. Do you really think we have a chance this time?"

"Please call me Seth, Sally. And yes, I think we do. But after I tell you what your part would be, you may show me the door."

"I doubt that," said Sally with an expectant smile. "And, by the way, I adore your wife. We discuss her sometimes in our classes when we look at contemporary women leaders. She is well-known among our students and admired by faculty members who know about her."

"Thank you, Sally. And since we are discussing reputations let me tell you straight out that we decided to contact you first because of your reputation and writings. I gave your article about the ERA in *The New Yorker* to the staff members of the small NGO we started as required reading."

Seth looked Sally straight in the eyes and started. "But let me cut to the chase. As I stated in my letter, Shy plans to introduce the ERA in the House, and a Senate colleague has agreed to do the same in the Senate. But unlike in past attempts, this time it will be attached to a bill as an amendment. In other words, it can't be sent off to committee to die from inaction. This time, it will have to be debated and voted up or down. That's where you come in. We want to form a special collegiate committee to help us plot strategy, and we want you to head it.

"Unfortunately, that is only the beginning. We want you to recommend nine other folks, regionally dispersed, who head departments like yours to join the committee."

"So far, so good, Seth, but I know there's more. How about some more coffee?"

Seth held out his coffee cup. "Please. I didn't get much sleep, and I had to get up in the middle of the night to stop by my office and get myself here through O'Hare. Anyway, our game plan depends on a lot of public education, some public affairs work with Congress, and maybe a bit of civil disobedience."

"Now I know I'm interested," deadpanned Sally.

"Good," continued Seth. "First, we want to organize at least five regional meetings of fifty colleges, each chaired by two of the chairs like yourself, two student leaders, and department heads from each school. During each of these two-day meetings, we'll explain our strategy and enlist support. Then you and your cochair and the two host chairs of the other four meetings would join a national planning committee that would include the heads of several feminist, advocacy, and service NGOs such as NOW, Ecumenical Women 2000, and several others. By then we also hope to have enlisted a few religious leaders and maybe even a few business leaders. We'll report on our work, plot strategy, and, hopefully, find the support and enthusiasm that will give Shiloh's colleagues the confidence to go forward. If all goes as planned, we'd hope for House and Senate action sometime in the fall of next year, before the election."

"That all sounds exciting," enthused Sally. "But you must know that college professors only have resources available for about two meetings per year and very little for students. Unfortunately, some colleges don't even have that."

"Sorry," Seth said with a smile. "I forgot to mention the good part. We have the funds for all of these meetings. As I said, we've set up a small NGO. It's called ERA Today, and it has a budget for all of the meetings that I've discussed and some funds for materials development, media work, and such as well. Several foundations joined forces and gave us a five-million-dollar grant, and more is promised if we get this little venture off the ground. And, while we do have paid staff at ERA Today, I'm not one of them. Shiloh and I will only pay for our travel from the grant. I recently retired and have a pension, plus I have a wife who keeps me in fishing lures and golf balls, neither of which I expect to enjoy for the next couple of years."

"I'm impressed," said Sally. "You can count me in. What are the rest of your plans?"

They talked for another hour and a half before Sally called a cab for Seth's trip back to the airport.

As he left her office, he smiled to himself. He couldn't believe how extraordinarily well that had gone. Now if only the rest of the process would go so smoothly.

* * * * *

Shiloh was waiting with a brick of sharp cheddar, crackers, olives, and chilled pinot grigio when Seth arrived at their townhouse that evening at ten o'clock.

"Wow," exclaimed Shiloh after hearing Seth's report, "you scored. Sally sounds wonderful. My day went well too with similar results."

They both worked very hard preparing for their first college meeting. Shiloh knew that Seth's team at ERA Today was in overdrive doing research, writing, designing pamphlets, and working on NGO contacts. As usual,

Shiloh was busy in Congress, and also as usual, she went back to her district every other weekend. Seth went with her once a month. They talked ERA on most nights, and Seth always got Shiloh's clearance on everything that he and his team were doing. It made her feel good to know that she had his support.

They would begin the college meetings in May before professors and students scattered for the summer. The Ecumenical Women 2000 developed an impressive list of potential NGO supporters that were added to the ERA Today list and reported that their member churches were eager to help. They even lined up a few notable religious leaders who were willing to be quoted.

In April, on a trip to Nashville, they drove to Tullahoma to talk with Barry about enlisting some of his former governor pals and any others he thought would help. He agreed to sign a letter for ERA Today when they got closer to D-day.

The trick would be to get all of this moving and then connect it to Shiloh's legislation when the time was right. The planning committee of leaders included the ten college professors led by Sally Cohen, ten NGO leaders, and the Ecumenical Women 2000.

* * * * *

In the meantime, Madame Congresswoman and Mr. Richards were enjoying a permanent honeymoon. She didn't know if they were making up for lost time or they were trying to make a basketball team of children. Their time together centered around two issues: the ERA and their constant love affair. She was so in love. They seemed to laugh most of the time they were together. She was happier than she'd ever imagined was possible. They were lovers, best friends, and totally relaxed together.

Shiloh snuggled up next to Seth. "Rather than lament about not finding you years ago, darling," said Shiloh. "I plan to use every minute we have together to enjoy what I've found.

Seth smiled at her. "Me too, sweetie, me too."

Chapter 10

Seth worked day and night with his small team to prepare materials. NOW had a treasure trove of historical materials and remained active in the quest for the ERA. Over the rest of the first year, Seth and his team attended the meetings of many of the college groups. Almost all of the 250 colleges had held successful meetings and had set up committees to plan events such as ERA days on campus, which included passing out materials at such venues as the student union and sporting events and putting up posters that had been designed by ERA Today.

Most of the colleges held or had plans to hold special ERA workshops, where they invited the member of Congress who represented the district where their college was located to speak about his or her position on the ERA. They also held ERA events where they invited professors from sociology, political science, anthropology, education, public health and health education, economics, history, and, of course, women's study departments. They were asked to lecture on women's rights, the ERA, women's health and education, international development, terrorism, trade, and other subjects relating to women and women's participation in society. There was a new buzz growing on campuses around the country.

The Ecumenical Women 2000 and NOW helped organize an NGO meeting for the winter, just after New Years. Shiloh and Seth had met again with the foundations in September and received a fresh infusion of cash. The foundation representatives were delighted with their progress. The representative that they had selected to join the ERA Today planning committee was even more effusive than Seth.

In October, they held the first meeting of the full ERA Committee in Washington DC, which included the ten regional faculty chairs and two student representatives of the five colleges that had hosted the five regional meetings, the Ecumenical 2000 group, NOW, and the foundation representative.

Seth was pleased with the good start. Now the hard part would come: bringing in NGOs from around the world and beginning discussions with governments from every region of the world. They held the NGO meeting at the Capitol Hilton in January. It included representatives of Ecumenical 2000, NOW, Sally Cohen representing the colleges, and ten carefully selected American NGOs, which met on day one in a small meeting room. The next day, they met in a large room with a group that included ten NGO representatives from each of the world's five regions: Asia, Africa, Europe, the Arab States, and the rest of the Americas. The Americas actually had twenty representatives, which included ten from the United States and ten from Canada and Latin America. Seth knew that the United States would be key, since that was the place where it would all begin.

On day one of the meeting, Seth and the leaders of Ecumenical Women 2000 and NOW sat at one end of the table with Sally and went through the agenda. Sally summarized the college report and Seth discussed plans for day two. The NOW representative gave a brief history of the ERA in the United States and referred to the packet of materials that had been prepared by ERA Today, much of which had relied on NOW materials and research. She suggested a strategy that the group could consider to get the word out in the United States, including a meeting in June when they would invite hundreds of NGO representatives from around the United States to meet with their senators and representatives to discuss women's rights, work on op-eds for local newspapers on the same subject, and organize a march in Washington after the ERA was introduced in the fall to demand that the ERA be passed by Congress.

The Ecumenical Women 2000 representative informed the group that her organization would hold a meeting with state representatives of the religious and other organizations that sponsored their organization and work, and that their group would also meet with their senators and Representatives and bring members from the states to join the fall march. They were presently working with ERA Today to develop materials that could be passed out in churches and other venues throughout the country and would join NGOs in coordinating op-eds.

"So far, so good," Seth had told Shiloh when she arrived home that evening. "Everyone seems excited. There wasn't a naysayer in the crowd—nothing but enthusiasm."

"You're doing all the work, Seth. When I told you that day a year and a half ago in New York about my dream, how did I ever think that I could have organized something like this? Without you I'd still be at the thinking stage." Shiloh reached for Seth's hand.

Seth smiled. "Without you telling me your dream, I'd still be a bureaucrat in New York."

* * * * *

The next day, the presence of the fifty other NGOs from around the world created an air of excitement.

Seth opened the meeting. "Friends, it's good to see all of you here today in frigid Washington. I expect the weather to be warmer for our next meeting. I hope all of you who are from warmer climes have warm coats."

There were polite chuckles. Seth knew that the folks who had not seen Shiloh were eager to see the lady from Tennessee who fought so hard for women's rights. Seth's run-in with Lawson had made the news around the world and had prompted replays of the Giles-Skyler affair that had catapulted Shiloh to her seat in Congress. He smiled. Today they got them both. Seth was at the head table representing ERA Today with Shiloh and other members of the planning committee.

"Not a bad first family," Seth overheard one of the Canadians whisper. "She would make a great president."

After finishing his housekeeping chores regarding the agenda, travel claims, and such, Seth introduced his wife. Shiloh stepped up to the podium and thanked Seth and then thanked the audience for their attendance.

She began, "Today, my friends, we are discussing a topic that is important to all of us and to the countries and regions we represent. Some of our colleagues here today, especially our friends from Europe and a few others are from countries where equal rights for women is already law and close to reality in practice. They can teach the rest of us much about how to win the battle for gender equality.

"Here in the United States, we have come a long way, but we aren't there yet. Fundamentalists in this country, as well as fundamentalists in many of your countries, demand the status quo. Some even want to go backward. It makes no sense not to move forward. It makes no sense to bide our time and wait. We have waited too long. It is time now to act.

"We have made progress for sure, especially with the great UN conferences of the 1990s. Women's rights were addressed in many of the documents produced by those conferences and were addressed again in the

UN's Millennium Development Goals. These victories, I am sad to say, are today, under the current administration, opposed by my own country.

"We are left in this country and in many others with the sad reality that much work is still to be done. While this issue has been successfully addressed at the international level, there are no teeth that require enforcement. There is nothing in any of these consensus conference documents that orders enactment. Poverty is the major goal of the Millennium Development Goals, and gender equality is a requisite requirement, like AIDS treatment and prevention and universal education. But how will it happen without accountability?"

Seth smiled. She was off to a great start.

"Have we seen noticeable improvements?" Shiloh continued. "A few but, not many. We have succeeded to get women's equality in many documents now, but there are no new proclamations out there that take the form of law. All of these documents are based on the good will of the signatory countries. Well, my friends, can you take a good, strong dose of good will to a bank and get a loan for a home or a business idea or a new car? No, you need collateral. In this case, collateral mean laws and policies that require gender equality.

"Let me discuss my own country for a moment. The United States is the world's strongest nation: militarily it is the strongest; economically it is the strongest; and it has been, in the past, a leader in issues relating to human rights and development. It was a valiant supporter of women's rights in all of the major UN development conferences. It did that without its own ERA for women. And without the ERA in this country, inequality abounds.

"And now, as many of you know from firsthand experience, its overseas aid policy is essentially reneging on its past international support for women's rights."

Seth looked around the room. Everyone seemed to be nodding his or her head in agreement.

Shiloh pressed on. "The United States has been generous recently with money to address the AIDS crisis, which is good, yet it pushes abstinence to the point of discouraging condom use to prevent AIDS. The rules are confusing, and programs for such things as mother-to-child prevention are cut back so enough money is available to meet the percentages devoted to abstinence-only programs. And who suffers most from this policy? Women. We do not adequately fund any foreign aid item based on our ability and our pledges."

"In the area of population assistance, which includes reproductive health—that is, family planning and maternal health care during pregnancy, including ensuring safe deliveries—the United States is a miser and dead last in terms of percentage of gross domestic product. Plus, it does not support the largest NGO in the world in that field or the largest multilateral organization due to fundamentalist pressures at home. Who pays the price for this? Yes, of course, women."

Shiloh had reached her stride, and Seth could tell she was enjoying herself.

"Regarding the ERA," she said, "it was well on the way to passage when the right wing in this country began a campaign that convinced our citizens that women's rights would destroy the family, force women and men to share public bathrooms, increase abortion, promote homosexuality, and take jobs away from men who must support their families.

"Unbelievably, some men in the U.S. Congress even attempted to approve Viagra for servicemen, while at the same time denying contraception for women in the military. My country is one of only a few that has not yet signed CEDAW.

"A clear example of our situation came in a 1983 argument before the Supreme Court when a Justice Department lawyer argued that a college ban on interracial dating violated the Fourteenth Amendment. The Fourteenth Amendment is an amendment to our constitution that supposedly grants equal protection and rights to all citizens. Yet, when a justice asked the attorney for the Justice Department if his argument applied to sex as well, the lawyer said, 'No, we did not fight a civil war over sex discrimination, and we did not pass a constitutional amendment against it.'

"Within the U.S. court system, women always have to prove their rights. With an ERA, that would not be necessary.

"In some of your countries, culture dictates principles that are violations of human rights, such as female genital mutilation, honor killing, and bride burning, even though they are against the law in most countries. Some even have rape laws that place the onus on women to prove the crime with a certain number of male witnesses. Sex trafficking is common, where parents sell their children for economic gain. And women's health, especially maternal health, is largely either ignored or given little importance in health budgets. We all know the consequences for women. And donor countries, even those with ERA laws, still make women's health last or almost last in their foreign aid budgets. That's where goodwill gets you. We need laws, and we need to foster an understanding that women's rights are not only essential for human development, they are ethically and morally proper."

There was a murmur among the crowd as many added their own commentary on the situation. *This couldn't be going any better*, Seth thought.

Shiloh's eyes traveled around the crowded room. Standing tall in her light gray suit, she took a glass of water from a glass stored under the lectern and continued, her voice strong and clear.

"In my country, individual behavior and social practices such as forced sexual relations in marriage, women being denied equality in sports and in certain jobs, and sexual harassment are illegal, but they are in fact practiced because there is not a constitutional provision that forbids it under any and all circumstances. In other words, it is tolerated by tradition.

"A woman is abused every six seconds in my country. Two women are killed in the United Kingdom each week by someone they know. Violence reaches one in three women, and one in five suffers rape or attempted rape in their lifetimes. The list of female abuse and inequality around the world is endless. There is not a universal cultural value that says women are equal under all circumstances. The ERA for women in all of our countries is the first step.

"It's time we change this system. It's time we change the law. Then with the enforcement of the law, we'll change practices. If that means changing culture, then we change culture. If that means changing tradition, then we change tradition. Women must be equal in all aspects of life."

"This will not change biology, it will not change motherhood, and it will not change chivalry. Seth will still open the door for me, won't you, dear?"

Seth nodded with a smile that provoked laughter.

"We will still be ladies and gentlemen. That has nothing to do with the gender roles we take regarding the upbringing of children, who cooks, and who mows the lawn or tends the fields. Couples will figure out these things as they do now. They will share the work and the benefits of their work. This has to do with equality: equality socially, economically, and politically. A 1977 rape study in my country found that 'all unequal relationships must, in the end, rely on the threat or reality of violence to protect themselves.'

"My friends, imagine if that violence was illegal, not just figuratively but also literally. Imagine if women were equal to men in all respects.

"It is our mission to throw out inequality globally. We can only do this if we stay the course. Many are fighting this fight daily. Many organizations fight for these rights, even if that is not their professed mandate. And NOW, an organization that has been harshly maligned by fundamentalists in my country, fights for the ERA every minute of every day.

"Our plan is simple. We will enact women's equality in all countries. Carrying out our plan is, of course, a bit more complicated."

Laughter and scattered applause filled the room.

"My friends," Shiloh said, "we will discuss the how for much of today and, hopefully, go forward with a strong commitment and a full understanding that we can make this happen together. We will help each other and enroll our sisters and brothers around the world to make equality for women a reality.

"Women do not wish to be superior; we do not wish for any more than our God-given abilities will allow us to achieve. All we want is a chance to live in peace and to do so with equality for all of humankind."

The crowd gave Shiloh a standing ovation.

The rest of the day included regional planning meetings to discuss the strategy that ERA Today had prepared. In the afternoon, each region reported back with their plan for moving forward. Seth told the group that ERA Today would translate all the materials that it had prepared into all the necessary languages and send out reports and educational materials to all regions and countries soon. He also said that his organization would serve as a clearinghouse. Finally, he pledged to put together an electronic newsletter to share information and asked if they would all e-mail their local news items to him for inclusion.

That evening there was a reception that included the House minority leader and her leadership team along with a few coconspirators from the Senate.

The minority leader took Shiloh aside. "I'm enthusiastic, Shy. You and Seth have done a great job getting this thing moving. We may actually be able to make it go somewhere. You know, of course, that word is beginning to get out around Congress."

"Yes, I do," answered Shy, "but I don't think that anyone knows our full plans. Do you think that they will come after us or wait until we fire the first volley?"

The minority leader frowned. "I'm not sure. They aren't known for their patience. I don't expect that it'll be long before our friends get restless. On the other hand, they are nothing if not cocky and overconfident."

Chapter 11

Seth went to New York to meet his old friends among the UN delegations. He had meetings set for three days, mainly with the donors group, which includes the Western Europeans, Japan, South Korea (ROK), New Zealand, Australia, and Canada. They were the ones with foreign aid programs. He excluded the United States because it had disavowed many key international agreements such as the 1994 population conference where Vice President Al Gore had led the U.S. delegation, the 1995 women's conference where First Lady Hillary Clinton had led the U.S. delegation, and many other global meetings. He also scheduled meetings with the representatives of each developing country group, namely the Africa Group, the Latin American Group, the Arab States Group, and the Asia Group. He didn't invite certain countries such as Sudan, Libya, Malta, Iran, and El Salvador because they had joined the United States in attempts to backtrack on global agreements regarding women and women's health.

Seth was liked and respected by the delegates. He had known many of them for years. The meetings were informal and friendly. Seth explained what he was working on, and the agreement from all groups was quick and enthusiastic.

The big meeting for Seth was his special meeting with the Dutch and Brits. They met for lunch at the Dutch Mission on Forty-fifth Street. Seth had talked with them briefly on the previous day after the donor country group meeting. Both representatives indicated that they thought they could do what he had asked but would have to check with The Hague and London to get permission from their foreign ministries.

As soon as Seth arrived, he was shown to the conference room where his Dutch and British friends were waiting. When he walked into the room, they all gave him a thumbs-up. They spoke off the record as friends, not as diplomats.

"We got the go ahead," the Brit exclaimed.

"Yes, indeed. We are on the way," added one of the Dutch participants.

"Great," replied Seth. "No worries about the wrath of my president, huh?"

The Brit spoke first. He was uncharacteristically frank. "Actually, we think that the Queen's government has given your president quite enough. We will not compromise on your domestic fundamentalism. Your country is the opposite of the country we have negotiated with on these issues since the 1968 Human Rights Conference. Our policies could not be any more different than yours."

"So," Seth queried, "you'll introduce it in the Third Committee in September as we discussed?"

"Yes," said the Dutchwoman, "and we'll try to get it to the General Assembly by early October. At least it will probably be in the press by then. Our minister wants to introduce it himself."

"And after that," the British man remarked, "we believe we can carry the day unless the U.S. gets nasty and threatens the poor countries, as your country has in the past. It can instruct its ambassadors to present démarches to withdraw aid and trade and who knows what. We won't do that of course, but we will, I believe, succeed on the merits as we have the past few years when you Americans tried to backtrack on language that you had originally supported."

"Terrific," enthused Seth. "You guys are great. Hopefully we can actually get my country and many others to pay attention this time."

They talked about strategy. Seth reported to them that many European NGOs were developing plans for a massive demonstration in Brussels, the home of the European Union, when the international version of the ERA went to the General Assembly. Seth also filled them in on the preliminary plans for other regions.

After they finished with business, they talked about how much the United States had hurt its image in the UN and around the world with its we-are-right-and-the-world-is-wrong attitude.

"It's really a sea change globally," said the woman from Holland. "Before, we all worked with the United States, not just because of their strength, but also because they were right. But now, even though they bully us and especially the poor countries, many are flipping them the bird. It's just too much: no compromise, no diplomacy. It is getting worse every day, ever since you left."

"I know," agreed Seth. "I could feel it when I traveled. Every place I go, people ask me what's wrong with my country. Why is it so belligerent? What could I say? One minister of a country that is a close ally with the U.S. told me, 'Your country has lost all pretense of diplomacy. We can't afford to have a public argument with them, but we catch hell from voters every time we agree with the U.S., even about things we support, including the war on terrorism.'

"He said that they get letters from citizens that say to hell with the U.S.: its war in Iraq; its lack of respect for the environment; the peanuts it appropriates for international development; its stupid, counterproductive rules about condoms for AIDS. Why do we have diplomatic relations with a country that tortures people and tries to push its religion with its foreign aid? The minister was irate. He said that the United States is even trying to interfere with the European Union on religious matters."

"Well," said the Brit. "You can imagine how much our citizens are raising hell. If the Tories had an ounce of charisma, our PM would be history. But he has been fairly good domestically and on foreign aid, which we believe that it is essential for development. It helps combat terrorism, and of course, it is morally appropriate."

They continued their discussion for another hour before Seth left for another meeting.

Seth couldn't wait to tell Shiloh about his successful three days. But as he sat in the shuttle, his thoughts were more on his country than on the ERA. He was sad for America. No one loved his country more than he did.

He had heard all the criticism of the United States before and agreed with much of it, but it seemed to get worse every day. There was so much more vitriol now.

The United States was described in terms reserved for school yard bullies. Its traditional friends and allies were plenty angry and overwhelmingly disappointed. These countries believed in multilateralism and global problem solving. The cold war was over. Why couldn't the United States join them in building a better world? The United States had spent fifty years fighting the cold war and building an inclusive foreign policy. Now his country seemed like the proverbial rotten apple in the barrel.

Seth was so deep in thought that he didn't realize that his plane was landing; he jumped when the wheels of his Delta 727 Shuttle touched down on the Reagan International tarmac.

He called Shiloh at home, but there was no answer. He called her office to discover that she was still there.

"What's happening, babe?" Seth inquired jauntily.

"Hi, sweetie, it's nice to hear your voice. Have you landed?"

"I'm in a taxi. Shall I swing by and pick you up?"

"No, not just yet, Seth. I need a bit more time, but I'll get home as soon as I can." Shiloh's voice sounded forced.

"Okay, is everything all right?" Seth could hear the stress in her voice.

"I think so. I'll let you know soon. I have some computer problems, and I need to see it through so I can understand what happened. It shouldn't be too long."

"Fine, darling. I'll rustle up some chow for supper and test a bottle of wine to see if it is suitable for congressional consumption."

Shiloh laughed. "You know how to hurry me, don't you? I'll hustle. I can't wait to see you."

* * * * *

It had been 7:45 p.m. when Seth had called. Shy didn't get home until 10:20. She hugged her husband and gave him a warm and affectionate kiss when he met her at the door.

"What is it, dear?" he asked. "You sounded tense when we spoke earlier. Is the majority leader making your life miserable again?"

"Let me get out of these clothes first and get a sip of wine."

"Fine," said Seth, "I'll pour you a glass and take some food into the living room where we can relax."

Shiloh arrived in the living room wearing an old Sewanee sweatshirt and cutoff jeans. "That shower perked me up, and even more helpful was that glass of wine the tooth fairy left on my dresser." She gave Seth another kiss and dug into the food he had placed on the coffee table. "Lawson somehow got into my computer. I was with a team of computer folks from special services trying to sort it all out."

"What?" Seth said a bit louder than he meant to. "You mean he tapped into your system? The U.S. government's system?"

"I'm afraid so. I got an awful call from him today."

"But that doesn't mean that he messed with your computer, does it? Your e-mail address isn't difficult to figure out. It is probably published somewhere, and your general office e-mail is in the congressional handbook."

"No, you don't understand. I get e-mails from constituents almost every day, although the general office e-mail gets most of them. No, Lawson somehow, probably with the support of computer experts according to our experts, installed spyware on my computer. Unfortunately, that can be done from afar. Thus he can read all of my mail."

"Damn," growled Seth. "Isn't that illegal? Can't you prosecute him?"

"Well, yes and no; it's hard to prove that he has done anything. Our system isn't quite that sophisticated. We have firewalls, but every day a better spy system is invented. The computer folks are still at my office working on it on-site and are connected back to their own offices where they are trying to eliminate the problem by cleaning the system, but it wasn't working when I left. In the meantime, they'll give me another computer and keep working on the hard drive of the old one."

"It's unbelievable that anyone can do that."

"Yes, Seth, it is. The FBI will warn him, but there isn't much they can do beyond that."

"What did he say?" inquired Seth.

"He was terrible, Seth. It went something like this: 'Hello, Catherine Shiloh Giles. I would recognize your baby killer voice anywhere. I have news for you, Miss Congresswoman. Sally Cohen, your Illinois ally for that little scheme you are working on is a whore. She has blasphemed God and tried just like you to subvert young women. She tells them that they are equal to men and that they can do anything they want. And what would that be? What, Miss Shiloh? Lesbians and whores?' His voice was so creepy, Seth.

"I responded by saying something like. 'Reverend Lawson, how do you know Ms. Cohen? What are you talking about?'

"He then said, 'You are so evil, Miss Shiloh, so evil, but I found you out. I know exactly what you're doing and now you will be stopped. I'll stop you, Miss Shiloh, because I have all your e-mail, every bit of it. It was easy.'

"I must admit that I stammered then. My mind was racing, thinking about the ERA e-mails and what he might do. I said, 'I don't know if you do or you don't, Reverend Lawson, but I can tell you that if you do, you have committed a federal offense and can go to jail.

"He said, 'Don't try to bluff me, pretty lady. You know I have you. Or do you want me to name the foundations that gave you money or maybe the churches that are involved with your little scheme?'

"I called Sarah on my cell phone and held my hand over the receiver and told her to come to my office. Then I wrote a note for her to call the computer folks immediately and that our system had been compromised. Then I went back to Lawson.

'Reverend Lawson, I must say you are clever, but what will you get out of this? Why do you hate me? Why do you have such contempt for women?'

"You should have heard his response. Then he said, 'Well, Miss Congresswoman, as a student of the Bible, surely you have read Leviticus and Deuteronomy. They spell out clearly women's roles, now don't they? It's too bad you were born a woman, but that's the way it is. God has a plan, and I'm following it. You're not part of his plan, and your life will guarantee that you'll never meet God or his beloved son. You, Miss Shiloh, are going to hell. You see, God made woman for man, but you have to be obedient and deserving.'

"That was enough for me. I just said, 'Thank you for the lesson, Reverend Lawson. I'm going now.'

"Then I hung up, and I was almost sick to my stomach. He was just so nasty, Seth, so scary."

Seth leaned over and hugged her. "Does the Bible say all that stuff, darling?" inquired Seth.

Shiloh grimaced. "There are some pretty nasty passages in the Bible about women. There are some about the subservience of women—burning your daughter, cutting off a woman's hand—some about women being inferior—that women should be silent, that girl babies are less valuable than boys and so forth. The Bible has some unbelievably bad passages. The sad fact is that many of these folks like Lawson think that way, literally. If the Bible says it, well, that's the way it is. This is the twenty-first century, and they are still living in BC."

"How do you answer such things?" asked Seth.

"Biblical historians agree that, in the times the Bible was chronicled, culture was such that women were not much more than chattel. In its extreme cases, it could be equated to the Taliban today. And of course, men wrote the Bible. In defense of women, scholars point to Genesis where God made humankind, male and female, in his own image.

"But the most salient arguments are the works and words of Jesus. Jesus never condemned or criticized women. He revered his mother, and there were women among his followers whom he talked with and consulted.

"He saved the woman who was about to be stoned for adultery with the famous, 'Let thou who is without sin cast the first stone.' Another example is the Samaritan woman that Jesus spoke to at Jacob's well. First, she was a woman, and second, her tribe, the Samaritans, was enemies of the Jews. Yet Jesus spoke to her respectfully. He told her that if she drank water from the well, she would still be thirsty, but if she drank of the water he offered, she would never thirst again. He went on to instruct her to go forth and spread his word among her own people. In essence, he made her a minister of his gospel.

"This argument can go on forever, and unfortunately, it has. The issue is more a question of culture than of religion, although the interpretation of religion and its refinement over time is the basis for the cultural arguments. Women would never vote, lead, or be anything but slaves if you listened to some of today's fundamentalists who believe only in strict interpretation. Of course, anyone can cherry-pick from the Bible to espouse whatever he or she wants.

"The bottom line is that Lawson seems to have a messiah complex. He would be an interesting study if he weren't so scary. He was probably influenced by his father, who at one time was a fairly well-known preacher who attracted a great number of devoted followers. Bill Jacobson actually met him a couple of times. And I've told you before about the president of his college who is of course well-known nationally.

"The results of the influence of the two men are not good. He's so focused on the bad in the world and vengeance that he can't see the good in people or his role to nurture the goodness out of those who, in his eyes, are bad. Who knows what he'll do next? What's so sad is that Jesus was such a kind and compassionate man. He tried to enlighten people, not frighten them to death," continued Shiloh.

"Don't worry," Seth tried to ease the tension. "We're doing well. They'll fix your computer, and we can ignore ole James Robert Lawson II."

"I know, Seth, but he is so spooky, so evil. Just imagine if his kind really took over."

"They won't. Their talk is beginning to wear thin. It'll take awhile, but I sincerely believe that we will eventually prevail. I have faith that we're on the right path, Shy. I just wish it weren't so painfully slow. When you're president dear, the world will really make headway."

Shy laughed. "No more wine for you."

Seth told Shy about his New York trip and the warm reception he'd received, which greatly improved her mood. They sat in the living room talking until almost 1:00 a.m. before going to bed.

When Seth came back from the bathroom, he reached over and held Shy's hand and was about to kiss her good night when he realized that she was sound asleep. He smiled and lay back on his own pillow, but sleep didn't come.

Seth lay in bed worrying about the enormity of trying to pull off the ERA and the millions of things that they still had to do. He also thought about Lawson. Once again he was angry for allowing himself the pleasure of breaking the SOB's jaw. He knew it was legal in strict terms, but it hadn't been the best decision.

Yet in his heart of hearts, he had taken immense pleasure in bopping Lawson. He had heard so much about him so often that he felt deep inside that Lawson had to be dealt with, and his alpha side couldn't handle just standing there.

Yes, he thought, *I was being protective, but most of all I wanted to rid Shiloh of this constant menace.* If he had learned anything living with her, it was that violence is not the way to solve problems. *Damn fool*, he thought. *Brawn over brain. Macho over reason.*

Yes, indeed, it is time for the ERA and for men to be real men rather than simpleminded macho bullies—me included, he thought, as he scrunched his pillow and rolled over for the umpteenth time.

* * * * *

The next day, Saturday, Shiloh notified the minority leader and all of her relevant contacts including the Ecumenical Women and NOW about the computer problem and the fact that the ERA plans were in the hands of their opponents. Seth notified the NGOs, his UN delegation friends, and the college groups.

Shiloh and Seth met later and drove to Cape May, New Jersey, to spend the weekend with Sam and Barbara. It was good to unwind with them and get away from Washington, if only for thirty-six hours or so. Although both were worried about the computer episode, they vowed during their drive to Cape May not to let it interfere with their weekend. There was plenty of time for that later.

The two couples were the only guests in a charming bed-and-breakfast. In Cape May, it seemed that every house was a bed-and-breakfast. Each was brightly painted and well appointed. It was a wonderful place to get away and forget the world, especially in the off-season when few tourists were around. They had agreed, at least for Saturday, not to discuss anything that had to do with politics, the ERA, or any other issue that would remind them of the real world. Sam had said that he would abstain from such talk on Saturday but that he and Barbara both wanted to get caught up over breakfast.

The men talked about the recently completed NCAA basketball tournament, while Shiloh and Barbara discussed the kids, who were now in their freshman and junior years of college. It felt good to walk on the beach. The weather was cool and the sea breeze constant, but the sky was bright blue. They loved being outdoors and together. They shared a bucket of steamers at a cozy beach restaurant and drank warm cider. By evening, they were back at their bed-and-breakfast, where their hosts had prepared baked scrod in a dill sauce with red potatoes and an endive salad. Dessert was peach cobbler topped with homemade vanilla ice cream. That evening they sat by the wood fire in the living room and enjoyed Irish coffee. They were warm, relaxed, and comfortable. It felt to Shiloh that the ERA and Washington were a million miles away.

As they sat drinking their coffee, Sam told a story about a divorce case he was working on that involved abuse of the woman by an alcoholic husband.

The woman had called the police three times, but they'd only come once, and even then, the woman thought they took the man's side.

"It's often difficult for women to get a fair hearing in these matters, which is one of the many reasons I hope you succeed with the ERA," Sam said. "I know that I'm not supposed to mention that subject until tomorrow, but I see the need every day …"

All of a sudden, Sam stopped. "You're crying, Shy. I'm sorry. I didn't mean to upset you."

"It's okay. I was just remembering things that happened in our family long, long ago."

"I'm sorry. I'm reminded all the time of Mom and Dad when I do divorces. I didn't know that it still bothered you so much."

"It didn't until recently, as I've become more and more involved in the ERA. I hear so many stories now and see the need for the ERA in just about every part of life. But mostly, Sam, I'm reminded of your courage when we went through the divorce. You helped me so much."

Thankfully intent on keeping the evening light, Sam changed the subject. "So, who wants another drink?" he asked, patting Seth on the shoulder. Then turning to Shiloh, he asked, "So, Shy, where did you find this turkey anyway?"

Barbara replied quickly, "How about a hot chocolate before bed? They left some in a thermos over on the sideboard."

Barbara and Seth served, as talk turned to the Yankees.

The next morning, Shiloh and Seth brought Sam and Barbara up to date on the ERA.

Sam said, "Let me know if there's anything I can do. I'm with you 100 percent."

"Me too," added Barbara, "and both kids want to help on campus."

They parted after a wonderful brunch, vowing to get together again for a weekend that included a Yankee game.

* * * * *

Lawson had immediately alerted his mentor in Virginia about ERA Today and the plans that were being cooked up by Representative Catherine Shiloh Giles. He sent him several of Shiloh's e-mails and told his mentor that they needed to move quickly. "This Giles woman is smart and popular," he had said.

Lawson was pleased that his mentor agreed that this ungodly effort must be stopped ASAP. He felt like he had finally done something significant, something that made his mentor proud. He had been irritated when his mentor had scolded him for talking to Shiloh and alerting her that he had pirated her plans.

The mentor told Lawson he was both worried and pleased with this news—worried because it seemed to be a well-thought-out strategy, which he hadn't seen from his leftie opponents before, but pleased because they had plenty of time to head it off. He told Lawson he was nothing if not confident, both in his abilities and in the mood of the country. We have come to a place, he said, where our work is paying great dividends. The other side is afraid of us. Every time they speak out, they get blasted. Our forces are strong now, much stronger than in the early days of the Moral Majority. We have television, we have radio, we have universities, and we have slowly but surely built a strong political base.

When his mentor had started talking about the future, Lawson had tuned him out. Lawson didn't see or care about the big picture. All he cared about was stopping his beautiful nemesis. She tormented him with her grace and beauty. The people in her district were under her spell, and as long as she was in Congress, she would lead the people away from God's teachings.

I'll get her now, he thought, *I'll get her now*. He imagined how much he would enjoy his carnal sin that night as he once again fantasized about Miss Shiloh.

* * * * *

"Yes, indeed," the mentor had said, smiling to himself as he spoke to his pupil. "We will smite the perverts, the homos, the bleeding heart liberals, the unchaste, and the proud and disrespectful women like this Giles woman."

Yes, he thought. *We shall prevail. And I will be the one to lead us.* He was as proud as a peacock that he would be the one who would tell the others. Once again, he would be the champion of the right.

* * * * *

A meeting was arranged for two weeks hence, in early April, with several of the mentor's nationally-known colleagues, including the woman who was credited with stopping the ERA just three states short of ratification in the 1970s. The meeting was held in the White House with the president's chief of staff and his political guru and strategist. There were handshakes, hugs, and backslaps all around. Even though White House time is measured in minutes, they spent time inquiring about health and family and talking over days gone by, including battles won and lost, lately mostly won. They were a formidable group.

The guru chaired and asked the mentor to "fill us in."

"Well, my friends, just when we thought we had them on the run, they up and get bold."

The guru smiled. "I see you don't read the papers or the polls, if you think we have anyone on the run."

The mentor brushed him off. "Yes, brother, I know what you mean, but in the social arena, we're on solid ground. Just look at what that wonderful legislature in South Dakota has accomplished just last month by formally outlawing all abortion in their state, which will likely force the Supreme Court to reconsider *Roe v. Wade*. We may not win this time, but with another good appointment to the court, we almost surely will. Other states will follow South Dakota. We're winning, brother. And as for the other issues, I know that you'll find a way to prevail there too."

"I hope so," said the guru, again smiling.

"My friends, some of the heavyweight liberal foundations are financing another ERA effort. They seem to be aiming, not only at this country, but at the rest of the world as well, through the UN. They have set up an NGO headed by a UN retiree who is married to a congresswoman from Tennessee, Catherine Shiloh Giles."

"Yes, I've heard of her," said the chief.

"She appears to be quite talented. Is anyone running against her?" asked the guru.

"No," said the mentor. "An exuberant graduate of mine ran in her maiden election and didn't do very well with his campaign or at the polls. Since then, except for the last election, she has been unopposed. She won 67 percent of the vote in a fairly well-contested race."

"Maybe we can do something about that," said the guru.

"No, I believe that it's too late to qualify; the deadline for filing is tomorrow, April 6," advised the mentor.

"There are other ways," offered the guru. "Let me think about it. Please continue, sir."

"Well," said the mentor, "they seem to be working with religious groups, some of the women associated with the so-called mainline Protestants, and of course NGOs, including feminist groups and similar folks in other countries. They've also enlisted several college women's studies departments. The minority leader in the House is in the loop; at least I've seen e-mails where she was copied, but nothing specific has come back from her that I've seen."

"How do you know all of this?" inquired the chief of staff.

"Not from the CIA, I can assure you, or from NSA's listening." The mentor chuckled.

His colleagues laughed, but their two hosts did not.

"Anyway," he cleared his throat, "Giles is careless with her e-mail. But that probably won't happen again. My exuberant colleague found this information, but just like in his earlier campaign, he couldn't constrain himself. So she knows that we know and will expect opposition sooner rather than later. That said, we should be able to figure out a way to head her off before this thing gets too messy."

"This is a tough one," said the guru.

He was immediately interrupted by one of the other leaders. "This isn't an issue we will compromise on, even in a difficult election year. Don't forget, as my friend and colleague said, we are on solid ground on social issues. And you have two more years, at least with this president, to correct many of the issues we care about."

"Well, somewhat solid. The women in Iraq wouldn't agree with you, and the women in the United States, according to polling, are beginning to pay attention," said the guru.

"No matter," said the leader, "we will not let Iraq dictate American values."

"Calm down, calm down," implored the chief of staff. "He didn't say it was impossible, just tough, right?" He looked at the guru.

"Right," agreed the guru. "But a lot depends on how much you folks are willing to do to help out. But before we discuss specifics, let's hear from the lady from St Louis who has more experience on this issue than any of us. She and her famous Forum, which she created in 1972 to fight the ERA, was our leader when we stopped state ratification at 35."

"You know the answer as well as I do," said the grand lady of the right, "family! Go to your members and talk about the family, abortion, and homosexuality. The ERA is a sure fire way to bring us same sex marriage. Talk about child support and parental responsibility; talk about children and their upbringing. There are many ways to turn this issue. Remind them what we've done over the past thirty years. Ask them if they really want high taxes and a social welfare system that rewards irresponsibility like most of Europe."

"That shouldn't be too difficult," said the chief of staff, "but is that enough?"

"Probably not if they're really well organized," said the guru, "but we can do other things as well. We can probably organize a 527 operation like the one that produced the Swift Boat ads during the last campaign. We can also use other TV ads along the lines we just discussed regarding specifics like abortion, welfare so forth. And maybe we can even do some work in Giles's district. I'm sure that we can count on you folks to find some money for this effort."

"Perhaps a little," one of the guests said reluctantly.

"Come on, fellows, you all own goldmines, especially for social issues like this one, which affects so many other issues near to your heart," said the guru. "We can put together an in-house domestic policy team to coordinate the effort. I'll get them started later today."

The mentor was beaming. "So it appears we're up and running. Who will be the domestic team focal point?"

"Probably Wesley Bragg," advised the guru. "He's smart, talented, and politically savvy. He also knows street rules."

"I beg your pardon?" queried the mentor.

"He's a tough customer," laughed the guru, "just like I've seen you behave over the years, old friend."

The meeting ended. The visitors were ready for battle when they left.

The hosts looked at each other with worry on their faces. "Here we go again," said the chief of staff. "Hopefully we can nip this one in the bud, although my sense is that they won't go down without a fight. The minority leader is looking for a way to get at us, and this may be it. Hit them where they're strong, right?"

"If we can," the guru said with a shrug. "But with so many groups involved, it won't be a walk in the park. We can certainly hit Giles hard though, and fast."

The guru went straight to Wesley Bragg's office in the Old Executive Office Building as soon as he left the chief.

"Hi, Wes, you got a minute."

"Sure," Bragg answered. "Have a seat. Coffee?"

"Yes, that would be nice."

"So, what brings our guru here on this bright spring day?"

The guru smiled. "You would never believe it, Wes, but the ERA is back. You're probably too young to remember the battles we waged in the 70s, but it's back, maybe in full force. This time it's a bit more serious than we've seen from the other party over the last several years."

"I remember a little," said Bragg, "but you're right, not much, just that it was going on. I was in elementary school then. My mother was all for it."

"That's not good," said the guru.

"She died a few years back," said Bragg.

The guru told him about the meeting that had just ended and asked. "By the way, how secure are our computers here?"

"Pretty secure, boss. We have the system checked every week, but of course technology is moving fast. Certainly ours are much better than the Congress has."

"Well," said the guru, "no matter; I don't believe that they have the time or capacity to come after our system. And even if they do, it won't make much difference once we get started."

"Am I getting an assignment?" asked Bragg.

"Yes, Wes. Pick a team to help you and let me know when you're ready for me to meet with them. In the meantime, my initial thoughts are to hit this Giles woman hard and fast. We need to check her and her husband out and see where they're vulnerable. We need to learn about her district. I think it's the Tennessee Fifth. It's Gore's former district."

"Roger that," replied Bragg. "I'll also contact the folks you met today and start twisting a few arms for some bread so we can get this thing rolling."

They talked for a few more minutes. The guru heard Wes call his secretary for phone numbers as he left to brief the president.

* * * * *

Across town, Seth was preparing for another meeting of the ERA Committee. The meeting would be set for early June when colleges were wrapping up their spring semesters. He was calling the principals to ask them to stay alert for opposition. He told each person he had just heard from a press contact that a few of the national fundamentalist leaders had been seen at the White House for what may have been, he surmised, a meeting to discuss a counter-ERA strategy.

"We're relatively sure," Seth told them all, "that these folks will be up to something. They hate the ERA and are riding a high now with this administration and the makeup of the current Congress. They have money, and they certainly have grassroots networks and the ability to make trouble, so please be alert. We've gone through all of Shiloh's e-mails, and we know they have a lot but not our timetable."

* * * * *

Meanwhile, Lawson's mentor called to inform him about the White House meeting.

"James, I am confident that your good work will bring results. But a word of caution: please let this unfold and don't get out front yourself. Let the pros work their magic. Whatever you do, don't contact Giles again. They know that we know; let's not let them know anymore."

"Yes, sir, I understand," said Lawson. "I'll let you know anything I learn, and I'm ready to help however I can."

Lawson was thinking, *Just like the Bible says, we will cast out the sinners. Women have their place as mothers and wives—not as members of Congress. I will stop Catherine Shiloh Giles once and for all. Her time as the abortion, homosexuality, and women's liberation leader will end this time.*

He smiled as he remembered his father. *He would be proud of me today. I am carrying out the mandate he gave me. I am God's lieutenant, and this time, I will cast out the sinners. This time I will beat Giles.*

Chapter 12

On Wednesday, May 15, Sarah brought in *The Tennessean* and laid it on Shiloh's desk, opened to page 8. Without saying a word, she pointed to the full page ad. Shiloh bent down to read it.

WHO IS CATHERINE SHILOH GILES?

CATHERINE SHILOH GILES is currently serving her sixth term as the representative to the United States Congress for the Fifth District of Tennessee.

She won her first term after being involved in an altercation when she was promoting abortion. She had no qualifications for the high office she holds. Since being in Washington she has supported many issues that are repugnant to all thinking men and women:

Abortion on demand, Expensive environmental laws, Increased welfare, Liberal immigration laws, Stem cell research, Homosexual rights, Funding for overseas abortion and coercion in china, Contraceptives for single military personnel, and Wasteful UN programs.

And she will soon offer the EQUAL RIGHTS AMENDMENT, which will destroy the American family and promote abortion and bless homosexual marriage forever.

She has voted against legislation that would:

Require abstinence education for our children and abstinence education to stop the spread of AIDS in US aid programs, Provide adequate funding for the war in Iraq, Allow the further exploration for oil in the U.S. that would make the U.S. less dependent on Arab oil, Remove unreasonable restrictions for U.S. businesses operating overseas, and Increase Medicaid funding.

Representative Giles has run unopposed for three of her five elections and is running unopposed again in 2006. She is wrong for the Tennessee Fifth District, and she is wrong for America.

BUT YOU CAN STOP HER.

Submit the sample WRITE-IN BALLOT below or secure a ballot at your polling place on Election Day. Write in the name of RAYMOND WILSON BOYD, who has been selected by the Republican Party for the Fifth District as its candidate.

Paid for by the Tennessee Republican Party and the National Republican Party.

Sample write-in ballot:

I _____, who resides at _____ _, cast my vote for Republican candidate, Raymond Wilson Boyd for U.S. Representative.

When she had finished reading the ad, Sarah flipped to the second page and pointed to this article.

Nashville, May 15 – On page 8 in today's edition, you will see a full page ad paid for by the Tennessee and the National Republican Party calling on the electorate to write in the name of Raymond Wilson Boyd as their candidate for the Fifth Congressional District seat, currently held by Catherine Shiloh Giles. *The Tennessean* interviewed Mr. Boyd and Congresswoman Giles last night.

Boyd, a well-known local banker and fund-raiser for the Republican Party, said, "I am honored to have been asked by my party to run against Shiloh Giles. I have been disappointed in the past when my party did not field a candidate against Giles. A write-in campaign will be difficult, but I plan to work hard starting tomorrow morning."

Boyd went on to say that he was for a strong economy, supporting our troops in Iraq, and an improved educational system in Tennessee and in the Fifth District. Boyd is prolife with exceptions for the life of the mother. He said that he was most definitely against the Equal Rights Amendment.

Giles was reached at her congressional office in Washington. She said that she was unaware of the ad that was placed in today's edition of *The Tennessean* but not surprised. When the ad was read to Giles, she said, "I would laugh if it were not so serious. Today's Republican Party is well-known for misstatements and misrepresenting facts. Look at what they did to Senator Kerry with the Swift Boat ads they inspired.

"I know of no votes, since I have been in Congress, regarding abortion on demand, for example. Yes, I did vote against abstinence education because it was abstinence-only education with no mention of reproduction and contraception. I am for abstinence, but I am also for lowering the abortion rate among our youth. I am not against abstinence education as a part of our foreign aid program to slow the spread of HIV/AIDS. But we must also supply sufficient condoms. I am for what is called the ABC approach: Abstain, Be faithful, and if you do have sex, use a Condom. Ten people are infected with HIV every minute, and half are women and girls; many of them get HIV from their husbands. That particular element of our foreign aid program is impractical and can, if taken to extremes, actually cause great harm."

Giles also said, "Yes, I was for contraceptives for our service personnel. Many of the members of Congress who voted against contraceptives voted for Viagra for military men. How is that for gender equality?"

Giles said that she too would run a strong campaign and was hopeful that the voters of the Fifth District would return her to Congress. When asked if she was planning to introduce the ERA as the ad implied, the Congresswoman replied, "I may. I've been looking into the possibility. Women in the United States have most of the rights that men do, but often, to enjoy those rights, women are forced to go to court to prove them. That isn't fair. Men do not have to go to court for equal pay or to get into a public school, as women have to do. And many women around the world do not possess the rights that are called for in international human rights documents."

In response to the ad's claim that the ERA would promote abortion and homosexual marriage, Giles said that such a statement did not square with the facts. She said, "Once again they have produced a statement that misrepresents reality. Several states have their own ERA laws and many also have abortion restrictions. So their argument doesn't fly."

When Giles was asked if she would debate Mr. Boyd even though he was a write-in candidate, she answered, "Yes, of course."

After reading the paper, Shiloh called Charlie.

"Hi, Charlie, is it bad? Do I have to wear a mustache when I come home for the weekends?"

"Well, I'm glad that your sense of humor is intact. I don't think that it's bad, but it's certainly vicious. We'll have to wait and see. I'm sure that you'll receive several letters and so will *The Tennessean* in response to today's article. At least they gave you a chance to respond. The TV ad is vintage pit bull. Brenda will e-mail it to you later today."

"Any advice?" queried Shiloh.

"Just don't worry. You're loved here. The Republicans are really pushing nationally on abortion, or at least the fundamentalist wing of their party is, but my sense is that the folks here are tired of the dirt that the other side loves to throw around. Plus, the president's numbers are down. Voters are getting weary of the mess the country is in today."

"Yes, Charlie, I'm thinking that too, but this group knows only one way: full out for the jugular. Anyway, Seth and I look forward to seeing you and Tom on Saturday night—especially now that we can discuss all of my many liberal sins."

As Charlie rang off, Shiloh heard him chuckle, and was glad that he appreciated her sense of humor.

Later that day, Shiloh received the TV ad. The ad started with an escort walking a woman into the Mid-State Women's Clinic with Operation Savior demonstrators in the background. This was followed by a news clip of U.S. troops in Iraq and ended with Raymond Boyd sitting at a table with his family in his backyard eating supper.

The voiceover said, "Shiloh Giles is not qualified to be in Congress. She is a radical feminist who wants to bring back the ERA, she does not believe in sexual abstinence for our children, she believes abortion is a child's right, she does not support our troops in Iraq, she supports higher taxes, and she does not support exploration for American oil reserves. She does not care that her actions make the United States more dependent on the Arabs for oil.

"Vote for Ray Boyd for integrity, honesty, and a strong economy. Ray Boyd supports America's military. You will be proud to have Ray represent you in Washington. He is a native of Nashville, a devout Christian, and a loving and dedicated family man. Be sure to write in Ray's name, that's Ray Boyd, when you vote for your congressional representative on November 7. Ray will bring good sense and American values back to Tennessee's Fifth Congressional District.

"Paid for by friends of Ray Boyd."

Then Boyd's voice said, "My name is Ray Boyd, and I approve this message."

Shiloh put her hand to her forehead. Charlie certainly had his work cut out for him.

* * * * *

James Robert Lawson II was in his office writing his letter to *The Tennessean*. He would take his mentor's advice and be calm.

> Dear Editor,
>
> I am writing to complement you on today's article on Raymond Boyd and that woman, who, for the present, represents the Fifth District in the U.S. House of Representatives. Raymond Boyd is a God-fearing family man who despises abortion and supports our troops in Iraq. That was well covered in your article. Giles has been in Congress for far too long. She is evil. The longer she stays, the more she will desecrate the values we all hold so dear: God, family, and country. Your article exposed her failings. She actually sounded proud of her actions. She mentioned misrepresentation. The real misrepresentation is her misrepresentation of the good people of the Fifth District.
>
> May God bless you all,
> Reverend James Robert Lawson II

* * * * *

Barry called Shiloh.

"Hi, Shy. I saw that vile ad and the article in *The Tennessean*. I sure do wish that Coffee County had not been gerrymandered out of the Fifth District. Maybe I'll move back to Nashville just so I can vote for you."

"Barry, relax." Shy was laughing. "I'm fine, but when you planned my run for Congress, you didn't tell me that I'd have to work so hard and that people would say bad things about me."

"I didn't know that you would be so mean to the other party, Tiger," said Barry. "Listen, there may actually be an election this time—probably not; but just in case, I plan to get a haircut and shine my shoes and bring my woman to Nashville to help you. The former governor may not be able to do much, but the former first lady can win a few votes."

Shiloh chuckled. "All help appreciated and accepted. How is Trudy?"

"Fine, but she wants to see her favorite daughter, and so do I. It's been too long."

"It has," agreed Shy. "Why don't y'all come up and spend the night with Seth and me on Saturday night? It's my weekend to be in the district. Charlie and Tom are coming to dinner, and I'll invite the Jacobsons too. We can talk about me instead of sports. How about it?"

"You'll win for sure, don't worry. And you just convinced us to come up for the weekend."

"Yes, you have," Trudy said from the extension that she had just picked up. "I can't wait to see you and that sweet man of yours. Are we having roast quail?"

Shiloh's spirits lifted. "Yes, since you like it so much. I'll put it in the oven when we arrive on Friday night."

"Great," replied Trudy, "and don't forget to make reservations at that nice Italian restaurant."

* * * * *

Shiloh called Seth to tell him the news. After she finished he said, "It sounds ugly in Nashville, and I'm sure there is more to come. Sally Cohen called to report that several of the department heads who came to our meetings have been told by their deans that they need to be careful.

"Apparently, some of the deans received visits from the IRS. The deans were told that they needed to make sure that their women's studies departments are aware of the line between politics and their school's tax-exempt status. The IRS agents, or whoever they were, said that routine checks had turned up what looked like a concerted effort by women's studies departments around the country to influence legislation. They warned them that such political activity could violate their school's 501(c)(3) tax status."

"My goodness," retorted Shiloh, "they do play hardball."

"Yes, but Sally said that most of the schools were not too worried. They were furious but not stupid. Sally said, and I quote, 'We're fine, Seth. Tell Shy that when the time comes, we'll be there. They aren't foolish, and they certainly don't want to jeopardize their federal grants. But it isn't just the IRS they need to worry about. The administration has many agencies and departments that they can call on.'"

"And," said Shy, "is there more?"

"Yes, there is. The churches have been warned too. But the churches are so irritated by what the fundamentalists get away with that they say that the stupid IRS warnings—their words, not mine—will be ignored."

"And the NGOs?" asked Shy.

"Nothing yet, dear. But we called most of them to let them know what was up."

"Good," said Shy. "Let's try to get home early tonight and have a nice bottle of wine and some creamy seafood pasta."

"That sounds great. By early you mean 7:30 to 8:00?"

"Maybe 7:00. Can you get away?"

"I'll be cooking when you get home. An evening with my wife with pasta and wine, I may declare a holiday."

"It has been busy, especially for you," said Shiloh.

* * * * *

It was nice to see the Whitfields and the Jacobsons that weekend. Seth cooked steaks, baked potatoes, and corn on the cob on their grill, and Shiloh made a salad. Susan brought dessert, and Barry and Trudy brought wine. Even Charlie brought something: Shiloh's new campaign posters and a pamphlet that extolled the virtues of his candidate and, in so doing, refuted the awful newspaper ad.

Seth told their assembled friends about the IRS trouble, which now included threats to the foundations and to three of the NGOs. "The lawyers that represented two of the foundations made them drop out, while the lawyers for the other foundations told their clients to hold pat. Three of the NGOs have now been threatened too. One of the NGOs has threatened to sue the IRS for harassment."

"What?" asked Bill. "That doesn't seem smart."

"I asked the same question," agreed Seth. "I was told that this IRS stuff was an old trick and that they had learned long ago to fight back. Somehow those three letters, I-R-S, don't scare them as much as they do the rest of us. However, two NGOs that receive U.S. international aid funds for development work were nervous, but so far they are also staying with us."

"I didn't know that the IRS could harass folks like that," said Susan.

"I'm not sure that it's the IRS," mused Seth. "It could be anyone with a government ID."

Barry offered his advice. "If I were representing them, I'd tell them to hang tough. It's very hard to hassle folks in the public domain. They can conduct audits and perhaps conduct reviews of senior level employee's taxes, but it's very difficult to go after an organization unless the violation is blatant. The press is often quite helpful with these sorts of cases too. I represented an NGO once that was battling the Feds over onerous accounting requirements. It was also based on politics. I filed a harassment suit and went to the press. The government immediately dropped the case."

"Can't their harassment cause problems though?" asked Susan.

"Of course. Anytime they come after you it takes time and money. And most NGOs live close to the margin."

"How bad is this Boyd candidacy?" Seth asked Charlie.

"I think we'll be okay. But it won't be pretty. Boyd's negative campaign will get some votes. But this is a write-in campaign and will be much harder. On the other hand, if the party spends more on TV ads, they could make it easier for Boyd to run again in the next election. We did a quick poll yesterday, and so far there isn't much effect. But the ads playing continually on TV will hurt. That's for sure. And that's why Shiloh will need to campaign hard this time, starting with a press conference in two weeks."

Barry changed the subject. "How is Sam, Shy?"

"He's okay. We see them fairly frequently since we live so close. Both their kids are in college now. Sam and Barbara are both interested in politics and especially the ERA. But mostly we spend our time together talking sports, don't we, Mr. Yankee?"

Seth grinned. "Guilty as charged."

The evening was a wonderful break for Shiloh and Seth. It helped them recharge their batteries for the battles ahead.

* * * * *

Two weeks later, Shiloh went to Nashville while Seth stayed in DC to prepare for the upcoming ERA Committee meeting, which would be held the following week. Shy arrived Thursday night and went straight to Charlie's office for a briefing.

"So, dear friend," inquired Shiloh, "is Tom moving back?"

"He is. I'm delighted. It's almost as if he never left. He's going back to his old job and he's moving in with me."

"I'm happy for you, Charlie, after all these years too. That's really great."

"We'll see. It'll take awhile to get used to each other again, but I have hopes. Now, my turn. The press conference will be held tomorrow at 10:00 a.m. at the Hyatt. You should make an opening statement about your work, including the ERA and why you are considering it. And then we go to questions. You'll get questions on the ads. Go get 'em, tiger. They'll want red meat; give it to them. Leave Boyd alone, but go for the dirt. Let's meet at 9:00 at my office and go from here. Okay?"

"Okay, boss, I'm ready."

"How about the Kiwanis speech and the drop by at the Banker's Association reception?"

Shiloh nodded. "I'm ready for those too."

"You won't be expected to speak at the banker's reception. Just work the crowd for a half hour or so, and we'll take off. Bill Sawyer will be there to take you around and do introductions."

"That sounds fine. I plan to spend the day at my office on Saturday. Wayne has several constituent appointments lined up. Then I plan to return to DC after church at All Saints on Sunday."

Shiloh went straight to her condo and slept. She was exhausted from her normal work in Congress and her constant interaction with Seth about ERA Today and its work. He insisted that Shiloh at least discuss, if not clear, all of ERA Today's work. She trusted him, and he knew that, but he felt more comfortable checking with Shiloh. It seemed like she had two jobs, but she was happy with the way things were going.

Shiloh went to the podium at the Heritage room of the Hyatt after Charlie introduced her. "Thank you, Charlie, and thank all of you for coming. As y'all know, I'm running for reelection this November. I've enjoyed my time in the House of Representatives and believe that I've served the interests of this district and of our country during my stay in Washington. I've tried to make sure that this district receives a fair return on its taxes, and I've been proud to assist individual constituents with various requests over the years. In fact, I very much enjoy that part of my work."

Shiloh stopped a moment to look at her notes and at her audience. Then she continued.

"I'm a proud sponsor of legislation that will help provide a state-of-the art rehabilitation facility for the American troops who have been injured and maimed in Afghanistan and Iraq. I believe that we were led into the Iraq War for political and ideological reasons. My position today is that we must leave Iraq as soon as feasibly possible. It is time for Iraq to run its own affairs. I also support the proposal you may have seen that splits Iraq into Shia, Sunni, and Kurdish semiautonomous regions under the common state of Iraq. If there isn't some sort of brokered deal like the one I just mentioned, Iraq could sink further into civil strife. It seems that a political solution is almost impossible at this time, and many think that is the best option for avoiding a bloodbath. It would take some intricate planning on issues such as sharing oil profits, a common defense force, and other institutional matters, but to me that is preferable to what we have today.

"It would be difficult for the United States to just leave, but we have sacrificed far too many Americans and spent far too much money on a war that was not necessary. I know that the Iraqis didn't start this war, and as General Colin Powell said, 'If we break it, we own it.' In addition, the Iraqi people and government have said many times that they support the ousting of Saddam. If so, then it's time for them to take charge and work out a settlement among the major groups. If there's a full-fledged civil war instead, then we don't belong there—not anymore than we did in the civil war in Vietnam."

Shiloh paused and looked around the room. It was stately and dignified. Elegant brocade gold drapes were held back by off-white mounts, exposing white shears over large windows. An unobtrusive, nondescript, green carpet covered the floor, where comfortable leather chairs with wooden frames were arranged in a theater arrangement. The Hyatt's staff was there to help, not intrude, which lent to the importance of the event. Shiloh felt at home at the Hyatt and relaxed. She smiled as she sipped her coffee and resumed her statement.

"The National Wildlife Refuge drilling bill. Its impact on our pristine wildlife refuge is not warranted or necessary. I'd rather work on conservation and support ideas like wind farms and the governor of Montana's suggestion to explore the use of the coal in his state to extract a cleaner burning fuel that would better serve our needs and lessen our environmental problems. I also support dramatically increasing the use of ethanol, but not without using land-banked acreage that is not now in production so that corn for food will not be decreased for corn for ethanol. Some of this is expensive, but we must start with a strong policy rather than just wishing for more oil and depending on others. Brazil has made great strides in that area. Its economy is sound now after years of hyperinflation and is no longer dependent on foreign oil. And we must intensify our search for alternative sources of energy."

Shiloh took a breath before continuing. "I'm appalled that we have tortured prisoners and violated the Geneva Convention. I want to stop terrorism, but I don't want to see our country lose its moral underpinning in the bargain. Torture is wrong.

"I'm against ignoring the privacy rights of American citizens by eavesdropping on their private conversations and reading their private correspondence without an appropriate court order. We need to be alert: a court order does not stop the work of our security agencies; it protects the privacy of American citizens.

"I voted for the prescription drug benefits for the elderly and would again, and I am happy to report that the instructions for its use have improved markedly.

"I want our country to be respected around the world as a champion of human rights.

"And finally, I support the ERA. It's wrong for any class of people in this country to be forced go to court to prove their rights. I'll be glad to take your questions."

One reporter asked, "Congresswomen Giles, what is your position on abortion?"

Shiloh smiled. She knew this one was coming; it always did.

"I agree with former President Clinton and many others that abortion should be safe, legal, and rare. We need to work hard to prevent abortion; abstinence-only education and cutbacks in contraceptive services are not the answers; nor is denying contraceptives to the poor and the young, as many other states are considering. Quite frankly, it angers me that mainly men make these decisions. That's the problem with women's rights.

"Why do we call them women's rights instead of human rights? Because women are not equal. One famous woman once said that, if men could get pregnant, birth control would be a sacrament. I expect abortion would be as well. Ask any man what he would do if he discovered that his wife, girlfriend, mother, sister, daughter, aunt, or friend came to him for help because she was pregnant and didn't want to be because of medical problems, age—too young or too old—rape, incest, her situation in life, or any other reason that the woman chose. What would he do? What would you do?"

Another reported shouted out, "Do you think that the newest members of the Supreme Court will make it possible for the court to reverse *Roe v. Wade*?"

Shiloh paused a moment before responding. "I don't know. I hope not. Some court watchers say the votes are there, while others disagree. I guess that we'll just have to wait and see."

The next question was an easy one. "Would you vote against the war in Iraq today?"

Shiloh spoke without hesitation. "Yes, I'd vote against the Iraq War knowing what I do now. I voted for the war because I believed that Saddam had weapons of mass destruction and would use them. I believed the intelligence we were given at the time. We have the strongest military that has ever existed. But we need to match our military strength with equally strong diplomacy. War should be the last card we ever play.

"I might add though that I support our troops. They deserve to earn a living wage. I voted for a higher raise for our troops than the president's budget requested, and Congress prevailed. We have American soldiers whose families need food stamps to get by, and that's wrong. They put their lives on the line; the very least we can do is provide a livable wage and superb medical services."

A reporter in the back asked, "You now have an opponent in this year's election, Raymond Boyd. He has announced that he will wage a write-in campaign against you. Do you know him, and do you know why he chose to enter the race so late as a write-in candidate?"

Shiloh shrugged. "I don't know, Mr. Boyd, but I welcome him to the race. This is a democracy, and I look forward to debating the issues we are discussing here today."

Someone asked, "Do you know why the Tennessee and National Republican Committees suddenly decided to run that tough newspaper ad and the tougher TV ad?"

"Maybe they want my seat."

The crowd laughed.

"Actually, I believe that it has to do with the ERA. I've been seriously considering reintroducing the ERA. Someone used some kind of spyware on my computer and learned about my plans. Maybe they want to keep me busy. Their record on women's issues, by the way, is atrocious."

A man near the front asked, "Do you know who broke into your computer, Congresswomen?"

Shiloh frowned. "I'd rather not say at this time—although he wasn't very smart about it. He called me and told me what he had done. Shortly afterward, the ads appeared, and Mr. Boyd announced his candidacy."

The man wasn't finished. "Why won't you say?"

"Because I don't want to give him a platform. It was a person, not the NSA. But it does make me appreciate even more why it is wrong to listen in on private conversations or read other people's mail without a need-to-know safeguard. We can't allow one branch of government to have such power as we do today."

A woman to Shiloh's right asked, "What is your view on gay marriage?"

Shiloh bowed. "Thank you for all the easy questions."

Laughter again.

"I won't introduce a bill in Congress for a gay marriage law, if that's what you're asking."

Someone Shiloh couldn't see asked, "Would you support such a bill?"

"That depends on the language. I favor gay civil unions that allow for spousal health insurance, inheritance rights, and other rights such as what the next of kin enjoy, like hospital visitation. If that means marriage, then I support it. Gays have human rights too. There are between fifteen and twenty million homosexuals in this country. They are not confined to any ethnic or social group. They could be your boss, your sibling, or the person who repairs your car or dry-cleans your clothes. The bottom line is that they are American citizens."

An older man asked, "Then you favor gay adoption?"

Shiloh took a moment to collect her thoughts. "I believe that it's better, ideally, for children to have a mother and a father. But nearly a third of our children are raised in households headed by women alone. I think that as long as children need homes, it is fine for them to have two parents of the same sex, as long as the parents can meet the requirements that all adoptive parents must meet. Children need love, support, and a good home life."

A woman in the middle asked, "How do you like being in Congress?"

Shiloh smiled. "Finally, an easy question. If you do your job right, Congress requires a lot of time, but I love it. I like being able to help constituents solve problems and negotiating with my colleagues and debating the merits of various issues. It's more difficult now with the White House and both houses of Congress being in the hands of one party. But it's still a job that I love, especially press conferences."

More laughter.

"I'll take one more question."

Toward the back, a young woman raised her hand. "Do you ever think about running for the Senate or governor or even higher?"

"No, not really. I like the House. Maybe someday, but I'm having fun and I'm acquiring seniority that will give me more power with which to help this district, especially if my party ever recaptures the House."

Charlie came to the mic and thanked the journalists for coming and said that Shiloh would be available for a few individual interviews before she headed for her speech at the Kiwanis luncheon.

Later over coffee, Charlie said to Shiloh. "They love you, Shy. You're easygoing and honest. That gay marriage question and the one about adoption will give Boyd some fodder, though."

"I know, Charlie, but I had to say how I feel. I do support gay marriage."

"Yes, and as a gay I thank you for saying so, but as your political adviser I'm not too thrilled."

When they arrived at the restaurant for the Kiwanis luncheon, they were not surprised to find Lawson and some of his followers outside the restaurant passing out copies of the ad that had appeared in *The Tennessean*.

Lawson glared at Shiloh and said, "You're an evil woman, Shiloh Giles, and so is that fag with you. You're going down this time. You'll never make it again, Giles, never again."

Shiloh stared at him. "Can't you at least be civil, Reverend Lawson?" Shiloh held out her hand to shake his.

Lawson backed away, growling, "Don't touch me; don't ever touch me."

When Shiloh and Charlie entered the restaurant, Charlie whispered. "God that man is creepy. I'd better hire some security for you."

Shiloh frowned. "That won't be necessary. He won't do anything but talk."

"I'm not so sure. I'd feel better with security."

"Let's wait awhile. This is still America. I'm not the president."

"I won't wait long, Shy."

Shiloh went to the head table and met the president of the Kiwanis Club.

"Good morning, Congresswomen. It's good to see you again."

"And you too, Joe. How's your family?"

"They're all fine. Thanks. That man over there is Ray Boyd." He nodded toward a man standing by one of the tables. "He arrived a few minutes ago and asked to speak. We had no choice but to agree."

"That's fine, Joe. Why don't you introduce me?"

At least Boyd shook Shiloh's hand, but he was not very friendly. *Oh boy,* thought Shiloh, *another man with a cross to bear.*

Boyd spoke first and spent ten minutes talking about the dreadful moral situation in America. He talked about abortion, gay marriage, and the young people who believe that it is okay to have sex before marriage. "We need leaders who will recapture the moral values that have made America great. We need to rid our Congress of members who encourage immorality, like my opponent." He looked over at Shiloh. "I'm here to offer you an option to vote for dignity and the family. To vote for morality and to send Congresswoman Giles back to civilian life. Vote for me, and you'll vote for decency and honesty. Thank you. And God bless you all."

Boyd received about five seconds of polite applause.

Shiloh thanked the president for his kind introduction and the audience for its warm welcome. She spoke about the war, taxes, the NSA scandal, her legislation for improving the medical care and rehabilitation of veterans, the military pay raise, the funds that she'd helped secure to improve the I-40 and the I-440 highway network around Nashville, and fairness in migration. She addressed the need to support the UN's Millennium Development Goals to reduce poverty, noting that the goals had been adopted by all UN members' heads of state, and said how much she appreciated the opportunity to serve as their representative.

She ended by thanking the group for past support and saying she hoped that she would receive their support for this reelection. She totally ignored Boyd's speech. When she finished, she was greeted with sustained applause.

The president of Kiwanis asked if the candidates would take questions. Both agreed.

The first question was for Shiloh. "Madame Congresswoman, do you think that y'all be able to get the funds for the Cumberland River recreational area?"

"Well the budget is tight," replied Shiloh, "but I'm working with our senior senator, and I think we have a good chance of getting it in during the House-Senate conference committee meeting for the appropriations bill. We'll do our best."

Applause.

Boyd raised his hand.

"Mr. Boyd, do you have something to add?"

"No, sir, but I want to ask Mrs. Giles why she avoided the abortion issue in her statement."

The president started to respond, and Shiloh signaled him to let her answer. "Mr. Boyd, you've already stated how I feel about abortion."

There were chuckles from the crowd.

"Actually, I don't like abortion. I do believe, though, that it should be safe, legal, and rare. But it will never be rare unless we do a better job with sex education and contraceptive services. I prefer abstinence, but not at the expense of more unwanted pregnancies, more abortion, and more young women starting their families in poverty."

Boyd tried to speak again, but the president cut him off and went to the audience.

"Thank you. Shiloh, why should we support the Millennium Development Goals with our tax dollars?"

"Hi, Ralph. Thanks for the question. First, because it's morally appropriate for America to help the world's less fortunate. It's the right thing to do. Second, it's pragmatic to help eliminate poverty. Almost three billion people live on two dollars a day, less than the cost of a cappuccino at this restaurant. Almost one billion of those folks live on only one dollar a day. They wake up each morning wondering how they will eat. Poverty breeds desperation and crime, maybe even terrorism. It brings with it a lack of sanitation, which can spread disease, possibly even to other countries.

"If people are healthy and educated and have an opportunity to utilize their God-given talents, they'll have a greater chance to enjoy a prosperous and happy life and to contribute to their society and its economy. Nations are less likely to go to war and more likely to want peace and security, which we all cherish. Trade will increase, and the world will be safer."

There were a few more questions for Shiloh. Finally the president thanked the two candidates and ended the luncheon.

Several people surrounded Shiloh. Only a few went to talk to Boyd.

On their way out, Charlie was ecstatic. "You were terrific," he enthused. "But I fear that we'll see more nasty ads. You'll get good coverage today, but I don't think that the race is over."

Shiloh frowned. "Nor do I—not with the help Boyd will get and not with Lawson lurking around to stir things up."

"What did you think of Boyd?" asked Charlie.

"It's too early to tell, but my first impression was not too favorable. He certainly isn't a Jake Sheraton. I'm sure that he'll get some coaching and will get better. He wasn't very collegial either. He'd fit right in with some of his party mates in Washington."

* * * * *

Lawson had sat at the back of the room and listened to the speeches and questions. The more he heard, the more distraught he became. When he returned to his church, he called his mentor and reported.

"It wasn't so good for us today, sir. Our candidate didn't do so well, and Giles is good at charming her audience."

"Don't worry, James," counseled the mentor, "we'll beat the ERA. All of the folks who met at the White House will be prepared to fight it the moment it is introduced. And the guru is working with his friends in Congress. Don't worry, son, we will prevail."

"But, sir, I want to beat this woman. I want her out of here. She's a disgrace and against all that we believe in."

"We aren't through yet, son," the mentor said, "but even if she wins, losing the ERA will make her more vulnerable the next time. Now, tell me about that flock of yours, James. Are they still supporting you?"

Lawson mumbled a positive answer and rang off as soon as he could.

That evening Lawson sat in his office brooding about Shiloh. His father had given him his name. He had anointed his son to carry God's banner. James knew that he could never mesmerize his congregation like his father had, and his little church was far too small for what his father had envisioned for his only son. In all the years he had been there, not once had he received an offer to go to a larger church. He knew it was because others did not share his total devotion and passion for God's exact words. He knew the words and lived by them. He was born to serve God. People did not yet understand his legacy.

But they will, he told himself, *they will.*

In his heart, he knew that he was failing. Losing to Shiloh Giles years ago had hurt his reputation. "If you can't even beat a woman, how can you lead a big flock?" he imagined the powerful people from big churches thinking. Shiloh Giles, a wanton woman, a woman from a fancy church, was setting a horrid example for God's children. And she continued to beat him. She must be stopped.

"My mission," he said out loud in the privacy of his office, "is to stop her. I know, Lord, that I am your instrument. I will find a way, Lord. I will honor my father's memory, just as your son honored you and gave his life for our salvation. Oh, God, give me the strength to prevail; shine your countenance upon me, Lord, and I will do your work. I will exact your vengeance, Lord God."

* * * * *

Seth held the full ERA Committee meeting the following week at the Capitol Hilton. They discussed various plans that had been worked out by the subcommittees representing each group. Seth and the smaller executive committee agreed not to discuss specific dates. They would keep that a secret as long as they could. This meeting was scheduled to keep everyone working to prepare for a busy fall. It was especially important for the college group to work hard. He hoped they would be able to rally the students like they had during the sixties for Vietnam.

The meeting went well, and everyone was excited. They all knew the ERA could be a defining issue, and they were all proud to be a part of it. If they won this battle for equality, it would be on the world's largest stages: in Washington, in New York at the UN, in Brussels, and at capitals around the world. It would be a global movement that would change history.

Seth thought to himself after the meeting ended and he'd headed home to see his wonderful wife that this was like being Ike before Normandy. He chuckled at the comparison. *What a turkey I am,* he thought. *General Richards goes forward leading the troops under orders from commander in chief Catherine Shiloh Giles.* It reminded Seth of daydreaming about being a football hero or making the winning shot in a basketball game.

* * * * *

When Seth got home, he was in a great mood.

Shiloh met him at the door with a glass of wine and a sweet, mysterious smile.

"You too, sweetheart?" asked Seth.

"Me too what?" inquired Shiloh with a smile.

"Do you feel excited too?"

"Yes, as a matter of fact I do. You first, darling."

"Me first what?"

"Why are you so happy, dummy?"

"Because I'm married to the commander in chief—a beautiful commander and chief, I might add. Actually, the meeting went very well. I'm sure that you could sense it at last night's reception.

"Yes, I could. The mood was great."

"And," Seth said as he smiled, "I was just daydreaming about leading your army. It was boy stuff. You know, feeling macho."

"You aren't making a lot of sense. I suppose that's the boy in you as well."

They were both giggly. "It's just with all of this Lawson, Boyd, majority leader, and other stuff, Shy, it was nice to have a real upper. It makes me want to stand here and hug you forever."

"Wait a minute. Remember I'm happy too. Do you want to know why?"

"Now you're being a little girl," retorted Seth. "Of course I want to know why. Did Boyd drop out?"

"No, much better."

"Did the president resign?"

"No."

"Okay," said Seth, "you have my attention."

Shiloh was smiling, her face was flush, and she was, Seth thought, quite pretty.

"It is big news, dear, very big news. You, my good man and devoted husband, will have a new title conferred upon you on about December 16. On that day, someone will arrive into this world who will call you daddy."

"Uh huh," mumbled Seth. Then like a bolt of lightening had hit him, Seth said, "What? Really? Are you Okay? How do you feel?"

"Happy is how I feel."

"Me too," blubbered Seth, "but how do you feel, feel?"

"I feel fine, darling, in every way."

Seth hugged his wife. He could hear her laughing and feel her tears on his cheek. Then they kissed deeply and with feeling.

Finally Seth pulled away and declared, "I am very, very happy, sweetheart—very, very happy."

They had a wonderful evening together discussing the future of their soon-to-be-expanded family.

* * * * *

Shiloh told her staff the next day about her pregnancy. They were full of good wishes and jokes about sleepless nights with her new baby. She truly loved her team of staffers. She had had many during her time in Washington, but Sarah and Carol were still there. Her current staff was especially good.

Over the years, Sarah had not only been Shiloh's chief of staff and friend; she was also her confidant. On this day she confided in her about the upcoming election. "I'm worried about this election, Sarah. They're really after me, and I'm sure it'll get worse. Now that I'm pregnant, I worry that the stress may hurt the baby. I'm forty-one now, so this is probably my last chance to be a mother."

Sarah was upbeat. "I wouldn't be too worried, Shy. You are strong, you exercise, and I've never met anyone up here in this madhouse who is calmer under pressure than you. I think it's just your maternal instincts taking over, which is natural. But I'll try to keep some of the more routine stuff off your desk from now on."

Shiloh sighed. "Thanks, Sarah. That helps a lot. It probably is maternal instincts. I'm so happy."

At that moment, the phone rang. It was Seth calling from New York, where he'd gone early that morning to meet with the UN contingent.

"Hi, darling. I thought I'd call and check up on my favorite mother to be and pass along some good news."

"Hi, sweetheart; Mama is good. Sarah is with me. Let me put you on speakerphone, and you can give us both the good news."

"I just finished a meeting at the Dutch Mission with the Brits and representatives of all the regional groups. After I told them about our good news, which required slaps on the back from all present, I learned that all was set for the introduction of our resolution in the Sixth Committee. Not only that, the Brits reported that the president of the General Assembly had agreed that the Sixth Committee report could be introduced in the General Assembly on October 5, which is the day you and the minority leader are aiming for your introduction down there. And as you may remember, the General Assembly introduction will be handled by the Dutch foreign minister."

Shiloh jumped up from her chair, deep in though. "Oh, Seth, that's good news. I just hope we can follow suit here. The minority leader figures that we will be behind as usual and that the fifth is as good a date as any to shoot for, judging from past experience."

"Congratulations, Seth," said an excited Sarah. "Everything is looking good—legislation, pregnancies, the weather."

"Yes, it's all good, sweetheart," said Shiloh. "Only now the clock is ticking on two important fronts."

Chapter 13

During the late spring and summer, Seth worked with his small staff to stay in touch with NGO colleagues around the world and the other groups from the colleges, religious organizations, and the governments at the UN. Shiloh worked as always in Congress and went to the district almost every weekend to campaign. Seth joined her when he could, and Barry came up from Tullahoma with Trudy and stayed with Shiloh when Seth couldn't be there.

Shiloh, along with the rest of her team, was surprised and a bit concerned that Boyd had reached 40 percent in the polls. There had been two more TV ads extolling the virtues of Raymond Boyd. They did not contain the anti-Giles vitriol of the first ad; they merely referred to Shiloh as Boyd's "unqualified opponent." Charlie alerted Shiloh that Boyd's handlers were saving the best for last. Shiloh knew that Boyd had added two young hotshots to his staff who had improved the candidate's speeches and performance. Charlie told Shiloh he was sure that the party had sent the newcomers, but he was still confident that his candidate would prevail.

She followed his advice and was able to maintain her twenty-point lead through the dog days of summer. She was greatly admired by her constituents and never slipped when she was out making speeches and attending events. She was smart, she was spunky, and she exuded confidence. Most of all, she had charisma, which, no matter how much coaching he received, would never be a word used to describe her opponent.

In July, before Congress took its August summer recess, the minority leader called a meeting of the Democratic Caucus. As Shiloh sat in the front row, the minority leader gave a brief history of the ERA and explained its current status. "Once again, friends, our colleagues in this Congress introduced the ERA in both houses of Congress, Kennedy in the Senate and Maloney and Leach in the House. Both were, like others before them, sent to committee where they died. Mr. Andrews also introduced a bill in this session requiring the House to take whatever action was necessary to adopt the ERA, if the required three states that were still needed from its original passage by the House and Senate in 1972 finally ratified the ERA.

"It is not likely that three states of the fifteen left that have not ratified the ERA will ever do so, unless there is an outcry from the electorate. And even then, the Andrews bill would be questionable because the time allocated for the ratification is long since past.

"The only reason there were time limits for 1979 and 1982 is because Congress was appeasing anti-ERA members by establishing a ratification time limit. The constitution is mum on the time issue. However, we do have precedence on our side. As you all know, it took 203 years for the so-called James Madison Amendment to be ratified in 1992. It was a part of the original group of twelve amendments offered as the so-called Bill of Rights amendments that were passed by the Congress and sent to the States in 1789.

"The first ten were ratified and became the Bill of Rights. One was not ratified and was dropped. Madison's last amendment was only ratified by the final state necessary for inclusion into the Constitution in 1992. It was then agreed by Congress, on May 7 of that year, that since it had been adopted by three-quarters of the states, it should be included in the Constitution. It became the twenty-seventh and, to date, the last amendment to be added to the Constitution.

"It is, by the way, the amendment that does not allow Congress to receive a pay raise until after an election cycle has passed. Congress decided that this amendment did not have a time limit, even though it took 74,003 days for the required number of states to ratify. Of course, an issue like this, which would prohibit Congress from giving itself in-session pay raises, would be popular in all quarters.

"Maybe it would be constitutional today if three more states ratified the ERA, maybe not," continued the minority leader. "And that is why we have the Andrews resolution. But with this Supreme Court and this Congress and fundamentalists ready to fight back any way they can, I have serious doubts that it would be added to the constitution even if three states could be found to ratify.

"Which brings me to our sister, the gentlewoman from Tennessee. Our colleague, Shiloh Giles, came to me almost two years ago, long before the last ERA resolution was introduced last year. She suggested that the ERA be reintroduced in a different way, which included developing an active, grassroots constituency. I advised her to develop her constituency and to come back to see me when she was ready. At that time, I told her, she would either have my blessings or not. As we all know, trying to get anything done by our party in this Congress is next to impossible.

"Well, I have attended two receptions involving the grassroots groups that Shy and her husband, Seth, have been working with, and I must say that I was impressed by the people I met and by the work that has been done.

"So, my honored colleagues, we are meeting today because I've given Shy my blessing. Shy has worked diligently to bring us to the place where the ERA could actually win, or at least again become a part of the national debate. So today Shy and I are here to seek your thoughts, and hopefully, your blessing. Shy."

"Thank you, Madame Leader, soon I hope to address you as Madame Speaker."

There were applause and "hear hears" from the assembled Democrats.

"Friends, first, I in no way meant to usurp the work that any of you have put into trying to pass the ERA," Shiloh began. "And I wasn't comfortable with keeping what I've been doing on this issue a secret. I was especially uncomfortable when many of you were asked to speak on the ERA at colleges in your districts. Our leader said that I could blame her for the secrecy, and I will."

The leader smiled at Shiloh. There were chuckles from her colleagues.

"This is what we—my husband, Seth, who many of you know—and I have done." Shiloh told them about the foundations, the establishment of ERA Today, the partners in the colleges, the NGOs, the churches, and finally about the UN and the agreement from all the political regions of the world. She discussed her hopes that all Democrats would try to convince as many of their colleagues in the other party as they could to support the ERA.

"My husband, Seth, has done most of the work. In fact, Seth retired early from the UN just to work on this. I thought it could be done if we were able to find significant support, and I believe we have. At the very least, this gives us an opportunity to reintroduce a largely forgotten issue back onto the national agenda. And, my dear friends, it will also serve to call attention to the dreadful policies and record this administration has established regarding women in this country and the deplorable conditions women face in many countries around the world.

"The downside is that the other side knows some of what we have been up to. A person from my district used some sort of spyware and was able to read many of the e-mails on my computer. I would never have known this, but he told me. Unfortunately, I'm sure that he told others.

"A few months ago, just a week or two after the person who read my e-mails called me, there was a meeting of fundamentalist religious leaders at the White House, which we have reason to believe resulted from my e-mails. I also believe that this is why the RNC is helping to finance and manage a write-in candidate to run against me in this year's election. Until then, I was unopposed. Then all of a sudden a write-in campaign was organized, and their first full page newspaper ad mentioned the ERA. Mostly, they have focused on family, abortion, staying the course in Iraq, and gay marriage—which leads me to believe that they are laying in wait for whatever might happen here on the Hill before going all out on the ERA.

"If we try to go forward with the ERA, I expect that they will open fire with clever ads and plenty of religious venom. This could affect each of you, which is why I wanted to mention all of this as part of your briefing today. That said, I sincerely believe that we have a shot to win on the ERA, or at least to put it back out there in the public square."

The leader thanked Shiloh and asked for comments.

There were several questions about the details of Shiloh's plan and whether she thought that all of the various actors would come through. And there were compliments and vows of support. A few of her colleagues worried that the issue could hurt if not handled well, but generally support was strong. In fact, most of Shiloh's colleagues were excited. Shiloh was glad that they too saw an opening to accomplish something that had long languished as a part of their platform.

The leader closed the caucus with a promise to keep everyone in the loop and said that they would have another full meeting closer to the time that it seemed right for introduction.

After the meeting, Shiloh accompanied the leader and her leadership team back to the leader's office. "I think that went well enough, don't you, Joe?" She asked the assistant whip.

Joe nodded. "But I believe that some of our colleagues are nervous about a few of the tight, red state districts. Maybe we can let the few that it could affect take a pass when it's introduced. By the way, when will it be introduced?"

"I don't know," said the leader. "Shy and I have discussed her introducing it as an amendment on one of the appropriations bills. I need to check with someone on the rules committee to see if that can fly. I think it can, but I want to make sure.

"But," she continued, "when our colleagues begin to talk to the other side, we'll need to be totally united. That's where you guys come in. We can be confident that the other side will use this in the election, but I believe that the country has heard enough of their fundamentalist garbage. I really believe that this could actually work, Shy."

"Yes, me too," offered Shiloh. "So far there has been plenty of enthusiasm, and the momentum seems to be building from all the support groups. It'll all depend on whether they hit the ground running on the campuses when the fall semester begins."

* * * * *

Shiloh reported her meeting to Seth that evening at home over a quiet supper of grilled salmon. "With all the allies you've lined up, I'm beginning to believe we have a real shot. My colleagues ranged from nervous to supportive to enthusiastic. I just can't believe that most American women won't come on board. They don't need to be told; they know they aren't equal; they live that fact every day."

"I don't know," replied her husband. "On the one hand, it seems logical that we could successfully appeal to our fellow citizens' consciences. Yet some people, mostly from disinformation, think that we have been too generous, with our foreign aid funds, for example, since that would eventually be part of this. And yet, we give less proportionally than any other industrial country."

"That's true," agreed Shiloh. "Polls indicate that most Americans think that our foreign aid expenditures are budget breakers when, in fact, they represent one-tenth of 1 percent of our GDP."

"When I was at the UN," agreed Seth. "I was embarrassed by the United States always complaining about its burden. In fact, its economy equals the combined economies of Japan, Germany, England, France, Italy, and most of Canada—the entire rest of the G-7. Yes, some folks see foreign aid as welfare and the countries who participate in it as do-gooders, but chipping in globally is right, and it is also a wise investment."

"I agree," replied Shiloh. "We're all better off when the world is better off, but that argument, like women's rights, has a tendency to fall on deaf ears. I guess it just isn't sexy enough to sell, but I know that you'll find a way, dear, to make all of this work, right?"

"Speaking of sexy," Seth chuckled.

"Hold on, tiger," appealed Shiloh. "First I want to discuss Sam and Barbara's visit tomorrow."

"Okay, since you asked me to suggest something, I was thinking of a stroll down the mall and maybe a peek at the new Rousseau exhibit at the National Art Museum. Then perhaps we can try that new Lebanese restaurant in Georgetown. Or do you have another idea?"

"Well maybe," said Shiloh. "Sam called a few hours ago and said that they have something that they'd like to discuss with us. Since he knew that I was busy at work he was wondering if we could spend some time together just talking."

"Of course. Is something wrong?"

"He didn't say," replied Shiloh. "I guess we'll just have to wait and see."

"Fine, I can go out in the morning and get something light for lunch and maybe some New York strips to grill for supper. What do you think?" asked Seth.

"Sounds good. Now, what were you saying about sexy? Were you referring to that skimpy thingy you bought me in New York, or is it that new grill that you want to buy?"

"Finally," smiled Seth, "my turn to talk."

* * * * *

Sam and Barbara arrived around ten o'clock Saturday morning. They all settled in the study where they shared a hot pot of Starbucks French Roast with bagels, a variety of cream cheeses, grapes, apples, nuts, and chocolate mints.

"I see we're dieting today," mused Barbara.

Seth smiled. "Wait until you see lunch. Pregnant women never seem to stop eating."

They discussed Shy's election campaign and of course the Yankees, until the conversation began to die down. Shiloh and Seth waited expectantly for Sam to say whatever he wanted to say.

He finally started. "Thanks for agreeing to stay in today so I could have my say. At least it's a typically hot DC summer day, so I don't feel so guilty keeping us inside for awhile. But I feel a bit like I should be sitting on a psychiatrist's couch today, and I think Barbara would second that."

Barbara smiled that instinctive smile that reminded Shiloh of a mother showing love and understanding to her child.

"I've been thinking a lot about my situation, rather our situation. Barbara is happy with her career, but she also supports what I'm going to talk about today. We are comfortable financially. I've been practicing law now for almost twenty years and have done quite well. And of course Barbara has a good income too. I guess, what I am trying to say is that we can afford to take a break, if we choose, without any undue burden.

Sam gulped and leaned forward, rubbing his hands together, and hurriedly continued. "As you know, Mario has been sick with alcoholism for quite some time now. He finally went to a treatment program earlier this year and is doing fine now. I love Mario like a brother; we have been through half of our lives together. But I need a break. I am sure that I have been driving him nuts. He is fine; he is strong and sober, and our other partners are solid. I need to do something that will help me, I don't know, remember Mom and my childhood.

"But I also want to do something to help people. I want to give back to society. I had a rocky start as a youngster, and many people helped me. So after talking with Barbara, I went to see Mario about me taking a sabbatical for six months or so."

Shy had tears rolling down her cheeks as she remembered her own childhood and her protective big brother who shouldered so much of the burden and the pain. She thought of the priesthood and the compassion she had felt for those she had counseled and how she always remembered Sam during those times.

"It isn't something that should make you cry," said Sam with a smile. "I look forward to doing something else for awhile, to give back a little of what I have received. In fact, you can help me, Shy, you and that handsome husband of yours."

Seth scrunched his face. "Now I'm worried."

Sam laughed. "Did I actually say handsome?" He continued, "I've often thought about our mother, Shy, about the hardships that she suffered and the hardships that women suffer every day because they are women—because they can be abused almost at will without much consequence for the abuser. So my request is this. I'd like to move here to Washington and help you with the ERA. Barbara wants to help too.

"I realize that having an alcoholic mother does not easily equate with women being killed and maimed in developing countries from desperate unsafe abortions or being abused or denied equal rights. But Mom was mistreated many times by men and was viewed her entire life as a sex object first and a person second. Anyway, what I'm trying to say is that, for the immediate future, I want to take a sabbatical."

Shy started to speak.

"Not yet, sis. I can't believe that I earn my living making cogent arguments. I am making such a hash of this one. I want to do something for my heart and perhaps my head. I'd like to help Seth. I'll work 24-7 if that's what it takes. I'll take out trash, sweep the offices, write memos, or water the potted plants. I'll do whatever would be useful.

"If my legal skills could help, that would be great. But I want to help because I need it for my own peace of mind and because I believe in what you two are trying to do. I present myself to you in humility. If I would be a burden, say so. After my ham-handed presentation just now, I could certainly understand it if you did. I rest my case." Sam sat back and rubbed his eyes.

Shiloh looked at Seth, and he nodded emphatically.

Shy stood and embraced Sam. "The answer is yes. Of course."

"Yes, Sam, it is; the answer is yes," echoed Seth. "I'm desperate for help. Maybe you can teach me how to do what I'm supposed to be doing,"

They all laughed, which relieved the tension.

"So," said Barbara as she brushed away her own tears, "more coffee anyone?"

Shy remembered Sam's courage during their childhood and how he had shielded her from many of the problems. One occasion stood out in her mind.

* * * * *

She had heard sounds coming from her mother's bedroom. Then she had heard a man's voice, "Come on, baby, don't go to sleep; come on, baby."

"I'm sleepy," Shiloh heard her mother say.

"Goddamn it, I said don't go to sleep."

Then Shiloh heard the sound of a slap, and her mother cried out. She ran to Sam's room.

"Sammy; wake up, Sammy."

"What is it, Shy? What's wrong?" said Sam as he became instantly awake.

"There's a man with Mom. He hit her."

Sam jumped up and grabbed his rifle.

Shiloh screamed, "No, Sammy, don't kill him."

Sam said over his shoulder, "Go back to bed, Shy."

She watched as Sam opened their mother's bedroom door. His mother was naked and drunk. There was a trickle of blood oozing from one side of her mouth. A naked man was straddling her, holding one of her arms down and trying to get her legs apart. Sam yelled, "Get off my mom, or you're a dead man!"

Shy, right behind her big brother, said in a teary voice, "No, Sam, please don't shoot him!"

The naked man, looking over his shoulder yelled, "Get the hell out of here! This is none of your goddamned business. Get out."

Sam moved to the end of the bed and reached behind himself to make sure that Shiloh was there. He leveled the rifle and pointed it at the naked man's head. "Mister," said Sam in an ice-cold, even voice, "get up now, or I'll blow your brains out."

Their mother was barely conscious; the naked man looked back at Sam and said, "I told you to get outta here. I'll take that goddamned rifle away from you and stick it up your ass."

Sam jabbed the man in the face with the rifle, cutting him just under his right eye. He worked the lever action, which slid a cartridge into the chamber. Glaring at the man, Sam said calmly, "Now."

The sound of the lever action and the calmness of Sam's voice worked wonders.

Shiloh didn't breathe; she could feel Sam's legs shaking. The naked man obeyed and stood.

Sam said, "Gather your clothes."

The naked man started to pull on his shorts. Sam was losing his patience. He poked the man in the side with the barrel of his rifle and shouted, "Pick up your damn clothes and move it."

The naked man complied, and Sam marched him to the front door.

"Out!" Sam shouted.

"Let me get dressed first."

"Get out, now. You can dress outside."

The man went out. Sam stood in the doorway and watched as the man fell down in a bed of marigolds trying to pull on his pants.

Shy snickered.

"Shiloh, you little devil. I thought I told you to go to bed."

They looked at each other, Shy in her pj's and Sam in his jockey shorts, and they both started to laugh. Sam knelt down and hugged his little sister. Shy remembered feeling so safe with Sammy protecting their mom.

* * * * *

Now as they sat together talking, she understood why Sam wanted to help. She loved her big brother and was proud of his accomplishments.

They all agreed to look for an apartment for Sam on Sunday, after he politely turned down their offer to stay with Shiloh and Seth. Barbara would split her time between Trenton and Washington, staying with the kids while they were there for summer break from college and finishing a project she was working on for her firm before she moved to Washington to join Sam. Sam would report for work at ERA Today the following week, just in time for Washington in August.

"Most people, including the politicians, leave town in August," said Sam as he laughed. "But I move in. Maybe it's a good time to take over."

"Someone needs to," offered Seth.

Shiloh was selfishly pleased about the turn of events with Sam and Barbara. She was sad about Sam's haunting memories about their mother. But there was a lot of work to do, and Seth needed the help. Plus, that meant there would be four of them to discuss strategy and share ideas and commiserate with when the going got tough.

She knew that this would be a busy fall for all of them. And there was that little matter of an election to win. She felt good about the election, but she was sure that her opponents would make her life much more difficult before it was over.

She was happy with her pregnancy. She didn't really have much in the way of morning sickness, and her doctor was pleased with her progress. She would have an amniocentesis soon to make sure that everything was okay.

Shiloh didn't care if she had a girl or a boy, as long as her baby was healthy. Her major concern was the load she had to carry during her pregnancy. She was still concerned about stress or anything that could harm the development of her child. She had always dreamed of being a mother, but she had thought that time had passed her by. Now that she had this opportunity, she didn't want anything to in any way harm her child.

* * * * *

Seth and Sam had discussed the campaign when Seth was tending the grill. They were both worried about the tone of the campaign and the reasoning behind it, and they were nervous about Lawson and any stunts that he might plan to disrupt things.

Plus, Seth was frightened about Lawson's capacity for violence. Thus the two men agreed that, no matter what, one of them would always be with Shiloh when she was in the district campaigning, once September rolled around and the campaign heated up.

Seth had talked to Barry a few times by phone and shared his feelings about the campaign. Barry had told Seth he was not only worried about Shiloh but also about Charlie. He worried that Charlie, who was living in a gay relationship, might be used in the campaign. He knew the other side would stop at nothing, and he didn't want Charlie to get hurt either physically or emotionally. He had volunteered to help in any way he could, including being available in Nashville to help Shiloh with her campaign.

* * * * *

Charlie wasn't too worried about the campaign, but he was about Lawson, especially with Shy's pregnancy. He would never forgive himself if Shiloh lost her baby because of some sort of emotional stress or a tussle of some kind.

* * * * *

For his part, Lawson was still brooding. Boyd had greatly improved after a dismal start, but Jimmy Bob Lawson could not accept anything less than victory. Giles had to go. She was a demon to him, a person who had to be stopped at all costs. His father would accept nothing less. God would accept nothing less.

* * * * *

In the meantime, Wesley Bragg, the devious and aggressive White House staffer the guru had selected to run their end of the anti-Giles operation, had been busy. He and his team were in touch with fundamentalist ministers around the country. They had developed numerous pieces of anti-ERA material for a variety of audiences: family-focused for the churches, abortion-focused for the right-to-life crowd, and antigay for all groups. He had enlisted conservative women's groups, and he was working on an anti-ERA ad for Shiloh's district. He wanted to keep her busy.

His biggest coup was setting up a 527 organization, which would also sponsor a national ad against the ERA. Money was not a problem. He had essentially been given a blank check. They would not only defeat the ERA, they would hang it around the necks of every Democrat who was up for election or reelection, all of those in the House and the thirty-three who where contesting in the Senate.

He was almost ready. Giles and her partisan leader would be toast when he was through with them. *Yes indeed,* thought Bragg, *it is going to be a busy fall.*

* * * * *

Sam walked in the door of the office at his first day on his new job. "Hey, bro, where can I plug in this laptop?"

"Welcome," replied Seth, "let me take you around to meet the team. I told them that we had more grist for the mill arriving today."

"Grist indeed. You're kind, brother-in-law. Just what Washington needs: another lawyer."

After the introductions, Seth showed Sam his office. "It's not the kind of place you had in Jersey, pal, but this is how we poor, bleeding hearts live."

"It looks great to me, boss. So what do you have for a lazy lawyer who is a bad typist?"

"Well, I was thinking of a few days of reading and some briefings from the team and then off you go around the world. You did bring your passport, didn't you?"

"Yes. What do you have in mind?"

"As you may remember, we're trying to make things happen in other countries when this thing goes down here and in the UN. It all depends on everything going just as we planned, which of course it won't. That's what you need to explain to our friends around the world. You see, what we hope will happen is demonstrations, press coverage, and calls for action from every corner of the globe at the same time. What you need to do is go over all of that again and advise them about the timing. And you'll also be delivering checks from the foundations, sample editorials, speeches, and talking points."

"This will be a whole new life for me," replied Sam, "but I'm ready to learn and do whatever you tell me."

Seth nodded. "Actually, this is also part of your high-speed, jump-start education. We desperately need what you'll do during your travels, but it will also serve as a crash course for you as well."

Seth spent the next two hours going over their work to date, who was involved, the committee structure, and their strategy.

Sam was impressed. "Wow, you've been busy. I feel a bit out of touch. The practice of law is challenging because it is constantly changing. You get new clients, new issues, and different twists. But it comes and goes, and we start again.

"This is a big-picture deal you have here. It's a chance to make something happen that is wonderful and long overdue. I knew that I wanted to be involved, but I didn't really know what that meant. Now I do. Or I should say, I'm beginning to understand the process.

"It's far more complex than I imagined. It's still difficult for me to fathom that my baby sister is at the center of this storm. I'm really proud of her. She's lucky to have a life mate who understands. Your early retirement, I must say, inspired me."

"I'm no saint," Seth said blandly as he took a sip from his long forgotten cup of coffee. "As much as I admire what the UN stands for and accomplishes, it is only as good as its members allow it to be. Quite frankly, it's a nice change of pace to work on something that doesn't require the blessings of an executive board, ECOSOC, and the General Assembly."

"What is ECOSOC?" inquired Sam.

"Never mind, pal. It is just UN alphabet soup. So much time at the UN is driven by process. Sometimes it is a real hassle: words, words, and more words."

"You sound a bit jaded."

Seth shrugged. "No, I loved my work, but it's nice to work on something that's moving forward every day with a rigid timeline. This exercise is measured by how much time we have to do our task rather than step-by-step with faints, combined with pitch, roll, and yaw, and then delays for consultation and so forth. Interestingly, the worst offender in the UN process is our good old USA. The United States want everything their way. And they usually get it, but it takes time and long, drawn out negotiations."

"But if it's okay, can I go back to what we were discussing last night, Sam? Shy's campaign."

"Yes," said Sam. "That's on my mind too."

"The other candidate isn't great," replied Seth, "but he has a lot of help and is gaining. Plus, there is that Lawson guy in the shadows. That's why I'm so happy that one of us will always be with Shy in September. That's when things will start heating up."

"I am delighted that I can help here and in Nashville, Seth. I look forward to all of it."

"I expect more attack ads soon," said Seth, "and when the ERA is introduced, I'm certain the attacks will intensify, but that will be in October. Charlie and Tom are there, and Barry comes up to stay with Shy some too, but with you there I feel much more comfortable."

Sam nodded. "Me too. But will Shy agree?"

"Probably not, but she'll be overruled by the menfolk on this one. What do you think?"

"I totally agree. I dearly love my sister and will do anything to help. And by the way, she has a great husband. She waited a long time, but she chose well, very well."

"I didn't say she was always smart," Seth said with a smile. "Thank you, Sam."

* * * * *

One day in late August, Shiloh called Seth from Nashville where she was campaigning during the August congressional recess.

"Hi, baby," answered Seth, "what's up?"

Shiloh sighed. "I'm just so depressed. It's hot, and I'm uncomfortable. The campaign is sheer drudgery. I'm just so tired of it all."

Seth thought about how to answer his wife. The iron woman was starting to feel the pressure that was her life these days. What could he do? He was swamped too. On the other hand, Shy was, as Reggie Jackson would say, the straw that stirred the drink.

"First, sweetheart, let me give you some good news. Sam just called from Bangkok and reports that each of his stops so far has been terrific. Our partners are enthusiastic, and Sam, to say the least, is running hard. He was absolutely ebullient, Shy. The other news is that I was going to surprise you and come down tomorrow for a long weekend. I was just about to call Charlie to ask him to give us three days to just chill out and relax. Will that help?"

"Oh, Seth, that would be wonderful. I know I can't quit and disappoint people who are counting on me, darling, but I just feel so exhausted."

"I certainly understand why. Let me call Charlie and get back to you."

Charlie readily agreed to clear Shy's schedule for a few days.

"Seth, I was about to call you," he said when he answered. "Shy hasn't been herself for the past week or so. She's doing well, but always being 'on' and dealing with such nastiness is tiring and depressing. Plus it's hot, and she's pregnant. I'm amazed at how devoted the other side is these days and how mean-spirited. That is taking a toll too."

Seth made his flight arrangements and made a few other phone calls. He would get in that night and spend the night with Shy at the condo, and they would drive to Sewanee Friday morning. He had made reservations at the Sewanee Inn for four rooms.

It was a bit cooler in Sewanee. They walked around the campus and spent an hour sitting in the quiet, cool cathedral. They talked about Shy's campus days and had lunch with one of her old professors. That afternoon, they went back to the inn and took a bottle of wine to their room and did what couples do when they are away from home in a hotel room alone with a bottle of wine, although only Seth could partake in the wine.

They drove over to Saint Andrew's School and walked around the campus. That evening they had a quiet dinner in their room at the inn.

Seth could tell that Shy was beginning to unwind. That evening they lay in bed and talked about names for their child. Her pregnancy was going well, but because she was forty-one, they were both worried about the amniocentesis that was scheduled for when she returned to the Washington. They held each other and enjoyed each other's closeness.

Shiloh snuggled in close. "You're wonderful. How did I ever survive without you? I can barely remember the time when you weren't with me."

"I feel the same way. We have something special. If I were to pass on at this moment, I would do so knowing that I had loved one of God's favorite angels. I can't imagine a better life."

"Oh, darling." Shy had tears in her eyes. "I love you so much. I'm so sorry that I've taken you away from Washington and our mutual work. I guess that I needed some pampering."

"Don't be foolish. I needed some too. You can call that pampering if you like; I call it lust for my favorite priest.

"But I was afraid," Seth continued, "that the woman I work for would scold me for being a lazy, dirty old man."

They fell asleep in each other's arms.

The next morning, they had coffee and pastries in the room. Seth had left the "Do Not Disturb" sign on the door to their room. Seth excused himself at ten o'clock to go get a newspaper and check on his arrangements.

He and Shy left their room at noon to go to lunch. Instead of the restaurant, they went to a small meeting room. Shiloh looked puzzled but said nothing and followed. When Seth opened the door, the Jacobsons, the Whitfields, and Sarah Bartlett and her husband, Abe, who were back home in Chattanooga for a two-week summer break, greeted them. Shiloh put her hand over her mouth as tears filled her eyes. She hugged everyone, and they all stood around and had a glass of wine, except for Shiloh, who had sparkling water, while waiting for lunch to arrive.

"This is quite a surprise," enthused Shiloh. "I see my husband brought in the National Guard to cheer me up."

"We all need cheering sometimes, Shy," exclaimed Bill. "Even hotshot politicians like you and our distinguished governor here."

"Goodness, yes," said Trudy, "when Barry wasn't moping around worrying about this problem or that, he was stewing over what words to use for a speech or how he could handle his life after his favorite staff member left him."

"Yes, I'm still stewing about Sarah leaving me," he chuckled.

Sarah smiled. "And everything's fine at the office, Shy," she said. "No one's there to cause any problems. Seriously, though, all is well, and we're ready for the fall, boss."

"I love you all," answered Shy, looking toward Seth, "even my sneaky husband."

* * * * *

They had talked about Shy's pregnancy, the campaign, and the upcoming ERA battle. But mostly they talked about All Saints, their families, and how much Shy was loved and respected by her constituents. It was just what Shy needed. Plenty of love and affection sprinkled in with a little praise, some joking, and a pledge from all to help Shy get through the next few months until the birth of her child in December.

That evening they had a long, lazy supper with more talk and much laughter. The three couples left the next morning after breakfast, while Shiloh and Seth stayed in Sewanee for another day before driving back to Nashville, where they had supper with Charlie and Tom. Seth flew back to Washington early Monday morning. Shiloh continued to campaign until the Wednesday before Labor Day when she returned to Washington.

Shy felt better now. The restful weekend with Seth, seeing her friends, and being away from the campaign for a few days helped Shiloh refocus and recharge. She was confident that she would win the election and the ERA battle. She was ready, and with a clean bill of health from the amniocentesis for her developing child, she was as happy as she could ever remember.

She and Seth invited the ERA Today team, Sam and Barbara, and Shy's congressional staff and their families over for a cookout on the Sunday before Labor Day. It was a late afternoon and evening of food, drink, and light conversation among friends. They all knew that this would be the last respite for a long while, so they made the best of it. The following Tuesday, September 5, would be the beginning of a long and tense struggle.

Chapter 14

Shiloh saw the new TV ad that started the day after Labor Day. It pictured Raymond Boyd at a National Guard armory, surrounded by American flags and speaking about his support for staying the course in Iraq, his respect for our men and women in uniform, and his commitment to a strong America that would lead the world morally, militarily, and economically in the twenty-first century. Then it showed a film clip of U.S. troops in Iraq, a shot of the trader's floor on Wall Street, and a series of pictures of churches.

The voiceover said, "Raymond Boyd will bring strong leadership to Congress. He is the man for the times. He is dedicated to American values. He is a religious man. He is a family man. He is a man of honor, who we in the Fifth District can trust.

"His opponent, Catherine Shiloh Giles, is not qualified. She wants to run from America's responsibilities abroad. She supports homosexual marriage. She supports abortion on demand, and her personal life is not appropriate for Congress. Giles must go. For honesty, for integrity, for morality, write in Ray Boyd for Congress on November 7.

"Paid for by the friends of Ray Boyd."

The ad ended with Boyd's obligatory, "My name is Ray Boyd, and I approve this message."

The screen faded with a picture of an absentee ballot with Boyd's name written in the appropriate space.

Shiloh was insulted, but she doubted that many people would fall for such trash.

Another quarter page ad appeared in *The Tennessean* with a write-in ballot in the lower, right-hand corner. Above it was written, "Clip out and use this write-in ballot to send Ray Boyd to Congress on November 7."

The ad copy parroted the TV ad.

But it didn't stop there. Even the vice president, the second most important person in the country, came to Nashville and spoke for Boyd the next week, followed the week after by the chairperson of the National Party. Boyd was getting ink that Shiloh couldn't match. She continued with her speaking schedule. She was in Nashville either Saturday through Monday or Friday through Sunday each week. Seth was with her the first two weekends.

Shiloh noticed that everywhere she went to speak there were demonstrators carrying signs: "Stop Giles," "Stop Abortion," "Stop Homo Marriage," "Support the Troops." The demonstrators were loud but peaceful.

Seth stayed close to Shiloh at every event. He and Charlie stayed on each side of her when she entered and left venues. Shy saw Lawson and told Seth to be calm, but Lawson was keeping back and did not try to provoke another confrontation.

Shiloh wasn't too bothered by the demonstrators or the ads. After that weekend in Sewanee, she'd gotten a second wind and was determined to work hard to win reelection. She was also thinking about the ERA, which was just about all she and Seth discussed. The only issue that really concerned Shiloh was Lawson, not for herself, but for Seth.

Every time they saw Lawson, Shiloh would say, "Be calm, darling," or "Stay cool, Seth." And every time, Seth would answer, "It's okay, Shiloh, I learned my lesson," or "Please don't worry, Shy. I know he's just a blowhard."

But Shiloh had overheard Charlie and Seth agreeing that Lawson had to be watched closely, and both were always alert to Lawson when he was present. They agreed that under no circumstance was Shy to be left alone. Even when she had to visit the ladies room, which was more frequent these days with her pregnancy, one of them would always take her to the door and wait. Even though she thought it was unnecessary, she appreciated that both men were always vigilant.

In spite of the nasty tactics and the demonstrations, Shiloh was always well received, and her speeches were well covered. Her standard stump speech focused on supporting U.S. troops, her work for the medical treatment and rehabilitation of the wounded, her support of a fair tax system that did not penalize the middle class, and her support for education and health care and an easy to understand prescription drug system for the elderly.

Shiloh spoke calmly and forcefully when queried by her audiences about abortion. "We live in a country where our citizens should be able to make their own decisions about contraception and abortion. We can lessen the need by making available options to avoid unwanted pregnancies. I don't believe that we'll ever see full agreement either way on the abortion issue because the sides are too entrenched. Let us do our best to help make it rare, and let us also remember that we live in a democracy, not a theocracy. The founding fathers were wise to disavow a state religion and to guarantee the free practice of religion. Let us as a nation today agree to disagree on certain social issues and be thankful that we live in a country where that is possible."

The polls tightened to 56–44, but Charlie was still confident. "Remember," he told Shiloh and Seth over coffee one evening after a day of campaigning, "it takes a lot of will to go to the polls and write in a candidate's name. Some churches, like Lawson's, will give instructions to their congregations, but most won't. It's hard enough to get people to the polls, much less to get them to execute a write-in ballot."

The three of them agreed that the A team from Washington had helped Boyd, but he was still less than charismatic. Charlie and Seth agreed that Shiloh was still Shiloh: articulate, smart, pretty, and poised. Shiloh laughed at their characterization.

"Well," she mused, "at least I know two votes I can count on."

* * * * *

Lawson would retreat to his study after demonstrating at Shiloh's events. He was always looking at polling data. *The devil woman will win again*, he thought. *Boyd will never catch her. Damn her. I must not allow her to go forth again with her blaspheming and her godlessness.*

Abortion rare, indeed. Homo unions, indeed. He would think of his father and his expectations; and he would think of his name and what God expected of Robert James's only son.

On days like today, he would lie in bed at night, haunted by the vision of Shiloh—at once a demon that must be beaten at all costs and still his own personal demon, for whom he lusted.

* * * * *

Sam accompanied Shiloh to Nashville the next weekend. Barry and Trudy, who stayed with the Jacobsons, joined him. At one event, Barry pointed out Lawson to Sam. Sam stayed behind at the door and watched Lawson for a few minutes.

Sam commented to Shy about watching Lawson. "Seeing him reminded me of a few of the opponents I met during divorce cases who were determined to exact some sort of punishment from their marriage partner that was beyond the law. One client told me, 'I don't care what it costs. I want to make the son of a bitch wish he were in hell.' As if alimony, child support, the house, and the bulk of the bank account weren't enough. Lawson seems just as determined."

Shiloh sighed. "Don't worry about him, Sam. He is a bit spooky, but what can he do? I worry about Seth when Lawson's here. I don't want to have to worry about you too."

"All we want is for you to be safe, Shy," replied her brother. "Just don't let your guard down, and we won't either. And don't worry, neither your husband nor your brother are about to provoke anything. But God help him if he tries anything."

Shiloh only laughed.

* * * * *

Seth had one last meeting with the domestic committee of the whole that represented all of the groups: religion, NGO, college, and foundation. They discussed the details of their plans, and then Seth introduced them to Judy Keller of the ERA Today team.

"Judy has set up a Listserv that includes all of you by group so she won't crash our system. She will send daily updates beginning next Monday, September 25. I will also meet with the regional NGO groups in two days and hope that we can keep them in the loop as well. We're getting close, friends. It all depends on what can be worked out in the House now. The UN schedule is on course."

He held a similar meeting with the foreign groups and visited his friends in New York one last time.

Shiloh had received a green light from the minority leader and was told to be ready. It looked like a go. Shiloh and the minority leader would meet with the Democratic Caucus in a few days. Then they would get ready for all hell to break loose.

After the foreign group left town, Shiloh and Seth had a quiet supper at home.

Seth raised his wine glass. "Here's to you and to a victory in October with the ERA and to your reelection in November. Time is moving fast now, but my confidence is high. I believe we can do both."

"That's quite a mouthful and quite a job you're doing with the ERA. Yes, I agree, we just might win the election, and if we don't win the ERA right away, at least the country, and perhaps even the world, will know what it is."

They were both tired, especially Shiloh, who was getting bigger by the day. But they were happy and eager for their plans to bear fruit.

* * * * *

"It's nice to see you again, Pam."

"Hi, Seth. Same here," answered Pam Bradley, the CEO of an NGO that specialized in media outreach, Concern Communications Group (CCG).

"I suppose that the word is getting out about what our little group is up to," queried Seth.

"More to the point, word is getting out about what your wife is up to," said Pam with a smile.

"I heard there were no secrets in this town," mused Seth.

"None," agreed Pam. "But I think that we'll be ready for liftoff."

Just then, a waiter came to take their drink order. They were sitting in the parlor of the Tabard Inn just off Connecticut Avenue on N Street.

Pam Bradley was a respected media pro in Washington. She had come to the nation's capital straight from college and had cut her teeth working for the women's movement. She could write, and soon she learned that she could also sell to the media. She could sell ideas, articles, and issues like few others.

Over the years, she grew restless working for other organizations and set up her own NGO, which in time became the place to go for other NGOs that needed help with the media. Pam's fees, while substantial, paled when compared to for-profit PR firms. Plus, she knew social and environmental issues and required little or no coaching. She could hit the ground running, while the big, expensive groups always needed time to learn the issue and its nuances. She was just what Seth needed.

With drinks in hand, Seth started his pitch. "As you remember, I called you in June and asked you if we could meet in a few months. I also asked if you would be available to run a very difficult campaign full time. Well the time has come. I would've wanted to meet you much earlier, but certain pieces had to fall in place before I could commit. Now, I want to see if you are still interested and if we can afford you."

"You don't have to worry about whether we're interested, if we're going to be talking about what I'm hearing, and if what I understand about your timing is true, you don't have many choices left."

"Touché," replied Seth with a timid smile.

"And, yes, you can afford CCG."

"I'm so sorry. We were sworn to secrecy, and I never really considered anyone else. Your reputation is superb. So, my friend, you have me over a barrel."

"That's true. You did wait awhile, and I think I know why." She was smiling.

Seth liked Pam's directness. "Okay, then let me explain why it took so long to get a green light," offered Seth. He explained the two-year process and what they had been up to with the various groups. By the time he had finished, they were seated at their table for supper.

"Wow, you've been busy. I admire your organizational skills and, even more than that, your and your wife's dedication. It's a reminder that Washington is really and truly an inside-the-beltway place. I knew from some in and around Congress that your wife, the congresswoman …"

Seth interrupted her, "Please refer to her when you meet her as Shy. She's not really that into titles."

Pam smiled. "I had heard that she was relaxed that way; some aren't you know."

She continued, "As I said, I knew from some that Shy was going to offer up the ERA and try to use a different approach. But I knew nothing about your grassroots and international work. You see, Seth, if it doesn't happen inside the beltway, it doesn't happen. Is there any wonder that most in Congress don't really know their constituents?"

Pam slowed down long enough to sip her drink and continued. "The gossip in this town is only about this town; thus I only knew a little about what you have been up to here. I'm impressed, very impressed. And I'm excited."

"I'd heard that," said Seth, "about Washington, but I didn't believe it could be so bad."

"It's probably a little exaggerated," said Pam, "but not much. What this means to me, what you have accomplished, that is, is that we can actually think about winning. I came here thinking that you wanted to get some key newspaper placements and then make some noise to rattle the opposition about women's issues before the election. But this has a real chance. Let's do it."

"I can't tell you how much that is music to my ears. I've been cloistered, thinking only about this issue for quite awhile now, inside the beltway for the most part. I understand that there is a war in Iraq."

Pam laughed and said, "Yes, I heard that too. Please let me hear more about your plans."

Seth explained what they needed.

When it was Pam's turn to respond, she reminded Seth of his drill instructor in boot camp. "I need a computer copy of all your partners, your press kit, which we will probably redo, and as exact a timing schedule as you can produce. Do you have anyone working on a national TV ad?"

"Yes," replied Seth, "the party is going to handle that. And remember, the Senate will introduce the day after the House."

"Great. I think we can help."

"But what about cost?" asked Seth.

"How much can you spend?"

"We have a million set aside for media work," he replied.

"That's more than enough. CCG will cost about four to five hundred thousand for what will be required, now that I understand the breadth and depth of what you want to do. I'll need to put a team on this full time. We'll likely need to use some of your leftover cash for ads and international buys and placements."

All of a sudden, they noticed that the staff at the Tabard were their only companions, and they all looked ready to go home.

"Oops," said Seth, "we'd better let these folks go home."

Seth walked Pam to her car and they shook hands.

"We're counting on you, friend," said Seth.

"And I on you. I've wanted this to happen for as long as I can remember. I'm proud to be a part of your team."

Seth walked away confident. Another piece of the puzzle had just fallen into place.

* * * * *

Seth went to Nashville with Shy that weekend, and Sam stayed in DC as they had agreed. Sam had to organize himself for his part of the gear-up for the final push.

In Nashville, the scene was still tense. The battering was steady. The ads in *The Tennessean* with the write-in ballot were now daily. And each day, there was new copy. Today's version was about Shiloh's disregard for Christian values and discussed her leadership on the appropriations committee for funding for population work in China. It claimed she supported coercion that included the worst kind of human rights violations. And it included her vote against abstinence-only sex education and her speech to add more Title X funding for family planning for the young and the poor in the United States.

Each day was a different angle. And each day it looked dreadful.

To a practiced observer like Shiloh, the fingerprints of the White House guru were everywhere. Shiloh's team knew that the real reason was the ERA.

The other party had plenty of more vulnerable seats to go after, but they wanted to keep Shiloh distracted. They wanted to discredit the woman who would introduce an issue that could, in the guru's mind, hurt his party.

* * * * *

Meanwhile, Wesley Bragg and his troops were ready. "Give us the signal and we'll move," he had told the guru. "The religious folks are ready. Just give us the word."

"Keep your powder dry, Wes. You'll know when it's time. We'll all know. The world will know," advised the guru. "Just keep up the pressure in Nashville."

* * * * *

The minority leader sat with the Speaker and the new majority leader to go over the legislative calendar. This was crunch time. Seven of the thirteen appropriations bills still needed to be passed. The members wanted to get it over with as quickly as possible so they could go home and campaign. Non-passage would shut down the government if continuing resolutions, which kept the government running at past budget levels, were not passed. No one wanted a shutdown, which would anger voters, or a continuing resolution, which would be seen as putting off till tomorrow what you were paid to do today.

The government shutdown during the Clinton years had angered voters, who in turn had closed the gap in the House, making the majority slim. The majority party of Congress was not known for cooperation, but with lesser numbers, they needed it now.

During the course of their discussion, the minority leader casually suggested October 5 for the Defense Department appropriations bill, which could be followed by the State Department, Health and Human Services, and on and on until all the others were passed. They had already passed the easier bills the two previous weeks.

* * * * *

The Democratic Caucus met and discussed their plans. When queried, several Republicans had told their Democratic colleagues that they could see themselves voting for the ERA. They knew the poll data and knew what an all-out effort could mean. However, they were worried about how their leaders would respond. Added to the mix were rumors that the White House would use all of its power to stop passage. But many of the Republican House members were in tight elections, some for the first time in years. Some of them were also tired of the heavy hand of the guru and their party leaders.

Political analysts were saying that the House could change hands in this election, and the Senate, though less likely, was even possible. It was a damned-if-you-do-and-damned-if-you-don't scenario. Of course, it could backfire on the Democrats if their opponents scored on the anti-ERA invectives. They had won before on issues that the public didn't support, such as environmental and gun control legislation. They knew that if the White House really wanted to stop the ERA, the battle would be tough. The guru was a master strategist. He had crafted an effective, no-holds-barred, winning, though many thought dirty, strategy for the presidential election of 2004. He was never to be taken lightly.

It is with that background that the minority leader discussed her strategy with the Democratic Caucus. "My friends," she said, "there are risks in going forward, but there's also a strong possibility for great gains. Women and politicians like us have been trying to move this agenda forward since the Women's Rights Convention in Seneca Falls, New York, in 1848. It is right to do it on merits alone. And I believe it's right to take the political risk at this moment in history.

"I've spoken to party leaders in the Senate and outside. We have their support. I hope we can work together on this. If you must abstain, do so. But a no vote is not acceptable."

She received strong applause.

"As you all know," she continued, "we will work on appropriations day and night for the next couple of weeks. We will take Fridays off for campaigning and perhaps Mondays if this drags out too long. But be here for our work. The leadership team will be in touch when the moment for action arrives. Shiloh will lead off the debate, and Carolyn Maloney will manage the floor."

There was an air of excitement as the members trudged back to their offices. This exercise would make history one way or another. Their words would be remembered, their vote recorded.

* * * * *

The next day, Shiloh went to the doctor for her semimonthly checkup. Her amniocentesis had told Seth and her that their baby was a girl as well as assuring them of her health. Today Shiloh would get her usual ultrasound exam, as well as the routine urine and blood tests.

When she got back to the office she called Seth to report.

Seth answered the phone. "Hi, babe. Pam just called and reported that the media was responding well."

"Great, sweetie, did you forget my appointment today?"

"Of course not," he lied.

"Good, your prodigy is doing fine. I could see her face today. She is so beautiful."

"Wonderful, darling. I hope the doctor gave you a picture to show me tonight."

"He did, and I won't forget it like I did last time."

"Seth, the doctor also said that I was okay but that he wants me to restrict my schedule and be careful. In fact, I have to see him every week now. I don't know if he has something to worry about or if it's because of my age and work schedule. But he definitely wants me to go a bit slower. And before you say anything, don't worry, I will. I don't want to risk any problems"

"Yes, I agree 100 percent, Shy. Shall I pick you up at work?"

"No, silly, walking home's about all the exercise I get these days. But we can talk about all of this tonight."

"Okay," said Seth. Then in a sheepish voice he said, "I didn't remember, dear. I completely forgot, but I couldn't let my little fib stand. Sorry."

Shiloh laughed. "I love you, Seth; you are so wonderful."

"I love you too, sweetie," Seth said as he hung up the phone.

* * * * *

That evening over supper Seth asked, "So why are you named Shiloh? Is it a family name, or did they just like the sound of Shiloh? I know I do."

"It's a long story, Seth," replied his wife as she pushed away from the table, put her dishes in the sink, and turned on the stove to heat water for some decaf tea.

"Well," said Seth, as he swallowed a mouthful of food. "Let's hear it."

"The short version," Shiloh began as she waited for her water to boil, "is that it is a family name. My Grandma Alice's father, my great-grandfather, had two wives. The first one, Victoria, had eight children and died at an early age. One of her sons fought in the Civil War and died at Shiloh. "

"And that's it?" asked Seth as he got a couple of cups from the cupboard for tea.

"No, that's just the beginning. My great-grandfather married another woman, a Cherokee woman named Tennessee Carolina, and she also had eight children. The first was a girl who he named Shiloh in honor of his son. Her last child was Grandma Alice, who was born in 1886. Shiloh was my father's favorite aunt. She pampered him when he was a boy, so he named me Catherine Shiloh. Catherine was for my mother's mother, and Shiloh for his aunt."

"Wow, that's quite a story. So you're part Indian?"

"Yes, but unfortunately the Gileses lost touch after my great-grandfather died."

"Did you ever meet the other Shiloh?"

"Heavens no. She died when my dad was a young boy."

"So then, our daughter will be Shiloh the third."

"Seth, please, I don't want her to feel any pressure to be like her mother. Besides I like Setharina better."

"Okay. Okay. I give up," Seth laughed. I'll check the Internet. I'm sure they have baby names there somewhere. But not until we finish the ERA and you are reelected."

Chapter 15

Shiloh was accompanied to the district on the weekend before ERA D-day by Sam. The campaign had reached a plateau. Polling was conducted weekly now, and the numbers were stable with Shiloh hovering between 56 to 57 percent.

Shiloh and Sam hosted supper at the condo on Friday night for Wayne Long and the Nashville district office staff. They also invited Charlie and Tom, the Whitfields, and the Jacobsons. She wanted to explain to her local staff and close friends what was about to happen.

Shiloh discussed the history of the ERA and the current situation. "The Florida attempt in 2003 was a hard fight," she explained. "The governor of that state referred to the ERA resolution being debated in the Florida legislature as 'retro' legislation. And yet, polling shows that the majority of the American people would like it to be in the Constitution.

"But like environmental and other issues where the public disagrees with this administration and its followers, the administration just does as it pleases and wins elections on issues like terrorism and unsolvable but highly charged social issues. Their clever tactics nullify serious discussions about education and health and personal issues such as child care and gas prices.

"We know equality in this country is much advanced, but women still have to prove their rights while men don't, like the case where a woman was trying to enroll at the all-male and publicly financed Virginia Military Institute. She had to go through the expense, the pressure, and the unwanted publicity to get in. And legislation to overturn hard fought gains such as Title IX, which addresses the equality of women's education, can be modified or even abolished by a majority vote of one in Congress.

"That would not happen if the ERA were an amendment to the Constitution. Sandy Oestreich, the woman who led the ERA movement in Florida, reckoned that women always having to prove their rights was like President Lincoln trying to pass the Emancipation Proclamation one plantation at a time.

"Anyway, I imagine that opponents will focus on abortion and same-sex marriage and any other divisive issue they can come up with to get at me here in the district and to stop the ERA nationally when it is introduced in the House and Senate. Around the fifth of October, I'll introduce the ERA in the House, and it'll be introduced in the Senate the next day. Sam will be staying here with you this week to help with the media. And Seth is working on ally support with colleges, NGOs, and religious groups from Washington."

Her staff was excited, and Bill was beside himself.

"Shy," Bill enthused, "when we discussed the growing domination of the right years ago, I never dreamed that you would be one of the leaders at the forefront to correct the course of the Good Ship America."

Shiloh blushed. "Oh, Bill, come on. It's nothing like that. I'm just one of 435 members of the House. We're working together. It's the minority leader who is doing the heavy lifting and others who have fought the good fight for years like Carolyn Maloney. I'm merely a member of the team."

"Yes," replied Bill, "a team for America's real values. Go for it!"

* * * * *

Seth and Pam Bradley were meeting almost constantly. He had been to her office several times. Seeing her staff of twenty hard at work was like watching an action movie. They were working almost 24-7 and loving it. They were tired but excited. Seth and Pam had met with the Democratic leadership to discuss their press strategy and had consulted with the colleges and several NGOs. It seemed that both were either meeting someone or on the phone constantly.

CCG had revised the ERA Today press kit and designed new covers in all the appropriate languages. They had developed several talking points about the ERA for their allies around the country and the world, which they shared with the Democratic leaders of both Houses of Congress. They had also written numerous one- and five-minute speeches for House members for the floor debate. Now they were working on press releases.

Finally, they were preparing a ten-page editorial memo that was going to over five hundred newspapers around the world. The editorial memos covered the U.S. situation, the global situation, history, statistics, personal stories, and the consequences for women in selected countries around the world. It also included references to the UN documents that mentioned gender equality and women's rights.

On debate day, an hour before the debate started, they would contact CNN and other major U.S. networks, along with BBC and numerous regional outlets throughout the world. They would also alert C-SPAN to expect urgent feed requests.

Seth thought Pam's brain was like a computer. Every time he thought that they had reached the point of maximum exposure, she would have several more suggestions and walk through her office looking for warm bodies to act on her latest impulses. Today she wondered about setting up a press conference at the Millennium Hotel across the street from the UN at 10:00 a.m. on the day after the ERA was introduced in Congress and, hopefully, passed by the General Assembly. The press conference would invite the UN press corps, as well as other international press that did not have offices at the UN, plus radio, TV, and magazine correspondents.

Seth heard her down the hall. "Get a room that will accommodate two hundred with theater-style seating, a riser with a long table, and a podium for the middle; get coffee, pastries, and all the usual electrical hookups necessary for radio and TV. Find a small adjoining room, and be sure they set up a few areas with blue backdrops for one-on-one TV interviews, a few partitioned off areas with tables and chairs for radio interviews and ..."

Seth chuckled as Pam continued her litany of instructions.

Then to another person, he heard her command, "Work with Seth to get all the contact numbers and names of the Dutch and Brits, the European Union Representative, and the current chairperson of all the global regions. Once Seth calls them we can follow up and make sure to get them to the press conference."

Pam came into her office where Seth was working. "You need to call your main actors at the country missions at the UN."

Seth interrupted, "I heard you down the hall. I'm on it. Good idea. I'll go to my office and finish up and then update our collaborators around the world."

Seth thought on the way back to his office, *Now I know what it must be like to live in a beehive or an anthill.*

He was pleased but on overdrive: too much to do, too little time.

* * * * *

Shiloh and Sam went over her statement Sunday after early services at All Saints. He took her to the airport at 4:00 p.m. for her flight back to Washington.

Shiloh said with a smile, "I can't remember if it's Delta through Atlanta or Northwest through Cincinnati."

"Neither," he said. "It's Mr. Green in the Conservatory with the candlestick."

When they arrived at the terminal, Sam looked at his sister. "How you feeling, sis? You're about seven months now, isn't it? You sure you aren't having twins?"

"I feel fine, except that I feel like I'm having an entire basketball team. Oh, I forgot to tell you when you returned that my last checkup went well. But the doctor wants me to slow down a bit."

Sam smiled. "Barbara told me. Look, Shy, you take care of yourself. Wayne and I will hold down the fort. You just try to take it easy and get your beauty rest … for both of you. Your speech is great; you'll be fine."

Shiloh nodded. "I just don't have words to tell you how much I appreciate your help on this."

"No need; I'm loving it. Maybe I'll move back to Tullahoma and run when this is over."

"That would be great. Count me in."

"No, not really, just teasing. But your life sure seems exciting."

"Why don't you come back and replace me so I can go off to a quiet little church and have a house full of babies?"

They hugged and said good-bye. As she got out of the car, Sam called Seth to tell him that Shiloh was on her way.

Shy called Seth from the airport. He met her at the door with a tall glass of cold, decaf iced tea.

"What I'd really like is a cold beer, darling. This is definitely a downside of pregnancy—no alcohol and very little caffeine."

"Don't worry, I'm upholding the family quota," said Seth as they embraced.

They talked for a while and went to bed early. They were both exhausted.

The next morning when Shiloh awoke, she found a note from Seth who had already gone off to work. He had left breakfast for her in the microwave. She felt good when she walked to the Capitol to begin her day.

When she arrived, Isabel Farmer, a friend from Nashville who had served with her on the local Planned Parenthood Board was waiting. Isabel had come to Washington a few years after Shiloh was elected. They still kept up with each other and occasionally socialized. This morning, Isabel made a wonderful offer to help Shiloh in Nashville the next few weeks as a volunteer. Shiloh readily accepted and called Sam with the good news.

"Great," he replied. "We could use some more trusted helpers. She can help answer some of the abortion letters we are getting."

They talked a few more minutes and got back to work. Shiloh spent the afternoon reading about the various appropriations bills. She would attend the conference committee on her own foreign operations bill the next morning and then wait in her office until the call came from the minority leader that it was time for Shiloh to come to the floor to introduce the ERA. It would be when negotiations started on the defense appropriations bill.

She went home by 7:00 p.m. that evening, tired but eager to make her speech.

She was sound asleep in her nightgown on the living room sofa with the new Lincoln book about his cabinet when Seth arrived at about 12:30 that evening. He covered Shiloh with a blanket and put a pillow under her head. She barely noticed.

He was gone again when she awoke at 6:15. She staggered into the kitchen to find hot coffee and a note:

Dearest Sweetheart,

Under normal conditions, if I came home and found you asleep on the couch in your nightgown, I would have had wild fantasies but not last night. I drank my beer and yours ☺ and ate a sandwich and stumbled up to bed. When I left this morning at 5:30, I blew you a kiss. You looked radiant and so peaceful. It reminded me for the millionth time why I love you so much. Today is the day, Shy. You'll be great, and I think our friends around the world will be great too. Break a leg, sweetheart. You can do it.

All my love,
Seth

Shy couldn't believe how lucky she was to have found such a wonderful man. She called Seth at work and told him that she loved him too. They talked a few minutes until Seth was interrupted by a phone call from Bogotá.

Shiloh ate breakfast and picked out a nice beige maternity suit to wear. First stop, conference committee. On her walk to the Capitol, she thought about how nice it would be when she and Seth could relax together after the election and wait for the birth of their daughter. They would be a perfect family. She was excited about the ERA and election, but at the top of her list, were her wonderful husband and their daughter to be.

After the committee meeting, which ended around 3:00, she went to her office to wait for the call. Her leader had told her to wait in her office and try to relax. Shiloh was waiting to make the biggest speech of her life.

Now, as she sat in her office and thought back on the many months since she had met her leader to seek permission to begin this endeavor, she felt good. She had found much more receptiveness than she'd ever imagined. Seth's offer to retire and help her had been unbelievable. She remembered when she first brought up the subject of the ERA with Seth. His first comment surprised her, but then in retrospect, she should have known better. His first words as they'd sat talking at his apartment in New York that Labor Day weekend were, "So, when do we start, sweetheart?"

Without him, this wouldn't have happened. He had helped her refine her plan and waited on pins and needles for her return when she had gone to see the minority leader for permission to go forward with her plan. Since then, they had been consumed by a whirlwind of activity.

Shiloh was half-watching the Senate on the C-SPAN Senate channel when her leader called.

"Hi, Shy. It's time. The whips are rounding up the others."

"I'm ready," Shy answered. She felt her pulse quicken as she called Seth.

"Hi, darling, it looks like we're on in about a half hour or so."

"Our TV will be on," he replied. "Break a leg, baby. I love you."

Shiloh knew what was happening; they had planned it all out. As soon as she hung up the phone with Seth, she knew that his staff had immediately started sending out e-mail alerts to various Listservs. Then Pam would start on the media, and Sam would alert Wayne and call the Jacobsons and Whitfields. Within minutes, hundreds of TV sets would be tuned in to the C-SPAN House channel.

Pam would call CNN again. They were going to do a live feed as breaking news. All the editorial memos would go out after Shiloh spoke and press releases were ready.

Shiloh sat quietly with Congresswoman Maloney on the front bench. *This is it*, she thought. *I wanted to do it, and this is it*. Her mind raced back to Grandma Alice, her mother, her dad, the valedictorian speech in high school; she even thought of Tennessee Carolina, who she had never met. This was the day she hoped would change history for women.

"I recognize the gentlewoman from Tennessee. Madame Giles, you have the floor," offered the minority leader, who was acting as chairperson of this session.

Shiloh was jolted from her reverie. She stood and moved to the lectern to address her colleagues.

"Thank you, Madame Chairperson. It's an honor to see you in the chair, and it's an honor to offer my amendment to the defense appropriations bill. My good friend and colleague, Congresswoman Maloney, will manage the amendment. Madame Chairperson, I rise this evening to offer the Equal Rights Amendment for Women as an amendment to the bill before this body."

* * * * *

At that moment, Wolf Blitzer interrupted *Lou Dobbs Tonight.* "Sorry, Lou, we have a breaking story. Representative Catherine Shiloh Giles of the Fifth District of Tennessee is speaking on the floor of the House of Representatives, where she is offering the Equal Rights Amendment for Women. She is offering it as an amendment to the defense appropriations bill. This is a highly irregular maneuver. Let's listen in."

* * * * *

"Madame Chairperson, my amendment is identical to the one that Congress passed in 1972," Shiloh said. "As we know, the 1972 amendment is still three states short of final ratification. When Congress passed the ERA in 1972, it included a time limit for state ratification. The initial limitation, seven years, was later modified, allowing three more years for a total of ten years for three-fourths of the states to ratify. But since the approval of the Twenty-seventh Amendment in 1992, which was passed by Congress 203 years earlier in 1789, the ten-year, congressionally imposed window for state ratification of the ERA is questionable, to say the least.

"Madame Chairperson, the ERA has been a part of our party's platform for over sixty years, and we have dutifully introduced it in every session of Congress since that time, except for the ten years after it was passed in 1972. Yes, the ERA passed once, and thirty-five states ratified.

"Since then, although it continues to be raised in some of the states where it was not ratified, nothing has happened. This is wrong. Women in this country still receive unequal pay for the same work as men; a woman earns an average of seventy-eight cents for the dollar a man earns in the same job. For a twenty-five-year-old woman today, that works out to be five hundred twenty-three thousand dollars less than a man would earn by the time they are both eligible to retire at age sixty-five.

"There are laws to prevent this inequity, but they are not enforced. Approximately six hundred eighty-three thousand women were raped in America in 1996 according to FBI reports, but only an estimated 37 percent of those rapes were reported. Fifty percent of all American women will experience violence from their male partners during their lifetime. Domestic violence laws are rarely enforced. Do we believe, as a nation, that these numbers are acceptable?

"Madame Chairperson, as I have said, we have laws on the books to handle the transgressions I've mentioned and many more, but we do not have the backing of the U.S. Constitution. To enforce these laws, women almost always are required to go to court. Have you ever heard of a man going to court because his pay was not equal to a woman's? It is deplorable that so many women must go to court to seek enforcement of our laws. This would be greatly reduced if the ambiguity of tradition were forever trumped by the ERA.

"We all remember a few years ago, Madame Chairperson, the celebrated case when a woman chose to enter the Virginia Military Institute and was denied because of her sex. The court later said that she was indeed eligible and she was able to enroll. She had to go to court because equal rights for women are not a part of our Constitution. Women every day must fight for rights that should be covered by law. Why, Madame Chairperson? Because, here in the United States, custom and tradition do not fully support gender equality. Far too many women do not find redress for violent abuse and rape. Most are even afraid to ask.

"It will take time for our laws to work because it's difficult to change our culture overnight. We must have the ERA to guarantee this change. The foundation for real equality in this country is the United States Constitution.

"The ERA would also prevent tampering with laws that are meant to ensure equality such as Title IX. That title, as we all know, guarantees equality in education, including sports and other activities. Madame Chairperson, I'm sure you remember when some of the members in this body sought to alter Title IX. Usurping laws meant to protect a certain class of people, in this case women, can be accomplished by a simple majority vote of one. Such despicable attempts to change these laws would never be introduced if we had the ERA.

"Women's equality is not mentioned anywhere in our constitution. Is that not on purpose, Madame Chairperson? The Fourteenth Amendment, which contains the equal protection clause, revolutionized civil rights in this country. But it was not used in a case for women's rights until 1971, ninety-seven years after it was adopted. Maybe that is because the second section of the Fourteenth Amendment limits representatives of Congress to 'male citizens.' The Fifteenth Amendment, which was adopted two years after the Fourteenth gave '*all men*' the right to vote, not women.

"Yes, that was changed with the Nineteenth Amendment fifty years later in 1920. My point is that men's rights have been mentioned in our Constitution but never women's rights until 1920.

"Why? Why is anyone against the Equal Rights Amendment? The citizens of this great nation support the ERA by a large margin. Yet, why does the minority opposition prevail? What are we afraid of when we send resolution after resolution for the ERA to committee, to be relegated to the dustbin of history? People say that the fundamentalist religious groups oppose women's equality. We know that they are considered to be the powerbase of one of our major parties. That other party, by the way, included the ERA in its platform until 1980. In fact, their support was quite strong back in the early days of this struggle. What happened in 1980 to change their minds? A powerbase that challenges the bedrock principles of our nation that are enshrined in our Constitution, in our writings and in our laws, came into play.

"We are the grand experiment in democracy. We are the model for other great democracies. President Carter made human rights a global issue. And yet women in America are not truly and unequivocally equal. This administration, Madame Chairperson, is engaged in a cultural war. It is blocking sex education. It is refusing to allow information on reproduction and contraception, even though research shows that education prevents abortion, which we all wish to do. Information about condoms, which can prevent AIDS, has been removed from government Web sites. This hurts both men and women—especially our neighbors in developing countries that are influenced by the United States. Why?

"Let us examine the situation women face around the world. Let us look at the situation with American eyes, with eyes that represent a nation that is generous and that believes in human rights.

"With a few exceptions, women today in industrial countries, mostly in Europe, enjoy better conditions regarding equality than their sisters here in the United States. And some developing countries are making great strides.

"But in other countries women live in virtual slavery. They can't chose whom to marry or when. Rape is too often common and can even be socially acceptable, though not legally so. In some countries, honor killing of women still exists. Fathers or other male family members may kill female family members for disgracing their families by being raped. This barbarous act, though not legal, is often overlooked in a bow to local, social mores.

"In addition, approximately two million children per year, mostly girls, are sold into the sex trade and are trafficked around the world. Our country should care about this more than our policy suggests that we do. Hundreds of thousands of young girls are genitally mutilated each year. Of the one hundred thirty million children who are missing out on primary education around the world, seventy-eight million of them are girls. Girls who receive primary education marry later, have fewer and healthier children, and have higher family incomes.

"I am pleased to announce good news from the United Nations, which I hope we can emulate now. In the United Nations General Assembly a few hours ago, a global ERA was introduced and passed."

Applause.

"Sadly, our country opposed it—yes, opposed, just as our Senate has opposed the global Convention on the Elimination of All Forms of Discrimination against Women. The past few years, our government has opposed the term reproductive health and rights in international documents. Previously, on a bipartisan basis, we championed such commitments. What are reproductive health and rights? Not abortion, as the United States claims in international meetings. Even if the term did include abortion, how can our country oppose something internationally that is legal in its own country? We have become a bully against women and against human rights.

"Reproductive health and rights, Madame Chairperson, according to international agreements that our country helped write are: the right to family planning, which about two hundred million women in developing countries want but do not have access to or cannot afford. Experts say that half of the pregnancies in the world are unwanted at the time of conception. This leads to forty to forty-five million abortions a year. Almost half are unsafe and lead to complications and death. Many would be prevented with family planning.

"Reproductive health also includes the right to the safe delivery of one's children. In its simplest form, that means that a trained medical attendant is present when a mother delivers her baby—not that she's in a hospital, mind you, just that a trained medical attendant—in most instances, a nurse or a midwife—is there. Sadly, 46 percent of all women who deliver babies in developing countries do so without medical assistance. Just imagine what that means.

"What would it mean to your mother, your daughter, your sister, or any other women you know and love? Delivering your baby at home with your family. Think about that for a moment. For most, that also means delivering babies without running water and with only a kerosene lamp for light. Imagine: one woman every minute dies from pregnancy complications—every minute. That is sixty per hour and over five hundred twenty-five thousand per year. A majority of these deaths would be prevented with family planning and safe deliveries."

Shy was becoming emotional; her voice had cracked with her last sentence. She thought of young women delivering in cold or sweltering huts in far off countries—and of herself delivering in that manner.

She took a deep breath and continued. "Madame Chairperson, I'm pregnant with my first child. My husband and I are full of joy and happiness. But what would it be like if I was one of the 46 percent living in the world's developing countries? My husband would be frantic. I would live each day in worry. We want so much to have a child and are excited every time we discuss the happy event. But if I had to deliver our baby without medical assistance, our happiness would be laced with trepidation.

"For couples all over the world at this very minute, that scene is playing out. Put yourself in the place of the father; feel the fear he feels for his wife and child. One of life's greatest joys is, for so many, also a time of fear and, for far too many women, a time of death."

* * * * *

Seth, sitting with his colleagues watching Shiloh speak on C-SPAN, could feel the tears silently rolling down his cheeks. This was it, he thought. This was what they were fighting for.

* * * * *

"In one African country," Shiloh continued, "when a woman announces her pregnancy, she says that she will be receiving a gift soon. But the words to describe the actual pregnancy mean a time between life and death. Her chance of dying is about one in sixteen. Here is the United States and in countries like England, it is about one in two thousand eight hundred.

"Madame Chairperson, the last element of reproductive health is the prevention of sexually transmitted diseases, especially HIV/AIDS. There again, our country is on the wrong page. Abstinence is what we all choose for youngsters, but the reality is that one-half of all new HIV infections occur in youngsters under twenty-five. That means that five out of the ten new HIV infections each minute affect the young. We provide condoms but not nearly enough. It costs just pennies for protection, and yet we restrict some of our aid funds to support abstinence-only programs. If that approach fails, as it too often does, who pays the price?

"This policy is not only impractical for young girls and wives who have little or no choice about sex, it is immoral. Women often pay the price for their gender. None of us, the financial policy makers, pay any price. We go have our martini, prop up our feet, and watch the pundits on TV talk about how many bills we've passed. Most of us will never meet one of these women.

"We have a policy that prohibits HIV/AIDS prevention support for sex workers in developing countries. Many are forced into that life and know no other. Others have no education and children to feed. Why do we have such ill-advised policies? Are we trying to stop a killer disease that is decimating poor countries, or are we making some misguided powerbase in our country happy? We preach fire prevention, but we forbid the use of water if there is a fire.

"We are the richest country in the world, the human rights champion of the world, and supposedly the most generous. Why are we condemning women and men and, even worse, little girls to death because of domestic politics? We know better. The God I worship finds that unacceptable. I find that unacceptable, and the majority of the American people find that unacceptable.

"Madame Chairperson, we need the ERA for the women in this country so that there will never again be a question about women's equality. No sleight of hand, Madame Chairperson, and no skullduggery of any kind—not in the work place, not in the homes, not in the schools. Nowhere, Madame Chairperson, should women in this country ever be anything but equal to men. By adding the ERA to the United States Constitution we will illustrate to the world that we are a nation that respects and reveres the human rights of all humanity regardless of color, creed, ethnicity, and sex. Our policies need to reflect that at home and abroad.

"My friends, we are Americans. Remember our own progress in civil and human rights. Remember your great-grandmother, your grandmother, and your mother. Could their lives have been better? Now think of the women in your lives today, especially the young women. Why should your daughter have to fight for equal pay, for punishment for violence or threats of violence committed against her, for an education she prefers and has earned? Think especially about women around the world: the poor, the young, and the abused. How can the greatest nation in human history not support equality for women? Worse still, how can we oppose it? What are we thinking friends? What are we thinking?

"I appeal to my colleagues to pass this amendment. If you do, you will be able to look into the mirror tomorrow morning and feel proud. You will be able say to yourself; I have made a difference. You will be able to look at the women in your own family and know you have done the right thing. You will have helped change human history. You will have struck a blow for freedom. You will have struck a blow for the half of humanity that throughout history has been treated like second-class citizens at best or chattel at worse. Women should be equal. Our constitution should enshrine gender equality and our global policies should reflect America's global commitment to all women. That is the way it should be, and that is the way we all know it could be. Thank you, Madame Chairperson."

Shiloh was exhausted. She moved away from the podium to sit back down on the bench when she began to hear a few people clapping. Then the applause became louder and louder until people were on their feet. She remained standing for a moment and nodded to her colleagues.

Carolyn hugged her and whispered, "Great job, Shy; you were inspiring, my friend."

Shiloh smiled and thanked her colleague. Then she sat down, welcoming the bench, which felt heavenly to her aching back. Once again, thoughts raced through her mind. She thought of Letty and her friends in the Philippines and women in America. *It is so wrong,* she thought, *that we have not done better sooner.*

And then she thought about racism in America, a problem that gnawed at the very soul of her country. *Why has equality been such a perplexing issue? What is in our DNA that makes us this way?* she wondered.

The chairperson banged the gavel and brought the House to order. "The chair recognizes the gentlewoman from New York. You have one hour for debate. Is there an opposing side? Seeing none, gentlewoman you may proceed."

Shiloh jolted back to the present.

"Thank you, Madame Chairperson, I have a five-minute statement, which will be followed by a series of statements from other supporters."

Shiloh received a note from the sergeant at arms. It was from her leader.

Shy, why don't you go back to your office and relax? You can watch on TV. I will call you if you are needed. Great job!!!

Shy smiled, looked up at her leader, and mimed a grateful thank-you.

As Shy was walking to the underground train that runs from the Capitol to the House and Senate office buildings, she realized how tense she had been. Her back was aching, but she was sure that a good night's sleep would cure her. *I've done it,* she thought, *this part is over.*

Sarah met her at the underground train platform on the other side with a big hug. Then she took her purse and briefcase. "I saw you leaving the floor on TV. You were great, boss. It went down very well. And it's being carried live by C-SPAN and CNN."

"Thanks. We've all worked hard for this day. But this is just the beginning."

"Yes, it is," beamed Sarah, "and we relish it. We're going to win this thing, Shy. I really believe we are."

They arrived to a party in progress. There were staffers there from several offices watching C-SPAN, munching cheese and peanuts, and drinking soft drinks and beer. When they saw Shiloh, they began to applaud. Then one of them chanted, "Hip, hip, hooray," and the rest joined in. Shy shook hands with them all and retired to her office.

Carol came in and said, "Voilà."

She was carrying a plate of food and a cold, caffeine-free diet Coke.

"You are the most wonderful person in the world," said a famished Shiloh.

Carol left Shiloh to her privacy and returned to work.

Just as Shiloh took the first bite, her internal phone rang.

It was Sarah. "Shy, we've had several press calls. You must have been seen on TV leaving the floor. I suggest that you have an impromptu press briefing in forty-five minutes or so in your office and close out after that."

Shiloh agreed, "Okay. I was about to call Seth, but I had to have at least one bite of this chicken first. Please give me twenty minutes or so and then bring Corrie and Alan in so we can discuss strategy before the press arrives."

"You got it, boss."

Shy dialed Seth, who answered on the first ring. "Hi, baby."

"Hi, sweetheart," said Shy with a mouthful of pasta salad.

"I can tell that you're eating, as usual. First, you were great. Second, Pam thinks that the CNN bit will guarantee a lot of overnight coverage. And you may even get a few press calls at your office."

Shiloh chuckled. "I have a press conference in about twenty-five minutes, darling, in my office."

"Oh, wow, that's great. Do you need help? Is there anything we can do?"

"No. I'm waiting for the debate to end to see if we vote or whether there is a problem. But when I end here, I may ask you a favor depending on how I feel."

"What's that?"

"Could you drive over and pick me up at the back door?"

"Of course, Shy. Are you okay?"

"Yes, I'm fine, just tired. Plus I may need to escape. The press folks keep coming."

They rang off, just as Sarah, her personal assistant, and her press secretary walked into Shiloh's office.

Alan Marshall, Shiloh's press secretary, spoke first. "It looks like about thirty journalists will show: all the biggies and a few internationals. Several of the TV folks wanted one on ones, but we begged off until tomorrow."

Her assistant, Corrie Cohen, gave Shiloh her talking points. "Here you go, Shy. I also included your speech."

"Thanks, guys. What questions are they asking?"

* * * * *

The minority leader watched as the cloakroom doors swung open. Her counterpart from the other party walked toward her briskly. Two of his staffers followed in his wake.

"Where did they find you?" she asked as he approached.

"Never mind that, just what in the hell do you think you are doing?"

"I believe it is the defense appropriations bill," she was trying hard to stifle a smile.

"Very funny," the majority leader fumed. "We didn't discuss this. You can't introduce anything that I don't okay."

"Maybe I can, and maybe I can't," the minority leader replied, "but I did."

"Well, stop it now."

* * * * *

CNN and C-SPAN ignored the person speaking and trained their cameras on the two feuding leaders.

"If there is no opposition, I plan to call for a vote. I think we have the required two-thirds for a constitutional amendment."

"You can't. I'll oppose all night if I have to," he roared.

* * * * *

The minority leader had been on the butt end of this House for a long time, and she was damned tired of the other party's heavy-handed tactics, but she had always respected the decorum of this great House of the people. She could see the red light of the gallery cameras, and they were pointed her way.

Finally she spoke. "This is certainly better than you deserve. I'll finish the proponent side of the debate and call a recess. We can start again tomorrow morning at eight. Don't be late."

He stepped off the podium and sat on the opposition bench with his arms crossed. His staffers were busily writing in their notebooks.

The next speaker was a Republican. "Madame Chairperson, I promised my mother that if this amendment ever again came to the floor of this House, I would vote for its passage. I am here tonight speaking for my mother and for millions of women in this country like my mother. My mom worked as a bookkeeper in a woolen mill for thirty-three years and helped put her four children through college. She worked for what amounted to slave wages."

The majority leader's face flushed with anger.

"Madame Chairperson," the speaker was saying, "I rise to appeal to my colleagues and to our country ..."

The minority leader smiled. "I wonder if the majority leader has a mother," she said under her breath, as she stifled another smile.

Chapter 16

During the course of the press conference in her office, Shiloh was handed a note from Carol that said that the minority leader had called. "She said that you should go home and sleep and be back for more festivities on the floor tomorrow morning at 8:00 a.m.," Carol explained.

Shiloh had seen the two leaders speaking at the podium on TV and guessed what had happened. It seemed that the press conference would last forever. There were forty-two journalists by the time it ended and six TV cameras. Finally after an hour and fifteen minutes, Alan Marshall announced that the press conference was over.

While they were milling around, Carol whisked Shiloh out her private door and down to the back of the building where Seth was waiting in the car.

Shiloh reported to her husband about the press conference.

"We also had several press calls, Shy. Pam said that she had received queries from numerous newspapers about the editorial memo and the current state of play. C-SPAN and CNN also inspired calls from other media outlets. As you know, the UN resolution passed with only the United States, Malta, Sudan, Libya, and El Salvador speaking against it. Malta bolted from the European Union, but Slovenia and Poland, who we thought might stray, stayed with the Union. In the end, it passed by consensus, without a roll call.

"The United States agreed to consensus to avoid further embarrassment, as it has on similar votes over the past few years. My team is still laboring away at the office, e-mailing and faxing NGOs around the world and fielding press calls. But, most importantly, I want to congratulate you again. You were fantastic. Once I get you tucked in, I need to get back to the office and help Sam, Barbara, and the others. We're going to win, Shy; I can taste victory."

* * * * *

"Did you go to bed last night?" inquired a sleepy Shiloh when she came down the stairs ready to go the next morning.

Seth nodded. "I got home around 2:00 or so and slept a few hours here on the couch."

He had showered and shaved and was ready for work. "The TV this morning is all about you and the ERA, dear. The press coverage is fantastic. And more are waiting outside."

"What?" exclaimed the congresswoman. Shiloh peaked through the curtains and saw an army of media folks milling around in front of their condo. "Goodness, I at least need some wake-up coffee before I can handle that."

* * * * *

The majority leader took over the podium and announced that appropriations bills were not the correct place to handle constitutional amendments.

"This particular amendment," announced the leader, "is presently in committee."

The minority leader asked for a point of order, which was denied.

"I will be pleased to schedule," rejoined the majority leader, "hearings for your amendment in the Judiciary Committee in the next session of Congress. You and your friends may testify then."

"Thank you, Mr. Chairman," replied the minority leader. "I believe that I'll be in position then to decide where this amendment goes, and it'll be to the floor of the House where it belongs, sir, not in the Judiciary Committee where your lackeys will kill it."

* * * * *

A group of senators tried to introduce the ERA, but the Senate Majority Leader was ready. Their effort failed.

* * * * *

By Friday, there were positive editorials in sixty-five newspapers, and more followed over the weekend, including a full column editorial in the

Sunday *New York Times* and a full page of coverage and Shiloh's speech and various press reports in the *Washington Post*. The *LA Times* and *Chicago Tribune* joined the *Boston Globe*, *The Atlanta-Journal Constitution*, and *The Baltimore Sun* in printing pictures and extensive coverage. Overseas coverage was also voluminous. There were demonstrations on over four hundred college campuses on Thursday and Friday. In Europe a huge "manifestation" was staged in Brussels, and a weekend vigil was planned in front of the European Parliament there. Over eighty capitals in developing countries witnessed demonstrations for women's equality. There were pledges from many quarters to continue until national ERAs were passed to match the one adopted by the United Nations.

Shiloh taped several interviews for the major TV networks that day for their evening TV newscasts. She was also interviewed for guest shots on all of the evening shows on CNN and MSNBC. She and the minority leader appeared on *The NewsHour with Jim Lehrer* and *Larry King Live* together.

When the day was over, the leader said to Shiloh, "I never dreamed that the ERA would take off like this. I expected coverage but nothing like this. You and Seth sure planned this well; women are uniting, and men seem to be coming on board as well."

"Yes, but I am sure that our 'friends'"— said Shiloh as she made quote marks in the air—"will be heard from."

"Yes," replied the leader, "but we have a leg up on them. If what you say happens regarding demonstrations and such, we may be hard to catch."

Sure enough, Shiloh noted that the televangelists were going strong, as were several right-wing radio talk shows. But mainstream media was clearly overwhelming the airwaves, and print media covered the ERA as front-page news, often with banner headlines. The question now was who would have staying power. Was this their fifteen minutes of fame, or was this an issue that had legs for the long haul?

Later that night, Shiloh watched the national 527 TV ad.

The 527 ad started with a distant clip of a woman walking with a young girl. The woman had a jacket on that had the word ESCORT printed on back. They walked to a doorway in a building where a woman in a nurse's uniform welcomed the young girl.

The voiceover said, "Catherine Shiloh Giles was elected to Congress with no qualifications. She won because of the publicity she received for escorting a woman into a clinic where she was allowed to kill her baby. Giles has now introduced a bill in Congress, the so-called Equal Rights Amendment, which will legalize abortion on demand for our children without parental consent."

There was now a clip of same-sex marriage ceremonies.

The voiceover continued, "This bill will also legalize same-sex marriage throughout America—in every state, every city, every town."

Now a clip of a family sitting down for dinner and another of well-dressed people entering a church followed by one of a Little League Baseball game played.

The voiceover said, "The family as we know it, which consists of a man, a woman, and children, will be destroyed. Our values, our religion, the very essence of right and wrong will be destroyed by abortionists, perverts, and atheists. America will suffer, its families will suffer, and we will become weak and godless, unless we stand up today for what is right."

Now clips of bar scenes showed young people with multicolored hair and scanty clothing and played loud music; another clip of young people drinking from what appeared to be beer bottles flashed across the screen followed by a scene showing a young man giving himself an injection.

"Our youth will resort to drugs, drinking, and immoral behavior," the voiceover proclaimed. "The American family will perish. Our values will perish, and God will turn his back on the American people."

As clips of the Jefferson Memorial, the Lincoln Memorial, the White House, and the Capitol appeared, the voiceover commanded, "Tell your Senators and members of Congress that you will not accept the ERA. America is God's country. We are God's people."

Shiloh only laughed. It was ludicrous.

In response, the minority leader gave the go-ahead for the Democratic Party ERA ad.

It featured a clip of the Capitol Building, then one of women in white marching for the right to vote in New York in 1919 and another of workers leaving an office building. There were men and women, all well dressed.

The voiceover said, "Throughout human history, women have had to fight to have equal rights with men. Millions of families in the United States are headed by women; women in America receive only seventy-eight cents for every dollar men make for the same work; women have to fight for their rights for education, for alimony, and for punishment of men who violently abuse them."

A clip of a woman in court standing before a judge, one of a young woman standing in front of the Virginia Military Institute, and one of a newspaper clipping was accompanied by the words, "A woman fights for the right to attend VMI."

Then there followed a series of women speaking into the camera saying, "I support the ERA," "I support women's rights," or "I am an American woman." The clips included twenty women of all races and ages, from grandmothers with white hair to a woman in a business suit to a woman at a meeting with a PTA sign in the background to a woman in a military uniform sitting in the pilot's seat of a helicopter to a woman in surgical greens to a woman in a kitchen cooking to a little girl sitting in a sandbox with other children playing on swings and other playground equipment in the background. The little girl said, "Are we not equal?" as the camera panned to a little boy sitting next to her in the sandbox.

The final clip started as a distant shot of a battle scene, perhaps from Iraq. As the camera moved closer, a woman came into focus. She was crouched behind a short mud wall as bullets zinged around her. "Medic" was written on her helmet. She was tending a young male soldier with a chest wound. The soldier looked into the camera and said, "I support the ERA."

When Shiloh finally went home that evening, she got on her computer and read about the ERA coverage. She was elated. She called Seth, who was still at the office, and reported everything she had seen and read in detail.

"Seth, I just can't believe that the ERA has become such a big deal. It's capturing the country's imagination. I hope that this will continue until we finally get the vote."

"Me too," enthused her tired but happy husband. "Pam expects it to continue for as much as a week as the number one news item unless we're attacked by Mexico or Canada."

"I hope so, darling," said Shiloh, ignoring Seth's humor, "but I worry about the cultural war. The ERA is another divisive issue that will lead to more bitterness. Yet we were left with little choice."

"That's right," replied Seth. "No action has led to big action. I'm so proud of you, Shy, and of all the folks who have brought this about."

"And my sweet, hardworking hubby is chief among them. I love you, Seth, I love you so much." She hung up the phone and breathed a huge sigh of relief.

* * * * *

Charlie had accepted a speaking engagement for Shiloh weeks before for that Friday at noon. Her audience would be a gathering that had been organized by the political science department at Vanderbilt University. Her speech, originally scheduled to take place in a large classroom in the political science department that seated two hundred, was quickly moved to the Memorial Gym, which seated over fourteen thousand.

When Shiloh, Charlie, and Sam drove across campus, they saw ERA posters everywhere but not many students. Nashville was experiencing beautiful fall weather. Usually at this time of day, the campus would be full of students sitting in the grass, reading books, throwing Frisbees, and soaking up the sun. Where were the students? They parked at the arena and went inside, not knowing what to expect. When they walked in, Shiloh was greeted by a standing ovation. The stands were full to the rafters, and the students were chanting "ERA, ERA, ERA ...."

The chairperson of the political science department introduced Shiloh. Shouts of "Shiloh, Shiloh, Shiloh" filled the air.

Shiloh was amazed and so filled with emotion that she had to take a deep breath to avoid tears. There must be students here from other local universities to fill this place, she thought.

Shiloh began. "This is a larger audience than I expected to hear a discussion about Chinese hegemony in the Pacific Rim." More chants. "I could switch that to a discussion about the Federal Reserve's latest assessment of the global economy if you prefer?"

Laughter and applause filled the room. Then "ERA, ERA, ERA ..."

"Okay, the ERAs have it." Shiloh spoke for thirty minutes and was interrupted by applause so many times that Charlie and Sam couldn't keep count. Afterward, she was taken to a holding room long enough for the arena to clear, and then she came back out into the arena for an impromptu press conference. A few hundred students had stayed back to listen. After the press conference, Shiloh spent over an hour with the remaining students. When they left, Shiloh was on cloud nine.

What a remarkable swing of events, she thought. *Last week I felt so down with all the angst created by the campaign, and now this.*

Suddenly she felt her baby kick, and she remembered that she had to be careful. She smiled and thought, *Maybe you, my precious little one, will be one of the first American women born into the new age of gender equality.*

"What do you think, Charlie? Do we concede now? Have we given the election to Boyd?" Shiloh was smiling.

"Yes and yes," answered her erstwhile campaign director. Charlie joined Shiloh's playful mood. "Why don't we drive over to *The Tennessean* and surrender?" Then Charlie became serious. "Boyd and his minders will try to use the ERA to the max, Shy. Their Swift Boat look-alike ad and the Democratic ad are playing here in the district constantly. The social-cultural war has reached a new and scary level."

"Yes, it has," agreed Shiloh. "Seth and I discussed that issue the other night by phone after the debate on the House floor. We agreed that if the citizens of this country seriously weigh the pros and cons, we will eventually prevail. Most Americans are for equality, and maybe this time they will speak up locally and in the voting booth."

Sam turned to Charlie. "How long will it last? What's your best guess?"

Charlie shrugged. "Hard to say. I have never been a part of something like this. From news coverage, it seems like a national fever. You heard the students, didn't you? They won't take no for an answer, and I don't expect the other side to blink any time soon either. This is indeed a cultural war, brought on, I would say, by the rigidity of our friends in the other party."

"I suppose so," said Sam. "But I sense that this time we have as many chips as they do, maybe more."

* * * * *

Shiloh had a dinner speech that evening with a combined Rotary group, which was quite unusual. Their meetings were usually at lunchtime, but this one was set for all Rotary clubs in the metro Nashville area. They would have upward of two thousand in attendance. It was in the ballroom of the Downtown Nashville Hilton.

Rotary had welcomed women members for several years now; thus there were many women present. When Shiloh entered the room, it was the women who stood first to greet her, joined quickly by the men.

The evening was another smashing success. She gave an abbreviated version of her normal stump speech and then switched over to the ERA. Her speech received sustained applause. Most questions were not as much questions as statements of support, and when that ended, she received another prolonged ovation. Many had said how proud they were that this new effort to pass the ERA had been initiated by their congresswoman.

Sam chortled, "This kind of excitement may make some of the potential presidential contenders begin to have second thoughts."

"Enough of that," replied Shy. "All I want to do is put my feet up and have a long, cold drink of iced tea and some food."

"Didn't you just eat?" teased Sam.

Shiloh glared at him. "Only a little. People are always talking to me, and I tend to wolf down my food before I speak, and then I feel lousy afterward. Plus, my baby likes her food well chewed."

The press left Shiloh alone after the Rotary speech. They covered her speech, but most apparently felt that they'd had enough for one day. Several said hello and a few asked questions, but most just went back to wherever they worked to write and edit film and finish their own long day.

As Shiloh and her team left, they went outside where a small group was holding signs against the ERA, abortion, and same sex marriage. Lawson was there. He was silent. He just stood there and glared at them as they walked out to the parking lot to find their car.

"Damn, that guy worries me," noted Sam.

"Me too," agreed Charlie.

When they got to the condo, Shiloh changed into her favorite expandable Sewanee sweat suit, and Sam took drink orders. Sam and Charlie had beer, and Shiloh had her iced tea. She nibbled on whatever she could find in the fridge while the men ate chips and peanuts.

"Well," offered Charlie, "soon we should get some idea about how this is all playing. Brenda will have our latest round of polling data by tomorrow night. And luckily, Shy, you only have one speech tomorrow."

"Where is it, Charlie?"

Charlie grinned. "At a church. Actually, it's at the parish hall of a church."

"Which one? I didn't see that on my schedule."

"That is because it's a surprise. Just be ready at five. It includes supper."

"Is it All Saints?"

"How did you guess?"

"Oh, that's wonderful. It'll be like going home."

Charlie nodded. "Bill has been planning it for weeks, Shiloh, so act surprised."

* * * * *

At a small church at the far reaches of the Nashville city limits, another speech was being penned. This one was a sermon for the Sunday service, and the author was Robert James Lawson II.

His fingers were flying as he wrote hellfire and damnation. "That is what will happen if this ERA madness ever becomes law. It must be stopped at all costs. Women must bear the burden of what happened in the Garden of Eden," he wrote.

After he finished, he went next door to his modest home and lay in bed. His mind was consumed with Shiloh. She was the Judas of the twenty-first century. She was worse; she was the Antichrist. It was her that his father had prepared him to face in battle. It was this evil woman whom he must stop.

He imagined himself in Gethsemane, and he prayed. "My father in heaven, I am not asleep at this hour of trial. I am here, Lord. I am ready to heed your command. I am not a sleeping sinner like your son's disciples. I am your warrior. My flesh is not weak. I am ready, Lord."

But soon his lust overcame him as he thought of Shiloh. He bit his lip until it bled, and he sinned.

* * * * *

Sam came into the condo stealthily. He had been out to get some pastries and *The Tennessean*. He was surprised to find Shiloh awake and having coffee.

"I'm sorry if I woke you when I left. I tried to sneak out so I could get the paper and some munchies," apologized Sam.

"Not to worry. Charlie called me with the good news. In fact, he had a lot of good news. Have you looked at the paper?"

"Not yet; what's up?" Sam asked.

"Well for starters, I'm back up in the polls, to 61 percent. And there are two editorials in *The Tennessean*; the lead endorses me for Congress, and the second and longest one endorses the ERA."

"Wow," enthused her brother. "That's great." He hugged his sister. "Here, have some orange juice and a pastry while I cook up some eggs and hash browns."

Just then, Charlie came in with more pastries. They all laughed at the abundance of food.

Charlie smiled. "Two weeks to go. The negative stuff seems to be backfiring. I won't make any predictions yet, but Boyd will need to walk on water with you in his arms to catch you now, Shy."

They all clicked orange juice glasses as Charlie began reading the editorials aloud.

* * * * *

The trip back to Washington was uneventful. When Shiloh and Sam arrived, Seth had more good news. The reports from around the world were looking good. NGOs were reporting several meetings with government officials and positive news coverage. And yes, there was some strong negative sentiment from religious quarters carried in the press.

"How could this happen?" a minister in Dallas was quoted as saying.

Others criticized the president for allowing this woman to introduce such a sacrilegious amendment in Congress.

"As if he could stop her," laughed Seth.

In some countries, those who opposed the ERA criticized the U.S. president for trying to spread "American religion" around the world and for interfering with the cultural prerogatives of other countries.

This made Shiloh laugh. "If they only knew," she mused. "This president is America's zealot in charge. They need to look at his policies and appointments."

* * * * *

The next day, the minority leader came to Shiloh's office. Carol jumped when she saw her. "I didn't know that you were coming, ma'am."

"Neither did I. I was over here for a hearing and decided to drop by," said the leader. "Is Shy in and free?"

"Oh, yes, ma'am, her chief is with her, but she's free. Let me call."

"That won't be necessary. No need to be so formal."

Shiloh looked up from the papers she was going over with Sarah and smiled. "Hi, boss, have you met Sarah?"

Sarah stood and extended her hand.

"Oh, yes, several times. Can I have a minute?"

Sarah excused herself.

"Coffee?" asked Shiloh.

"Yes, that would be great."

After coffee arrived, the leader asked Shy, "So how was this weekend in the district?"

"Good. No, actually great. My numbers are up, there seems to be strong support for the ERA, and *The Tennessean* gave me its endorsement as well as an endorsement for the ERA. How about elsewhere?"

"Mixed, I'm afraid. Good for most of the Dems, but the other side has been able to take a little starch out of their pro-ERA colleagues. We've lost several of our votes from what I hear. Certainly we don't have two-thirds anymore. The fundamentalists have set up a letter-writing campaign, and phone calls from the districts are pouring in. While they are a decided minority on the ERA, they almost always vote together, and that carries a lot of weight with the party."

"What do you think the majority leader will do?" asked Shiloh.

"Well, he can't exactly call for a vote since he's already on record questioning our tactics. But he may have someone else do it from the floor; and he could accede, since there is such a groundswell, although the time is past for that since we are working exclusively on appropriations. But he's in the driver's seat at the moment."

"But if the country is for it, isn't he worried that he may push too hard and lose? If I were him, I'd just wait until after the election," exclaimed Shiloh.

"Me too," said the leader, "but he's an arrogant and unpredictable SOB, just like his predecessor. He may try. If so, he probably won't try to move tomorrow. More likely, he would try to do it Wednesday or Thursday after he has had time to meet with his caucus. Whatever he decides, I'm sure that we'll know in advance from one of our friends."

On Wednesday afternoon, Charlie called to report that Boyd had accused Shiloh of planning to introduce a constitutional amendment to legalize abortion and a second amendment to legalize homosexual marriage.

Charlie snickered. "Not same-sex marriage, Shy, but homosexual marriage. And according to an ad agency friend of mine, he has an ad ready to go that shows gays in drag walking with little children with a voiceover asking, 'Would your children be safe with these people?' And then it goes on to a picture of a woman crying and saying, 'I killed my baby. I will burn in hell. Please don't make the same mistake I did.' Then it ends with something like, 'This is what Congresswoman Giles wants. Vote for morality. Vote for Boyd.'"

"What next?"

"I don't know. These people he has working for him are getting advice from the party. But this kind of hardball is wrong and anti-American. We are a tolerant country; we are a democracy. They are going too far, and it scares me."

"Me too. Those guys really are inciting a cultural war. This is way beyond dirty politics. This is gutter fighting, and the sad part is that it's not even true."

As soon as Charlie hung up, Shiloh received a call from Sam.

"I have bad news."

"What is it, Sam? It couldn't get much worse."

"The FBI came to the office an hour ago and padlocked it. They said that our phones were being used to contact known terrorist sympathizers. Seth and Jennifer were arrested, and everyone else was sent home. I tried to go with them. I told the head guy that I was a lawyer. But he told me that they were going in for questioning and that Seth and Jennifer would be able to call me later. They also said that the phone calls from here had been picked up by routine NSA checks and regarded national security. I'm on my way to your office now."

Shy called the minority leader and reported Sam's conversation.

Her immediate response was, "Ouch."

"Now what?" asked Shiloh.

"Let me make some calls, Shy. I'll call you back."

The minority leader called back just as Sam walked into Shiloh's office. "They're being questioned at a detention center of some kind at FBI headquarters. I talked to a friend who was a staffer here years ago. He said that the whole thing was a farce. Apparently they're claiming that some of the NGOs that Seth's working with are anti-American. The person with Seth, Jennifer something ... "

"Jennifer Smith, she is one of ERA Today's staff members," interrupted Shiloh.

"Anyway," continued the minority leader, "Jennifer has said some derisive things about the policies of the U.S. government."

"So have I," exclaimed Shiloh.

"Yes, we all have, but not to people in the Middle East, not that that makes a difference."

Sam called a senior partner of one of the big law firms in Washington who he knew from law school and asked him for advice. Shiloh called Pam, who said that she would bring in Seth's other staff members to her office the next day so that they could keep working.

"You don't have to do that, Karen. You may get in trouble too."

"Screw them. This is still America, Shy."

All members were called to the House floor on Thursday to consider a special bill. Shy knew what was coming as she trudged to the capitol with several of her colleagues.

The majority leader is going to get even and vote the ERA to defeat. Power corrupts, she thought, *and absolute power corrupts absolutely.*

Why is it so hard to do what is right? What a bastard. Shiloh smiled to herself, knowing that if she had said that out loud Seth would have teased her forever. Then she grimaced, thinking that her husband was still being held, essentially for being an American.

When she arrived, the majority leader was in the chair. "I call upon that gentleman from South Dakota. You have the floor, sir."

"I rise, Mr. Chairman, to introduce the Equal Rights Amendment for Women."

"Point of order," said the minority leader from the Democratic lectern in the well. "Mr. Chairperson, we are supposed to be considering the State Department Appropriations bill. Your rules dictate that we may not at this time introduce other bills before this House due to the crush of time and the necessity that we all have to keep the government running so that we can return to our districts and campaign."

"Madame Leader, I say to you and to the party in opposition that you lead that I have the prerogative as the leader of the party in power to set the agenda, and I do so now to assuage your desire and your party's desire to put this matter before the House."

"You know full well, Mr. Chairperson, that I'm not ready to move this bill at this time."

"But, Madame Leader, I am."

With that, the minority leader left the floor of the House, followed by the members of her party. The session continued, and the amendment to the constitution brought by the gentleman from South Dakota was defeated.

Shiloh was sad that women were being sent to the back of the line once again. And she was incensed at the arrogance of the majority leader. *What a bastard*, she thought again, only this time she didn't smile. She was ready for battle.

* * * * *

Late that night, with the help of Sam's friend, Seth and Jennifer were to be released from detention. But they were told to stay at home.

"They'll be under house arrest," Sam reported to Shiloh.

He and Barbara came to the condo and waited with his sister for Seth's arrival.

Seth came in and hugged Shiloh, Barbara, and Sam and poured himself a double scotch.

"Long day," he said with a sad smile.

"I really can't believe that we no longer have privacy in this country," he continued. "We're trying to do something to help women in this country and around the world, and they say that we are working with known terrorist sympathizers. And poor Jennifer, she criticized U.S. government policy. What next?"

"Oh, darling," sighed Shy. "I want to fight, but sometimes I think, *why*? Just go to a nice church and work with everyday problems and talk about a God who is loving and kind. Why is it so hard to try to do what is right?"

"Yeah, and the hell of it is, we have to keep plugging away, or they win, and then what? More lies, more of their religion dictating policy, more heavy-handed garbage," declared Seth.

They sat a minute, each with their own thoughts.

"So how was your day?" inquired Seth.

His trio of listeners burst out laughing. "Great!" they said in unison.

Then Shiloh explained what had happened in the House and how Sam had worked with an old friend to spring Seth and Jennifer.

"This really screws things up," replied Seth. "I'm scheduled to go to Nashville with Shy, and you're supposed to speak at a rally in Brussels, Sam."

"Yeah, I know," replied his brother-in-law. "I've asked Sally Cohen from the Illinois State University to stand in for me in Brussels, and I'll replace you in Nashville."

The phone rang and Shiloh answered.

"And," continued Sam, "Wayne Long is coming up from Nashville and will go to CCG to handle our staff. Pam offered to take us all in there until the padlock is removed from the front door of ERA Today. Wayne will stay in touch, and you can work from here until this mess is cleared up."

"You've been busy. But can Wayne be spared? Doesn't Shiloh have the debate this weekend?" exclaimed Seth.

"Yes," answered Sam, "the debate is on Saturday night, and she has a speech to a group of union folks on Friday night at the Opryland Radisson. But Wayne's team is able to operate a few days on their own, and remember that Isabel is there helping out along with several volunteers."

"Shy's debate history is checkered, to say the least. Or mine is anyway. Don't leave by the rear door, pal," said a smiling Seth as he remembered his run-in with Lawson four years earlier.

Shy hung up the phone.

"What's up, sweetheart?" said Seth.

"That was *The Tennessean*. Apparently the ERA is still hot news. The chair and the senior minority member of the Judiciary Committee were on *The NewsHour with Jim Lehrer*, the minority leader and Carolyn Maloney were on *Larry King Live*, and the majority leader was on Fox."

"Why weren't you called for any of these shows?" asked Seth.

"I begged off so I could rest as much as possible for Nashville. The leader said that she and Carolyn would handle press calls for me. My office sent all queries from the press to them so I could stay off of my feet. After the election, I was thinking about taking the next six or so weeks off, or at least only going in for major votes. I spoke to my doctor today, and he told me that he didn't want me to travel anymore more after the election until I delivered. In fact, he isn't too happy that I'm traveling now."

"Great, sweetheart. I agree with your doctor. Maybe you should call it a campaign after this weekend. Wayne could announce as much next week," said Seth.

Shiloh nodded. "Maybe I will. I want to make sure that I carry to term. So far, so good, but I don't want to tempt fate."

* * * * *

The next morning, Seth was up and working the phone just like he was in the office. Shiloh printed an article off her computer to read to Sam on the way to the airport. Sam came by at noon to pick up his sister. Before leaving, Shiloh embraced her husband and told him not to work so much, and he in turn told her to rest as much as possible.

They held each other a long moment in silence.

"Take care, darling," whispered Shiloh.

"You too, sweetheart, you too."

When they got into the car, Shiloh read the front-page article from *The Tennessean* to Sam.

> Giles Ahead in the Polls; Strong Support Nationwide for ERA
>
> Nashville, October 27 – According to a recent *Tennessean*/Vanderbilt Political Science Department poll, Catherine Shiloh Giles has a comfortable lead in her campaign to be reelected as the congressional representative for the Tennessee Fifth District seat she has held since 1996. The polls, which have varied little for the past two months, find Giles with a commanding lead of 62 percent, less than two weeks before the November 7 election. Giles, reached at her home last night, was pleased with the news and thanked the people of the Fifth District for their continued confidence and support. Giles, who is over seven months pregnant, said that she would campaign as long as she could and then would slow down and stop traveling before the birth of her first child, which is due in early December.
>
> Giles said during her interview last night that she was saddened but not surprised about the defeat yesterday afternoon of the ERA in the House of Representatives. She explained, "This was a case of the majority leader using his power to change his own rules after browbeating his party to introduce and then defeat the measure. I am confident that when we win back the House on Election Day, the new Congress will pass the measure with the required two-thirds. I am also confident that there will be a similar vote in the Senate."
>
> The majority leader, after disrupting the vote on the ERA last week, "brought the amendment back yesterday, he said, to teach the minority party a lesson," according to a Republican member who did not wish to be named quoting internal discussions.
>
> Another *Tennessean* source said that the majority leader informed his colleagues in a pre-session, closed-door session, "I remind all of you that our party has an official stand against the ERA."

And, according to other sources, he "threatened that anyone who votes for the ERA will lose party campaign funds and support."

The minority leader tried unsuccessfully to delay the vote. She led her members out of the House in protest when the majority leader refused to accede.

A national poll conducted by *USA Today* found that a majority of 78 percent of the American people supported the inclusion of the ERA in the Constitution.

* * * * *

Lawson's eyes were drawn to the picture of Shiloh on the front page. He quickly read the article. By the time he was finished, his face was red with rage. She never loses. *Why can't people see her for what she is? She is there for all to see: Satan's disciple. That woman's amendment is popular now because of her. People don't understand what it will mean. God will punish us all if she wins that awful amendment. God proscribes women's role in society, not that demon Giles.*

What would my father say if he saw how I have failed? I have let him down; I have let down my father who spent his life saving sinners, and I have let down my father in heaven, he thought as he made his way into his closet.

"There it is on the shelf," he said to himself. "There is my instrument of justice. It feels good. I will do God's bidding. He will grant me salvation. I will have a special place with him next to my father."

Lawson lay down in his bed and looked at the ceiling. He could see his father looking at him. He could see the disappointment in his eyes. *You will be proud soon, Father.* Jimmy Bob knew that soon his father would feel great pride for his only son.

Lawson shook his head, and the image disappeared from the ceiling; and for a final time, his lust for Shiloh again dominated his being. His eyes now focused on Shiloh. She was sensual in her white, low cut dress. He could see the swell of her breasts and the roundness of her hips. She looked into his eyes, as he shivered and began to breathe in gulps …

Chapter 17

It was rainy, dreary, and insufferably muggy when Shiloh and Sam arrived in Nashville.

Shiloh shrugged as they walked off the plane. "Well, brother of mine, back to our sweltering homeland."

"Yes, it's almost as bad as Washington. At least I can't get pregnant," teased Sam.

"Oh, didn't you know that male pregnancy is part of the ERA? That's why so many men oppose it," laughed Shiloh.

They walked to the baggage claim where Charlie was waiting.

"Welcome home, friends," Charlie smiled as he greeted Shy and Sam.

"Hi, Charlie, what's up? I hope better weather," deadpanned Shiloh.

"It's supposed to clear in a few hours, just for you. It's hot for this time of year."

"Actually, Charlie, I'm quite happy today. In spite of all of our difficulties, the election will soon be over, and I'll get to focus on being a mother. I'm so excited, and so is Seth."

"So are we all, Shy, so are we all. This has been a humdinger, but soon we can all take a little break. Then we'll start planning the political career of that little daughter you're about to hatch."

"I hope she runs from a place with a cooler climate," chimed in Sam. "What do you think Charlie, governor first? House, Senate, president?"

On the drive to town, Charlie filled them in on the schedule. "You have the speech tonight, Shiloh, with the combined group of unions at the Opryland Hotel. A press conference is scheduled for tomorrow at noon at the Hyatt, and then of course the debate is tomorrow night at Tennessee State.

All things considered, you have a relatively light schedule. I've refused the usual drop bys and hand-shaking events. I know you like those, Shy, but you need some downtime so you'll be well rested for what you do have."

"Thank you, Charlie. I appreciate that. I like the lazy schedule. So does my baby."

"Lazy?" exclaimed Sam. "It sounds like a bunch to me."

Charlie grinned. "In normal years, even when unopposed, your sister goes twelve to fourteen hours a day on her campaign days, but not this time. Folks understand. They know she's pregnant. But most of all, they know she cares about them."

Shiloh called Seth to report that they had arrived and that she was sipping, actually gulping, iced tea. He filled her in on what was going on.

"I've been busy on this end, sweetheart, and so has the rest of our team. Many colleges have events planned next week. The NGOs are planning a huge march in Washington right after the election, and the word from overseas is good. We're still alive, dear. And I believe that we can still eventually win the ERA."

"Great. Just a few more weeks, and maybe we can take time off to eat, drink, and be lazy."

"All you do is eat, sweetheart. If I followed your lead, I'd weigh three hundred pounds. But I'm happy to be the designated drinker."

"Deal," laughed Shiloh.

"I love you. Be safe and come home soon," Seth said.

* * * * *

They arrived at the Opryland Hotel at 6:15. When Shiloh entered the ballroom, it exploded in applause. She worked her way to the head table, shaking hands with the standing union members. She sat next to the hostess, the president of the state teachers union. Charlie sat next to her. Union dignitaries joined Shy and Charlie at the head table.

Sam was at a round table just in front of the head table that was reserved for special guests. His tablemates included the mayor and two members of the city council and, to Sam's delight, the Jacobsons and the Whitfields. They ate supper and talked about the campaign, the ERA, and UT's upcoming game for the SEC Championship.

As dessert was being served, the hostess clicked her glass. "Ladies and gentlemen, the main event. But first I would like to introduce the former governor of our great state, the honorable Barry Whitfield and the distinguished mayor of our beautiful host city, Bettye Anderson."

Applause filled the room.

"We have many other distinguished guests here tonight, but if I introduced them all, there wouldn't be enough time for our very special guest to speak. It is now my honor and my pleasure, friends and colleagues, to introduce to you our little-known and timid friend, Shiloh Giles."

Laughter and applause followed.

"Shiloh, an Episcopal priest, also has another job, which requires her to occasionally commute to our nation's capitol. Shiloh, who will become a mother soon for the first time I might add, has put us on the map here in the Fifth Congressional District of Tennessee. She introduced the Equal Rights Amendment in Congress recently."

The hostess was interrupted again by loud applause.

"And I for one say, it's about time," she continued. "Shiloh has been a great representative of this district for ten years and will soon start, after a little formality in about ten days, a sixth term as our congresswoman. My friends, Catherine Shiloh Giles."

Shiloh was welcomed by a standing ovation.

Shiloh took a slight bow as she reached the podium. "Dear friends, it is wonderful to be here tonight. And thank you, Kate, for that exaggerated introduction. I admire the work that unions do for our working families, for our economy, and for our state and nation. And it is my hope that, early in the next term, when our party regains the majority ..."

"Hear hear," offered many in the audience.

"That we will pass a new minimum wage bill and that the new Congress will finally pass the Equal Rights Amendment for Women," Shiloh continued.

Thunderous applause rang out.

"It is so nice to look out into the audience this evening."

* * * * *

As Shiloh continued, Lawson, who had been sitting far in the back, away from the view of people who might recognize him, made his way around the side of the ballroom toward the head table.

No one was paying attention to him, as waiters and waitresses quietly bused the supper dishes and served dessert.

"I remember when I first went to Congress," Shiloh was saying. "I was newly elected and ready to roll up my sleeves and go to work. But I quickly realized that, to succeed, you had to work together and sometimes compromise with the other party to get things done.

"And for my first several years, even though we were in the minority, I felt like we were making at least some progress for the country. Today, compromise and progress are almost impossible.

"Now, my union friends," continued Shiloh.

Lawson moved steadily closer to the head table; still no one noticed.

* * * * *

As he ascended the riser, Sam saw something out of the corner of his eye that caught his attention. He focused on Lawson, just as the man raised the gun. Sam yelled, "Shy!"

The .38 Caliber Smith and Wesson exploded with a loud bang that caught Shy in the middle of her right side, just below her breast. The first response from the crowd was to duck. Dishes crashed as many scrambled to find cover under the tables.

Charlie jumped up to assist Shy, who was clinging to the podium as she sunk to her knees.

The second bullet was accompanied by Lawson's shout, "Queer," as Charlie was hit on the left side of his back. The force of the bullet threw him to the floor. Sam, who had run for the head table when he yelled, and a man seated at the head table wrestled the gun from Lawson and pinned him to the floor. Sam handed the gun to another man and rushed to his sister. He cradled her head in his arms as she lay on the floor bleeding. She was unconscious. The hostess and another woman from the head table were attending Charlie, who was also bleeding heavily. Charlie was still conscious.

Within seconds, the police who were at the back of the ballroom were on the scene. Medical attendants arrived within minutes and began attending to the two gunshot victims. The hotel located a doctor among its guests, who also rushed in to assist. They loaded Shiloh and Charlie onto stretchers. Sam asked Barry to call Seth and to find Brenda and Tom. Sam went in the ambulance with Shiloh and Charlie.

Barry, who had immediately stepped into his governor's role, reached Seth. He spoke plainly and evenly. "Seth, I have very bad news. Shiloh has been shot. Charlie too. They're both alive. Shiloh is unconscious. Sam is with her in an ambulance on the way to the hospital."

Seth wailed, "God no. No, Barry, it can't be."

"You'd better hurry down here, son. Call me when you get a flight, and I'll be waiting at the airport."

Barry hung up and called Brenda to tell her and to ask her for Tom's number and the number for Charlie's mother.

* * * * *

Seth didn't know what to do. He started to put some clothes in a bag; suddenly he stopped and ran to the phone and called information to get the phone number of an airline so he could get a ticket. He was confused and scared. He was on hold, listening to the airline's menu.

"Damn," he said out loud. "Damn it, hurry up."

He took a deep breath and scolded himself. *Shy wouldn't like my choice of words*, he thought with a weak smile.

He started packing while he held the receiver. In a few minutes, there was a knock at the door. Seth opened the door.

"Hi, I'm here to help. I know about your wife." It was Special Agent Dan Farrell of the FBI.

"Screw that house arrest," said Seth.

"I agree. We dropped it. I was coming over to tell you when I got the call about your wife. I'm embarrassed that it ever happened; we all are. Do you have a flight?"

"No, no one answers the damn phone," Seth growled.

"Don't worry; just pack. I'll call the office, and they'll get you on the next flight out."

Agent Farrell drove Seth to the airport. The FBI got him a ticket on United to Chicago with a connection on Delta to Nashville. He arrived in Nashville at 12:15 a.m. Barry was waiting. The airport was closing. His plane was the last flight in for the day.

"She's alive, son. She has been transfused. They are trying to save her and your baby. Sam is with her now."

"Is she conscious?"

"No. She's in intensive care. They're waiting for you."

They followed a police escort to the hospital.

"How is Charlie?"

"He's going to make it. He was standing up to help Shy. If he had stayed seated, the bullet would've likely blown his head off. He's still critical, but the doctors say that he'll survive. Brenda and Tom are at the hospital, and Trudy is also there with the Jacobsons."

"Thank you, Barry," Seth said through his tears.

Barry reached over and squeezed Seth's arm. "If you know any prayers, son, now is the time to say them."

They arrived in the intensive care area of the hospital. Sam was standing at the window. The curtains were drawn around Shiloh's bed as two doctors and a nurse gave her another transfusion.

Sam turned when Seth and Barry arrived. "She's fighting, Seth. She's trying to live."

Both men cried as they hugged each other.

Finally, the doctors came out. The nurse stayed in a chair next to Shiloh's bed.

"This is her husband, Seth Richards," Sam said to the doctors as he nodded toward Seth.

"How … how is she?" Seth stammered.

"We've given her two pints of blood so far, sir. She's leaking blood internally, but we can't go in and stop the bleeding or go after the bullet until she stabilizes. Her pulse is weak, and she's in shock. We have given her the appropriate medication and are keeping her warm."

The other doctor spoke. "The baby seems okay. She is, of course, depending on her mother, but she appears to be okay. If her mother dies, we'll have to try to save her immediately. She's still tiny."

"May I see my wife?" Seth blurted.

The doctors looked at each other.

One of them answered, "Come with me and scrub and put on some greens and a mask. You can go in for a minute."

Seth did as he was told and walked in and stood next to Shiloh.

"Come on, sweetheart. You can't leave me now. Fight hard." He put his hand under the covers and held her hand. She felt cool. Seth's eyes again filled with tears.

The doctor touched his shoulder. "It's time to leave. Mr. Richards."

He took one last look at his wife. She looked pale but peaceful. He leaned over and kissed her forehead through his mask. Seth left the room and said, "Give me a minute please."

He walked to the end of the hall to a window and looked out at the still, peaceful night. He prayed.

* * * * *

On Sunday afternoon, Seth and Sam visited with Charlie for a few minutes. He was still in intensive care but stable. Charlie asked about Shiloh, and Sam reported that there was no change. Charlie said that his entire body ached but that he felt better.

Neither Seth nor Sam left the hospital. Barry brought them some toiletries, and they took turns showering and shaving in an empty hospital room. Susan and Trudy brought food, and Susan filled them in on the news.

"There's a vigil outside the hospital. The hospital is issuing statements twice a day. Nationally, the news broadcasts are covering Nashville, and the ERA is being discussed constantly. The clip in her speech the other night, when Shy mentions passing the ERA in the next session of Congress, is being played over and over. So, unfortunately, are the shootings."

Barry spoke. "Seth, you need to think about saying something to the press."

Sam nodded. "Shy would want us to say something, to thank people."

A bewildered Seth sighed. "I know. I've been thinking about that. Every time I do, my mind drifts to Shiloh. Please help me with some words."

"It just so happens that I wrote out something this morning," said Barry.

That broke the tension, and they all chuckled.

"Politicians," exclaimed Trudy with a smile as she reached out for her man's arm.

"Will you come with me, Sam?" Seth asked.

"Of course I will."

"I'll get them ready," Barry offered. "Take a few minutes and prepare yourself, Seth."

When they went to the press area, the journalists had attached microphones to the hospital podium that was set up under the roof that covered a side entrance to the hospital. It had been closed for the duration of Shiloh's stay for press briefings. In the nearby parking lot, a rope line has been installed for the vigil. The police were monitoring the approximately seven thousand people who were there.

Barry introduced Seth.

Seth spoke, "My wife is struggling to live. I'm sure that you've heard the doctor's periodic reports. And our baby who she is carrying is also alive. It's difficult to know quite what to say. My mind is up there in intensive care with my wife and soon-to-be-born daughter. But, I know that Shy … Shiloh would appreciate knowing that you care so much for her and her values. Shiloh is a fighter. She is fighting now. When she recovers, she'll continue her fight for justice, for a strong and compassionate America, and for the Equal Rights Amendment for women."

The people straining against the rope applauded at Seth's mention of the ERA. Another group further back watched a handheld TV that was tuned to CNN's live broadcast and also applauded.

"I thank you all for your thoughts and prayers. Hopefully, Shiloh will soon be out of danger." Seth paused. He couldn't think of anymore to say. "This is Shiloh's brother, Sam Giles, Sam."

Barry smiled at Seth. "Great job, son." He put his hand on Seth's shoulder.

"I can't add much," said Sam. "I know that my sister is fighting hard to live. She told me last week that she can't wait," Sam said with a smile, "to see her husband, Seth, change diapers."

Seth smiled weakly as tears rolled down his cheeks.

"I admire my sister and her husband. They've worked tirelessly to adopt a national and international ERA for women."

There was applause from both groups within the crowd.

"I hope all of you and the citizens of our great country and the world will join their campaign for justice. Please continue to pray for my sister and for the success of her work. Thank you."

* * * * *

Monday morning dawned, and still there was no change in Shiloh's condition. The doctors were debating whether to try to save the baby. She was sapping her mother's strength and vice versa. Seth wanted to wait as long as possible before they tried to deliver the baby with a C-section. It would be traumatic and may be too much for Shiloh to bear. They could also abort the baby, which would be less invasive and may help Shiloh.

Seth was facing a dilemma. He would save Shiloh first, but he did not want to lose their daughter unless that was the last resort. He grimaced as he thought that such an abortion, called partial-birth abortion by those who opposed a woman's right to any abortion, might someday be against the law. Just another example of how ideology and politics conspire against women, he thought, as he paced the hallways of the intensive care unit.

* * * * *

The minority leader was in her office meeting with her leadership team. It was Tuesday, October 31, Halloween day and one week before Election Day 2006.

"I spoke with Shiloh's brother last night," she opened the meeting, saying, "and he told me that her condition is essentially the same: weak vital signs, comatose, and still bleeding internally. They are trying drugs to slow the bleeding but so far without significant results."

After a reflective moment she said, "Anything to report, Joe?"

"The majority leader is in a pickle," replied the deputy whip. "With students boycotting classes in hundreds of colleges across the country, his troops want to revote the ERA. But he is holding firm, saying that this will pass. I understand that one of his leadership colleagues said yes, Mr. Leader, and we may too."

The chief whip chimed in, "I sure as hell hope so."

They all laughed.

"Also, NGOs and students are working together organizing vigils at state capitals asking for their state legislatures to intercede with their senators and

House members to demand that they take action on the ERA," reported the chief whip.

"How many of our members are here this week?" asked the leader.

"About half," Joe answered. "But we can get them all here for a vote within twenty-four hours?"

"Okay then, let's let the other side stew in their own juices a day or two before we try to force the issue. But go ahead and get our colleagues back here by tomorrow night, Joe. Okay?"

He nodded as the meeting ended.

* * * * *

In the meantime, at the Executive Office Building, the guru was walking into Wesley Bragg's office. "Where are we on the ERA thing?"

"We have everything ready to go for the final push," answered his protégé.

"And?" asked his boss.

"And I think that we're in deep shit. Don't you?"

"Maybe. What do the fundamentalists say?"

"Fight on, of course. One of them even had the balls to say that Giles got what she deserved and that God was letting us know he's with us, that we're following his divine word or some such."

"Damn, those crazy bastards even scare me sometimes," lamented the guru.

"I told the stupid turd not to ever say such a thing publicly," retorted Bragg.

"Good. And the FBI thing—I think we need to call off the dogs there."

"We don't have a choice, boss. The FBI pulled the plug itself on Friday."

"Oh really. Well, make sure you stop that new slimy ad that we did for the guy in Tennessee running against Giles."

"I did that yesterday," reported Bragg.

"Okay, just sit still for now. Let's give it a day or two."

"Yes, sir. Will do."

But when the guru left the office, Bragg mused, "Ain't no way we gonna win this one, man."

* * * * *

"I just got off the phone with several of the fundamentalists pooh-bahs, and they say to stay the course, that this is a fight that we must win," reported the majority leader to his leadership colleagues on Wednesday morning.

"Have you looked outside on the front lawn lately? There are more than ten thousand of them out there camping, and their numbers are growing by the minute," the chief whip retorted. "What now? Hang on while those fundamentalist reprobates sail us down the river?"

"Look," the majority leader replied angrily. "They are the ones who brought many of us to the dance, and they have worked hard to keep us here. They'll deliver next Tuesday. Just hang on for another day or so, and we'll see what happens. And damn it, have the Capitol Police remove that crowd. They aren't supposed to be where they are, certainly not camping out. It's against the post-9/11 security protocols."

"No way," answered the chief whip. "That'll just make matters worse. They won't move. Think of the headlines for a minute: 'Capitol Hill Gestapo Removes Women's Rights Advocates from Capitol Grounds.' TV coverage would be even worse than it already is if we did that. Just ignore them. Don't look out your window."

* * * * *

At Lawson's arraignment on Wednesday morning, which had been delayed for two days due to the defendant's psychotic behavior, Lawson eagerly admitted his guilt.

"I am the avenging angel of the Lord. God told me to smite that evil woman and her queer," he effused. "God is my witness. God will cleanse the land of this evil and put women in their rightful place. Crucify me if you must. I am the son of God."

His lawyers tried to keep him quiet, but there was no stopping James Robert Lawson II. He had finally lived up to his name. Jimmy Bob was now at peace with his father and his God. His name would be revered among all true believers.

A Tennessean reporter at the hearing scribbled in his notebook. "Crazy!!!"

* * * * *

At noon, the Senate majority leader walked into his counterpart's office and closed the door. "I think it's time we voted on the ERA," he said without hesitation.

The minority leader stifled a smile. "Agreed! It's lunchtime now. How about at 1:30, which gives us time to round up our colleagues."

"Fine," replied the majority leader as he turned on his heel and left the minority leader's office with the look on his face of a person who had just eaten a green persimmon.

The minority leader broke out in laughter as soon as he closed the door.

Senator Kennedy introduced the exact amendment that had been passed by the Senate and House thirty-four years, seven months, and ten days before, on March 22, 1972. It passed by a vote of seventy-one "Yes," zero "No," with eighteen senators abstaining. The two-thirds majority for passage was met. The eleven senators who were absent were in their home states campaigning for reelection in tight races.

The European Parliament voted overwhelmingly that morning to adopt a Euro-wide ERA for its twenty-five member countries. ERA amendments had been passed in Kenya and Ghana and debates were on going in Japan, India, Egypt, Mexico, and Columbia. Parliamentary debates were scheduled in twenty-six other countries over the next two weeks to consider an ERA law or an amendment to their respective constitutions.

* * * * *

At the hospital that evening, the hospital spokesperson gave his second briefing of the day to the press.

"Charles Bates is improving rapidly. He was moved from intensive care to a private room early this afternoon. Catherine Shiloh Giles is still in critical condition. She received her eighth transfusion this morning. Her vital signs are stable but still weak. I'll answer questions now.

"Bill."

"Can't the doctors perform a cesarean section and save the baby?"

"No, Bill, not at this time. Such a procedure could be too traumatic for Congresswoman Giles to survive. That's why they have not tried to fix the wound that is causing her to leak blood internally. She is being kept warm and is receiving nutrients, antibiotics, and a drug used to assist coagulation, but she's too weak for major surgery now.

"Would an abortion be traumatic?"

"Yes, Lois, but not as bad. It would not require invasive surgery, since it could be accomplished through the birth canal."

Lois on follow-up asked. "So why not an abortion then? Isn't the baby sapping her strength?"

"Because, Lois, the doctors say that even an abortion would be traumatic, just not as traumatic as a C-section. If she improves slightly, the doctors may recommend an abortion to save her life. If her condition deteriorates, then they may recommend trying to save the baby. There are no easy answers.

"Sandy."

"What are the chances that Congresswoman Giles and/or her baby will survive? Can you give us a percentage?"

"No, Sandy, no percentages. Both are in grave jeopardy. I would not venture a prediction either way."

"Tess."

"How is the family holding up?"

"They're all holding up as well as can be expected. They're very close. Father Jacobson, who is rector of All Saints Episcopal Church here in Nashville, has held a Holy Communion service every day for the family.

"By the way," said Brian as he was leaving. "Congresswoman Giles has received hundreds of flower arrangements here at the hospital. They have come from organizations and individuals from around the world. There are flowers everywhere in the hospital, including in all the patient rooms. It is incredible. Good night, friends."

* * * * *

The hospital reports were carried live by CNN and MSNBC. Many nervous people in Washington watched the hospital report, as vigils around the country prayed for Shiloh and her baby. Students in colleges in every state marched this night. They carried candles in silence. There were American flags everywhere as well as ERA Today signs and signs with the words:

PRAY FOR SHILOH AND HER BABY TONIGHT, AND PRAY FOR WOMEN EVERYWHERE WHO HAVE SUFFERED FROM VIOLENCE.

* * * * *

At about 5:45 a.m., Shiloh's blood pressure dropped, and her pulse became weaker. The ICU nurse called the physician in charge of Shiloh's care.

"Shiloh's failing, doctor."

He rushed to the intensive care unit, followed by two doctors who were working the emergency room. He checked her vital signs and called to have an operating room prepared.

He walked out to the waiting room, where Seth and Sam were drinking coffee and quietly talking. The Whitfields were asleep on two waiting room couches.

"Seth, I'm afraid that your wife is slipping away."

Seth felt a lightning bolt of nausea course through his body as tears welled up in his eyes.

"What? What about the baby, Stafford?"

"At this age she depends totally on her mother. There's a slim chance, but I have to try to save her immediately."

Seth was crying freely now. "Can you abort the baby and save my wife? Is there any chance at all for her?"

The doctor shook his head. "Shiloh's injury was too much. I'm dreadfully sorry, Seth," Stafford responded.

The hospital team rushed Shiloh to the operating room. The family waited. The baby was removed by cesarean section at 6:05 a.m. and rushed to intensive care.

The doctor came to the waiting room. Seth waited for him to speak.

Dr. Stafford Dodd's eyes were compassionate as he spoke. "Seth, your daughter is in intensive care. She seems normal, but she's in critical condition. All I can say at the moment is that she has a chance. Your wife is being moved to intensive care in a few minutes. You'll be able to visit her and anyone else that you wish may also be with her."

Seth's shoulders slumped. He thanked Dr. Dodd with a weak voice and walked over to await the arrival of his beloved Shiloh. It was 7:20 a.m. when she arrived. Seth looked over to the others and nodded. They joined him at Shiloh's bedside.

* * * * *

At eight o'clock sharp in Washington, the House majority leader was in his office meeting with his party's leaders when the Speaker burst into his office.

"I want the ERA on the floor at 9:00 a.m."

"I don't think that's necessary," the majority leader stated emphatically.

The Speaker glared at his friend. "I don't care if Abraham, Isaac, and Jacob appear on the Capitol steps with anti-ERA signs. I want that damn amendment passed. Now move it—9:00 a.m. I will chair."

The Speaker and the leadership team scattered to alert their colleagues about the session.

The majority leader sat in his office brooding.

* * * * *

Father Jacobson administered the absolution. "The almighty and merciful Lord grant thee pardon and remission of all thy sins and the grace and comfort of the Holy Spirit. Amen."

Seth leaned over and kissed Shiloh's forehead and held her hand. "I love you so much, Shiloh. I'll miss you and cherish you forever. Our little one will make it, Shy; little Shiloh will be fine. I know she will. I'll give her all of my love and attention. Sam is here with you, and so are Barry and Trudy and Bill and Susan. We all love you, Shiloh. We all love you."

They stood together in silence.

Seth was looking at Shy's peaceful face when she stopped breathing. He was holding her hand and felt her pulse stop.

He bowed his head. "Father," Seth choked, "she's gone."

Father Jacobson read the commendatory prayer from *The Book of Common Prayer*. "Into thy hands, O merciful Saviour, we commend the soul of thy servant, now departed from this body. Acknowledge, we humbly beseech thee, a sheep of thine own fold, a lamb of thine own flock, a sinner of thine own redeeming. Receive her into the arms of thy mercy, into the blessed rest of everlasting peace, and into the glorious company of the saints in light, Amen."

It was 7:55 a.m. in Nashville and 8:55 in Washington.

* * * * *

At 9:15, the Speaker banged the gavel. "I call this House to order," he said with a strong voice. "I recognize the House chaplain."

The House chaplain offered a brief opening prayer, asking for the House to be blessed with wisdom in their deliberations.

Then the Speaker looked at the minority leader and asked, "Is there business before this House?"

"Yes, Mr. Speaker," said the minority leader, who was standing at the Democratic lectern. "I rise, Mr. Speaker to ..."

At that moment, her chief of staff handed her a note. The minority leader hung her head as tears welled up in her eyes.

After a moment, she raised her head. "Mr. Speaker, it is my sad duty to report that a member of this House, our friend and colleague, Catherine Shiloh Giles, has expired. She passed on at 8:55 a.m. Washington time, in Nashville, from complications from the gunshot wound she suffered last Friday evening. Her child, a daughter, was successfully born at 7:05 a.m. Washington time by cesarean section. She is in intensive care and is in critical condition. Mr. Speaker, I request a recess of five minutes so we can each, in our one way, contemplate the life and work of our departed colleague."

"So be it, Madame Leader."

At 9:35, the Speaker called the House to order and recognized the House chaplain, who prayed for God's mercy for the soul of Catherine Shiloh Giles, for the life of her daughter, and for God's blessings for Representative Giles's family and friends at their time of grief.

The Speaker then recognized the minority leader.

"Mr. Speaker, I rise to offer an amendment to the United States Constitution."

She read the proposed amendment:

The Equal Rights Amendment for Women

Section 1. Equality of rights under the law shall not be denied or abridged by the United States or by any state on account of sex.

Section 2. The Congress shall have the power to enforce, by appropriate legislation, the provisions of this article.

Section 3. This amendment shall take effect two years after the date of ratification.

"Mr. Speaker, I ask that the report for this session refer to this bill, the ERA for Women, as The Giles Amendment. Thank you."

The minority leader stayed at the lectern.

"I see no need for debate, Madame Leader," said the Speaker. "Nor do I believe that we need a role call. The chair moves that this amendment be approved by voice vote."

"I second," said Carolyn Maloney, the gentlewoman from New York who was sitting on the bench behind the minority leader.

"I see no objections," said the Speaker. "All in favor, say 'Aye.'"

There was a thunderous, "*Aye!*"

"Opposed, same sign," bellowed the Speaker.

Silence reigned.

"The ayes have it. The Giles Amendment is adopted. The states will be notified immediately." He looked out at his colleagues. "Being no other business, the House is adjourned," the Speaker said as he banged down the gavel.

He leaned over to his assistant. "I screwed up. Things fell apart on my watch."

He hung his head and walked slowly back to his office

* * * * *

It was 10:30 Saturday morning. Seth and Sam were seated in the waiting room of the intensive care unit talking about arrangements for the funeral, which would be held in Tullahoma on Thursday, November 9, two days after the election. They were both dressed in suits and would leave shortly to go to the Tennessee Capitol Building, where Shiloh's closed casket would be placed at noon in order for the public to pay its last respects.

Dr. Dodd entered the waiting room. Seth held his breath.

"I have good news, Seth. Your little girl has been removed from the critical list. We believe that she'll be fine. She'll need to stay in the incubator for several weeks, if not months, until she grows a bit more, but in a few weeks, you'll be able to hold her for a few minutes each day."

Seth hugged Dr. Dodd. "That's great news. Just wonderful! May I see her?"

"Yes, but just for a few minutes. Let me get you a mask to wear. Sam, maybe it would be wise if you waited a few days to see your niece."

Sam nodded. His smile matched Seth's.

Seth entered the intensive care room. His daughter was in an incubator, hooked up to all sorts of wires and tubes.

"Hi, sweetie. My name is Seth. I am your dad. Your mother can't be here just now. Her name is Shiloh, just like yours. Your name is Shiloh Giles Richards. You are beautiful, just like your mom. If you work hard, sweetie, you'll be just as smart too. Just know I will always love you and take care of you. And soon I'll tell you all about your mother and your Great-grandma Alice, your Uncle Sam, and your Aunt Barbara, and all the other people who love you. I can't wait to hold you, sweetie. I have to go see your mom right now." Seth's eyes filled with tears. "But I'll be back soon. I love you, Shy."

He lingered a moment by the door with his head bowed. Finally, he raised his head and smiled. As Seth left his daughter and walked out of the intensive care unit, he was at peace. He knew that his beloved Shy would be proud. And he knew that she would approve of the name he had chosen for their daughter.

Epilogue

Reverend James Robert Lawson II was confined to an institution for the criminally insane. He would live out his life knowing that his martyrdom of Catherine Shiloh Giles provided the spark that emboldened male politicians to finally do what was right.

Sam Giles went back to New Jersey and his law firm. He continued to work with his partner, Mario, who remained sober. Five years after Shiloh's death, Sam and Mario opened and fully financed a halfway house for recovering alcoholics and drug addicts and the Catherine Shiloh Giles Center for Abused Women.

The Whitfields and Jacobsons enjoyed long retirements. For many years, they would get together once a month in Nashville, September through February, and attend a movie, a sports outing, a lecture, or a cultural event. From March through August, they would spend a weekend each month in Tullahoma and go fishing. Seth and his daughter, Shiloh, frequently joined them at both venues.

Seth and his daughter moved to Nashville where he taught women's studies at Vanderbilt University. He was a frequent guest on national and local radio and TV shows. He wrote a best-selling book about the love of his life entitled *Shiloh Giles: Champion of Justice*.

The state of Tennessee became the first state to ratify the 2006 version of the ERA on November 10, 2006, the day after Shiloh was buried.

Raymond Boyd asked voters to drop his name as a write-in candidate for the 2006 election the day after Shiloh was shot. In spite of her death, Shiloh won the election. The governor appointed Charlie Bates to fill Shiloh's seat until a special election could be held. Charlie Bates defeated Raymond

Boyd in the special election with 56 percent of the vote. Both men ran clean and spirited campaigns. Seth, Sam, and Barry worked tirelessly for Charlie's election. Charlie went on to serve in Congress until he retired at the age of eighty.

Shiloh Giles Richards asked her father, a stooped but spry ninety-nine-year-old, to hold her Bible, which had belonged to her great-grandmother Alice, when she was sworn-in, in 2053, as the third woman to be elected president of the United States. Her husband Marc, and her two daughters, Ruth and Mattie, stood with Seth for the grand occasion.

Wesley Bragg became a hedge fund trader and was indicted for issuing false statements that devalued the stock of a thriving company. He served three years in federal prison.

Printed in the United States
131988LV00001B/82/P

9 780595 470914